D1518214

The Indian Imagination

The Indian Imagination

Critical Essays on Indian Writing in English

K. D. Verma

St. Martin's Press
New York

ISBN 0-312-21139-2

Library of Congress Cataloging-in-Publication Data
Verma, K. D.
    The Indian imagination : critical essays on Indian
writing in English / K. D. Verma.
        p.   cm.
    Includes bibliographical references and index.
    ISBN 0-312-21139-2 (cloth)
        1. Indic literature (English)—20th century—
History and criticism.   2. India—In literature.
I. Title.
PR9489.6.V46   2000
820.9'954'0904—dc21

                                                              99-057757

First edition: May, 2000
10 9 8 7 6 5 4 3 2 1

Contents

Acknowledgments

Journal of South Asian Literature, Michigan State University, for permission to use the revised versions of the following papers: "Myth and Imagery in Nissim Ezekiel's *The Unfinished Man:* A Critical Reading," *Journal of South Asian Literature* 11.3–4 (1976); "Balachandra Rajan's *The Dark Dancer:* A Critical Reading," *Journal of South Asian Literature* 22.2 (1987); "Observations," *Journal of South Asian Literature* 24.1 (1989); "Sri Aurobindo as a Poet: A Reassessment," *Journal of South Asian Literature* 24.1 (1989); and "Ideological Confrontation and Synthesis in Mulk Raj Anand's *Conversations in Bloomsbury*," *Journal of South Asian Literature* 29.2 (1994). *The Toronto South Asian Review* to reprint the revised version of "The Social and Political Vision of Sri Aurobindo," *The Toronto South Asian Review* 8.3 (1990). *The International Fiction Review*, University of New Brunswick, for permission to reprint the revised version of "The Metaphysics and Metastructure of Appearance and Reality in Arun Joshi's *The Last Labyrinth*," *The International Fiction Review* 21 (1994). *Ariel: A Review of International English Literature*, the Board of Governors and the University of Calgary for permission to reprint the revised version of "Alienation, Identity and Structure in Arun Joshi's *The Apprentice*," *Ariel* 22.1 (1991). *South Asian Review* for permission to use "Understanding Mulk Raj Anand: An Introduction," *South Asian Review* 15.12 (1991). *Littcrit*, University of Kerala, for permission to reprint the augmented version of "Sri Aurobindo as a Critic," *Littcrit* 22.2 (1996). Anita Desai, the author, and William Heinemann, Publisher, to quote from *Baumgartner's Bombay* by Anita Desai. Vision Books and the Joshi Foundation for permission to quote from *The Apprentice* and *The Last Labyrinth* by Arun Joshi. Mulk Raj Anand and Arnold-Heinemann Publishers for permission to quote from *Conversations in Bloomsbury* by Mulk Raj Anand. Nissim Ezekiel and Writers Workshop, Calcutta, for permission to quote from *The Unfinished Man* by Nissim Ezekiel. Simon & Schuster for permission to quote from *The Dark Dancer* by Balachandra Rajan. Copyright © 1986 by Balachandra Rajan. Sri Aurobindo Ashram Trust for permission to quote from *Sri Aurobindo Birth Centenary Library Edition of the Collected Works*.

Preface

The *Indian Imagination* is a study in the structure of consciousness of the colonized and decolonized imagination in a broad sociohistorical and cultural context. The fundamental conception of consciousness as liberty, whether one invokes the definition of consciousness ad advanced by Hegel, Nietzsche or Aurobindo, is essentially moral and philosophical. Any authentic inscription of India presupposes a direct confrontation with the moral and philosophical incongruities and unresolvabilities of history. Thus the sociohistorical and sociopsychological process of confrontation—and of a possible synthesis—must include, amongst other things, the narcissistic incursions of the imperial imagination, the newly formulated aspirations of the emerging civil societies and the characteristic representations of the decolonized imagination. If it is significant to invoke Fanon's psychoanalytical presumptions about the colonial situation, it must also be equally significant to examine the psychological formulations of the postcolonial mind. Can Art and Time mediate between various oppositional strands and affect some sort of cathartic symbiosis? In the idealistic imagination of the poet of *Savitri*, the awakening of Satyavan from the death-state is allegorical of the awakening of humanity. Can India aspire to that level of Aurobindo's vision?

Amongst the numerous moral and philosophical unresolvabilities that this work has tried to address are the British imperial possession of India, the Indian struggle for independence, the partition of India and the establishment of new India as a free nation. Ironically, the independence of India was yoked to the partition of the country. But one of the cruelest and inerrable barbarities of history—the large-scale massacre of men, women and children—still remains the severest indictment of the neuroses of a civil society. It is not surprising that Mulk Raj Anand's Bakha in *Untouchable* and Munoo in *Coolie* are metaphors of universal human oppression and suffering. Needless to say that the intellectual debate on the British colonization of India and the dissolution of the imperial governance is not as yet fully concluded. In examining the legacy of the European intellectual thought and cultural traditions, one must understand the genesis of the politico-economic phenomena of colonialism and imperialism. In the process of theorizing these several issues one must ask: if the history of the colonized people is the history of human alienation, can the decolonized imagination recover its identity? Considering that Indian writing in English belongs as much to imperial history as to the postcolonial era, can there be some sort of synthesis between India's past and the aspirations of the present? If post-coloniality is merely a contestatory theory, can it adequately deal with Indian literary and cultural issues in a universal and global context? And what after postcoloniality and postmodernism?

It must be recognized that India's literary map is defined by its multilingualism and cultural and regional diversity and that several Indian languages, including Sanskrit, have extremely rich literatures of their own. It has now been generally accepted that all authentic Indian literatures have their origin in the universal Indian temper and that modern Indian literature have gone thought a sociohistorical process of cross-fertilization. In the case of Indian writing in English particularly, one must consider the steady impact of cross-fertilization and vernacularization. Doubtless to say that Aurobindo's signal contribution a s a poet, philosopher and critic, as the discussion in chapters 2, 3 and 4 shows, is to suggest boldly the applicability of the Indian aesthetic of *rasa-bhava-ananda* to the progressive evolution of modern English poetry. This cultural-linguistic amalgam of Indian literatures is a significant aspect of Indian writing in English that deserves a detailed study; the vernacularization of Indian writing in English, starting with Kipling, is a distinct characteristic of its own. It must be recognized that if Indian writing in English has made a significant progress during the last fifty years to deserve international acclaim, it is most certainly not at the expense of other indigenous literatures.

The writers included in this study represent varying patterns of consciousness, but it must be understood that my choice of these six writers has not been governed by any specific criteria. Undoubtedly, there is a large number of very talented Indian writers writing in English whose work needs careful and close attention. In fact, I am fully aware of the rich crop coming from India and other former British colonies.

I take this opportunity to thank the University of Pittsburgh at Johnstown for awarding me a summer research grant and a sabbatical to facilitate work on this project. Initially, Michael Flamini and Maura Burnett of St. Martin's Press had extended enthusiastic support to the conceptual design of this study. To the late Professor Sisirkumar Ghose, former chairman, Department of English at Santiniketan, and Mulk Raj Anand, I am greatly indebted for a generous and stimulating exchange of ideas. I am also gratefully obliged to numerous South Asianists and my colleagues at the University of Pittsburgh at Johnstown for their intellectual understanding and encouragement. Professor John Hawley of Santa Clara University liked my essay "The Social and Political Vision of Sri Aurobindo" and included it in his *Through a Glass Darkly: Essays in the Religious Imagination*. Jean Sedlar read the chapter on Anita Desai's *Baumgartner's Bombay* and gave me the benefit of her extensive knowledge of European history and India. Jerry Wemple also read this chapter and gave me the benefit of his knowledge of the European war theater and multiculturalism. Richard Strojan has been unusually generous with his time; he read several chapters of the study and gave me the benefit of his criticism, especially of his vast knowledge of Conrad and Forster. I am specially thankful to: Jodi Nicotra, my former student, who graciously volunteered to read early drafts of several chapters; Priscilla Stump who has persistently stood by me in preparing quite a few drafts and also the final manuscript; Charles Darr who was always available with his expertise in the use of computer technology; and Jeffrey Pruchnic, my student, who has proved to be a valuable and tireless helper in the various stages of the study, both in research and proofreading the manuscript. Last but not the least, I am thankful to the editorial and production staff at St. Martin's Press for their help and graciousness. Kristi Long, my editor, obliged me by her very perceptive and encouraging comments on the first draft of manuscript. Meg Weaver virtually saved the manuscript by her dedication, thoroughness and keen sense of judgment. Ruth Mannes, production editor, has been extremely patient, understanding, and helpful at all stages of the production process.

The Indian Imagination

Chapter 1 ⬖

Indian Writing in English: Structure of Consciousness, Literary History and Critical Theory

I

he Indian Imagination is an interdisciplinary study in the humanities and a critical discourse on patterns of consciousness. Essentially a work in twentieth-century literature, this book focuses on literary developments in English both in the colonial and postcolonial periods of Indian history. Six divergent writers—Aurobindo Ghose (Sri Aurobindo), Mulk Raj Anand, Balachandra Rajan, Nissim Ezekiel, Anita Desai and Arun Joshi—are studied as representations of a consciousness that emerged from a confrontation between tradition and modernity and from a deep sense of tradition during the colonial and postcolonial periods. British India is a historical configuration of the European fantasy of colonialism and imperialism, the fantasy that was finally dissolved in the first half of this century but only to be reinstituted by another fantasy or dream, of the restructuring of sociohistorical reality of an independent India, a sovereign nation-state. Aurobindo and Mulk Raj Anand are active participants in the representation of these two sides, the colonial India and the postcolonial India. And so is Balachandra Rajan, the well-known Miltonist. Nissim Ezekiel, Anita Desai and Arun Joshi are youthful voices of new India. The study argues that the two phases of history—as also the two characteristic phases of Indian writing in English—are a combined representation of the sociohistorical process of colonialization and decolonization and of the affirmation of identity and that no reasonable interpretation of postcoloniality can be sustained in the larger debate on human freedom without a presumptive reference to coloniality. This study goes far beyond the so-called rhetorical formulations of "third-worldism"[1] or of postcolonialism as subculture. While the work examines the impact of European intellectual thought, it traces the historical and psychological process of a cultural and ideological confrontation and synthesis of East and West.

Despite the incisive work of scholars like K. R. Srinivasa Iyengar,[2] the literary history of Indian writing in English remains a virgin territory. One would naturally assume that the origin and development of Indian writing in English are directly traceable to the firm establishment of British colonial India as a part of the British Empire.[3] By this time the philosophical basis of colonial governance and the repressive psychological process of colonization, including the Macaulayan system of education, had succeeded in erecting a confrontational cultural divide and in arousing radical nationalistic sentiment. While the general impact of European intellectual thought over the years cannot be denied and while the matter of India's inheritance from the British Empire is still being debated by historians, one cannot help noting the emergence of two seemingly contradictory cultural phenomena: the revolutionary nationalism that had unequivocally rejected the idea of the empire, and cultural pluralism that made the idea of progress rationally acceptable. Thus while progressive elements of Indian society accepted modernity in principle, they outrightly and vociferously rejected imperial subjugation. It is important to remember that although the Royal Asiatic Society of Bengal was founded by Sir William Jones in 1784, the general image of India portrayed in the European Orientalist discourse on India, with the notable exception of the ideas of some "Brahmanised Britons" like Jones and Munro,[4] was one of backwardness and despotism. It is against this historical background that one would consider the structure of the Indian imagination. Raja Rammohan Roy, the first advocate of progress, also happens to be the first great master of English prose. "The renaissance in modern Indian literature," maintains Iyengar, "begins with Raja Rammohan Roy,"[5] who is also known as the founder of the Brahmo Samaj.

Indeed, Rabindranath Tagore and Aurobindo Ghose (Sri Aurobindo) belong to the early phase of Indian writing in English. Tagore's reputation as a poet was well established and he was awarded the Nobel prize for literature in 1913. While Tagore's imagination is characterized by universalism, humanism and cosmopolitanism, Aurobindo's vision as a poet and a philosopher is much more erudite and comprehensive. The criteria used by T. S. Eliot in the assessment of Goethe as a European poet—abundance, amplitude, unity, universality and wisdom[6]—are truly applicable to both Tagore and Aurobindo, especially the latter. Aurobindo's *The Life Divine* is the greatest contemporary work in Indian philosophical thought and the poem *Savitri* is undoubtedly an important epic venture compared by some to Dante's *Divine Comedy*. In the history of English poetry in India one finds that Henry Derozio (1809–31) and Michael Madhusudan Dutt (1827–73) are early practitioners of English verse and were followed by Toru Dutt, Manmohan Ghose (Aurobindo's older brother), Sarojini Naidu and Romesh Chander Dutt. The enviable achievements of Romesh Chander Dutt as a poet are comparable to those of Manmohan Ghose, who had earned recognition as a poet during his stay in England and who, having considered England as the nurse of his early intellectual growth, is known to have struggled between the two exiles.[7] But the names of Tagore and Aurobindo stand in a different category: while critical assessments are still being made about the progress made by Indian writers in the field of English poetry, it is difficult to think about a contemporary Tagore or an Aurobindo. The contemporary poets of the post-1947 era, including well-known names like Dom Moraes, A. K. Ramanujan, P. Lal, R. Parthasarathy and Nissim Ezekiel, mostly share the modernist tradition of English poetry. Lately, the "New" poets' "scornful" attitude toward Aurobindo has undergone an interesting dramatic change; the situation in many ways reminds one of the treatment of Milton in the history of English literature and of Harold Bloom's theory of the anxiety of influence.[8] The "New" poets' relationship with Aurobindo, which Iyengar compares with T.S. Eliot's criticism of Milton and the Romantics can be understood by the following statement:

> Sri Aurobindo happens to be our Milton, and Toru Dutt, Sarojini Naidu, Manmohan Ghose . . . our Romantic singing birds. They provide sufficient provocation to experiment afresh, set new standards, preserve what is vital in the tradition and give a definition to the needs of the present.[9]

The reconstruction of the Savitri-Satyavan legend into a cosmic myth is Aurobindo's greatest achievement in *Savitri*. One does not have to be an ideologue or a member of a particular school of thought in order to recognize Aurobindo's achievements as a poet, philosopher and critic. His evolutionary philosophy is essentially concerned with the progress of humanity, transformation from "animal humanity into a diviner race."[10] His vision of India may be termed idealistic but certainly not trivial or undignified: "India has existed for humanity, and not for herself, and it is for humanity and not for herself that she must become great."[11] "Aurobindo," affirms Langley, "is primarily a poet and most of his early writing is poetical."[12]

II

The Indian novel in English as compared to novels in other Indian languages, remarks Mukherjee, had a relatively slow start.[13] Starting with K. S. Venkataramani's *Murugan the Tiller* (1927), essentially a work in Gandhian economics, we witness the arrival of the famous trio, Mulk Raj Anand, Raja Rao and R. K. Narayan. The history of the English novel in the eighteenth century from Daniel Defoe onward shows that the novel as an art form is essentially a social document. The Indian novel in English, which seems to have followed the track of the early English novel has its immediate context in the nationalist movement; some of the major themes treated by various novelists are nationalism, the East-West conflict, Gandhian ideology, the struggle for independence, and various social and economic issues such as casteism, poverty and industrial development. In the post-independence era, however, the dramatic shift was to the colonial period, reexamination of imperialism, multiculturalism of Indian society, psychoanalysis of national identity and emergence of India as a sovereign nation. But these sociohistoric developments in India are not much different from those in the erstwhile colonies, including America, Australia, Canada and the Caribbean. In *Cat's Eye,* Margaret Atwood raises the issue of national identity in a newly evolving cultural mosaic of Canada: are Canadians Brits?[14] What can one possibly make of the continued homelessness of Mr Biswas in V. S. Naipaul's *A House for Mr Biswas?* Against the background of the homelessness and exile of Mr Biswas and the unresolvable conflict between order and disorder there is the allegory of the impoverished and alienated writer. Naipaul's poignant treatment of the history of 300 years of struggle of the East Indian indentured labor in Trinidad shows that the capitalist-colonial structure, with its attendant gifts of poverty, ugliness and class structure, has permanently destroyed the potential of Mr Biswas as a writer, thus siphoning him into the irreversible state of alienation, fear and despair.[15]

The sincerity, forthrightness and intensity with which Naipaul examines sociohistoric conditions, especially the colonial person and colonial reality, are also seen in the novels of Mulk Raj Anand and Raja Rao. While Mulk Raj Anand and Raja Rao are directly involved with the sociopolitical realities, R. K. Narayan remains aloof, completely shutting off all possible incursions of Western history or discourse. But the achievements of Bhabani Bhattacharya, Manohar Malgonkar, Sudhin Ghose, Kamala Markandaya, Khushwant Singh and Ruth Prawer Jhabvala cannot be swept aside. In terms of their inevitable preoccupations with the history of pre-independence India and the issues of social reality, one can readily see some sort of common ground between Bhattacharya and Malgonkar. Bhattacharya's *So Many Hungers!* (1947) still remains a classic fictional narrative of the war years. Malgonkar's *A Bend in the Ganges* (1964) is a historic narrative, much in the tradition of Walter Scott, dealing with the collusive impact of World War II, British colonialism and India's struggle for freedom. Khushwant Singh's *Train to Pakistan* (1956), with its imaginary creation of Mano Majra, is indisputably a significant work on the subject of India's division.[16] Undoubtedly, Khushwant Singh is a realist, and so is Mulk Raj Anand: the important difference is that Anand's realism derives its strength and direction from his humanism. The treacherous brutality in Khushwant Singh is comparable to Anand's more dense and blatant unearthing of the lowest depths of life in its utterly naked form, somewhat resembling the tradition of "dirty realism" or the French "misérabilisme."[17] Mulk Raj Anand's first five novels, *Untouchable, Coolie, Two Leaves and a Bud, The Village* and *Across the Black Waters,* simply endorse the critical judgment that Anand returned from England after 25 years as a well-established novelist. Anand, a Kantian scholar, is a prolific novelist, an essayist, an art critic and a thinker. He is still writing in an attempt to complete the biographical series; the hero Krishan is a unique creation, not like a Shelleyan Prometheus but more like a Byronic figure.

I have said elsewhere, and would repeat unhesitatingly, that *Untouchable* still remains his best work. E. M. Forster's preface is one of the most significant critical statements on the literary merits of the novel and on Anand as a novelist:

> Avoiding rhetoric and circumlocution, it has gone straight to the heart of its subject . . . and it is to the directness of his attack that Mr. Anand's success is probably due . . . *Untouchable* could only have been written by an Indian, and by an Indian who observed from the outside. No European, however sympathetic, could have created the character of Bakha . . . And no Untouchable could have written the book, because he would have been involved in indignation and self-pity.[18]

Forster's emphasis on Anand's objectivity and directness should help one remember that he does not glamorize India and life in general; on the contrary he, as Nagarajan remarks, "sees life in the raw and exposes it mercilessly. . . ."[19] In revealing the hidden, repelling and horrifying spaces that define the destiny of caste-out people, Anand challenges the moral conscience of the upper-caste Hindus for castigating and permanently subjugating a segment of community. Anand's greatest contribution as a literary artist is that he has been able to place the repugnant issues of untouchability and casteism in the open before the caste-ridden Hindu society and its colonial master.[20] The novel *Coolie* was also warmly received both in England and in India. The two metaphors, untouchable and coolie, are sociohistoric metaphors of enslavement, subjugation, servitude and dispossession.

Balachandra Rajan, an eminent scholar of Milton and an academician, presently resides in Canada. Of the two novels he has written, *The Dark Dancer* for one is as tragic as the times it portrays. The East-West confrontation that Forster dramatizes in *A Passage to India* is represented in the struggles of the Cambridge-educated Krishanan who has returned to India, his native home. But it is not the main point of the narrative; it is Krishanan's search for identity in the post-independence India. During the course of his search he encounters two tragedies, the tragedy of Kamala's death and the tragedy of the partition of India. The book must remind one of the novels of Manohar Malgonkar and Khushwant Singh, and the historicism of the Indian novel in English. If the East-West conflict is only a political statement, what about the issues of race and gender? Krishanan's struggle for identity reminds one of Yeats' s lines: "Many times man lives and dies / Between his two eternities / That of race and that of soul. . . ."[21] Does a writer have a national label? What about a writer's worldview? The fictional character of Krishnan could be allegorical of Rajan himself, of a Manmohan Ghose, a Nehru and a score of other Western- educated Indians whose minds have been developed by European intellectual thought but whose hearts have remained devoutly Indian.

It is somewhat surprising to note that the post-independence era has witnessed the emergence of a large number of eminent women novelists. The work of such writers as Kamala Markandaya, Ruth Prawer Jhabvala, Anita Desai, Attia Hussein and Nayantra Sahgal simply shows that Indian women writers have vigorously and effectively responded to conflictual developments in a newly evolving postcolonial culture. One may wonder if this unique structure of feminine sensibility possesses special psychosociological and psychobiological characteristics and if this literary phenomenon is any way related to developments in contemporary feminism. Indeed, Markandaya, Jhabvala and Desai are the three most outstanding novelists and their novels show imaginative depth and highly developed sensitivity to the art and craft of the novel. Markandaya's first novel *Nectar in a Sieve* (1954), which has been linked to Pearl S. Buck's *The Good Earth* and Venkataramani's *Murugan the Tiller,*[22] deals with Indian peasants. The thesis is partly Rousseauistic and Wordsworthian and partly Gandhian. In the five novels that have followed Markandaya presents the picture of Indian life emerging from a struggle between tradition and modernity. While there is a sense of loss, frustration and anxiety in both Markandaya and Desai, Jhabvala closely watches as an outsider the confusion of life resulting from cultural conflicts in the urban middle-class families. Among the women novelists, Anita Desai's originality of vision and unmatched artistry put her in a unique position as a novelist. She has been compared to Jane Austen and Virginia Woolf. Meenakshi Mukherjee maintains that Desai's "language is marked by three characteristics: sensuous richness, a high-strung sensitiveness, and a love for the sound of words."[23] But there is a side of the artist Anita Desai that one sees emerging in *In Custody* and *Baumgartner's Bombay;* it is her vision of history that makes these two works universal representations of history and human consciousness. However, in *Baumgartner's Bombay* she merges the histories of India and Europe into a substantially larger theme of human destiny, misery and desolation against the composite background of British colonialism, German fascism and the twin gifts of the independence and division of India. But it must be remembered that the distinct quality of the representation of history makes Rajan's *The Dark Dancer* and Desai's *Baumgartner's Bombay* outstanding achievements of Indian fiction in English.

In the untimely death of Arun Joshi, India has lost a novelist of great promise. His novels deal with the complexities and inextricabilities of modern urban industrial culture; the refulgence of conscience is followed by the moral and psychological process of self-rehabilitation. Iyengar makes the following observation about Joshi's heroes: "Arun Joshi's heroes—Sindi Oberoi, Billy, Ratan, Som Bhasker [*sic*]—are all 'outsiders' after a fashion, making desperate attempts to silence the insidious bug within and reach a rapport with the world."[24] While Ratan Rathor attempts self-rehabilitation in the manner of a Dostoevskian hero, Som Bhaskar is a very Pascalian figure.

There is no doubt that the Indian novel in English has made significant progress, but extensive critical effort is needed to assess the nature and quality of this progress, to determine possible trends and schools in relationship not only to other Indian literatures, but also to world literatures, and, above all, to identify a work of universal significance. Has it followed the categories established by Mulk Raj Anand, Raja Rao and R. K. Narayan? One would have naturally assumed that Desani's *All About H. Hatterr* (1948), a Joycean experiment that had appealed to T. S. Eliot,[25] could have become the trendsetter. Desani's novel, one of the most ingenious fictional narratives, was republished with a sympathetic introduction by Anthony Burgess. Indeed, the mad Hatterr, the antihero, is, as Williams notes, "Desani's great achievement."[26] But the creation of Banerrji, the facetious Bengali intellectual, the lover of English literature, without whom the parodic design of the novel will not be complete, is not any lesser achievement. Surely, one feels the overwhelming presence of Swift, Sterne and Rabelais in Desani's liberal use of lampoonery, parody, caricature, satire and irony, but behind the obfuscatory mad pursuits of Hatterr and the facetiousness of Banerrji is Desani's knowledge of Buddhism, which lends its controlling voice to madness, grotesqueness and absurdity—and hence to the unreality of life. The writer who seems to resemble Desani in certain special ways is Sudhin Ghose, but the real extension of Desani is seen in Salman Rushdie's literary artistry in *Midnight's Children*. Anand is the first Indian novelist who experimented with the idea of the antihero, and he along with Raja Rao is a pioneer of the political novel. A serious reading of Desani and Rushdie shows that they are hardly apolitical. Situated in sociohistoricity and postcoloniality, Naipaul's and Rushdie's novels are supposed to be trendsetters. Anand, Rao and Narayan are still writing, and one would wish that a work like *Conversations in Bloomsbury*, an original experiment in sociohistoricity and literary history, could be the trendsetter. Indeed, I am raising the question of influence, tradition and continuity, but I am also thinking of a novelist of promise, wisdom and originality. One could hardly disagree with Rushdie that "on the map of world literature, too, India has been undersized for too long,"[27] but a bumper crop of writing in English has emerged from the non-imperial postcolonial cultures, especially from India. One would simply hope that the younger group of Indo-Anglian novelists is able to represent India in a broad cultural context of human civilization, showing a marked advancement of the Indian novel in English.

III

Although the fundamental consideration in this study is Hegel's conception of history and consciousness, I have been eclectic in the choice of an approach or approaches to the reading of a particular author or a work. I am fully sensitive to the methodology of New Criticism, according to which the integrity of the text, the structure of language and the evolution of literary form are interactive units for the study of meaning. Should criticism serve the end of ideology, philosophy, history or moral science? I am raising this question as a sequel to Murray Krieger's rhetorical observation:" . . . how can writing itself be other than a moral act . . . ?"[28] What does a work of art mean? How is that "whatness" of a work determined? Does the totalizing vision of a work pertain to its meaning in relation to a tradition, a structure of consciousness, or an ideology? Should the question of "whatness" lead us to consider the use of various tools from amongst academic disciplines—history, psychology, sociology, philosophy, anthropology and political science—that will illuminate the "stubborn structure"? If the function of literature or an aesthetic production is to aid in the social reconstruction and the improvement of culture, should literature then become subservient to what Frye calls "concern" and "anxiety"?[29] Of course, the inherent paradox in such formulations is that communal good or social reconstruction is not an extraneous moral value but an integrative function of the imagination. It could be argued that if concern and anxiety are simply advocated as extraneous values and not as mythic, typological or some other form of linguistic structure, we would then be talking about a political ideology.

If criticism is a "structure of knowledge,"[30] can areas of knowledge such as metaphysics, religion or another discipline from the humanities be excluded from a discourse? How will one attempt a postmodernist or postcolonial reading of Tagore and Aurobindo? I have suggested elsewhere that the conflation of Aurobindo and Marx will provide a nontraditional but intellectually expansive reading, for after all both Aurobindo and Marx are theorists of social reconstruction.[31] It is not surprising that Fredric Jameson, a Marxist critic, finds the critical methodology of Northrop Frye based on the medieval schema of the four levels of meaning acceptable, for it is community-centered.[32] Jacques Barzun's conflation of Darwin, Marx and Wagner convincingly suggests the direction an enlightened critic can take; as a work of criticism his book that treats three revolutions—the biological revolution, the social revolution and the artistic revolution—as a unity is a significant contribution to the history of ideas.[33] This is also the case with Northrop Frye's *The Critical Path,* in which his commentary on Marxism shows his own Romantic liberalism.[34]

New historicism, combining the ideas of Foucault, Williams and others, has emerged as an important critical theory. It may be argued that the representation of history is an issue for literature, but that the discovery of history is an issue for an historian. "Fiction," maintains Conrad, "is history, human history, or it is nothing."[35] In equating fiction and history, Conrad's controversial statement equates historical reality and fictional reality. Hegel's view of history, Marx's view of history and most other important views of history, conveniently summarized by Georg Lukács in *The Historical Novel,*[36] show if the identity theory can hold out in reaffirming that the truth of history is the truth of literature. It is important to consider Jameson's Marxist interpretation of history in *The Political Unconscious:* " . . . that history is *not* a text, not a narrative. . . ."[37] Although history and text are not identical, "a narrative . . . [is] a retextualization of History. . . ." Admittedly, then, the structural principle of a narrative is to superimpose a form, possibly by the world of desire, on history which has its own form. Thus the world of desire finally achieves its control over the causality of history. But the Nietzschean thesis of the degenerative influence of history must not be forgotten: like the Book of Revelation, Nietzsche's presumption of the coming of the superman is based on the annihilation of the past. Should the past, like an Indian *yuga,* become a self-integrative part of history? Hegel's progressive view of history constitutes the basic formulation of this study, for in one particular sense it helps to articulate Aurobindo's view of history, especially that of evolutionary progress of man and society. But in Hegel as in Aurobindo the word "consciousness" holds the currency in understanding the relationship between art and consciousness and art and history. Art, for Hegel, "is *a mode of consciousness* of the Idea, but it is not a *representation* of it."[38] It is this modality of consciousness that in turn determines the quality of art.

Hegel also relates the idea of consciousness to the dialectic of the master-slave relationship where it is the master who has been reduced to the subhuman level; for the slave, through his work, is the creator and the knower of "the world of reality." Thus "the slave becomes a universal consciousness through his work." The true fulfillment of desire, the realization of self-consciousness, consists of the twin process of annulment of otherness or foreignness and the recognition of others as human beings, for Hegel maintains that "self-consciousness attains its satisfaction only in another self-consciousness."[39]

Although postcolonial critical theory is still in its infancy, it seems to be making important strides in clarifying and defining itself. Helen Tiffin points out that Raja Rao and Achebe have been successful in the dismantling and unmasking of the Western master narrative of history.[40] But it would be only logical to assume that total freedom from imperial vision and the perverse mechanism of hegemony is a long sociopsychological and historical process of continuous decoding. We cannot forget the circuitous repetition of history: the imperialism and colonialism of the first world to which the countries of the third world had been subjected manifests itself as the present first-world cultural imperialism, a postmodernist phenomenon, which has enveloped the third-world mind under the name of materialistic progress. Evidently, the assumption is that under the pretext of global economic structure no third-world nation can seek to foster independent progress and self-identity.

No discourse on postcoloniality can be considered with its complete and full meaning without taking into account the history of the colonial period. But if postcoloniality should emerge only from the actual colonial condition, then it "can be best thought of as a form of contestatory/oppositional consciousness. . . ."[41] One of the dangers of this kind of formulation is that the discourse may have its scholarly limitations. What is needed is a hardheaded scholarly theorization of the structure of colonial consciousness, the empire-building enterprise and the history and psychology of power that must subjugate others by a process of deprivation and dispossession. In a sense, the history of coloniality, as Bhabha explains, reveals the limitations of Western metaphysics and humanistic thought.[42]

The term postcoloniality with all its "semantic instability," may be defined as a structure of consciousness of the decolonized mind in history, but most certainly it is simply not a reactionary and empty combative "cannon-fodder,"[43] or a Blakean negation. Undoubtedly, it absorbs certain elements of postmodernism,[44] but its immediate context is provided by the psychoanalytic and sociohistoricity of coloniality.

IV

Jerome McGann refers to Frantz Fanon's concluding argument that "'the fate of the world depends upon' whether the first two worlds, and especially the first world, are able to operate from a non-colonialist imagination," inferring "that the first world must be forced to realize its obligation not merely to allow the Third World its independent development, but also to assist actively in that development, and with no strings attached."[45] Surprisingly, but very correctly, however, McGann juxtaposes Fanon's Third Imagination with that of Benjamin (ironically equating Fanon's and Benjamin's imaginative voices) who in his famous thesis states that "there is no document of civilization which is not at the same time a document of barbarism."[46] Will the first world, wonders McGann, examine its past of violence and domination? The Third Imagination's perception of the first world's barbarity and its history of imperial dominance, power and violence, as McGann convincingly argues, lead us, through multiple and conflictual voices, to the unfaltering poetic voices of Blake and Shelley. While Blake's radical imagination boldly rejects the empire-building ideology, Shelley's imagination liberates Prometheus, one Humanity, from the despotism of Jupiter. But in Blake's scheme of things in *Milton,* the third world, as McGann notes, becomes "appropriated to the missionary zeal of an Elected design," which for Blake is "not merely moral righteousness" but actually "political imperialism."[47] McGann's new historicist reading, combining Foucault and Fanon, appropriates Blake's categories to the contemporary division of the world into first, second and third worlds. The first world of the imperializer and the colonizer is the world of the Elect, where religion and empire join to create a cultural other, which is the third world. One wonders if the "non-colonialist" imagination will become a contemporary cultural reality.

Considering the amazingly heteroglossial nature of the discourse on India, one must ask: what would constitute a true and honest representation of India? We are well familiar with a vast variety of imperial representations of India, from William Jones to James and John Stuart Mill to Kipling and Forster, and the indigenous representations of India from Rammohan Roy, Tagore, Aurobindo, Gandhi to Mulk Raj Anand. Whose representation of India is more faithful? Goethe's India, Hegel's India, Southey's India, De Quincey's India, Shelley's India, Kipling's India, or Forster's India! How does the European Orientalist discourse, as problematized by Edward Said, Homi Bhabha and other postcolonial critics, give, or rather not give us the voice of truth? And what about the literary representations of India by Indian writers of the pre-independence and post-independence eras? Can history or literature—we must not forget Conrad's identity theory—communicate the truth of India, colonial India and postcolonial India? It must not be forgotten that the picture of colonial India in history—India as a backward and inferior culture—has been considered the British Empire's greatest defense for the dramatic conversion of the East India Company, merely a trading company, into an imperial possessor. And yet there is another view advanced by Indian historians like Mazumdar, according to which the East India Company, following its success in the Battle of Plassey in 1757, had nurtured territorial ambition for the occupation of the rich subcontinent.[48] This is not to suggest, however, that the conduct of the French and Portuguese colonists in India was any different.

James Mill's *The History of British India* (1818), which remained a standard reference source and also a textbook for the training of British colonial officers to be stationed in India has not stood the test of time. As John Clive remarks: "Mill's attempt to show the subordinate position occupied by Indian culture and civilization on the scale of human progress is hardly in accord with twentieth-century opinion."[49] The value of Mill's *History* has been greatly debated both by the Utilitarians and Orientalists. H. H. Wilson who edited Mill's *History* in 1840 calls it "evil in tendency." William Thomas maintains that eventually "many of Mill's most serious contentions have been discredited, no less than Burke's." But historically of course Mill fully shared the developments at home, especially the victory of evangelical movements, with the passage of the Charter Act in 1813, and the consequential reshaping of the English attitude toward India: "From then on the evangelizing aims of the missions and the anglicizing aims of the succession of aristocratic governors-general who followed Cornwallis went hand in hand, to encourage Englishmen in an attitude of contempt for the civilization they were called on to rule."[50] Despite the "profound gulf between their actual practising ideas," notes Eric Stokes, "the assumptions of the Evangelical theology and the Utilitarian philosophy were remarkably similar."[51] Blake, as McGann notes, was probably right that the empire by assigning the third world to the Elect actually assigned it to evangelicalism. Mill's *History* thus proved to be a collusive document of power and knowledge on the one hand and of history, education and politics on the other. One may simply have to speculate the immense capacity of such a document to produce in the colonized mind the precipitous conditions of fear, violence and repression, the unchecked psychoses of colonial governance.

That India became a laboratory for practicing Bentham's Utilitarian philosophy is indeed true.[52] But in order to reach the truth of the Utilitarians' general attitude towards India, one needs to examine the positions of Burke, Macaulay and the Orientalist Sir William Jones. After all, Mill's *History* is considered to be a combative response to Jones's romantic philosophy of Orientalism. Mill, as Thomas points out, "leaves unexplored Burke's conviction that there was a vast East India Company interest eating away the liberties of the Parliament." Significantly, Macaulay, whose signal contribution to the British Indian governance is his famous Minute on Education, later on came to admire Mill's *History.* In fact, Macaulay had sincerely endorsed "James Mill's statement that any form of representative government was utterly out of the question."[53] Whatever the ramifications of Mill's political ideology and his adherence to Utilitarianism at home, in so far as India is concerned, Mill's views, as Thomas points out, "were firmly on the side of the soldier-administrators who ruled the country by the sword." He could have never accepted the fundamental principle in Jones's philosophy and Burke's and Hastings's—"that Englishmen in India were the guests of a civilization." On the contrary, underlying Mill's *History* is his fundamental conviction that "the overthrow of native culture, especially Hindu culture, [is] not only inevitable, but desirable."The Anglicist strategy of assiduously denigrating and condemning indigenous cultural traditions—metaphysics, art, language, education and sociology—and replacing them with European cultural structures more or less defines the ideology of subjugation and imperial domination. But this psychological formulation of the ideology of colonialism and imperialism, based on the principles of conversion, subjugation and replacement, was initially rooted in the social biology of race—that Asiatics or Orientals are basically inferior.

It remains a matter of intellectual puzzlement and embarrassment that John Stuart Mill, one of the most radical liberals and the last of the English Utilitarians, who remained an active participant in most forms of revolutionary political changes in England and who is credited with an enlightened discourse on the moral and political significance of liberty, should have persistently opposed India's right to freedom. Undoubtedly, the younger Mill had unreservedly endorsed his father's position on the British governance of India by power and stern authority, and had categorically "declared there to be no other practical alternative to a pure and enlightened despotism."[54] As a result, the British colonial government in India had reportedly "approached most nearly Hobbes's ideal of the Leviathan, 'that immortal god to whom we owe, under the immortal God, our peace and defence.'[55] In the case of India, the "greatest happiness principle" of Utilitarianism became as dysfunctional as some of the other experiments in the refinement of moral and political freedom—Fabianism, Chartism and Owenism.

The overwhelming evidence of the historical continuity of the superiority of racial consciousness in the imperial mind in the writings of Carlyle, Thackeray, Charlotte and Emily Bronte, and later in the works of Conrad and Kipling, displaces the fortuitous assumption that the arts, the Word, will be the intercessor in the tyrannous reign of human domination and slavery. How in a modern humanistic enterprise can one nation with power and knowledge justify the enslavement of another nation in the name of backwardness, racial inferiority, or political expansionism? One must recognize the intrepidness and honesty with which Edward Said questions the European and British humanistic enterprise, cultural and literary, in its astounding failure to deal with the phenomenon of imperialism and its relation to culture and its formulations.[56] Said does not refer to the early political writings of Aurobindo or Tagore. Both Tagore and Aurobindo have persistently and vigorously denounced the political ideologies of British humanism and liberalism that became instrumental, either by an inexplicable silence or by an aggressive reformatory zeal, in the formulation of the colonizer's repressive and authoritarian policies and attitudes toward India as a colonial possession. Basically, it is this psychosociological contempt directed at intellectual and emotional desiccation, the idea of cultural denigration that underlies the theoretical formulations of Orientalism. Mulk Raj Anand in *Conversations in Bloomsbury* enters into a series of confrontational discussions with T. S. Eliot, E. M. Forster, D. H. Lawrence, the Woolfs and other members of the Bloomsbury intellectual elite on their perceptions of the general imperializing process and India's right to freedom. I have tried to show in chapter 6 the imaginative subtlety with which Anand evokes his memory to parody and satirize the British humanist attitude toward the colonized subject. But the matter of India's political freedom and her prolonged struggle against her colonial masters is one of the common topics in Indian fiction written in English.

The newly emerging conceptualizations of nationalism as a form of political expansionism or legitimization of the political desire of a group of people to aspire to a more cohesive structure by seeking an Other must indeed examine the process of "nation-making," of seeking some supernational identity. But the imperialization of desire means possession of the Other, and not its creation, as a separate cultural identity. Thus in the cultural umbrella the political governance of the empire became divided into two categories, one set of socioeconomic and sociopolitical structure for the metropolis and another for the rural constituencies of the empire. The foundations of the moral and political structure of the metropolis were rooted in the conceptual formulation of nation-making, but the structure of the rural territories was conceived on the fundamental principles of divisiveness, disunity and disintegration. The moral and political legitimization of this sort of instrumentation could only rest on the idea of empire-building as a fulfillment of national hubris. This complex political formulation of the relationships between the empire and the colonies leads us directly to the early English debate on the conception of the state and the relationship between state and culture. While Burke had proposed "political trusteeship" for India, he wanted Ireland and America to be bound "to Great Britain and the British Constitution by the same ties of affectionate loyalty and honorable self-interest as was naturally operative over the hearts of Englishmen."[57] Was Burke's relentless tirade against Hastings prompted by his genuine concern for India and by the idealistic conception of the relationship between the mother country and the colonies, or by some other political motivations? Burke's position on India needs further scrutiny, but it is important to remember that the colonies were regarded as no more than "tributary states." Ironically, Coleridge would regard state as "a spiritual community cohering by virtue of an inner necessity."[58] If the state is conceived as a spiritual or religious community or a national community, what will be the role and place of an Asian or African rural constituency in this political structure? Apparently, whatever positions have been advanced on this subject by Kant and Hegel in Germany, and by Burke, Coleridge, Wordsworth, Southey and Eliot in England, one could say more confidently that these idealistic conceptualizations were unrelated to the Asian and African territories of the empire.

V

The role and place of Sir William Jones, the founder of the Asiatic Society of Bengal, can hardly be underestimated in any careful examination of the beginnings of Orientalism's discourse in the eighteenth century and the modern developments in Indian studies, or "scholarly orientalism," a term used by S. N. Mukherjee. Whatever one might think of Jones's work in Indian jurisprudence, languages, literature and metaphysics, his impact on Indian and English writers, especially the English Romantic writers, still remains a subject of scholarly interest.[59] Of course Jones, as Mukherjee points out, shared with his fellow compatriots the usual English attitude of being radically liberal at home but militaristic and authoritarian in India.

The fundamental hypothesis in Said's critical theory, derived from Gramsci's conception of hegemony and Foucault's philosophy of power and knowledge, is the relationship between empire and culture; in this complex relationship the discourse of Orientalism is produced by the primary center as a manifestation of latent Orientalism. While the primariness of the European-piloted oriental discourse is forever guaranteed, the secondariness of the non-European subject becomes rooted in the racial divide. Orientalism as a body of recrafted knowledge of the Orient must be distinguished from the objective, scientific or poetic and philosophical discourse on the Orient. Despite the problematization of power, knowledge and value, one must consider truth, not ideology, the ultimate objective of a humanist discourse. In that sense alone, knowledge produced as pure knowledge in the humanistic strain should help abolish categories known as "Orient" and "Occident."[60] Criticism as "critical consciousness" is a filial and affiliative process, both intellectually and culturally; thus "criticism modified in advance by labels like 'Marxism' or 'liberalism' is . . . an oxymoron."[61] Note Said's explicit affirmation: " . . . criticism must think itself as life-enhancing and constitutively opposed to every form of tyranny, domination, and abuse; its social goals are noncoercive knowledge produced in the interests of human freedom."[62]

It should be remembered that even though Christian missionaries and British administrators who did any significant work in Oriental studies were an integral part of the imperial ethos and pathos Indian nationals had conveniently used Jones's work in defense against the implacable hate and belittlement of their civilization. The development of the European interest in India from the eighteenth century onwards, from the Romantics to the Victorians and to the modernist era, is directly related to the political significance achieved by India as the nerve center of the larger imperial design. Ironically, India for the British Empire had become "the jewel in the crown." Nevertheless, it is probably logical to assume, as Edward Said does, that the entire discourse on Orientalism, with the exception of the work of "Brahmanised" scholars like William Jones, Anquetil-Duperron and Raymond Schwab whose scholarship is free from ethnic and racial considerations, is a byproduct of collusive and hegemonic engineering of the European power and knowledge. The sentimental presumption, if it be so characterized by a certain degree of intellectual skepticism, that classical Indian metaphysics, art, literature and religious thought had suddenly aroused a powerful interest in the nineteenth century and then later in the modernist era, must be validated against the social, economic and political realities of the colonial status of the possessed. While classical Indian thought has attracted such great minds as Schopenhauer, Nietzsche, Yeats, Eliot, Jung and Hesse, colonial

India had become a battlefield for testing the moral and political conscience of the empire.

Anquetil-Duperron, Jones, Colebrook and other members of the Asiatic Society are usually regarded as ameliorists and pioneers of a burgeoning movement to introduce Indian civilization to the European mind. But the body of Orientalism, as it emerged later in Europe, presents a picture of a cultural stereotype, representing an Oriental variously and severally, as sensual, despotic, weak, effeminate, racially inferior and indolent. Thus, the two contrasting impressions, one cultivated by Mill's *History* and the other by Jones, have traveled together since then. History needs to determine if the sociopolitical and psychological subjectification of an Oriental to a position of secondariness was prompted either by anthropological considerations of race or by a quaintness of Wordsworthian primitivism and rural simplicity. The Romantic discourse on India seems to have followed the trajectorial development outlined by the Asiatic Society. The German mind's interest in classical India, from Hegel to Deussen, has been considered much too sincere and dispassionate to be doubted and distrusted, for it was at least free from the taints of any direct German colonial interests in India. While Hegel and Schlegel associate the Indian view of things with a variety of pantheism, Deussen, as Inden points out, hypothesizes that "the inner, imaginative thoughts of the *Upanishads,* was the origin of both the Eastern and Western philosophy," a hypothesis that has been challenged.[63] Northrop Frye, it should be noted, is quick to suggest that Blake was eager to align his thought with that of *Bhagavadgita*.[64] Goethe looked upon India most poetically and here one may think about the case of Shelley whose interest in Indian metaphysics and mythology helped him in poetic syncretism and archetypal perception.[65] The Prometheus-Asia construct has an Indian bearing and so does the universal conflict between Jupiter and Prometheus. Robert Southey, who wrote *Thalaba* and *The Curse of Kehama,* had, as Cobban points out, changed his affiliative position as a pronounced Tory on the subject of England's relationship with the colonies and "had seen the vision of the British Empire as a Commonwealth of Nations as early as the year 1812."[66] Significantly, Coleridge had accepted the civilizing and redemptive mission as a moral duty of Great Britain. Marilyn Butler while advocating the reinclusion of Southey in the English canon and the importance of historicism maintains that Southey in *The Curse of Kehama* "gives a violently unfavorable account of Hinduism," believing that "Hinduism is a cruel, politicized religion, the tool of hereditary rulers."[67] But Byron and Shelley, much against Butler's deep consternation, justifiably believed that Southey's information about India and Hinduism was derived primarily from Christian missionaries' accounts and perhaps from a primary narrative like Mill's *History* and that the poem as such "implicitly justified British empire-building there." Indeed, it is not Southey but Blake who rightly understood the perverted philosophy of empire-building and had categorically declared the incontrovertible truth of liberty: "Empire is no more! and now the lion & wolf shall cease."[68] In questioning Byron's and Shelley's reading of Southey's poem, are we saying that history will give us the apodictic truth from which then the truth of the text can be adduced? But which reconstruction of history, and whose history will convey incontrovertible truth? Gyan Prakash notes Edward Said's assertion that for revealing the relationship between culture and empire, "we must reread the cultural archive 'not univocally but contrapuntally,' reading Jane Austen and John Stuart Mill alongside Frantz Fanon and Amilcar Cabral."[69] Can a genealogical structure of knowledge as theorized by Foucault produce truth that will be universally accepted by all disciplines in the humanities and social sciences? Indeed, these problems of textuality, contextuality and intertextuality help design epistemological and pedagogic approaches to knowledge, and hence to a possible juxtaposition of the world of desire and the world of reality.

VI

Such works as Coleridge's *Kubla Khan* and Shelley's *Alastor* show that for the Romantics India was a world of fantasy, exoticism and desire. Hegel's characterization of the Indian view of things as "universal pantheism" and that of Schlegel as "illusory pantheism," essentially issuing from the imaginative faculty, can only be contrasted to De Quincey's representation of India. Historically related to the exacerbated British interest in India, De Quincey's schizophrenic opium dreams portray the imperial fear of the soul of the Orient; in these dreams he sees the conflated images of India, China and Egypt—the barbarity of the people and culture of India, the psychotic horror of the Oriental character (the turbaned Malay), the swarming millions of people and the highly exaggerated images of the Hindu divinities based on readings of Maurice's *History of Hindostan,* Moor's *The Hindu Pantheon* and Jones's essays in the *Asiatic Researches.*[70] But despite these and later developments in the nineteenth century Mill's *History,* as Inden points out, remains "the oldest hegemonic account of India within the Anglo-French imperial formation."[71] As Inden explains the situation: "He [Hegel] and Mill, along with other political economists, were also the intellectual ancestors of another hegemonic figure, Marx, who reproduced much of what they said but with an emphasis on the economic rather than the political . . . they consolidated and dispensed a discourse on oriental despotism and the Asiatic mode of production."[72] Undoubtedly, Thackeray's Jos Sedley in *Vanity Fair,* Charlotte Bronte's St. John River in

Jane Eyre and Emily Bronte's Heathcliff in *Wuthering Heights* are resounding echoes of the hegemonic discourse on the colonial desire, fantasy and
history. Thackeray, himself of the Anglo-Indian descent, had understood
that evangelicalism, commerce and colonialism are the three major pillars
of the British Empire. "To the writer who substituted individualistic mor-
alizing and racial stereotyping for politics, however," maintains Patrick
Brantlinger, "India appeared only as it does in *The Newcomes*—a field for
potential *British* achievement, conquest, and fortune making and a background of changeless oriental deceit, lasciviousness, and obsequious bow-
ing and scraping to the master race."[73] But the Victorian images of India
are a representation of the dominant colonial thinking of people like Disraeli, Carlyle and J. S. Mill. The three prominent figures in the Victorian
discourse on India are Marx, J. S. Mill and Matthew Arnold. "Despotism,"
maintains Mill, "is a legitimate mode of government in dealing with barbarians, provided the end be their improvement, and the means justified by
actually effecting that end."[74] Apparently, for Mill the colonized subject
races are these barbarians who unless they affect self-improvement for liberty must be subjected to an "implicit obedience to an Akbar. . . ."
    Shelley's "The Mask of Anarchy," a work that was dear to Gandhi, treats
this despotism, and most certainly one should not have any difficulty in
seeing in the history of India's struggle for independence the self-destructive power of such a subversive doctrine of political governance. That a
civil society would on the one hand argue for bestowing liberty on its citizens and on the other advance politically expedient justifications for le-
gitimizing violence and repression is a gross violation of moral and social
conscience. It is somewhat amazing that Mill's reference to barbarians is an
ironic reversal of the metaphor used by Arnold in his *Culture and Anarchy,*
a major document in the culture industry after the ideas of Burke and Coleridge on the subject. Arnold's barbarians are in fact the wealthiest class of
people who like Blake's elect have violated the populace by abandoning
them. Culture, according to Arnold, is the pursuit of perfection. The
progress of civilization thus envisaged by Arnold is supposed to achieve a
classless society, harmony and stability. Strangely, however, Raymond
Williams maintains that Arnold's work "may be said to have generated the
very philistinism it wished to vanquish."[75] The conflictual argument probably centers on Arnold's inability to reconcile the difference between the
spiritual aspects of the social process of culture and the philistines' uncompromising commitment to industrial culture. While the disinterested pursuit of perfection is "an *internal* condition," an inner process of becoming
something rather than in having something, the triumph of the philistines'
realm of industrial culture means the triumph of colonialism and other
similar endeavors of collectivity. Is culture merely a "social idea" or a utopia

embedded in a dreamlike space? What are these "men of culture" who are also "the true apostles of equality?" "The great men of culture," remarks Matthew Arnold, "are those who have had a passion for diffusing, for making prevail, for carrying from one end of society to the other, the best knowledge, the best ideas of their time. . . ."[76] But Arnold's master plan of culture, however idealistic and revolutionary one might term it, was focused on the progress and unity of England and the European community and did not include colonial spaces like India.

Marx's view of the British occupation of India and of the imperial design of turning the Indian colony into an efficient and productive unit of the empire should be weighed against his fundamental convictions: that imperialism, being "the highest stage of capitalism," will write its own tragic end, that any British plan for regeneration will in return nurture the movement for Indian "self-emancipation," and that the creation of newly educated Indian natives will simply expedite the speedy annexations of "[t]hat once fabulous country . . . to the Western world."[77] But Marx had no illusion that the British "aristocracy wanted to conquer it [India], moneyocracy wanted to plunder it, and the millocracy to undersell it," and that the capacity and motives of the British bourgeoisie to achieve progress in India had their limitations. Undoubtedly, Marx's analysis of the colonial governance of India, primarily based on the Hegelian master-slave relationship, takes a predominantly economic view of things. It is rather perplexing to find that Marx would endorse the British policy of destroying the rural village community structure because of its possible historical association with Indian despotism.[78] The British plan had also included the systematic destruction of the Indian cottage industry as a prerequisite for the transformation of India into an industrialized productive unit of the empire. But as a philosopher of history Marx is a reconstructionist and it is not surprising that he had favored the British colonization of India in the interest of modernization and progress.

It can be safely argued that Marx's philosophical model of the expansion and collapse of capitalism in India has psychoanalytical implications. Although the colonial possession of India had been dramatically turned into imperial dependence, the fact remains that Britain's renewed mercantile interest in India's development only helped to intensify the national struggle for independence from foreign dominance. If the imperial possession of the Indian Other had meant a permanent displacement of the creative potential of India, would then the deliverance of the Other or the true creation of the cultural Other mean that India could ever reconstruct itself as a free society? But one would argue that such a construct of Indian civilization is still mapped out by the design and expectations of a neo-imperialist structure. That India as the feminine self was to be possessed by European imperialism is ultimately a commentary on Indian civilization. Indeed, the fateful dismemberment of the Mogul Empire and the occupation of India by the East India Company should be as much a matter for a philosophical disquisition on history as the disintegration of the British Empire. Should the redivivus India be redolent of the Mill-Macaulay policy of India as an imperial possession, of Burke's theory of the limited trusteeship for India, or of Marx's model of the collapse of capitalism? Or should one say unhesitatingly in the interest of an objective theorizing that the birth of new India or splintered India—and here one may remember the writings of Tagore, Aurobindo, Tilak, Gandhi, Nehru and other political leaders of the insurgency movement—was the inevitable result of the struggle of the nationalist movement?

But while the imperial discourse on India was formulated in Europe it is not until the beginning of the twentieth century that the inscriptions of India took a dramatic turn, especially with the appearance of a large body of political writings by Indian nationalists like Tilak, Gokhale, Tagore, Aurobindo, Gandhi and Nehru. However, the three major literary works that have brought the issues of imperialism and culture to a concerted focus are Conrad's *Heart of Darkness,* Kipling's *Kim* and Forster's *A Passage to India.* How are these texts to be read? What do these texts mean?

Conrad's interpretation of the sociology, history and anthropology of colonization of England extending over to the colonization of Africa is undoubtedly imperialistic. His anthropological distinction between the conquerors and colonizers does not go very far to justify the conflation of Kurtz's double-edged desire for white ivory and his youthful African mistress and the politicized philosophy of colonization. Thus it is not utterly surprising that Chinua Achebe characterizes *Heart of Darkness* as a racist document. But how would one answer Achebe's serious charge without dismissing it on simple grounds of nationalism? And how does one read Kipling and Forster? Indeed there are divergent critical interpretations of Kipling and Forster;[79] I have argued in chapter 6 that the Kipling of T. S. Eliot is markedly different from that of Mulk Raj Anand. Edward Said has attempted to formulate the critical problem:

> All the energies poured into critical theory, into novel and demystifying theoretical praxes like the new historicism and deconstruction and Marxism have avoided the major, I would say determining, political horizon of modern Western culture, namely imperialism. This massive avoidance has sustained a canonical inclusion and exclusion: you include the Rousseaus, the Nietzsches, the Wordsworths, the Dickenses, Flauberts, and so on, and at the same you exclude their relationships with the protracted, complex, and striated work of empire. But why is this a matter of what to read and about where? Very simply, because critical discourse has taken no cognizance of the

enormously exciting, varied post-colonial literature produced in resistance
to the imperialist expansion of Europe and the United States in the past two
centuries. To read Austen without also reading Fanon and Cabral . . . is to
disaffiliate modern culture from its engagements and attachments. That is a
process that should be reversed.[80]

Presumably, the question about the problematic of imperialism is equally
addressed to writers, and the kind of sweeping question, especially the way
it has been formulated by Said, should remind one of Georg Lukács's question about the emergence of Hitler: "The classical type of historical novel
can only be aesthetically renewed if writers concretely face the question:
how was the Hitler régime in Germany possible?"[81] This is precisely where
historicism, aesthetic and psychoanalysis are blended to create what Lukács
calls "social type." How imperialism has become a gigantic enterprise in the
midst of all the strides made by Western humanism is an important dilemma
for students of history, moral philosophy, literature and psychoanalysis.

What is the function of criticism? We are indeed reminded of two
major statements, Matthew Arnold's "The Function of Criticism" and T. S.
Eliot's essay of the same title—and in fact of all major statements from
Plato to the modernists and postmodernists. In *The Failures of Criticism*
Henry Peyre has helped raise some very important questions about the
limitations of critical theory. What team of critics or school of criticism
would be considered competent to interpret a work of art and to deal with
imperfections, contradictions, deviations and discontinuities?[82] Historically,
literature and art have been the preoccupations of high culture. Said places
hegemony and imperialism in the center, so that in the interest of truth,
knowledge, freedom, equality and human dignity, critical discourse, by
using various tools such as philosophy, sociohistoricism, Marxism and psychoanalysis, can decenter the imperializing power. Thus the function of
criticism in this context is to decolonize the minds of both the colonizer
and the colonized and to help recreate a civil order where knowledge does
not become an expedient tool of hegemony and imperial subjugation and
domination. If the problem of critical reading of a text can be solved by
designing combinatorial groupings of relevant social texts outside the national and parochial boundaries so as to ensure contrapuntal response, can
it then be reasonably ascertained that we are on the road to discovering
truth and a sense of universalism and humanism? Surely, Fanon's *The
Wretched of the Earth* is the foundational text, but can other works by indigenous writers, if "nativism" be not such a derogatory term, be placed
alongside of Fanon? In a polyphonic reading of Forster's *A Passage to India*,
can works of Tagore, Aurobindo and Nehru and of history, sociology and
philosophy be also added to the reading list? Should Kipling's *Kim* be read

along with Tagore's *Gora* and Mulk Raj Anand's *Untouchable* and *Coolie?* If literature can effectively communicate ideals of liberty, equality, universality and truth and if it can foster a broader intellectual understanding, a sense of universal humanity without walls and boundaries, ethnic, racial or geographical, there is every hope for a better civil society.

One would be justified in assuming that critical theory can effectively deal with imperialism, colonialism, nationalism, patriotism, racism and ethnocentrism—all these stultified expressions of the hubris of collectivity. Yeats's poem "Leda and the Swan" dramatizes the highly complex idea of the allegorical relationship between the imperializing power of a god and the subjugation of the mortal Leda. The god's possession and rape of the otherized Leda is at one level the story of colonial conquest and subjugation. The violent sexual act reinforces the sense of moral violation of the victim of desire. The violent sexual union with Leda is the expression of desire for the possession of the female body, the spatialized and sexualized space. In the fulfillment of this desire even a god can suspend his moral judgment. But the poem, according to Ellmann, expresses Yeats's strong feeling "that power and knowledge could never exist together, [and] to acquire one was to lose the other."[83] One of the eggs of this incestuous union produced Helen who became the cause of the Trojan War and the other egg produced Clytemnestra who married, and destroyed, Agamemnon. Yeats, unlike Burke, strongly believed that Ireland as a colony of the empire was possessed and raped and that the consequences of such a colonization, rather conquest, must be tragic. Yeats's poetization of his feelings is redolent of the feelings of Tagore, Aurobindo and Nehru. In fact, Nehru says quite candidly that India was raped. The poetic symbolism of Leda and the Swan are dialectical representations of Yeats's sense of history, aesthetic and moral philosophy. Leda the mortal woman is like the effeminate figure of India that was possessed, raped and abandoned. The intellectual history of British colonialism, especially the relationship between England and India, needs to be debated more candidly and intensively so that it becomes an acceptable theoretical discourse in the sense that it reveals the truth of history and the inestimable operations of power. The intellectual ascendance of an historic event to the level of an idea is what lends it credibility, permanence and universality. The story of Oedipus is significant, but ultimately it is the idea of Oedipus that gives permanent and intellectual interest to the fable. This is exactly where the greatness of Goethe's *Faust,* Shelley's *Prometheus Unbound* and Aurobindo's *Savitri* lies.

VII

The role of the Indian nationalist movement and the colonial regime's treatment of the nationalists are also important matters in assessing the moral basis of imperial governance. Both Tagore and Nehru had openly voiced their strong disappointment at the embarrassing poverty of the Indian masses and at the indifference of the colonial government to this and other similar issues.[84] How does a literary artist—a Dante, a Shelley, a Tagore, an Aurobindo or a Mulk Raj Anand—represent history? The earlier discussion on the relationship between the world of history and the world of desire focused on teleology and axiology of history and the capacity of the literary artist's imagination to reconstruct paradigms of human amelioration. It is important to remember that each artist's creative consciousness experiences the facts of history psychologically— their repressiveness, barbarity and obsolescence—and then recreates in the crucible of the imagination an art form that integrates sociohistoric reality, universal humanistic values and concerns and aesthetic.[85] Thus in the several different perspectives of historicity, from simple and direct historicization to a more complex mythicization, what ultimately matters is the literary artist's vision and its shaping power. The theorization of the French Revolution by Hegel, Burke and other Romantic writers in continuation of Rousseau's idea of the formation of "a human political community" should be as good a model as the ones discussed by Georg Lukács in *The Historical Novel*.[86] Scott's treatment of Britain's relationship with Scotland puts the entire Anglo-Scottish history in a different perspective; the imaginative and reflective recreation of history becomes evocative of memory and moral consciousness without showing any possible conflict between the historical representation and its imaginative rendering. In Wordsworth's case, however, "the representation of reality as a historical event" is mediated by the power of the imagination. After all, Coleridge calls Napoleon a "usurper:" "In his usurpation," remarks Coleridge, "Bonaparte stabbed his honesty in the vitals."[87] In a sense, Dante's *Inferno* is an allegorization and mythicization of the sociohistoric conditions of Italian society. But Kipling's *Kim* is a direct representation of colonial consciousness; its sociopolitical narrative is an imbrication of potent but mute facts. While Kipling, caught in the maelstrom of imperial politics, sees history as a fulfillment of the colonialist-imperialist fantasy, Forster's dramatic encounter with the ironic realities of British India is humanistic. Forster's *A Passage to India* is a polyphonic forum on the interiority and exteriority of colonial India, where Forster's sharp sense of the historical process of reality is fused with the philosophical view of reality. Mulk Raj Anand's *Untouchable* and *Coolie* have given us a naked picture of India being doubly subjugated; at another level, however, Bakha and Munoo are universal metaphors of the sociohistoric reality of the exploited and the dispossessed segments of humanity. Raja Rao's political consciousness and literary genius find ex-

pression in *Kanthapura,* a fictional discourse on the Gandhian moral philosophy of nonviolence. Raja Rao is a philosophical writer who like Aurobindo has attempted to strike a synthesis of several world cultures and
philosophies in his three novels. "If Raja Rao," remarks Iyengar about the
nature of synthesis in Raja Rao, "has moved from the *Puranic* 'form' to
the *ithihasic,* and from the *ithihasic* to the *Upanishadic,* there has been a
parallel movement too: from *karma* in *Kanthapura* to *jnana* in *The Serpent
and the Rope,* and on to *bhakti-prapatti* in *The Cat and Shakespeare.*"[88]
Whereas Gandhi's moral philosophy of love and nonviolent radicalism is
sometimes attributed to Shelley, Raja Rao relates it to the conception of
karma in Hinduism. Here is Raja Rao's provocative philosophical rejoinder to the European discourse on India: " . . . India has, I always repeat, no history. To integrate India into history—is like trying to marry
Madeleine. It may be sincere, but it is not history. History, if anything, is
the acceptance of human sincerity. But Truth transcends sincerity; Truth
is *in* sincerity and *in* insincerity—beyond both. And *that* again is
India. . . ."[89] This is a rejoinder to the historicist as well as to the colonial mind that has perceived India as a muddle or a jungle.

Gyan Prakash's argument for the unobtrusive return to "the site of
colonialism" rests on the assumption that it will "release histories and
knowledges from their disciplining as area studies; as imperial and overseas
history; as the study of the exotic other that seals metropolitan structures
from the contagion of the record of their own formation elsewhere—in
fantasy and fear, in cultural difference and uneven and entangled histories,
in contingency and contention."[90] Prakash quotes Whiskey Sisodia from
Rushdie's *Satanic Verses:* "The trouble with the English is that their history
happened overseas, so they don't know what it means."[91] Will the contemporary enterprise on India, colonial and postcolonial, fully empowered
by the new freedom given to disciplines in the humanities or social sciences, create a body of original and authentic structures of knowledge? For
example, will we ever know if the empire's economic might was fundamentally derived from the colonies and if Great Britain had a long-term
plan for the economic, industrial and educational development of India,
comparable in some measure to developments in the metropolis? How did
commerce and evangelicalism become unholy partners in the political
governance of colonies? While the knowledge of colonial history must be
reconstituted with the opening of the gates of knowledge that had been
hitherto closed, one can hardly disagree with Young's argument that rather
than digging in the colonial archives the entire thrust should be on the
strengthening of the theoretical basis of knowledge that will not only sustain but also enlarge the scope of discourse on coloniality and postcoloniality beyond the basic groundwork. After all, what is the reality of

knowledge that has been packaged and repackaged on the philosophical and methodological models of Western discourse that once invented and fantasized the phenomenon of Orientalism? Young quite aptly deals with Homi Bhabha's interventionist corrective to Said's Foucauldian position on Orientalism; there is the incontrovertible assumption that Said himself probably "set up the possibility of Orientalism working at two conflictual levels . . . distinguished between a 'manifest' Orientalism, the conscious body of 'scientific' knowledge about the Orient, and a 'latent' Orientalism, an unconscious positivity of fantasmatic desire."[92] If the fundamental basis of Orientalism is Europe's uncontrolled fantasy of the Orient, then the discourse on Orientalism must be focused on the fusion of the psychoanalytic of the fantasia of desire for the Other and the rational knowledge of history. Thus in trading with the Other the commercial trading of things or of bodies becomes an integral part of "sexual exchange"; hence in the newly evolved cultural anthropology and sociology of knowledge, miscegenation and hybridity become both the process and the product of a prolonged exotic fantasy of the Other.

It is still difficult for the West to understand how the Gandhian philosophy of nonviolent civil disobedience could awaken Indian masses to an unprecedented rebellion against the world's largest colonial empire and how the awakened monster of collectivity stood morally disciplined only to rebel but not to resort to violence.[93] Fanon has psychoanalyzed his countrymen's violent struggle against their French colonial masters, but it remains to be seen if some of the general conclusions arrived at by Fanon about power, subjugation, violence and freedom[94] are also applicable to the Indian situation. But the Indian struggle for independence demands an intensive study of the repressive and brutal use of power and its possible regressive effects on the consciousness of people in general. The creation of the Indian army and the Indian police is indeed a definitive statement on the repressive use of power. The issue of untouchability and the caste system is as significant as the study of subalternity carried on by the *Subaltern Studies* group. Students of history must determine the extent to which the native elitist groups—maharajas, rajas, nawabs, zamindars and the wealthy Indian business class—joined hands with the imperial power structure to create subalterns who would not speak. Gayatri Spivak thinks that once a subaltern starts speaking he is no longer a subaltern.[95] One may say that the hegemonic complicity of the Indian elite in creating subalternity and marginality was in fact intended to strengthen the pillars of the colonial empire. The general strategy of building the Indian military and other such structures was a means of enlisting complete loyalty. But some of these programs, one can argue, draw their fundamental support from the divide-and-rule policy of the empire which was primarily based on religion, racism and gender. There is hardly any doubt that the conversion of the natives to the religion of the colonizer, an act of complicity between the empire and religion, was politically motivated; its purpose was to seek undivided and unquestionable loyalty to the empire. Ironically, however, "Native Christians," as Gauri Viswanathan points out, "were left floating in a nebulous space, neither Hindus nor Christians in their social existence."[96] The unmatched political adroitness with which classes of people were designated as minorities and with which economic and educational benefits were to be distributed was aimed at enlisting class or group loyalty that in strict moral terms was a bartered loyalty based on the stereotypical representation of the colonized and converted native.

VIII

Mitchell is correct in observing that while a heavy crop of creative writing is coming from the former imperial possessions the bumper crop of critical theory has come from Western imperial centers.[97] But does such an observation imply that the aesthetic productions of former colonial possessions will continue to be "charter'd," to use a metaphor from William Blake,[98] by the imperial mind's hegemonic theoretical constructs? If chartering means curbing, controlling or directing, does it then mean that a former possession like India should reject Western critical theory that still remains aligned to the imperial center? How can the psychosociological gap between the language of aesthetic production and the language of criticism be bridged? This gap, determinate or indeterminate, actually refers to the difference in the levels of consciousness. Can criticism as a structure of knowledge rise to the level of pure and disinterested knowledge that is totally freed from colonialist and neo-colonialist incursions? In other words, can the first world receive the aesthetic productions of the third world with the sincerity and openness of a decolonized mind? Undoubtedly, the Indian literary scene, long dominated by the schools of Arnold and Leavis and the modernist tradition, is examining the relevance of contemporary developments in Western critical theory, including poststructuralism and postmodernism, in relation to its own traditions of indigenous literatures. The combining of Indian literary and philosophical traditions and Western thought and literatures, as pointed out in my discussion of Aurobindo, should be considered an intellectual and civilizational imperative to expanding consciousness and to experiencing universality of human experience. Aurobindo and earlier Goethe and Arnold have advocated such an approach: its cultural and pedagogical benefits are eminently visible in the efforts of Emerson, Jung and Hesse. While Indian literatures, including Indian writing in English, must retain their claim to individual identity, they should also affirm their uncompromising commitment to freedom, truth, universality and cosmopolitanism.

How should one read Aurobindo's *Bande Mataram: Early Political Writings,* his philosophical works *The Human Cycle* and *The Ideal of Human Unity* and the epic poem *Savirti?* One of the important principles in Aurobindo's philosophy and poetry is the principle of synthesis of various forms of knowledge—and of East and West—as a means of achieving *lokasangraha,* world unity. The conception of synthesis is a transliteration of his philosophy of integralism. But the principle of synthesis or the Hegelian reconciliation of opposites does not mean coerced acceptance, nor does it imply any hegemonic alliance. Note Aurobindo's fierce judgment of Lord Morley, the "radical philosopher, the biographer of Voltaire, and Rousseau": " . . . for the life of John Morley is a mass of contradictions, the profession of liberalism running hand in hand with the practice of a bastard imperialism. . . ."[99] (*BCL* 1.863) Tagore firmly maintains that the famous statement, "The East is east and the West is west and never the twain shall meet," is clearly an expression of "arrogant cynicism."[100] In *Is There a Contemporary Indian Civilization?* Mulk Raj Anand states:

> Now one of the concepts which helped to give a strong base to the national movement was the doctrine of synthesis put forward by Raja Ram Mohan Roy, Rabindranath Tagore, Mahatma Gandhi, and later by Jawaharlal Nehru. They have all believed that modern India will benefit from the belief in the sanctity of the individual conscience that had survived in the best minds of the past. Also, they [had] hoped that the learning of Europe would strengthen the belief in the sovereign individual. And that the wisdom of India, as well as the contemporary anarchist emphasis on the development of the individual, would give the necessary strength of character. . . .[101]

Synthesis, properly understood, is an intellectual process, not of diffusionism,[102] but of theorizing the possible limits of knowledge and the truth of existence. It is this principle of synthesis, and not of blind imitation of the West, that was to pave the road to progress for India. Indeed, one of the most troublesome philosophical irresolvabilities in the discourse on India and in the development of postcolonial critical theory is the fundamental conception of synthesis. The cruel irony is that most western-educated Indians, other Asians and Africans are now questioning the very truth and universality of the European intellectual tradition that at one time had shaped their thinking. This is also largely true of the writers and scholars of the diaspora who are confronted with the question of psychosociological identity, since like Yeats they cannot settle the puzzle of national or racial identity. Can East-West synthesis be achieved by an increased focus on the truth of history and human civilization? In the fearless intellectual examination of ideas, can we go beyond parochial and self-constricting wars and apprehend the meaning of the Buddhist parable: "Go then, O Pourna: having been delivered, deliver; having been consoled, console; being arrived at the farther bank, enable others to arrive there also"?[103]

Chapter 2 ⟨⟩

Sri Aurobindo as a Poet: A Reassessment

I

It is no exaggeration to say that Aurobindo Ghose (Sri Aurobindo) is one of the greatest minds of the twentieth century. Aurobindo the mahayogi, Aurobindo the philosopher, Aurobindo the poet, Aurobindo the interpreter of Indian thought, Aurobindo the critic and Aurobindo the radical politician—all these hats fit him. I would argue that a proper and comprehensive revaluation of Aurobindo's work and vision as a poet must take into account all aspects of his genius and achievement, for they are integrally related to the making of Aurobindo the poet. In the midst of the manifold twentieth century developments in literary theory and criticism—modernism, postmodernism, structuralism, poststructuralism, sociohistoricism, psychoanalysis and postcoloniality, to name only a few major ones—one must raise the age-old question: what criteria, if any, will determine the greatness of a poet? In a letter Aurobindo comments on the achievements of the world's greatest poets and classifies them into "three rows": Homer, Shakespeare and Valmiki are assigned the first row; Dante, Kalidasa, Aeschylus, Virgil and Milton the second row; and Goethe the third row.[1] The front benchers, Homer, Shakespeare and Valmiki, have, according to Aurobindo, "at once supreme imaginative originality, supreme poetic gift, widest scope and supreme creative genius" (*BCL* 9.521). What is fundamentally universal and uniquely original in the poetic consciousness of each category? Why would the highest rank go to Homer, Valmiki and Shakespeare? Is it Homer's view of progress and history, of mankind in general, that earns him a superior rank to that of Dante or Milton? Apparently, Aurobindo's intriguing commentary focuses on the scope and magnitude of the poetic vision in each category. Indeed, these judgmental criteria are extremely relevant to defining some key issues, not only of literary taste and critical theory but also of a poetic consciousness that is unobtrusively committed to achieving social amelioration and moral and spiritual consciousness.

The psychobiographical history of Aurobindo's upbringing and education is extremely pertinent to any serious examination of his work. Born in 1872 in Calcutta, Aurobindo, the youngest child of K. D. Ghose, a physician, was sent to the Loretto Convent. Dr. K. D. Ghose, who had obtained his M.D. from a Scottish university, later sent his three sons to England where Aurobindo was brought up and educated by the Drewett family in Manchester.[2] In 1884 Aurobindo was admitted to St. Paul's School in London. The Reverend Drewett had given to the young Aurobindo an excellent grounding in classics, and after matriculating from St. Paul's, Aurobindo won a scholarship for admission to King's College, Cambridge. Despite the pecuniary difficulties that the three brothers faced because of their father's unexpected failure to support them, Aurobindo was able to distinguish himself at the King's College. In 1892 he passed the classical tripos in the first class. Because of his failure to pass the riding test he had been disqualified from the Indian Civil Service. Deeply immersed in Western thought and tradition, Aurobindo returned to India in 1893 as a stranger to his mother tongue, Bengali, and Indian languages and literatures, including Sanskrit. He had been introduced to the Maharaja of Baroda, and immediately upon his arrival in India he entered the Baroda Civil Service. In the Maharaja's service Aurobindo worked in several capacities, from a revenue officer to an acting professor of English and from an acting principal to a secretary to the Maharaja. Aurobindo was married to Mrinalini Bose in 1901, but she did not accompany him to Pondicherry. Widely read in classical literatures, European intellectual history and English literature, the early Aurobindo was a radical thinker. But the Aurobindo of the Baroda period had undergone a dramatic change in two major directions. His early political sympathies dating back to the Cambridge days had been nurtured into fiery radicalism. And he had become deeply interested in Indian culture—Indian literature and religious thought. The intervening period, the period between the Baroda and the Pondicherry days, was the period of intense political activity and writing: during this period Aurobindo was imprisoned, charged with sedition, tried and acquitted. Of course, it is the Pondicherry period that, no doubt, had disappointed political activists, but which indeed witnessed an unprecedented flowering of a great genius. These various stages of development that read somewhat like Wordsworth's stages of spiritual growth in "Tintern Abbey" are significant for the understanding of the psychospiritual formation of Aurobindo's mind, the structure of his poetic consciousness and the struggle between his self and his idealism for reconciling sociopsychological and historical reality and imaginative reality. Aurobindo, himself a student of the yoga and social psychology, is known to have understood the intricate relationship between ego and culture and the process of recognizing—and transforming—one's ego.[3]

One might say somewhat condescendingly that Aurobindo readers fall into two broad groups:[4] those who are followers of Aurobindo and those who are fascinated by his extraordinary genius and achievements. And yet there are other readers like Kathleen Raine who consider Aurobindo primarily a philosopher and an interpreter of Indian thought.[5] Undoubtedly, Aurobindo is very clear about the relationship between philosophy and poetry and his position is somewhat Aristotelian rather than Platonic. While rejecting outrightly Houseman's "exaltation of pure poetry," Aurobindo maintains "that philosophy has its place and can even take a leading place along with psychological experience as it does in the Gita."[6] Indeed, there are Miltonists, Blakeans, Shelleyans and Aurobindonians, but a genuine admiration of a Milton or a Blake must be based on scholarly objectivity and authenticity. Aurobindo himself was an astute critic and a keen student of literary history, very much in the tradition of Coleridge, and would not have been happy with an approach that is wanting in critical judgment. If criticism is supposed to produce a body of sound knowledge and if the quality of that knowledge must be considered a measure of an enduring cultural progress, the critical methodology so devised must meet these expectations.

The problem in Aurobindo scholarship is further complicated by an unfortunate reluctance on the part of some to recognize a "third-world poet," even though scholars are faced with the formidable task of dealing with the 30 volumes of published works plus the unpublished material.[7] As a criterion of cultural progress and intellectual freedom, critics have been quick to recognize the place of cross-cultural and transnational studies as integral parts of the sociology of knowledge: in fact, a civilized mind is compelled by its own achievement to go outside the tradition in order to create a new body of knowledge. If multiculturalism, pluralism and transvaluation as contradistinguished from ethnocentricity and parochialism suggest, among other things, a process of disinterested (Matthew Arnold's term) intellectual inquiry, one will undoubtedly anticipate the emergence of a critical methodology that will recognize a progressive synthesis of several traditions. The cases of Dante, Milton and Goethe are different, since they belong only to the European tradition. But Aurobindo's canvass—Schopenhauer, Jung and Hesse fall in this category—is much larger. In Aurobindo one finds a unique synthesis of the East and the West, a synthesis that does not exist in the works of Kipling and Forster.

The Future Poetry contains Aurobindo's intriguing and bold argument for the application of classical Indian aesthetic to the progressive development of English poetry. Without indulging in critical platitudes, Aurobindo sees this synthesis as a practical possibility, especially because of the newly evolving structure of human consciousness. Can modern literary theory, in its bold but inchoate attempt to create a structure of knowledge, go beyond the ethnic and national boundaries and adequately examine the experiences of a poet like Aurobindo? Significantly, however, the popular leads of Arnold, Leavis and Eliot and those of various other schools of criticism have not been of much help. Can the meaning of a literary work be determined with some degree of finality? Does this meaning in any sense or manner relate to the author's intent? Added to this list of some of the most excruciating questions confronting modern literary theory is the one that concerns us the most: "Can we hope to understand works which are culturally and historically alien to us?"[8] The "otherness" of culture and history is perhaps symptomatic of an ideological attitude or limitation, but the assumption is that the methodology of history or of culture-study will at least facilitate a legitimate and fruitful intellectual discourse. However, it is difficult to guarantee that the perceptibility of truth and the significance of a work itself may not be lost to the force of history. Indeed, one might consider the critical methodology of comparative literature, but that methodology in itself is dysfunctional, at least partly, if not wholly, in dealing with Aurobindo.

It is true that deconstructive criticism and other poststructural theories have attempted to demolish the boundaries erected by ethnocentrism and have extended the scope of criticism to a much larger context—a context redefined by contemporary psychological, philosophical and historical approaches. But the overbearing tyranny of tradition still conceals the power of the word. The process of dissemination of knowledge is the process of unconcealment of truth, *aletheia,* as Heidegger calls it.[9] But the word corrupted by historical and social process—stipulations, assumptions and boundaries—loses its power to conceal and unconceal truth. Ironically, however, the revolt against tradition, far from being nihilistic or escapist, is a creative expression of the social and historical process of reality, and of the urge to seek continuity with the past by recognizing and reconstructing it in terms of the present. Students of literary history know that English Romanticism was essentially a revolt against an otherwise untenable tradition; and that the revolutionary displacement of myth[10] and values has continued to occur through the twentieth century, though not enough ground has been broken to deal with such phenomenon of modern civilization as calls for a synthesis of different traditions and conventions and the transmittal of knowledge resulting from such an attempt. If Aurobindo

has created a new poetic mythology, we must attempt to decipher its structure and meaning—analogies, images, metaphors and symbols—in the
context of the vision it projects.

II

While Aurobindo the philosopher and seer has drawn wide acclaim and
recognition, the discovery of Aurobindo the poet, much like the discovery
of William Blake, has been a slow but startling phenomenon. We are perhaps well familiar with the tributes paid to Aurobindo's spiritual genius and
philosophic vision by Rabindranath Tagore and Romain Rolland. Tagore
is reported to have told Aurobindo: "You have the Word and we are wait-
ing to accept it from you. India will speak through your voice to the
world. . . ."[11] Rolland sees in Aurobindo "the most noble representative of
this Neo-Vedantic spirit" as well as "the completest synthesis that has been
realised to this day of the genius of Asia and the genius of Europe."[12] A review of Aurobindo's *Collected Poems and Plays* in the *Times Literary Supple-
ment* of July 8, 1944 contained the following warm praise:

> Of all modern Indian writers Aurobindo—successively poet, critic, scholar,
> thinker, nationalist, humanist—is the most significant and perhaps the most
> interesting. . . . In fact, he is a new type of thinker, one who combines in his
> vision the alacrity of the West with the illumination of the East. To study his
> writings is to enlarge the boundaries of one's knowledge. . . . He is blessed
> with a keen intuition. Like Coleridge and Heine, he displays a piercing and
> almost instantaneous insight into the heart of his subject; and, what is no less
> important, his immense and exact knowledge of the thought and feeling of
> both East and West—he is an accomplished scholar in Sanskrit, Greek, Ital-
> ian, French, English and Bengali—gives his judgments balance and poise. He
> knows that a man may be right, but not wise. He treats each word of his as
> though it were a drop of elixir. In all this he is unique—at least in modern
> India.[13]

However, we must take into account the other side of the picture. For example, Aurobindo's greatest poetic achievement is *Savitri,* the longest epic
poem written in the English language. While the West has been more
sympathetic in recognizing the poetic merits of the poem, some Indo-
Anglian writers have criticized it and other works of Aurobindo on
grounds of verbosity, superficiality, the Miltonic, Romantic and Tennysonian imitations, the bejeweled diction of the Decadent poets and the
lack of authentic experience.[14]

The following two appraisals of *Savitri,* one by Piper and the other by
Ronald Nixon, deserve attention. According to Piper:

[*Savitri*] is the most comprehensive, integrated, beautiful, and perfect cosmic poem ever composed. It ranges symbolically from a primordial cosmic void, through earth's darkness and struggles, to the highest realms of supramental spiritual existence, and illumines every important concern of man, through verse of unparalleled massiveness, magnificence, and metaphorical brilliance. . . . *Savitri* is perhaps the most powerful artistic work in the world for expanding man's mind towards the Absolute.[15]

Comparing Aurobindo with some of the greatest poets of the Western world, Nixon says:

Perhaps the last great Western poet to have made any real attempt to grasp the inner unity was Dante, and even he made use of merely traditional myth—and somewhat degenerated myth at that—for most of his structure, while Milton who came later used even more degenerated myth for purposes which it is not unfair to describe as theological apologetics. Still later, Blake, a genuine but undisciplined seer, attempted to recover the lost unity but lost his way in uncharted private worlds.[16]

Apparently, Nixon assumes that *Savitri* contains a new myth of inner unity and that it is a cosmic poem.[17] I would not quarrel with these observations, but they point to a familiar trend in Aurobindo scholarship. Whereas Piper's comments focus heavily on Aurobindo's metaphysics, Nixon's criticism of Dante and Milton is self-defeating, since it merely expresses an anxiety to establish the superiority of *Savitri* by a reductive comparison.[18] As critics of Milton, the English Romantic poets, especially Blake and Shelley, were outspoken in openly questioning Milton's Protestant theology and in believing that it dulled his poetic genius, a view with which Aurobindo himself agrees.[19] But shall we say that Dante and Milton were theologians first and poets after and that Coleridge's metaphysics has nothing to do with his greatness as a poet? This is hardly the place to square up an old issue; admittedly, criticism has shown its inherent weaknesses in dealing with this difficult problem. Nevertheless, one might say that in their anxiety to defend Aurobindo, most critics of the Aurobindo circle seem to have emphasized his metaphysics and mysticism as a priori, a situation which is partially responsible for creating a feeling of discomfort among readers to whom theology and mysticism are an anathema. But both positions are subjective and colored, and have therefore obscured the central issues in assessing Aurobindo's true greatness as a poet. Why not study the whole man in relation to the literary tradition and in the critical vocabulary of disinterested and creative criticism, a criticism that, according to Northrop Frye, serves as an instrument of creating a coherent body of knowledge?[20]

In *A Defence of Poetry,* Shelley maintains that a great poem is the cooperative work of all poets.[21] What Shelley implies is that a work of art owes its true greatness, both in terms of its vision and form, to the relationship it bears to the total body of literature or knowledge created by all poets, that its vision participates in the continuity and universality of tradition, and that it is never finished. Undoubtedly, Shelley's conception of historical and cultural unity in literature includes critical issues of intertextuality or what Bloom calls the anxiety of influence.[22] We should therefore approach Aurobindo's work not only in relation to the tradition to which he belongs but also in relation to other similar works. If what gives stature, an enduring greatness to a work of art and its author, is the comprehensiveness and profundity of vision—cosmic consciousness, authenticity and totality of experience, and the nature and quality of the poetic concern with the human condition—then Aurobindo and especially his monumental work *Savitri* satisfy all these and other criteria. Aurobindo is a mythopoeic and visionary poet whose poetic combines several traditions in Indian and Western literatures. While Aurobindo is undoubtedly part of the English literary tradition—he is post-Romantic in the sense that Swinburne, George Russell, Yeats and Tagore are—his one foot is firmly in the European and Indian classical traditions. He has his affinity with Homer, Virgil and Dante on the one hand and with Blake, Shelley, Keats, Goethe and Whitman on the other. (Recent studies have compared him with Shakespeare, Milton and Goethe.[23]) In Indian literature his indebtedness is traceable to Kalidasa and numerous other Sanskrit poets. It should, however, be noted that the contemporary English literary scene was heavily punctuated by various movements and trends that leaned toward experimentalism. The Romantics in their passionate search for a new poetic had openly rebelled against the eighteenth century; likewise, the Georgians, the Imagists and the Modernists attempted to break away from Victorianism, though not with the intensity and exuberance of the Romantics. But, significantly, underneath the various literary movements of the late nineteenth and twentieth centuries, there was a strong and unchecked revolt against modernity itself. The experimentalism in the works of Yeats, Eliot and Pound is indeed laudable, but their distinct greatness as poets lies in their poetic visions and in the unconscious urge to align with tradition. No doubt, Aurobindo was quite familiar with these movements, but because he leaned heavily to the classical tradition, because he believed with the Romantics in the continuously evolving nature and function of art, and because he had sufficiently developed his own theory of overhead poetry, he was able to draw upon several traditions, yet retaining the uniquely original character of his own art. These intellectual traditions are relevant to establishing a comprehensive critical base and scholarly objectivity, so that we can reasonably assess not only Aurobindo's vision and art in a broad-based cultural, philosophical and religious context but also his place as a poet, especially his contribution to literature in general and to humanistic learning in particular.

III

Savitri, variously described as a Miltonic, Romantic and Tennysonian poem, expresses Aurobindo's conception of epic and of poetry in general. Not only does the poem show Aurobindo's keen interest in the epic tradition, both Eastern and Western, and especially in the epic ventures of Vyasa, Homer, Virgil, Dante and Milton, it also shows that even in such badly fragmented and hopelessly puzzled modern times as ours a successful epic could be written. In fact, Aurobindo's interest in epic poetry goes back to *Ilion.* Written in quantitative hexameters, *Ilion* marks Aurobindo's most successful experiment in "naturalizing" the power of the ancient hexameter to gain certain desired effects of modulation, intonation, and, hence, of power and harmony, that correspond with the movement of thought and feeling.[24] "*Ilion,*" remarks Sethna, "is a true epic in breadth and depth and height."[25] The greatness of *Ilion* lies in its profound epic vision, in its uniquely innovative hexameter and in its synthetic character. Whereas *Savitri* is a philosophic epic written in blank verse, *Ilion* is a truly Homeric epic based upon Homer's theme in the *Iliad.* The significance of *Ilion,* although a fragment, is twofold: first, it was Aurobindo's first great epic poem in which he exhibits his genuine interest of attempting a modern epic on a convincingly ambitious scale, an epic that could be successfully adapted to both the theme and meter of Homer; and second, it was a poem where Aurobindo provides us with a clear conception of the tenets of a classical epic, and of a progressive basis for a modern epic. Although the structure of *Savitri* is intricate, self-defiant and elusive, the poem is extremely well unified and tightly knit. The nature of its unity is not literal but symbolic, that is, the unity of form and meaning.

In its highly concentrated power and appeal, created by Aurobindo's treatment of mythos and *dianoia, Savitri* shows a distinct advancement over *Ilion.* What gives *Savitri* its well-merited place among such great epics in literature as *Aeneid, Divine Comedy, Paradise Lost* and *Paradise Regained* combined together, *Faust,* and *Prometheus Unbound* is its cosmic and humanistic vision of man's total redemption and of complete transformation of this earth into a living paradise. *Savitri,* we are told, is a personal poem that Aurobindo wrote for himself to verify poetically, to envision on a different plane, and to dramatize some of the central issues contained in *The Life Divine.*[26] It may well be that some readers would regard *Savitri* as a companion piece to *The Life Divine,*[27] but actually the unified power of verse and vision, and myth and drama, give the poem a uniquely independent character of its own. Although the allegorical nature of the poem cannot be denied, *Savitri* immediately transcends the literal level: it is an anagogic poem in which the heroine emerges as the archetypal symbol of the Universal Mother, the embodiment of the shakti of Brahman, that redeems the world of flesh.[28] The epic vision, which is purely gnostic, focuses upon the evolutionary view of man, and his infinite capacity to realize inner unity and to experience the absolute.

The central myth in Aurobindo's poetry is the myth of freedom. Based on the dialectical struggle between the worlds of appearance and reality, matter and spirit, evil and good, and death and divine life, the myth emphasizes the evolutionary view of human nature. It focuses upon the quest of the soul to realize the state of being by an intuitive process of self-discovery and awareness of the infinite; to ascend from the inconscient state to the wakeful state by spiritual journey through the stairs of the world, the manifold planes of existence, the states of becoming; and to experience complete identity with substantive reality and the totality of being by inward expansion and synthesis. This view of the soul's ability to experience infinitude and to attain liberty from a deterministic order of lower nature—a view that is typically Indian and Romantic—constitutes the core of *Savitri*. But while Aurobindo's luminous vision emphasizes freedom and unity of consciousness, it never loses its firm grip on reality. In fact, his imagination envisions earth as humankind's ideal home, where one's soul, by losing its egotistical selfhood in complete self-surrender and by merging, through common humanity, with the universal consciousness, experiences joy and fulfillment. The concern for individual freedom is, therefore, the concern for the liberation of total humanity. The myth of liberty is a genuine myth of concern—the kind of concern that art is best able to express and dramatize. Aurobindo's poetic vision of liberty, truth and bliss, and of a new order in which human beings are able to expand their consciousness and to attain psychic integration and wholeness, is essentially optimistic; and evidently it has its roots in his metaphysics. Therefore, whatever the fine polemical distinction between the poetic vision and the philosophic visions, the total, integral vision of Aurobindo, like that of Coleridge or Goethe, does not preclude his metaphysics.

In Aurobindo's treatment of the Mahabharata legend of conjugal love,[29] Savitri's struggle is twofold. On the one hand, in human form she undertakes the process of realizing her inner unity through a rigid discipline of yoga, such that the divine energy reveals itself in her. This revelation of the divine in her signifies her own infinitely expanded consciousness, the *virat* form, the transcendent wisdom, the gnosis, with the help of which she wages an all-out war against Yama, the god of death and of a lower order of nature. Her father Ashwapathy, too, has committed himself to the rigorous discipline of yoga, though more for personal deliverance. Yet, on the other hand, Savitri as the power of love (so she calls herself in the epilogue) has a truly important role of redeeming the universe from the tyranny of Yama and of restoring to earth the paradisal vision of life and of an ideal communal existence. Significantly, however, the two roles of Savitri are indistinguishably blended. In fact, Satyavan to whom she is married is the phenomenological reality, the manifestation of truth in the external world; and his death is only one point in the natural cycle of change. Yama, the prototype of Blake's Urizen, is the false god of this mutable and transient universe, and, hence, of inconscient matter. In this lower level of existence, human beings with their fragmented consciousness become aware of evil, sin and ugliness; they create and worship external deities under fearful repression of rewards and punishments, thereby denying themselves true awakening into the world of spirit. The submission to the death-state, as we may conclude from the polemic between Yama and Savitri, is submission to the state of matter. In Savitri's triumphant attempt there is the unmitigated affirmation that the spiritual reality and natural world are not contradictory and that the current state of the natural world, symbolized by Satyavan's death-state, must be redeemed for the ultimate benefit of humanity at large. Aurobindo's concept of creative evolution, however, implies that although duality between matter and spirit apparently exists, complete unity between matter and spirit is possible by a continuous process of divinization. The divinized humans will no doubt return to the One, but in a more progressively evolved form and not as a primal substance. The simple return of a primal being to a primal state, according to Aurobindo, means the acceptance of a deterministic order in which one denies oneself the freedom to exist.[30]

The mythic conflict between Savitri and Yama, with all its other ramifications, of course, actually contains two myths: the myth of individual freedom or inner unity, and the myth of social or collective salvation. In the first myth, we see the esoteric vision of Aurobindo the seer who believes in the creative evolution of human beings—the discovery of the true self by transforming the ego self[31] and, hence, by ascending to the Supreme Saccidanand. And in the second myth, the esoteric side of Aurobindo the socialist is more than apparent, since individual or personal salvation has no meaning without collective or communal salvation. It may be noted that during his stay in England, Aurobindo was an agnostic and a leftist. He had read Darwin, and was familiar with Bergson.[32] Undoubtedly, he was well acquainted with Nietzsche, especially his view of man, according to which man is basically unfinished but has the potentiality of becoming a superman. His early political radicalism is undoubtedly motivated by his un-compromising commitment to the ideals of liberty, equality and fraternity and by his optimistic faith in the ability of human beings to become per-fect. The transformation from this direct political anxiety and commitment into a much more universal and comprehensive concern for true human freedom and a new world order was the result of his progressive self-real-ization, during the course of which he saw his earlier radical socialist sym-pathies in complete harmony with his evolutionary view of human nature. Undoubtedly, the sociohistoric reading of the allegory of Satyavan's death-state suggests, among other things, the political subjugation of India and colonial despotism. Aurobindo seems to share with Hegel the fundamen-tal assumption that a higher form of consciousness must emerge from his-torical tragedy and destruction. The two prose works, *The Human Cycle* and *The Ideal of Human Unity,* provide us not only with one of the most subtle analyses of human nature and society but also with a unique vision of human progress. In *The Human Cycle,* Aurobindo maintains that, since human beings and nature will continue to evolve, no system can claim to be absolutely perfect and universally valid, and that humanity's journey through various evolutionary stages marks the process of its divinization. While human beings are certainly entitled to freedom, equality, fraternity and justice, neither the political man, nor the aesthetic man, nor even the ethical man possesses wholeness. The spiritual idealization of humanity, maintains Aurobindo, is the true basis of freedom, equality and fraternity, and, hence, of a future community of humankind. Speaking about Au-robindo's concept of evolution, Zaehner says: "More concretely he sees evolution both in political terms and in terms of ever greater awareness—a progression from apparently inanimate matter to life, from life to con-sciousness and mind, from mind to what he calls Overmind, and from Overmind to Supermind, which . . . is pure *cit,* pure consciousness, oper-ating in the world as *sakti* or power."[33] This shakti, pure consciousness, manifests itself in Savitri who exhibits the same concern as is reiterated by Aurobindo: "Heaven we have possessed, but not the earth; but the fullness of the Yoga is to make . . . 'Heaven and Earth equal and one.'"[34]

One of the most significant contributions made by Aurobindo to hu-manistic thought is the theory of evolutionary progress.[35] As a creator of knowledge, as a philosopher of history and as one who is seriously con-cerned with progress and unity of the human race, Aurobindo belongs to such great geniuses as Nietzsche, Marx and Freud. For all intents and purposes, Aurobindo is a reconstructionist. That human consciousness can be expanded by inner discipline, that different strands and techniques of thought can be integrated into a unified consciousness and that the structure of civilization can be continuously revamped and upgraded are extremely relevant to understanding Aurobindo the poet. But the disengagement from lower consciousness and the ascent to the next higher level of consciousness is a precondition for the progress of civilization. Both Aurobindo and Teilhard de Chardin recognize the existence of a psychic force—Aurobindo calls it "Sakti" and de Chardin "Force"—which impels all existence in the evolutionary process.[36] It may be construed that this shakti in a certain special sense is similar to Bergson's élan vital or life-force, but Aurobindo in his concerted analysis of the philosophy of history, as Maitra suggests, goes far beyond Bergson and Spengler.[37] Whereas Spengler who has based his theory of the decline of Western civilization on Bergson's idea of the élan vital emphasizes the principles of destiny and the cyclical view of history, Aurobindo's focus is on the emergence of humanity. It is important to remember that Aurobindo rejects both these philosophical assumptions, including the idea of regression, for any of these notions is utterly inconsistent with the conception of continuous and upward progress of the human race. It is pertinent to emphasize that Aurobindo does not accept any form of determinism, Indian or Western, religious or scientific. That is why in his conception of liberty Aurobindo rejects the idea of the four *yugas* in the cycle of history and the karmic theory of ethics in the Indian philosophical thought. It is also important to remember that Aurobindo rejects the theory of illusionism or Maya. In Aurobindo's philosophy of history the idea of a permanent cyclical dip, irreversible regression or decline is in direct contradiction to the idea of a creative evolution and the emergence of a spiritual religion of humanity. Thus Savitri cannot abandon hope of Satyavan's restoration; indeed, she must expand her mental capacity and recognize her higher self, the suprarational principle of the universe that Goethe calls the Eternal Feminine,[38] the principle of progress to which we are driven.

We must note the earth-centered restorative vision of Aurobindo loudly echoed by Savitri: "My soul and his [Satyavan's] indissolubly linked / In the one task . . . / To raise the world to God . . . / To bring God down to the world . . . / To change the earthly life to life divine" (Bk. XI, Canto 1). Indeed, such an important statement affirms the reconciliation of the world of social reality and the Ideal. Whatever one may make of Aurobindo's metaphysics, especially in contrast to that of Sankara, it is abundantly clear that he does not dismiss this life and universe as merely a false or empty illusion or Maya: "To be is not a senseless paradox; / Since God has made earth, earth must make in her God" (Bk. XI, Canto 1). The incessant search for the unity of the finite and the infinite is the key to grasping Aurobindo's vision of human salvation. That Savitri can triumphantly challenge time, history and death and that she as the "eternal Bride" can salvage from the death-state "the soul of the world called Satyavan," "the eternal Bridegroom," essentially define the integrative process of the epistemology and metaphysics of the "life divine." It must be noted that in her mental search Savitri goes to the very source of her own creation and seeks expansion of her spiritual energy by yogic discipline, by a process of mental seeing, by annihilating the ego-self and by dissolving the Kantian divide between *verstand* and *vernunft*. Indeed, there is one thing fundamentally common to the study of Dante's *Divine Comedy*, Goethe's *Faust*, Blake's *Jerusalem*, Shelley's *Prometheus Unbound* and Aurobindo's *Savitri* and that is the vision of the Eternal Feminine.[39] It must be understood that whereas the Faustian nature of Savitri's search is clearly recognizable, Goethe's Eternal Feminine and Dante's Beatrice belong to another world outside the context of temporal reality. In contrast, Savitri's dramatic awakening coincides with her immediate return to the earth to undertake the salvation of Satyavan, this life and this world. Aurobindo's conception of Satyavan in *Savitri*, Blake's conception of Albion as cosmic man in *Jerusalem* and Shelley's conception of Prometheus as One mind or Humanity in *Prometheus Unbound* are not drastically dissimilar, but it is Savitri's role that is distinctly different from that of Beatrice, Jerusalem or Asia in one particular sense. Savitri in her human form participates in the redemptive process more actively and directly.

Aurobindo emphatically rejects the Hobbesean thesis of the origin of evil as well as the conception of original sin. The direct contrast is between the risen consciousness that transcends good and evil and *sees* these as unity, and the fallen consciousness that is the egotistic and ratiocinative perception of things. Hence, Aurobindo emphasizes the importance of cleansing one's self of egoism and the divinization of the stuff of which human beings are made. Significantly, the solution offered by Savitri is rather very existential. This earth will be a happy and harmonious place, free from all suffering, pain and evil, only if humanity learns that "*to love is to live.*" This vision of love in *Savitri* implies both love as *philia* and love as Grace. According to Aurobindo's conception of the evolutionary progress, however, it implies cosmic consciousness, the Logos. In this state, the whole universe becomes alive and every thing responds to others in a pantheistic rapport. Inasmuch as *Savitri's* anagogic vision of the Saccidanand, the Logos[40] or cosmic consciousness concerns humanity as a whole, it is a cosmic epic, for it denies private and personal salvation as an end in itself. Religion is no longer a personal matter; nor can an experience of the absolute, for that matter, be considered a private experience. Aurobindo's cosmic vision of humanity is the vision of humanity-divinity in its fully liberated and integrated form.

IV

If there are planes of consciousness, levels of mental seeing, will there be corresponding verbal structures of comparable intensity and power that will adequately communicate imaginative experiences of reality? Can the highest form of wisdom, as Steiner asks, be communicated by language that is essentially a spatial medium?[41] Indeed, we can unquestionably vouch for the illimitable capacity of the poetic symbol or image to body forth the highest form of truth. From a more positive viewpoint images of the Virgin Sophia as Divine Wisdom in Jacob Boehme, of Shakti as *Sabda-Brahman* in Indian thought, of Beatrice as Divine Love in Dante, of Jerusalem as love and liberty in Blake, of Asia as love in Shelley's *Prometheus Unbound,* to mention only a few prominent experiments in the perception of reality, readily affirm the identity of the highest form of truth and the incarnate word. We may also refer to the intricate and powerful symbologies of the Word in the Bible and of *Vak* and *Aum* in Indian thought. Aurobindo's symbol of Savitri as embodiment of Shakti, a synthetic vision of the highest consciousness, rightly belongs to these clusters.

Aurobindo like Coleridge is a keen and formidable theorist of poetry. In *The Future Poetry* and elsewhere, Aurobindo deals with some of the issues mentioned above, especially those pertaining to the limits of language and the identity of consciousness and language. Aurobindo defines poetry as "the *mantra* of the Real"[42] (BCL 9.9). "The Mantra, poetic expression of the deepest spiritual reality," explains Aurobindo, "is only possible when three highest intensities of poetic speech meet and become indissolubly one, a highest intensity of rhythmic movement, a highest intensity of verbal form and thought-substance, of style, and a highest intensity of the soul's vision of truth" (BCL 9.17). The poet, according to Aurobindo, *sees* the highest form of Reality, the Saccidanand vision of unity in the nature of things and then communicates *ananda* or aesthesis through the medium of *Pashyanti Vak* (the all-seeing word). And yet we must assume Aurobindo's familiarity with the famous complaints of Dante (at the end of *Paradiso*) and of Shelley (at the end of *Epipsychidion*)[43] about the inadequacy of language to communicate the highest form of truth. When does language fail to approximate the level of vision? Assuming rather optimistically that there is a correspondence between what is seen and what is poetically spoken, Aurobindo grants Blake the sight of a seer-poet but feels that he lacks the language to communicate his vision.[44] Aurobindo, it appears, believes that a poet has to find the language of his perceived identities. "The poetry of the future has to solve," as Aurobindo maintains, " . . . a problem new to the art of poetic speech, an utterance of the deepest soul of man and of the universal spirit in things, not only with another and a more complete vision, but in the very inmost language of the self-experience of the soul and the sight of the spiritual mind" (*BCL* 9.283).

In *The Future Poetry* Aurobindo deals with the conception of aesthesis in classical Indian poetry and suggests somewhat boldly its possible adaptations in English poetry. If *ananda* or aesthesis is an essential accompaniment of a poet's vision and if a higher *ananda*—there are degrees of *ananda* corresponding to the levels of consciousness[45]—the "creative principle," that *ananda* must find expression in the language of poetry. In fact, all poetry must direct itself to the achievement of this end: the communication of the highest pleasure through the experience of beauty. Evidently, Aurobindo is in general agreement with the Romantic aesthetic, especially of Blake and Keats.[46] Since *ananda* and truth are inseparable, one simply does not exist without the other. Poets as arbiters of truth no doubt build high domes of mental pleasure, but in the epistemology of poetic truth and in the process of poetization their aesthetic knowledge and spirituality become mutually inclusive. A greater aesthesis or ananda results from the deepest and the highest concentration of the mind, from the total "felt reality," and from the identity of beauty and truth deemed to be "the essence of poetry." *Rasa* in classical Indian literature is, according to Aurobindo, "a concentrated taste, a spiritual essence of emotion, an essential aesthesis, the soul's pleasure in the pure and perfect sources of feeling" (*BCL* 9.243). Presumably, it is this felicitous experience of *ananda* that finally impregnates the poetic word with magical and incantatory power. "For the nearer we get to the absolute Ananda," remarks Aurobindo, "the greater becomes our joy in man and the universe and the receptive and creative spiritual emotion which needs for its voice the moved tones of poetic speech" (*BCL* 9.248).

It is utterly erroneous to suggest that Aurobindo has boarded the bandwagon of religion: Aurobindo's emphasis, it should be noted, is not on religion but on spirituality as a basis of his vision of evolutionary progress.[47] In Aurobindo's vision of human progress and universal humanity, such conception of culture that is rooted in religion and that, consequently, becomes constrictive by the very context it seeks to evoke is self-defeating and contradictory.[48] Eliot's conception of tradition and the role of religion in defining tradition is a case in point where the view of culture and cultural progress is limited to a segment of humanity. Aurobindo's philosophy of evolution, his conception of integral yoga as a spiritual discipline of expanding one's consciousness and his uncompromising belief in the capacity of human beings to make progress speak, variously and severally, of his fundamental concern for the human condition. The multiple allegory in Aurobindo's vision of humanity, that in many ways is reminiscent of Freud's *Civilization and its Discontents,* unequivocally affirms that civilization can be saved and that a better world order can be created. Admittedly, the restoration of Satyavan, suffering humanity, back to life, especially by a woman, is a significant ideological statement. In fact, *The Human Cycle* and *The Ideal of Human Unity* contain an elaborate account of Aurobindo's philosophy of social reconstruction and of a unified world order. It is important to remember that the notion of determinism, scientific, social or religious, is utterly and fundamentally incompatible with Aurobindo's philosophic vision of human salvation. Furthermore, Aurobindo also does not subscribe to the wasteland vision of Eliot. In his essay on Eliot, E. M. Forster maintains nonchalantly and demurely that *The Waste Land* is "about the fertilizing waters that arrived too late."[49] Eliot treats the water symbolism somewhat ambiguously and skeptically, but in *Savitri* Aurobindo's treatment of this symbolism, as Iyengar points out in *Dawn to Greater Dawn*,[50] is indubitably affirmative and optimistic. Aurobindo's worldview is much too formidable and comprehensive to warrant a narrow labeling or categorization; in fact, poets like Aurobindo defy such efforts, even the ones made with the best of intentions. The integralist vision of Aurobindo is an all-inclusive and timeless vision of unity, reintegration and spiritual freedom. Aurobindo fully participates in what Frye calls the myth of concern,[51] but the dimensions and parameters of Aurobindo's myth are radically demanding and incredibly complex: they ultimately focus on the epistemology of truth, on the human ability to seek freedom from darkness and on the vision of an ideal order of human unity.

Whether one thinks about human progress in Rousseauistic or Hegelian terms, civilization's recovery of the next stage in its advancement should inarguably define the vision of hope. Historically and culturally, Satyavan's death and recovery, very much like the fall and redemption of Blake's Albion and Shelley's Prometheus, clearly show that human suffering, whatever its ideological and theological contexts, is not a permanent condition of human existence and that the most important role of the poetical imagination is to eradicate evil. Langley rightly maintains that "Aurobindo is primarily a poet,"[52] for it is in the powerful vision of human salvation dramatized in *Savitri* that one sees the intensity and magnitude, translucence and perspicacity, finally discovering that the truth of poetry is greater than that of philosophy or history.

Chapter 3

The Social and Political Vision of Sri Aurobindo

As a prophet of Indian nationalism, Aurobindo occupies an important place in the history of Indian political thought.[1] When we recall the early Aurobindo, we think of a fiery, aggressive and uncompromising revolutionary who had cast his lot with the larger destiny of India and her people. His active involvement in the struggle against the British Empire in general was an expression of his staunch conviction that imperialism and colonialism, whether mercantile or political, are manifestations of repressive egoism or hubris on the part of a nation or a group who simply happened to possess an expedient superiority of means over its relatively less favored subjects. The Caesars and Napoleons of history have been guilty of exercising this hubris, of perpetuating slavery, tyranny and injustice in the world, of devising and enforcing negative and immoral political, economic and social systems, and, hence, of denying man his basic freedom and individuality. Man, as Aurobindo believed right from the very beginning of his involvement in politics, is entitled to freedom, equality and basic human dignity. He fully shared the ideas of Rousseau, Voltaire and other thinkers of the European Enlightenment, and the bases of the French Revolution, although later on, especially as one finds in *The Human Cycle* and *The Ideal of Human Unity*, his ideas of liberty, equality and fraternity assumed a much larger metaphysical and philosophical dimension. The early Aurobindo believed quite religiously that nationalism is an immediate and irrevocable necessity, an inevitable phenomenon, much like the powerful thrust of a destined natural cycle of change.[2] He further believed that revolutions in the history of mankind are healthy and fruitful expressions of the creative energy in human beings and that they occur and would continue occurring unchecked and uncontrolled at predicated successive intervals of history. The psychology of history of human progress was later fully developed and synthesized by Aurobindo in his evolutionary philosophy of human growth. Readers of Blake may remember the conflict between Orc and Urizen: the revolutionary energy, symbolized in the figure of Orc, manifests itself in the cycle of human destiny as a formidable agent of change against tyranny, oppression, the law and decay. Himself a fiery Orc of Indian nationalism, Aurobindo was resolutely determined to help the peoples of India not only in getting rid of the foreign yoke but also in achieving for them a happy and honorable condition of existence.

Evil, according to Aurobindo, appears at various periods during the course of evolutionary growth of man, nature and society, but it has no permanent existence of its own. The pattern of evolutionary progress, as envisaged by Aurobindo, is no doubt cyclical, but it does not admit the Spenglerian regression and pessimism.[3] The young Aurobindo, as Zaehner notes, was "a left-wing politician," and had evinced "sympathetic interest in Marxian socialism," perhaps fully sharing the Marxian prophecy of a possible materialization of a new social order "in which the free development of each is the condition for the development of all."[4] Whatever the nature of the obvious similarity between Aurobindo and Marx,[5] we know that Aurobindo's emphasis is on the divinization of man and of this earth and on the ultimate liberation of man. In Aurobindo, the two dreams, one of individual freedom, and the other of collective salvation, are integral parts of the one unified dream; and national independence or nationalism is only a preparatory condition to the realization of the larger dream.

For the Indian intelligentsia, especially for men like Aurobindo, Gandhi, Nehru and others who were educated in England and steeped in Western intellectual thought, it was not difficult to comprehend the meaning and significance of nationalism. One can argue that modern nationalism is a typical European phenomenon and that it emerged in India mainly as a reaction against British colonialism and racism.[6] In England, of course, nationalism had been imbued with powerful religious feelings: as a result of this amalgam of religion and nationalism, the English have always regarded themselves as God's chosen race, and the monarchy as a divine institution. It is this overpowering sense of nationalism that later outgrew into colonialism and imperialism. France and England, as Murray remarks, fought the Hundred Years' War "for a prize of incalculable worth, the headship of the colonial world."[7] Ironically, Blake thought this inchoate and expedient mixture of politics and religion as infectious perversion and clairvoyantly prophesied the fall of the empire. But Disraeli, Mill and Carlyle were happy colonialists:[8] underlying their pious convictions was perhaps the paternalistic assumption that God's chosen people had the moral obligation to spread light—to educate and reform the savages and natives, to devise means of introducing European education and civilization and to ensure progress and advancement. If this sanctimonious principle had effectively dictated the governance of India, much of the history of the British Raj in India would have been written entirely differently. But the fact remains that the British colonialism—and European colonialism for that matter— was an expression of the powerful urge to gain political and economic supremacy; and it had the blessings of "feudalized Christianity."[9]

As the colonial umbrella grew phenomenally bigger and more unmanageable, the English politicians at home became overly concerned with the problems of unity, homogeneity and consolidation of the imperial power. People like Lord Morley thought that the "empire was united, if it were united, by community of interest, whereas Seeley conceived it as bound together by community of race and religion."[10] The phrase "community of interest" is no doubt dubious, but it is pregnant with rich irony: it certainly did not imply uniform interest of people or national units within the empire. Earlier, of course, Edmund Burke had formulated the clear possibility of forming one commonwealth more expediently and readily by the states of Europe rather than by the racially heterogeneous nations; and for Burke nationalism was the key element in the unification of the European states. Burke, like Coleridge, had accepted the metaphysics of Divine Providence, but he was vehemently opposed to the use of divine authority by England for the gratification of "the lowest of their passions."[11] That is why Burke who was in favor of preserving the integrity of the Indian civilization and maintaining peace in India had proposed a political trusteeship for India. But the questions that intrigued Indian intellectuals like Aurobindo pertained to fundamental humanistic values and moral principles underlying the essential structure of British colonialism. Why is the principle of absolute sovereignty of a people, even if it were the most genuine and authentic expression of their will, not universally and unreservedly acknowledged? If the English as a nation have the absolute right to assert their sovereignty, why should Great Britain deny the same right to Canada, Ireland or India? Why is the Christian ideal, according to which the denial of human rights is supposed to be an offense to God, generally considered to be compatible with the political reality of colonialism? Does colonial politics, especially when its authority and sanction are explicitly derived from religion, have any moral basis?

It is abundantly clear from Aurobindo's early writings that he was very distrustful of British justice, for the British, in their injudicious and oppressive governance of India, were essentially led by their boastful pride— "the pride of race, the pride of empire, [and] the pride of colour" (*BCL* 1.904). The unpropitious school of Toryism and conservatism had made its political views on India too sharply pronounced to incite any feelings of hope and trust, but Aurobindo was equally suspicious of the British liberals.[12] In the history of Benthamite Utilitarianism, the emerging character of imperialism, as Eric Stokes notes, had successfully fused in its philosophical genesis the ideas of power, ambition, racism, conquest and evangelicalism.[13] Thus in J. S. Mill's conception of political liberty, which was undoubtedly shared by most Utilitarians and liberals, the idea of civil liberty for the Indian colony was considered untenable. In fact, the younger Mill was in complete agreement with his father in affirming the belief "that India could still be governed only despotically,"[14] mainly under the conflagrant pretext that India's civilization could not function rationally. The surreptitious imperial design of the European Nation, with its focus on power, control, supremacy and profitability, coupled with the mythical rhetoric of white man's burden, as Tagore argues, not only created an antagonistic and adversarial relationship between East and West, but also prevented "a free flow of knowledge" from the governing nation.[15] It is rather puzzling to note that in the larger intellectual debate on the moral and political basis of the empire subjective justifications have been sought for the denigration of liberty to power and for the continued existence of autocratic imperial rule in India. Such parabolic and insensitive vocabulary of colonial consciousness as indubitably defines the incongruous relationship between Prospero and Caliban, the master and the slave, and the ill-conceived obsession of Kurtz ("Exterminate all the brutes!"[16]) is only reminiscent of the unchaste collective guilt and of the self-destructive political reality that writers like Conrad and Forster were to dramatize in their works. Aurobindo was convinced that the colonial rule, in its lustful intent and approach, was engaged in robbing the subjects of their national and cultural identity and that it had, in the due course of history, firmly established a bureaucratic and despotic system based on fear, repression and tyranny. Because of the rapid debilitation of Indian consciousness prompted by racial bigotry and because of the pervasive colonial hubris, Aurobindo remained vehemently opposed to the idea of India becoming a satellite province or otherwise a confederate state of the empire.

Metaphysics and religious thought had played a significant role in shaping the political ideas of Dante, Milton and Coleridge. Likewise, in the case of Aurobindo—a poet, a radical, a philosopher—it goes without saying that his political vision of India's nationhood and sovereignty derives its essential outline from his spiritual vision of man's freedom and enlightenment. In fact, both Aurobindo and Gandhi were inspired by Indian spiritual thought,[17] although it is a well-known fact of history that Aurobindo did not share the Mahatma's position on several issues.[18] Aurobindo was an out-and-out revolutionary—he was dubbed as an "extremist"—who did not believe in the policy of mendicancy, appeasement and compromise. His vociferous criticism of the moderate position centered on their psychological vulnerability to the repressive and intimidating measures of the despotic regime and to the self-defeating programs of the Raj. It was practically the same sort of political process that had made people like Sir Syed Ahmed Khan support the colonial regime.[19] "To recover possession of the State," reiterates Aurobindo categorically and emphatically, "is therefore the first business of the awakened Indian consciousness" and not "to revive the old dissipation of energies, to put social reform first, education first or moral regeneration first and leave freedom to result from these" (*BCL* I.882).

Later, it turned out that the disastrous historical tragedy, the partition of Bengal, not only enabled the radicals to consolidate their own strength, but also forced the moderates to see the truth of Aurobindo's vision. The moderates, it seemed, had followed Burke's exhortation to the Irish of preferring the path of pacific resistance to that of an open rebellion. Aurobindo's spiritual vision had enabled him to invest divinity upon his country, his land and his nation, to see in each man the sleeping divinity that needs to be awakened, and to believe firmly that the solemn and unequivocal affirmation of the will of people can wipe out the stains of slavery. It is this unique vision of divine nationhood or of India as Mother that gave him the inspiration and strength to wage an incessant struggle for the sacred cause of freedom. Aurobindo believed that once India regains its nationhood, the task of strengthening national consciousness and of achieving progress will be much more relevant to the larger goals, for those who have been enslaved and subjugated too long would not otherwise know the meaning of true liberty.

During the period of his active political involvement, Aurobindo advocated the idealistic position—a position that admitted no compromise with the colonial rule on fundamental principles and which called for an equally firm and unequivocal commitment to a comprehensive program of revolutionary action. For Aurobindo, nationalism was a *dharma*, and the revolution was a *yudha*. "*Dharma*," as Aurobindo explains, "is the Indian conception in which rights and duties lose the artificial antagonism created by a view of the world which makes selfishness the roots of action . . ." (*BCL* 1.760). This *dharma*, the selfless act, *nishkam karma* of the *Gita*, is "the basis of democracy which Asia must recognise . . ."(*BCL* 1. 760). Since the struggle was not merely political but ethical and spiritual, he could, therefore, morally justify the use of violence as a means of achieving the larger ends. In the beginning, however, most of his ideas on freedom, nationalism and revolution were inspired by manifold experiments in the West, especially the long, intrepid struggle of the peoples of

Europe to attain basic human dignity. Rousseau and other European thinkers, we may remember, did characterize slavery as immoral. The entire history of the French Revolution and the European Romantic movement, especially in its unswerving commitment to the cause of liberty, had a moral basis. Some of the English Romantic poets, especially Wordsworth, viewed the French Revolution as a fulfillment of the biblical prophecy contained in the Revelation. In the history of European political thought and particularly at the time of the American and the French revolutions clear-cut distinctions had been drawn between morality that is politically functional and expedient and morality that has its reference to larger and more fundamental humanistic values. Undoubtedly, Aurobindo considered the latter the only justifiable basis of a revolution that was inspired by a comprehensive vision of liberty.

Liberty for Aurobindo did not mean simply the abolition of the foreign rule and the achievement of self-government based upon the blind imitation of the West. Nor did it mean the attainment of empty and selfish materialistic progress hitherto sought by great nations. Nationalism meant the true awakening of the "Indian proletariat" to a collective vision of such cultural greatness as would enable India to contribute to the progress of human civilization:

> . . . we advocate the struggle for Swaraj, first, because Liberty is in itself a necessity of national life and therefore worth striving for its own sake; secondly, because Liberty is the first indispensable condition of national development intellectual, moral, industrial, political . . . thirdly, because in the next great stage of human progress it is not a material but a spiritual, moral and psychical advance that has to be made and for this a free Asia and in Asia a free India must take the lead, and Liberty is therefore worth striving for the world's sake. India must have Swaraj in order to live; she must have Swaraj in order to live well and happily; she must have Swaraj in order to live for the world . . . as a free people for the spiritual and intellectual benefit of the human race. (*BCL* 1.465)

While egotistical nationalism is morally destructive, true nationalism, as is evident from this lucid exposition of the larger responsibilities of freedom, is neither callously selfish nor inherently antagonistic: on the contrary, such nationalism as marks the intellectual and cultural growth of a nation or a group of people is directly and positively related to the welfare of the entire community of mankind. Swaraj (self-rule) is an inner discipline, both at the individual level and the national level, and it cannot be realized without cleansing one's perceptions. Aurobindo maintains that "the true source of human liberty, human equality, [and] human brotherhood" is in the freedom of man's inner spirit (*BCL* I.759). Liberty, equality and fraternity are teleological and epistemological concepts, and their place in a social structure is dependent on man's ability to perceive the truth of each of these concepts. In the structure of political reality envisaged by Aurobindo, the recognition of the constitutional or legal rights of liberty and equality is not enough, for the ideal of liberty is not fully achieved without equality and fraternity, and more importantly without fraternity. Teleologically, of course, the term "swaraj" simultaneously refers to nationalism and liberty.

Aurobindo considered "political Vedantism" to be the basis of the struggle and the strategy: this "political Vedantism," the wisdom of the Vedas, and especially of the *Gita,* not only spiritualized the struggle but it gave him a much more profound and authentic political vision of liberty. The kind of swaraj that Aurobindo envisioned was not merely a political liberty; and the kind of struggle that Aurobindo championed was again not merely a political struggle, but a total and endless struggle for true freedom. Generally speaking, most revolutionary struggles are viewed as reactionary insurgences or temporary volcanic eruptions. But for Aurobindo the revolution meant more than a series of sporadic boycotts, fiery protests and violent demonstrations: it included a large-scale program of political, economic, educational, social and spiritual reconstruction. As a *dharma yudha,* it must be continuously fought simultaneously on several planes.

Aurobindo's early political radicalism was motivated by his uncompromising commitment to the ideals of liberty, equality and fraternity and by his optimistic faith in the ability of man to become perfect. Indeed, his early political writings are an important contribution to Indian literature and thought; but, significantly, as he progressed in his self-realization the direct political anxiety and commitment were transformed into a much more universal and comprehensive concern for true human freedom and a new world order. The later Aurobindo, that is, the Aurobindo of the period following his dramatic exit from the active political scene,[20] has given us not only one of the most subtle analyses of man and society but also a unique vision of human progress and perfection.

One no doubt gathers from *The Human Cycle* and *The Ideal of Human Unity* that Aurobindo is a close student of history, but his philosophic vision is not centered in history, that is, in the past. Aurobindo is essentially an evolutionist, and the evolutionary theory (which, in spite of some of its obvious similarities with scientific and materialistic theories of evolution, is not Darwinian) implies that man, forms of society and other structures must continue evolving. Since man is capable of realizing his true divinity, the form and level of perfection arrived at by man at one particular stage is not absolute. Nor is any one pattern or form of society perfect for that matter. In fact, in *The Human Cycle,* Aurobindo, using Karl Lamprecht's phraseology, conceives five psychical stages in the evolutionary development of the human race: symbolic, typal, conventional, individualistic and subjective.[21] The movement from the symbolic to the subjective marks a process of divinization of man. However, Aurobindo does not believe that there is a linear or straightforward path that the process of development follows. Nor does he think that man should become overly dependent upon either the past or the future, although for the purpose of immediate development the past and the future must coalesce in the present, such that the point of history absorbed in the present becomes only another point in history. As Aurobindo states:

> It is true that the world's movement is not in a straight line; there are cycles, there are spirals; but still it circles, not round the same point always, but round an ever advancing centre, and therefore it never returns exactly upon its old path and never goes really backward. As for standing still, it is an impossibility, a delusion, a fiction. (*BCL* 16.317)

Since man is capable of becoming perfect, the highest point that he is capable of achieving is the highest point of his divinization only at one particular stage. Similarly, society is not merely a stagnant and abstract political structure; its progress depends upon the degree and nature of perfection achieved by its individual members. In a true sense, an ideal society is a community of mankind, a brotherhood that apprehends the individuality of man. But since none of the political structures so far invented by man allows any one of the two possibilities to be realized in the most ideal sense, political solution alone is no satisfactory solution of the problem of human existence, individual or collective.

While the movement from the symbolic level to the typal and conventional levels may ordinarily be regarded as symptomatic of man's fall from unity, in Aurobindo it characterizes an essential phase of continuous human advancement without the slightest implication of any pessimistic regression. At these levels, the law is established and enforced strictly according to the dictates of rational and empirical reason. Also, at these levels, the age of scientific advancement has made some of its major claims: our priorities here are confined strictly to the external world of material existence. What is valued more is the shastra (that is, established rules and the logical order), and not Atman, the spirit. The Urizenic government of the shastra (coded morality) is primarily created to safeguard man in his fallen condition of disorder and disunity. No political structure based upon this constrictive reason, however ideal—and be this democracy, communism or socialism—will apprehend the true individuality of man. Under these various political and social systems, whatever liberty and equality are granted are given according to the law, the code, and are not consistent with man's fundamental right to be absolutely free and with his evolutionary nature. For example, in a democracy, political liberty or political equality is what is conferred upon an individual at the pleasure of the philistine majority. Therefore, even a democracy, and still worse of the mediocre kind, is limited in scope and nature; and at best it gives only political freedom. In any political structure, including democracy, absolute freedom breeds egoism; and whether it is individual egoism or national egoism, it will destroy the ideal conception of liberty. As Aurobindo says:

> Freedom, equality, brotherhood are three godheads of the soul; they cannot be really achieved through the external machinery of society or by man so long as he lives only in the individual and the communal ego. When the ego claims liberty, it arrives at competitive individualism. When it asserts equality, it arrives first at strife, then at an attempt to ignore the variations of Nature, and, as the sole way of doing that successfully, it constructs an artificial and machine-made society. A society that pursues liberty as its ideal is unable to achieve equality; a society that aims at equality will be obliged to sacrifice liberty. For the ego to speak of fraternity is for it to speak of something contrary to its nature. . . . (*BCL* 15.546)

Indeed, Aurobindo's concern with the nature and scope of liberty is teleological. And he advocates absolute freedom:

> . . . man cannot build greatly whether in art or life, unless he can conceive an idea and form of perfection and, conceiving, believe in his power to achieve it out of however rebellious and unductile a stuff of nature. Deprive him of his faith in his power for perfection and you slay or maim his greatest creative or self-creative faculty. (*BCL* 15.609–10)

If man's salvation, as Aurobindo maintains, lies in "a religious or spiritual idealisation of a possible future humanity" (*BCL* 15.609), man must continue to evolve, by means of the synthetic discipline of yoga, to the apex of what Blake would call human form divine. Aurobindo, like Blake, is not advocating licentious freedom with which man nourishes his titanic ambitions (*asura pravriti*) into egoism or hubris, be it Apollonian or Dionysian. But while most political systems are inherently fearful of such egoism, their repressive and sanctimonious laws, paradoxically enough, become a fertile soil for the nefarious perversion of ego as well as for the loss of individuality. After all, political slavery is only one kind of slavery, but the most frightful form of slavery is mental slavery—which is what the passivity of the spirit really means. It hardly needs to be stressed that any amount or degree of political freedom given to an individual whose mind has been conditioned by the language of laws and rights is not only use-less but also harmful. That is why Nietzsche, while advocating intellectual anarchism, proposes the annihilation of the stubborn structure of the obsolete system. If absolute freedom implies anarchism, political or intellectual, this kind of freedom, in a sense, is a negation of that divinity that entitles man to seek his freedom and that when realized is in itself true liberty. In the anarchist thought on the whole, we are talking about only partial or one kind of liberty, and not of total and comprehensive freedom. The conception of superman, according to Aurobindo, suggests the fully integrated and realized whole, a heroic consciousness. Therefore, neither the Apollonian man nor the Dionysian man is a whole man; and for the same reason, neither the ethical being nor the aesthetic being is a whole being. Such wholeness and realization as Aurobindo proposes are not anarchical in character, for his conception is based neither on the rejection of history nor on a self-centered alienation from the body of the universe. Rebellion against the yoke of law and its manifest tyranny and general "putrid waste" is a significant step forward toward a program of social reform; however, a total rejection of history and of law as generally emphasized by a variety of anarchist thought suggests not only an unnatural discontinuity and disruption in the process of evolution but also a refusal on the part of the systems to recognize man's achievement.

Here we may emphasize a significant difference between a political revolutionary and a karm yogi. In Aurobindo's *Savitri,* King Ashwapathy is a karm yogi, but Savitri is both a karm yogi and a radical. Savitri's heroic consciousness enables her to wage a successful war against the god of death and of a deterministic order of lower nature and to restore to the earth the paradisal vision of life and happiness. The heroic man, according to Aurobindo, is charged by his own consciousness to create paradisal condition on earth: such heroic souls as Plato's men of gold are agents of the Brahman engaged in the redemptive act of regenerating this virile universe. The individual belongs to mankind on the whole, and his true *dharma* is *manav dharma:* the principle and the process that bring him together with his fellow man are summed up by the word *lokasangraha*—which means "the holding together of the race in its cyclic evolution" (*BCL* 15.59). Man creates his new higher self by participating in the good of others. He enjoys absolute freedom and equality, but with one imperative—that is, brotherhood. The vision of one consciousness, and of reintegration and wholeness, places Aurobindo in an enviable company of such great figures as Plato, Dante and Shelley. But, most significantly, he shows the practical way of making this earth a paradise.

In Aurobindo's vision of human freedom and unity, as a nation's freedom and progress basically depend upon the nature of individual consciousness, so does the progressive movement toward one-world community depend upon the quality of the "aggregates" of people. Aurobindo maintains that people should be able to organize themselves into nations or "aggregates" in accordance with the principles of free association and unity. As free and equal people are brought together by a communal consciousness, so are free and equal nations brought together, not as a conglomeration of "imperial aggregates" that are motivated merely by political and commercial designs of expansion and aggression, but as "an ideal aggregate of humanity" that aspires to a vision of spiritualized community. True nationalism will lead, not to antagonism, domination and confrontation, but to understanding, collaboration and cosmopolitanism—and, hence, to creating a better and happier community of mankind. Since Aurobindo's vision of universal humanity is based upon the spiritualization of man, all forms of national and imperial egoism, including such racial egoisms as Europeanism, Asiaticism and Americanism, must be overcome. Man will cooperate with fellow man, not because he is a *homo economicus* or because he is a political or social animal, but because he has the inner urge to establish a spiritual brotherhood. It is abundantly clear that Aurobindo does not accept the Hobbesean thesis of a basic distrust in man's capacity to become free and of an avowed supremacy of the state. Nor does he regard Utilitarianism, Marxism and Socialism as sufficiently powerful structures for resolving the problem of human suffering. Most social and political theories of contractual obligation and entitlement are fundamentally inconsistent with the larger vision of human freedom, since several conceptions of contracts and rights are essentially founded on inveterate prejudices, especially fear, distrust and hatred, that in turn provide a pretentious basis of human subjugation and exploitation, economic, political and social, and, hence, of an invidious social anarchy.

Evidently, Aurobindo's conception of human freedom is very bold and radical. Aurobindo tells us that man is the author of social and historical destiny and that all forms of social, political and religious structures are hindrances to his freedom and creativity. The idealist position, beginning with Plato, recognizes the divinity of state: in *The Republic,* the soul's liberation from the cycle of existence is ultimately dependent upon social good. Kant, of course, considers individual freedom more important than an unequivocal commitment to the state, although Hegel's belief in the divinity of a nation, which incidentally constitutes the basis of his social ethics, is the direct opposite of the Kantian position. But amongst the English thinkers it is, indeed, Coleridge who emphasizes the divinity of state, categorically affirming organicism—not the Spencerian organicism but Romantic organicism—according to which man, nature and society evolve together discovering "the transcendental and divine force of life."[22]

In his conception of the evolution of a new society, Aurobindo, as might be construed, takes a daring leap beyond social morality, rational ethicism, nationalism and statism. In a message delivered on August 15, 1947, Aurobindo says that "Nationalism will then have fulfilled itself; an international spirit and outlook must grow up . . ." (*BCL* 26.403). While Burke will still insist upon the need of nationalism as the basis of a European common community or a confederation of nations, Aurobindo envisions the formation of an international brotherhood, a new community of man, where voluntary fusion of cultures takes place, where nationalism and its militancy will have outlived its usefulness and where narrow national boundaries will eventually become redundant. It is somewhat paradoxical that nationalism or the state as a moral entity carries only a limited value in Aurobindo's vision of the progress of human society: the divinity that was once attributed to the state is now vested in mankind as a whole, the divine humanity. We must note this significant difference between the early Aurobindo—the fiery, youthful and uncompromising radical—and the Aurobindo of the Pondicherry period—the serene, contemplative and philosophical mind. In his vision of human freedom, Aurobindo may be called a spiritual anarchist, but he is not a nihilist. He is a reconstructionist and a progressive thinker who believes that all precipitous impediments to human progress, whatever their generic form, must be overcome, and that modern socioeconomic and scientific progress and spiritual growth must not be considered incompatible with each other. Undoubtedly, behind this vision of affirmation is the hope and belief in the unhindered progress of man to the highest possible point in the human divine image: obviously, on a projected scale of continuous evolution, state, religion and other institutional structures, because of their regressive conservatism and cryptic inertia, do not remain compatible with man's progress. That is why Aurobindo stresses the need for newer forms of social and political structures that will eliminate the problem of historical obsolescence and redundancy and help in the fusion of tradition and modernity.

Since evil belongs to history and the order of nature—and, hence, to the world of Maya—it appears at periodic stages in the evolutionary process of life.[23] In a sense, evil, as Aurobindo would have us believe, is a fortuitous agent of beneficial change, and, hence, of good, since without evil the redemptive appearance of good will not take place. But moral evil and physical evil are real, not illusory; and Aurobindo deals with the problem of evil with full force in his philosophy of evolution. At the individual level, however, it is egoism that breeds evil. In *The Life Divine,* Aurobindo's view is clearly monistic: evil and falsehood, according to Aurobindo, result from ignorance (*avidya* Maya), but there is no absolute evil as there is no absolute ignorance. Evil and falsehood, as Aurobindo observes, "are a by-product of the world-movement: the sombre flowers of falsehood and evil have their root in the black soil of the Inconscient" (*BCL* 18.598). The world or life as a whole is not evil; nor is man inherently evil. This conception of evil, which essentially comes from Aurobindo's view of human nature, has unmistakably shaped his vision of liberty, equality and brotherhood and of man's salvation—and, hence, of a progressive journey from political freedom to spiritual liberation. One of the most significant elements in Aurobindo's social and political vision is that there is no room for repressive measures and laws based on a system of rewards and punishments. Nor is there any room for negative and punitive religious morality governed by the fear of evil and the self-dissipating bigotry of damnation. Religion that rejects life in preference to the overzealous pursuit of other-worldliness and esoteric goals and rituals, that creates an unwarranted division between life and spirit, and that promotes pain, suffering, fear and retribution is an exercise in spreading ignorance and as such does not hold any hope for man. In *The Human Cycle,* Aurobindo addresses "the historic insufficiency of religion as a guide and control of human society" (*BCL* 15.165): while sharply distinguishing between institutional religion and the spiritual religion of humanity, Aurobindo maintains that neither religion nor industrialization should be permitted to thwart human progress and world unity. Hence, it is clear that the way to resolving the problem of evil is not rational and orthodox religion but spirituality. As Aurobindo explains "the idea and spirit of the intellectual religion of humanity":

> Man must be sacred to man regardless of all distinctions of race, creed, colour, nationality, status, political or social advancement. The body of man is to be respected, made immune from violence and outrage, fortified by science against disease and preventable death. The life of man is to be held sacred, preserved, strengthened, ennobled, uplifted. The heart of man is to be held sacred also . . . The mind of man is to be released from all bonds. . . .
> (*BCL* 15.542–43)

Such a cohesive and profound vision of unity and progress of the human race is not utopian: on the contrary, it directly focuses on the intricate muddle of human existence in a comprehensive context and on the ultimate goal of life. Aurobindo's political vision is compatible with his spiritual vision of man's total freedom:[24] political freedom provides a fertile soil needed to pursue the path of spiritual awakening and to discover that intelligent principle that binds men together as a unity and that enables them to evolve into one divine humanity. But politics, education and religion are merely tools of facilitating man's evolutionary progress and his search for Reality and Truth, and are not ends in themselves. An ideal political structure that guarantees such individual freedom as enables man to pursue his search for truth voluntarily, unreservedly and fearlessly is an expression of the most genuine self-assertion and the will of awakened minds, but not of the philistines and the bourgeoisie. In this sense, Aurobindo is a fearless and astute champion of individual freedom and human dignity: in the struggle between collectivity and the individual, the state, as Aurobindo asserts with Kant, has absolutely no right to force an individual to surrender his freedom, whatever the pretext. The individual has the unquestionable right to strive to achieve the highest form of wisdom, since it is only by awakening divinity in oneself that one would know how to apprehend divinity in another. The recognition of this underlying principle of unity clearly implies that Caesarism, imperialism, colonialism, racism and other forms of repressive and hegemonic politico-economic structures will be rejected and that an individual and clusters of people can hope to coexist in the world today in a fraternal trust of love and hope without being trampled, devoured and vitiated. This vision of human freedom and progress and of realizing an ideal condition of human existence on this earth is not a devaluation of the political vision[25] but a fulfillment of the larger and more comprehensive vision of human freedom.

Chapter 4 ❖

Sri Aurobindo as a Critic

To interfere with the imperfections of the great poets of the past is a hazardous busi-ness—their imperfections as well their perfections are part of themselves.

—Aurobindo

I

Radhakrishanan has called Aurobindo "the greatest intellectual of our age."[1] Is this tribute meant to recognize the poet of *Savitri,* the prophetic mind of *The Life Divine,* the philosopher of *The Psychology of Social Development* (*The Human Cycle*) and *The Ideal of Human Unity* or the interpreter of the *Gita?* Indeed, Aurobindo is mostly known as a philosopher and a poet, but his stature as critic remains somewhat unassessed—and deeply undervalued—and perhaps overshadowed by the unsurpassed brilliance and originality of his work in other areas.[2] What-ever the merits of the three long essays in *Significance of Indian Art,* this volatile document shows Aurobindo's successful attempt to offer his inter-pretation of Indian art based on his theory of the expansion of conscious-ness and the Indian idea of *rasa-bhava-ananda,* derived from Bharata's *Natya Shastra.*[3] Aurobindo has used these ideas in *The Future Poetry* (1917–20) on a larger scale, but this time the subject is the English language and litera-ture, especially poetry. One must say unhesitatingly that *The Future Poetry* is an important and unique document in literary history and critical the-ory. In the introductory essay, Aurobindo straightforwardly and candidly refers to his reading of James Cousins's *New Ways in English Literature,* that possibly provided the immediate context to a series of essays in the *Arya.*[4] Aurobindo admits that since his "departure from England quarter of a cen-tury ago" all connections with contemporary English literature had come to "a dead stop" and that he had kept abreast only with contemporary continental literature. His last discovery of a poet in English literature, states Aurobindo, was Meredith.[5]

In some respects, Aurobindo as a critic is comparable to Samuel Taylor Coleridge, the father of English criticism. The one single work in English literature to which *The Future Poetry* can be compared is Coleridge's *Biographia Literaria*. Coleridge's indefatigable genius has traveled literally into several directions—"Logician, Metaphysician, Bard," as Charles Lamb notes.[6] Both *The Future Poetry* and *Biographia Literaria* have comprehensive philosophical bases and they are sharply analytical. One of the significant features of *Biographia Literaria* is that Coleridge has seized an opportunity to introduce German thought to the English mind. Likewise, in *The Future Poetry*, Aurobindo has boldly proposed the application of certain aspects of classical Indian thought to the future developments of English poetry. It must be noted that Aurobindo as a theoretician of literature and a philosopher is also a successful practitioner of verse. There is a little doubt that Aurobindo confronts some of the perennial critical issues: What is poetry? What is a poet? What is the function of art? But Aurobindo places these and other significant issues in the larger philosophical context of the evolution of human civilization. Elsewhere I have stated that "*The Future Poetry* contains Aurobindo's intriguing and bold argument for the application of classical Indian aesthetic to the progressive development of English poetry" and that Aurobindo sees "this synthesis as a practical possibility, especially because of the newly evolving structure of human consciousness."[7] Without being repetitive and overassertive, I would suggest unhesitatingly that the intricate argument of *The Future Poetry* can be understood only in the context of Aurobindo's philosophy. However, one must not forget at the same time that Aurobindo's inheritance contains two operative pasts: the colonial past against which he had fiercely fought but that bequeathed him the ineluctable legacy of the English language and literature, the legacy he willingly accepted; and the ancient Indian tradition, its philosophy and literature, which he tried to interpret in relation to other traditions in which he was thoroughly steeped.

One could possibly suggest a comparison with Matthew Arnold, a poet–critic and a moralist, whose critical theories have dominated the Indian literary scene for a long time. But it must be noted that Aurobindo considers Arnold's definition of poetry as criticism of life incomplete and inadequate. Dryden and Pope are also poet-critics, but their criticism and poetry would not stand the test of Aurobindo's criteria of future poetry. A comparison with Dr. Johnson may not hold out for obvious reasons. One could go back to Sir Philip Sidney's Renaissance ideals as expressed in *An Apology for Poetry*, but Sidney's essay at best is an apology. In the twentieth century, one would certainly think of T. S. Eliot's philosophical and critical ideas that have been instrumental in reinforcing the ideology of New Criticism and the moral approach to literature. Admittedly, Aurobindo's canvas is much wider and richer; the most common point among these figures is that they all are theorists of literature, enunciators of critical theory and practitioners of art. In Aurobindo's case especially, one does not have to belabor the point that Aurobindo's position as a philosopher remains unquestionably superior. And this is precisely the reason, at least for our purpose, for an objective valuation of his position as a critic, for, since most Western criticism has its roots in the philosophical ideas of Plato and Aristotle, it is simply felicitous to presume that there is a close relationship between Aurobindo's philosophy and his critical theories. In fact, modern and postmodern developments in criticism show the continued and heavy impact of philosophy and ideology on critical theory and practice.[8]

Can Aurobindo the poet be placed in any one particular literary tradition? And what about Aurobindo the critic? Is it somewhat difficult to identify Aurobindo with any one school or movement within the broad spectrum of post-Nietzschean critical theories? How would New Criticism, structuralism, poststructuralism and deconstruction respond to a document like *The Future Poetry* or the letters appended to *Savitri?* In the heavily diffused landscape of contemporary critical theory, especially in view of the phenomenal explosion of a multiplicity of theories, movements and approaches—Myth and Archetypal criticism, New Criticism, structuralist criticism, psychoanalytical criticism, poststructuralist criticism, Marxist criticism, feminist criticism, anxiety-of-influence criticism, reader-response theory, new historicist criticism, postcolonial theory and various other forms of post-postmodernist "isms"—where does Aurobindo fit? Can the critical geniuses of Samuel Johnson, Coleridge, Wordsworth, Shelley, Arnold and Eliot still retain their validity and relevance? And what about Aristotle, Kant, Hegel, Kierkegaard, Nietzsche and a host of other philosophical minds in history? Aurobindo's literary criticism comes close, in many ways, if not entirely, to the school of Myth and Archetype, with which the names of Freud, Jung, Frazer, Mann and Frye are commonly associated.[9] And yet Aurobindo's criticism is deftly grounded in philosophy. Aurobindo would certainly concede the necessity of structural analysis of a work as the first step, but would he agree with the general premise that criticism must become a means of creating "a systematic structure of knowledge?"[10] In his comments on *New Ways in English Literature*, Aurobindo approves Cousins's "positive criticism," while strongly disapproving his "negative and destructive criticism" of J. M. Synge. Here is a crucial statement: "For the light we get from a vital and illuminative criticism from within by another mind can sometimes almost take the place of a direct knowledge" (*FP* 3).[11] One may be tempted to suggest certain commonality between Aurobindo and the new critics like I. A. Richards and F. R. Leavis, but Aurobindo's concerns as a critic are far too comprehensive. For one thing, Aurobindo does not accept the autonomous character of a work as rigidly demanded by formalism. In terms of the relationship between critical ideology, metaphysics and other philosophical writings, one would inevitably think of a sort of parallel with modern hermeneutics, especially with Gadamer's idea, according to which the text is not an autonomous unit.

II

"The poet," maintains Aurobindo somewhat in the manner of Coleridge, "creates out of himself and has the indefeasible right to follow freely the breath of the spirit within him, provided he satisfies in his work the law of poetic beauty" (*FP* 38).[12] The poet's cultural milieu and the sense of history and tradition are important, but they must not hinder the "free play of his poetic spirit." While rejecting "the theory of the man and his milieu or the dogma of the historical school of criticism which asks of us to study all the precedents, circumstances, influences, surroundings," Aurobindo reiterates that we should "come straight to the poet and his poem" (*FP* 38–39). After all, the poet is "a soul expressing the eternal spirit of Truth and Beauty" (*FP* 39). While the soul of the poet is the "impersonal" creator and interpreter of beauty, the reader too like a "true critic (*rasika*)"[13] is "the impersonal enjoyer of creative beauty." Aurobindo's idea of the "impersonal" in the poet and the reader is a brilliant adumbration of Keats's idea of Negative Capability, an idea that Eliot transliterates as depersonalization. But Aurobindo concedes that "there is a truth in the historical theory of criticism," perhaps for ascertaining "our intellectual judgment of a poet and his work" (*FP* 39). Thus both the poet and the reader contemplate the universal, the infinite through their inner, subjective imaginations. Obviously, Aurobindo has attempted to resolve two major problems of critical theory: (1) the ability of historical criticism to deal with biography; and (2) the relationship between the poet, the text and the reader. Aurobindo's focus on the relationship between the personality of the poet and the personality of the reader should remind us about the psychological and philosophical basis of the contemporary reader-response theory.[14] Evidently, Aurobindo, in rejecting the autonomous character of a work, obviates the undue emphasis placed by Victorian critics on the ability of history and biography to contain truth.

Aurobindo seems to accept Shelley's distinction between the man and the poet,[15] maintaining however that there is "a larger movement . . . of the general soul of mankind" (*FP* 41) to which the poet, the reader and the poet's work must belong. We are told that the evolution of art form, the evolution of poetic consciousness and the evolution of general consciousness are constituent parts of an integral organic process. Coleridge's organicism and Wordsworth's theory of Nature essentially point in this direction, but the inevitable conclusion one would be compelled to draw from this sort of theoretical model is that the point of reference to a work of art and its total meaning essentially lie outside its body. Furthermore, since neither the text nor the poet's personality is an autonomous entity, the total meaning of a work is the integral and cumulative meaning of the various constituent parts.

<h1 style="text-align:center">III</h1>

Aurobindo's eloquent and perspicuous analysis of the dominant characteristic of various cultural and racial groups, the Anglo-Saxons, the Celts and the Scandinavians, and their impact on the origin and development of English poetry from Chaucer to the modern time is historical and psychoanthropological. In particular, it shows a strong psychological tendency in Aurobindo's mind to philosophize history in universal terms. Although Aurobindo devalues the temporal aspect of history as a principal method of critical formulation, he considers the struggle between the two aspects of time vitally significant in the process of creating universal and cosmological structures of historical consciousness. Aurobindo's view of history and man, it must be noted, is fundamentally embedded in his philosophy of evolutionary progress as fully enunciated in *The Life Divine*. Aurobindo as a philosopher is essentially looking at the total corpus of history very much like Hegel in *Philosophy of History*, but with one tangible difference in that Aurobindo's philosophical view of history is focused on man's social, psychological and spiritual progress. Indeed, Marx's view of history is centered on the dialectic of materialistic philosophy and on scientific objectivity, but Aurobindo's view is based on the psychology of human development and on spiritual subjectivity. Of course, we must recognize that with the exception of certain fundamental differences both views of history are inevitably geared towards the reconstruction of an ideal social order and the general amelioration of the human condition.[16]

It is erroneous to believe that Aurobindo like Shankara rejects materialism in preference to any form of transcendental idealism, illusionism or other worldliness.[17] In fact, it must be emphasized that as a theorist of society and civilization Aurobindo considers the integral relationship between matter, life and mind an essential condition for the development of unified consciousness. Thus in Aurobindo's metaphysical system, history becomes a universal pattern of evolution, sociohistorical reality and human civilization. In the evolutionary process of civilization, Aurobindo's conceptualization of total world history, following Lamprecht's groupings, consists of the following stages: the Symbolic, the Typal, the Conventional, the Individualist and the Subjective.[18] One might wonder if knowledge and the will of man could possibly direct the total course of history. In other words, can nature and the mind of man contain the truth of history? In his discussion of Nietzsche and Christianity, Karl Jaspers classifies the world's luminaries into two categories: those who like Pascal, Kierkegaard, Dostoevsky and Nietzsche became "heroic victims of a historic change in the human condition" and those "exceptional thinkers" who like St. Paul, St. Augustine and Luther "shaped the world."[19] There should hardly be any doubt or ambivalence about Aurobindo's place.

It must be noted that in *The Future Poetry* Aurobindo's analysis of the development of English poetry is based on the aforementioned philosophy of world history. According to this metaphysics of reality, the various stages of involution and evolution are not only integrally related but also mutually inclusive. In Aurobindo's thought spirituality means not any form of propitiatory withdrawal from, and renunciatory indifference to, life, but the highest form of awakening of the self, that will give some meaning to dull existence. Thus sociohistoric reality, the empirical view of history or a certain category of human experience does not become irrelevant and meaningless; on the contrary, it assumes its meaning and significance in relation to the total structure of reality. Aurobindo, himself once a staunch radical during the pre-Pondicherry years, would, for example, readily asseverate certain tenets of new historicism, Marxism and colonial and postcolonial discourses, but would strongly advocate the inadequacy of materialistic approaches. He would have no difficulty in understanding Stephen Greenblatt's new historicist reading of *The Tempest* and the treatment of colonialism in history, but would have vehemently argued for a more comprehensive and philosophical view of history.[20] Oswald Spengler's thesis in *The Decline of the West* is centered on destiny as the moving principle of history that will eventually destroy "the Apollinian [sic], Faustian and Magian soul." Maitra observes that in Spengler the periodic hardening of lifeforce marks advancement from culture to civilization; likewise in Bergson the slowing down of élan vital produces the state of matter. But Aurobindo does not accept the cyclical view of history, nor does he consider the principles of causality and destiny tenable.[21] Furthermore, he does not even accept the traditional Hindu view of karma or any other form of determinism. His historical perspective is directly fused into his philosophy of evolutionary progress: the highest state of human progress, spiritual subjectivism or supramentalism, finally leads to the Saccidanand vision. Aurobindo's vision of human progress is not linear: it contains an intricate structure of the stages of involution and evolution.

Thus it must be clearly understood that in Aurobindo's philosophy of evolutionary progress the highest stage is the subjective state, the time when man achieves the state of spiritual subjectivity, supramental growth, both individually and collectively. While the Age of Chaucer marks an abrupt beginning, the Elizabethan Age is the age of extraordinary exuberance, vigor and resurgence. "The Elizabethan poet," remarks Aurobindo, "wrote in the spacious days of its first birth into greatness . . . but it may be that the richest powers, the highest and the greatest spirit yet remain to be found and commanded" (*FP* 57). Aurobindo discusses the characteristic achievements of Milton, which were only followed by the regressive age of Dryden and Pope. The Romantic poets Blake, Wordsworth, Coleridge, Byron, Shelley and Keats, called the "poets of dawn," ushered in a new era that was soon to be eclipsed by Victorian intellectualism and smug materialism. However, Aurobindo maintains that the Romantic poets "have a greater thing to reveal than the Elizabethan poets, but they do not express it with that constant fullness of native utterance or that more perfect correspondence between substance and form which is the greatness of Shakespeare and Spenser" (*FP* 111). In the continued strain of a philosopher of history Aurobindo notes the growth of "strenuous intellectuality" and the contributions of Emerson, Carlyle and Ruskin in building "a bridge of transition from the intellectual transcendentalism of the earlier nineteenth century across a subsequent low-lying scientific, utilitarian, externalised intellectualism . . . over to the age now beginning to come in towards us" (*FP* 179). But it is the "prophetic mind" of Whitman, asserts Aurobindo, that "consciously and largely foresaw and prepared the paths" to future poetry:

He [Whitman] belongs to the largest mind of the nineteenth century by the stress and energy of his intellectual seeking, by his emphasis on man and life and Nature, by his idea of the cosmic and universal, his broad spaces and surfaces, by his democratic enthusiasm, by his eye fixed on the future, by his intellectual reconciling vision at once of the greatness of the individual and the community of mankind, by his nationalism and internationalism, by his gospel of comradeship and fraternity in our common average manhood, by almost all in fact of the immense mass of ideas which form the connecting tissue of his work. (*FP* 179)

This critical valuation of Whitman is centered not so much on the apparent affinity of Whitman's vision of life and nature with Wordsworthianism as on the democratic and universal spirit of Whitman's imagination—in fact, the expansiveness, immensity and unity of Whitman's consciousness, corresponding to the American landscape. It is Whitman's cosmic vision of "the community of mankind," of liberty, democracy and universality, that seeks to reconstruct a new progressive future by disengagement from, and subversion of, the past. Significantly, Aurobindo examines these issues of literary history and criticism with Arnoldian disinterestedness and intellectual objectivity, putting aside issues of class, race and nationality.

It is rather ironic that Aurobindo sees hope and light in the modern experimental period, although poets like Eliot had succumbed to the wasteland mythology of despair and pessimism. The twentieth century is the period of self-destructive anxiety, when the human mind is known to have experienced its most extrusive impotence in confronting discontents of a fractured civilization and when the words "progress," "soul" and "civilization" seem to have lost their currency and authenticity. But Aurobindo looks optimistically to the prophetic moment, to an emerging evolution, when poetry will become the language of mantra, the powerful rhythmic expression of the soul in its contemplation of the Saccidanand vision. The word "epic" had most certainly slipped out from the soporific vocabulary of the modernist imagination, except of course in the case of Ezra Pound whose ambitious work *The Cantos* seems to have been modeled after Dante's vision of the *Inferno*. The eighteenth century had experienced a similar decline of sensibility and found out that the only kind of epic it could rationally and justifiably conceptualize was *The Dunciad*.

IV

It is fairly reasonable to suggest that Aurobindo's discerning criticism of Romantic art and aesthetic deserves a much more comprehensive scrutiny than permitted by this discussion, especially in the provocative context of modernism and valuations of English Romantic writers. Admittedly, Aurobindo's treatment of the "poets of the dawn" in three chapters is the best section in *The Future Poetry*. A close reading of this section should leave no doubt in the reader's mind that Aurobindo's most favorite poet is Shelley, although elsewhere Aurobindo calls Blake "Europe's greatest mystic poet" (*BCL* 9.529). Blake, according to Aurobindo, is a seer who, very much like Coleridge, lives in the "middle-world" of the imagination, but is "unable to translate his experience to our comprehension" (*FP* 125). Blake's "power of expression," maintains Aurobindo, "is not equal to his power of vision" (*FP* 125). It is somewhat surprising that Aurobindo whose poetic method bears a close resemblance to that of Blake should complain about the problem of unintelligibility.[22] However, it must be recognized that Aurobindo's criticism in general is a reverberation of a common problem voiced in early Blake scholarship. After all, the discovery of Blake that started with Rossetti and Yeats did not reach its apex until the appearance of the monumental works of S. Foster Damon, Northrop Frye and Kathleen Raine.

Aurobindo is aware of Byron's "prodigious reputation" on the Continent. Undeniably, Aurobindo must have been familiar with Goethe's unreserved admiration of Byron: the English "can show no poet who is to be compared to him [Byron]. He is different from all the others, and for the most part greater."[23] But Aurobindo firmly contests Taine's misjudgment of Byron and considers Wordsworth "a much higher poetic mind" (*FP* 119), of course taking fully into account the two principal categories of Byron criticism, Byron at home and Byron on the Continent. Aurobindo's criticism of Byron is balanced and objective and it is abundantly clear that it does not share T. S. Eliot's moralistic denunciation of the poet.[24] Aurobindo recognizes that both Wordsworth and Byron had an extraordinary fund of energy: Wordsworth's domineering urge for metaphysics and Byron's overwhelming and intimidating Titanism are forms of expression of this energy. Aurobindo clearly sees Wordsworth as a poet of Nature, but will his critical judgment consider that "Wordsworth is Rousseau moralized, Christianized, and, as it were, transfigured by the light of imagination,"[25] that the essential doctrines stated in the preface to *Lyrical Ballads* and elsewhere in the prefaces would have been unacceptable to critics like Dr. Johnson, and that modern critical theory in English literature has its origin in the ideas of English Romantic writers, notably Wordsworth, Coleridge and Shelley?[26]

Aurobindo's focus is not on Coleridge the critic but on Coleridge the poet, especially on the role of metaphysics in the growth of the poetical faculty. Aurobindo's point is that "the poet in him never took into himself the thinker" (*FP* 124). Coleridge, according to Aurobindo, had an abundant supply of "intellectuality," but "he squandered rather than used it in discursive metaphysics and criticism . . ." (*FP* 124). Such a view is a part of the standard criticism of Coleridge's lapses as a poet, and in fact Coleridge himself brings this Kierkegaardian problem of despair in the open in "Dejection: An Ode."[27] It is however agreed now that the period of the "Dejection" Ode was purely a temporary one in Coleridge's life.[28] It could be argued that Coleridge's excessive interests in theology and metaphysics became an insurmountable impediment in the growth of his poetic faculties. Or, perhaps, his extraordinary interest in metaphysics and theology finally diminished his interest in poetry. Whatever the truth of the matter, it must be acknowledged that Aurobindo himself has debated some of the problems confronted by Coleridge, and perhaps none other than Aurobindo the philosopher and the poet could estimate the psychological truth about the disruptive nature of metaphysics and philosophy in the growth of a poetical genius. To assert that Coleridge seems to be supportive of the Platonic position about the superiority of philosophy will be an unfair assessment of Coleridge. But one cannot underestimate the gigantic mind of Coleridge, "the greatest religious philosopher" whose major undertaking, according to Julius Hare, "was to spiritualize, not only our philosophy but our theology. . . ."[29] Whatever the repercussions of Coleridge's predominant interests in metaphysics, one can unhesitatingly and unreservedly share Herbert Read's affirmative judgment "that philosophy directed the course and determined the ends of Coleridge's criticism."[30]

It should not be difficult to see why Shelley receives the highest grade from Aurobindo:

> He is a seer of spiritual realities, much more radiantly near to them than Wordsworth, has, what Coleridge had not, a poetic grasp of metaphysical truths, can see the forms and hear the voices of higher elemental spirits and natural godheads than those seen and heard by Blake, while he has a knowledge too of some fields of the same middle realm, is the singer of a greater and deeper liberty and a purer and nobler revolt than Byron, has the constant feeling of a high spiritual and intellectual beauty. . . . He is at once seer, poet, thinker, prophet [and] artist. (*FP* 126)

Aurobindo rightly mentions *Prometheus Unbound* and *Epipsychidion* as "two of the three greatest works of Shelley," the third being *Adonais*. One must not have any difficulty in seeing in Aurobindo's penetrating judgment of Shelley's imagination the significance of the powerful symbols of Asia and Emily—and hence of some sort of affinity of the two poetic minds in their symbolic representations of the feminine principle. Aurobindo boldly questions Arnold's impulsive criticism of Shelley as he does Carlyle's "ill-tempered and dyspeptic" attack on Keats. Can Aurobindo's assessment of Shelley stand against T. S Eliot's pertinacious deprecation of the poet? It appears that amongst the three major categories of Shelley criticism—Shelley the idealist, Shelley the Humean skeptic and Shelley the "ineffectual angel"—there is the fourth category of critics like Rossetti, Yeats, Aurobindo, Cousins and Spender[31] who firmly believe in the spiritual and classical character of Shelley's poetic genius, especially in its ability to reach the highest limit of consciousness. Browning, it must be remembered, calls Shelley the "Sun-treader,"[32] a judgment that is distinctly different from that of Arnold. That Shelley "has to deny God in order to affirm the Divine"

(*FP* 128) is Aurobindo's most profound and perceptive judgment of Shelley's philosophic imagination.

V

Aurobindo appropriates the Vedic and Upanishadic term "mantra" for future poetry. "The theory and practice of *mantra,* Sri Aurobindo's vision of poetry and poetry of vision," remarks Sisirkumar Ghose, "are surely his most appropriate gift to the life of an evolving humanity."[33] The mantra, explains Aurobindo, "is a direct and most heightened, an intensest and most divinely burdened rhythmic word which embodies an intuitive and revelatory inspiration and ensouls the mind with the sight and the presence of the very self, the inmost reality of things and with its truth and with the divine soul-forms of it, the Godheads which are born from the living Truth . . . it is a supreme rhythmic language which seizes hold upon all that is finite and brings into each the light and voice of its own infinite" (*FP* 200). Earlier in *The Future Poetry* Aurobindo states that "the Mantra, poetic expression of the deepest spiritual reality, is only possible when three highest intensities of poetic speech meet and become indissolubly one, a highest intensity of rhythmic movement, a highest intensity of verbal form and thought-substance, of style, and a highest intensity of the soul's vision of truth" (*FP* 17). Evidently, Aurobindo as a theorist of literature has firmly and clearly laid down the criteria for future poetry: the deepest, the most intense "vision of truth" remains the only justifiable criterion of ascertaining the quality of poetry. Aurobindo has elaborately specified that "an intuitive revealing poetry of the kind which we have in view would voice a supreme harmony of five eternal powers, Truth, Beauty, Delight, Life and the Spirit" (*FP* 203–04). Properly understood, Aurobindo believes in the inestimable capacity of the mind to continue to evolve. Surely, in this matter Aurobindo participates in the Romantic discourse on perfectibility, consciousness and unity. Epistemologically, poetry as mantra is the expression of the highest state of consciousness and it expressly calls for a systematic discipline of the mind to achieve the unity, the fusion, the depth and the intensity that Aurobindo has repeatedly emphasized as essential characteristics of a heightened poetic consciousness. In Aurobindo's theory of the mind, as explained in *The Life Divine,* there are levels or forms of consciousness; the Higher mind, the Illumined mind, the Intuitive mind, the Overmind and the Supermind.[34] These are stages of an individual's development in the evolution of consciousness. While the Overmind "sees larger possibilities," the Supermind "sees the plurality and unity" as an essentially integrated structure of reality. Undoubtedly, Aurobindo's conception of mental growth far surpasses the possibilities allowed by the Kantian view of Pure Reason and Hegel's idea of universal consciousness.

It can be said that for Aurobindo the most important criterion for crowning a poet is his poetic vision of *ananda,* its depth and magnitude to see and create forms of beauty and truth and its illimitable capacity to unify and harmonize. Aurobindo classifies the most important poets in three rows: the first row includes Valmiki, Vyasa, Homer and Shakespeare, the second row Dante, Kalidasa, Aeschylus, Sophocles, Virgil and Milton and the third row Goethe.[35] Evidently, Aurobindo's rich and extensive background in European and Indian literatures gives him an enviable position as a critic: in one large sweep he has put together eleven great poets in order to seek validity of his criteria of a poet's greatness. Despite Voltaire's disparaging criticism of Shakespeare and despite Goethe's enormous popularity on the Continent, Aurobindo considers Shakespeare not only the greatest poet of the English language but also greater than Goethe. But Goethe as a representation of modern progress and as a poetic category stands alone. Interestingly, Aurobindo maintains that if the volume of learning, the sheer amount of erudition in plain and simple terms, were a criterion for determining the greatness of a poet, surely Browning will be a greater poet than Shakespeare. Aurobindo grants "divine afflatus," the Overmind inspiration of the highest order to Shakespeare and other front-benchers of the first category. But what is uniquely characteristic of Aurobindo's penetrating critical genius is the formulation of a theoretical model based on his conception of the levels of Overhead consciousness, that would assign Shakespeare a position along with the authors of *Mahabharata, Ramayana* and *The Odyssey.* It is the same criteria that relegate Milton to the second row and Goethe to the third. Is this type of criticism that assigns categories and ranks to works and poets reliable and objective, especially in the context of contemporary critical theory? Since the days of Plato's *Republic,* criticism has been attempting to understand the matter of Homer's peremptory expulsion from the utopian vision of the ideal state. In *Adonais,* Shelley ranks Milton as "the third among the sons of light," the other two epic poets being Homer and Dante.[36] But Virgil and Shakespeare are not even mentioned. In the *Inferno,* Dante includes himself as one of the six sons of light, with Homer being the leader of the band.[37] Lately, Eliot's devaluation of Shakespeare and Milton and his glorification of Dante and Dryden remain an inexplicable critical strategy.[38] Of course, Eliot has given the utmost recognition to Virgil and not to Dante. Frank Kermode rightly points out that Eliot's cosmopolitanism and globalism are limited only to his conception "of a single cultural tradition, and that a Latin tradition,"[39] the builder of which is Virgil. That is why it is Virgil, not Dante, and certainly not Shakespeare or Milton, who is the bridge between the old Roman Empire and the Papacy. Is it simply a matter of exhibiting an independent and "disinterested" spirit of intellectual inquiry or would it be a matter of exercising judgment and taste in accordance with a certain tradition? Arnold's unprecedented elevation of Burke for the latter's capacity to pursue the path of "profound, permanent, fruitful, philosophical truth"[40] is an amazing expression of Arnold's own criteria of critical objectivity and intellectual playfulness of the mind—and also of "the Indian virtue of detachment."[41] As compared to Arnold and Eliot, Aurobindo's criterion of judging a poet's greatness is the quality of his total poetic vision.

It is no doubt true that Aurobindo's criticism of Milton in *The Future Poetry* and elsewhere is one of the most illuminating appraisals of the poet,[42] but it is here that Aurobindo tries to grapple with the criteria of greatness of a work or a poet. Aurobindo declares laconically that Milton's greatness as a poet is directly attributable to the greatness of *Paradise Lost*. "*Paradise Lost*," states Aurobindo, "is one of the five great epical poems of European literature, and in certain qualities it reaches heights which no other of them had attained . . ." (*FP* 83). While noting the unique poetic greatness of the first four books of the poem, Aurobindo categorically declares that "if the rest [of the poem] had been equal to the opening, there would have been no greater poem, few as great in literature" (*FP* 84). This structural flaw, maintains Aurobindo, is occasioned by Milton's defective theology and the lack of "inner greatness in the poetic interpretation of his materials" (*FP* 85). "Milton's structures" are intellectually conceived and not poetically envisioned. "To justify the ways of God to man intellectually," remarks Aurobindo, "is not the province of poetry; what it can do, is to reveal them" (*FP* 84–85). Evidently, there are certain similarities between Aurobindo's critical assessment of Milton and that of Blake or Shelley.[43] Shelley states that *Paradise Lost* "contains within itself a philosophical refutation of that system, of which, by a strange and natural antithesis, it has been a chief popular support" and that "Milton's Devil as a moral being is far superior to his God. . . ."[44] In the poem *Milton* Blake has recreated his own Milton. Harold C. Goddard has succinctly phrased the critical question pertaining to Blake's understanding of Milton: "Why did Milton, without intending to, make Satan a sublime and magnificent figure, and God in comparison a pale and ineffectual one?" And in answer he refers to the following lines in *The Marriage of Heaven and Hell*: "The reason Milton wrote in fetters when he wrote of Angels and God, and at liberty when of Devils and Hell, is because he was a true poet and of the Devil's party without knowing it."[45] While Aurobindo's admiration for Milton's "grand style" never stopped, he, like most Romantic poets, believed that his theology remained unintegrated with his poetic imagination. It is extremely important to understand that Aurobindo spiritedly participates in the discourse on Milton, from Dryden to post-Freudians, and that he would still assign him a lofty place along side of Dante and Aeschylus, but below Shakespeare and certainly above Goethe. Significantly, Aurobindo's crowning of Milton is in sharp contrast to the devaluations of the poet by such modern critics as Eliot and Leavis.

Is criticism a psychological process of acknowledging or denying poetic influence or "poetic legacy" of Vyasa, Homer, Valmiki, Dante, Shakespeare and Milton? Is criticism an epistemological device of recognizing "the grandeur of the past" and of reconstructing an outline of the history of civilization? The matter of determining the influence of Milton on major poets like Blake, Wordsworth, Coleridge and Shelley, especially those who are both poets and critics—and here one must include Aurobindo—essentially involves the inextricable issue of historical and literary continuity, of intellectual recognition of what Walter Jackson Bate calls "the burden of the Past."[46] Harold Bloom's *The Anxiety of Influence,* a Nietzschean-Freudian document, theorizes the matter of poetic influence: the moral and aesthetic categories of poetic influence, according to Bloom, simply reverberate the story of the "battle between strong equals, father and son as mighty opposites, Laius and Oedipus at the crossroads. . . ."[47] Does the psychoanalytic and morality of theoretical structure of the Laius-Oedipus story give us a convincing pointer to the understanding of the nature of the influence of Homer, Shakespeare, Milton or Goethe? Do we see in the uncanny reenactment of the Oedipal drama a clear affirmation of the authority of the past or a dramatic recreation of the past in the present, such as the one attempted by Blake in *Milton,* which is more a radical subversion and displacement than a direct transmittal? Can poetic past be appropriated somewhat selectively and arbitrarily in order to create an enduring present and to ensure the probability of a better future? Or must it be rejected in its entirety in the larger interest of freedom, hope and progress? Is there a "constructive principle" of creating a unified verbal structure, which makes Shelley say that a "great poem" is "like the co-operating thoughts of one great mind," that "the poetry of Dante may be considered as the bridge thrown over the stream of time, which unites the modern and ancient World" and that poets are "the mirrors of the gigantic shadows which futurity casts upon the present. . . ."[48]

Although Aurobindo has persistently argued for "supreme harmony" of the five suns of poetry, one might ask which one of these could possibly be the most significant element? What is the nature of truth, beauty and pleasure poetry should communicate? The mimetic theory of literature has laid down the twofold criteria of truth and pleasure as the main objectives of art, although we should remember that in *The Republic* Plato has directly questioned the ability of art to represent the highest form of truth. The Romantic aesthetic that finally centers on the representation of the Idea or the Absolute as the highest form of consciousness had finally found its interpreter not in Hegel—and certainly not in Kant—but in Schelling.[49] The concluding lines of the chapter "The Sun of Poetic Truth" in *The Future Poetry* seem to be awfully close to the conception of unity and identity of consciousness suggested by Schelling:

> The Veda speaks in one of its symbolic hints of the fountain of eternal Truth round which stand the illumined powers of thought and life. There under the eyes of delight and the face of imperishable beauty of the Mother of creation and bride of the eternal Spirit they lead their immortal dance. The poet visits that marvelous source in his superconscient mind and brings to us some strain or some vision of her face and works. To find the way into that circle with the waking self is to be the seer-poet and discover the highest power of the inspired word, the Mantra. (*FP* 222)

The "inspired word" is the mantra uttered by the seer-poet whose prophetic vision has ascended to "the fountain of eternal truth." The presumed identity of language and consciousness is made possible only by the power of the poet's vision of truth, the source of which is "his own superconscient mind." That reality or universal consciousness as Idea, to use Hegel's phraseology, can be perceived and then effectively communicated by a spatial structure of language still remains an extremely controversial point in literary theory and in the history of language. Several critics, including Derrida, have attempted to deconstruct the logocentric structure of reality, its essentialism whereby words are assigned a certain fixity of meaning to denote conventional or received forms of truth.[50] The crucial issue concerning the identity of consciousness and language focuses on the unresolvability between the infinite and the finite: can that which is infinite be finitized? Apparently, a more intricate aspect of this unresolvability is rooted in the epistemology of truth or reality. Can Truth be known in its highest and the most universal sense of the term? The mystical intuition, the supramental consciousness, Aurobindo seems to argue, will be the tiebreaker in this philosophical debate: the mantra as an art form is the rhythmic expression of the unified vision of consciousness, truth and language.[51]

VI

Aurobindo maintains that "poetry and art are born mediators between the immaterial and the concrete, the spirit and life [and that] [t]his mediation between the truth of the spirit and the truth of life will be one of the chief functions of the poetry of the future" (*FP* 205). In this sense alone, art becomes a multiple medium of epistemology, exegesis and psycho-analysis. Regarding the role of beauty and *ananda*, Aurobindo immediately places art in the psychological center of the contemporary human condition: "It is the significance and spiritual function of art and poetry to liberate man into pure delight and to bring beauty into his life" (*FP* 206). What is the nature of poetic truth? One might further press the point: can the four voices, the truths of poetry, religion, philosophy and science, be combined into one unified voice of eternal truth, the truth of intuitive poetry? Can a poet's soul help him to see his own "undiscovered self" (Jung's phrase) and the spiritual truth? Can a modern poet reach the "high achievement" of those "ancient deep-thinking men who discovered the profound truth that all existence derives from and lives by the bliss of the eternal spirit, in the power of a universal delight, Ananda"? (*FP* 236) If one would examine these and several other similar issues in the context of Aurobindo's theory of the mind, the obvious answer is that a poet's imagination must reach the level of the Overmind consciousness, a condition that all the eleven poets in the three categories have met. The Overmind, which has higher levels of ascent within its own ambiance "thinks in a mass; its thought, feeling, vision is high or deep or wide . . ." (*BCL* 29.806). "It is more properly," as Aurobindo explains, "a cosmic consciousness." But there is still a higher plane of consciousness, the supramental as the Saccidanand consciousness, the state in which the poet sees infinite unity and harmony. Evidently, therefore, the broad argument about the nature and function of poetry leads us to Aurobindo's metaphysics of reality, truth and *ananda*. In the highest state of consciousness, the universal *ananda* functions as a creative principle, a directional force, unifying all forms of truth—philosophic truth, moral truth, aesthetic truth and scientific truth—into a vision of universal truth.

Aurobindo's metaphysics of *ananda* essentially centers on the revelatory discovery of truth and the aesthetic experience of beauty. Aurobindo is fully cognizant of the spiritual barrenness of the modern mind, its inability to grasp truth and to experience beauty and delight. He could have quite appropriately referred to Coleridge's "Dejection" Ode where the clogged mind of the poet can experience neither beauty nor joy.[52] At the highest level of consciousness, however, beauty and truth become synonymous as they do in Keats's "Ode on a Grecian Urn." Of course, this metaphysical view of absolute beauty or absolute truth is incompatible with the Kantian notion of the feelings of pleasure as an aesthetic experience of beauty. Note the following observations by Aurobindo:

The poet is then something more than a maker of beautiful word and phrase, a favoured child of the fancy and imagination, a careful fashioner of idea and utterance or an effective poetic thinker, moralist, dramatist or story-teller; he becomes a spokesman of the eternal spirit of beauty and delight and shares that higher creative and self-expressive rapture which is close to the original ecstasy that made existence, the divine Ananda. (*FP* 241)

This "original ecstasy," "the divine Ananda," is indeed eschatological in nature, for it is fundamentally rooted in the ascent of the soul to its divine home. The classical Indian term *rasa* used by Aurobindo means, among other things, aesthesis; the process of "the soul's essential aesthesis" is the process of sinking deep in "the spiritual emotion of the seeing of truth and the abiding spiritual experience." "The ancient Indian critics," states Aurobindo, "defined the essence of poetry as *rasa* and by that word they meant a concentrated taste, a spiritual essence of emotion, an essential aes-. thesis, the soul's pleasure in the pure and perfect sources of feeling" (*FP* 243). The universal *ananda,* "the parent of aesthesis," according to Aurobindo, "takes three major and original forms, beauty, love and delight . . ." (*BCL* 29.810).[53] The Overmind contains "firm foundation of the experience of a universal beauty, a universal love, a universal delight" (*BCL* 29.810). In his lucid discussion of the role and place of beauty, delight and truth, one finds that Aurobindo keeps returning to his theory of the mind and that the incontestable measure of a poet's vision is finally determined by the nature of the mental ascent, especially its experience of *ananda.* Thus various types of *ananda*—"spiritual *ananda,*" "greater *ananda,*" "absolute *ananda*"—define the magnitude, intensity and breadth of a poet's vision. "For the nearer we get to the absolute Ananda," declares Aurobindo affirmatively, "the greater becomes our joy in man and the universe and the receptive and creative spiritual emotion which needs for its voice the moved tones of poetic speech" (*FP* 248).

One laudatory element in Aurobindo's post-Romantic argument as a poet-philosopher and as a critic is his firm conviction in the ability of man to make progress. Thus his view of evolutionary progress frees him from a possible entrapment in the debate between progress and modernity. As a poet-critic, his exhortation to the modern mind is not to become blinded by tradition but to forge ahead on the path of progressive experimentalism. Yet one may find it somewhat paradoxical and even puzzling to note that Aurobindo himself happens to be one of the boldest and the most lucid expositors of the classical traditions, Indian and European. His perspicacity and lucidity enable him to present exegetical and hermeneutic models of synthesis between Western intellectual thought and classical Indian thought. As a poet-critic, his is the first major attempt not just to propose hypothetically the use of classical Indian aesthetic theory but to show its actual application. That the future English poetry will be intuitive and subjective, that it will come from the deepest inner self of a poet, that it will truly be a fusion of truth, beauty, love, life and spirit, that it will be directed by the highest aesthesis as the essential creative principle, and that it will sing the greatness of human spirit are indeed some of the new directions given to the regressive mood of the twenties. But what about the moods of the thirties, the forties and the fifties, especially the post–World War II period? The focus on the external world is important, but it is "spiritual subjectivity," not egotism, that will give a universal and cosmic meaning to the external world of history. The Overmind or the supramental vision will absorb external reality and history in the revelatory iconography of the poetic word. Poetry as a spiritual discipline, *tapsaya,* gives not only the most exalted consciousness with which to comprehend the metaphysics of truth, existence and reality but also the eternal paradigms of unity, identity and freedom. Thus in reading the following lines in Shelley's "Hymn of Apollo," "I am the eye with which the Universe / Beholds itself, and knows itself divine . . ." one may not find the model of unifying the two levels of consciousness, human and divine, to be logical and rational, but certainly Shelley's supramental or cosmic consciousness enables him to absorb the two levels into a single unified structure of reality.[54] Shelley would argue that the realization of unity and identity of consciousness is a function of the poetic imagination and not of the analytical faculty.

VII

It must be admitted that Aurobindo's critical and poetic theories and his philosophical writings are an attempt at the "widest globalization" of the English language. Whatever the historical and cultural ramifications of colonial and postcolonial developments in the world, the writing in English outside the British Isles bears the indelible mark of the history of the emergence of a consciousness, a new tradition in the world order, with which contemporary critical theory has thus far failed to deal convincingly. In his "Introductory Memoir" to Manmohan Ghose's *Songs of Love and Death,* Laurence Binyon refers to an observation by Oscar Wilde: "His [Manmohan Ghose's] verses show how quick and subtle are the intellectual sympathies of the Oriental mind, and suggest how close is the bond of union that may some day bind India to us by other methods than those of commerce and military strength!"[55] Oscar Wilde's general feelings pertaining to the "commerce and military strength" in the history of colonial governance have been shared by humanists like Conrad and Forster. It is generally true that the European mind, especially beginning with the Romantic movement, is known to have established a serious intellectual dialogue with India. And it is equally true that numerous other modern minds like Yeats, Eliot, Jung and Hesse have exhibited a unique urge for an intellectual discourse with Indian thought. Such an open and uninhibited discourse as envisaged by Oscar Wilde is the only inevitable course open to a world community of free, progressive and civilized minds. Aurobindo's vision of universal human progress includes a healthy confluence of the colonial past and postcolonial aspirations: genuine and authentic criticism as "a structure of knowledge" must focus on the moral and spiritual experiences of the human mind, excluding therefore from its ambiance any form or type of animadversion, paroxysmal negations and "critical dandyism."[56] Thus colonialism and postcolonialism should not be misconstrued merely as metaphors for "fighting" in the confrontational dialogue between history and national identity. The early Aurobindo had clearly understood the repugnant politics of imperialism and colonialism in the larger historical context of the "shifting of the centers of power," but despite his inexorable opposition to the unsavory ideologies of human subjugation and empire-building he had openly championed the role and place of the English language in India. The later Aurobindo, while fully anticipating a recrudescence of Indian classical thought, had taken a more philosophical view of colonialism, perhaps as a phase in the involution-evolution continuum and hence as an ineluctable basis for defining the aspirations of the postcolonial Indian mind. But Aurobindo's vision of the evolution of the English language and literature is essentially that of a pluralist and a comparativist, and this guiding principle must underscore any attempt to the examination of his critical theory.

That literature can serve as a powerful means of establishing an enduring intellectual bond amongst structures of civilizations, cultures, nations and groups of people toward the emergence of an enlightened world community is in itself the most enviable and ambitious ideal ascribed to any one single human endeavor. Literature may be considered to have special "complicity" with political developments and the ideologies of revolutionary change in one special sense, and that is the unique recognition given to the ability of literature to cultivate an illuminated consciousness in its reader.[57]

Aurobindo as a critic and theorist of literature has gone in several directions in order to define the nature of literary taste, especially the critical measure of determining the greatness of a poet and the legitimacy of discourse. There is no doubt that the complexity of his theory of literature can be understood only in the light of his philosophy of evolutionary progress, the theory of the mind, the conception of the Saccidanand consciousness and the directive principle of universal *ananda*. It hardly needs to be emphasized that Aurobindo's evolutionary philosophy includes a comprehensive vision of human progress. The poets are no doubt arbiters of truth, but they are also what Shelley calls "the unacknowledged legislators of the world."[58] The nature of truth or consciousness realized by a poet is personal, but certainly not private like a Wittgensteinian experience, for it must seek its validity in a universal and cosmic context. The profundity and magnitude of a poet's vision and hence of a work of art essentially lie in the principle of supreme harmony, universal *ananda*. Thus the highest level of spiritual subjectivity or the supramental state does not mean self-indulgent, egotistic privatization of experience. Even in the revolutionary Marxian context, Aurobindo may be legitimately characterized as a revisionist. Despite Marx's declaration that reality is material and not spiritual and that a culture's ideological structure is usually synonymous with "false consciousness," Chattopadhyaya maintains that Aurobindo's "thought-route to utopia is not apparently very different from that of Hegel and Marx."[59] Such a presumptuous assumption may be logically unconvincing in the first instance, but it retains its full validity in another context. As Chattopadhyaya explains:

> The historical rootedness or situatedness of ideologies and utopias can well be presented in a different way. By highlighting the self-exceeding character of man it has often been argued that yearning for better, larger and nobler forms of life is an integral part of the human nature itself. The establishment of Kingdom of God on the Earth or the realisation of the *Divine Life* or the supramentalization of man is claimed to be the fulfillment of a promise which we have in our inmost being. This is substantially a line of argument of the thinkers like Sri Aurobindo, Samuel Alexander and Chardin.[60]

Needless to say that Goethe's *Faust*, Blake's *Jerusalem*, Shelley's *Prometheus Unbound* and Aurobindo's *Savitri* are poetic models of a promise and a hope for the "supramentalization of man" and hence for the "establishment of the city of God upon earth." But the precondition to the realization of this vision is our clear understanding of the source of "the kingdom of heaven." Speaking about Blake's emphasis on the function of the creative imagination, Frye remarks: "It is not, or not only, the entire structure of knowledge as an order of words, as represented by the Bible. It is rather the expanded vision that he [Blake] calls apocalypse or Last Judgment: the vision of the end and goal of human civilization as the entire universe in the form that human desire wants to see it, as a heaven eternally separated from hell."[61] In such a conceptual paradigm, the expanded vision integrates the world of art, the world of social and moral anxiety, the world of religion and all other similar worlds into a utopian order of ideal human civilization. Thus we arrive at one very important conclusion: the meaning of a work of art cannot be circumscribed by a limited value judgment. By examining various structures of civilizations created by poets, criticism participates in the global debate for determining the legitimacy of intellectual discourse of human reconstruction. In this respect alone, criticism and creative imagination must be deemed both as inseparable and complimentary.[62]

Chapter 5 ⊠

Mulk Raj Anand: A Reappraisal

I

Mulk Raj Anand can be rightly characterized as a Renaissance man, a novelist, an essayist, a literary critic and a thinker. His status as a novelist has been widely debated since the appearance of his classic work *Untouchable*. Although it has been customary to consider Anand along with Raja Rao and R. K. Narayan, three stalwarts of Indo-Anglian fiction, the first Indian novelist to receive wide acclaim is Mulk Raj Anand. Whatever the strengths and weaknesses of *Untouchable*, E. M. Forster's striking valuation of the "prose-poem" and his decision to write a preface to the novel can hardly be discounted by any student of Anand. The critical reputation of *Coolie* has not been any less striking. In his review of *Coolie*, Ronald Dewsbury maintains that although the novel deals with the "evils of exploitation and graft," it "goes much further by showing the inhumanity of man to man, proletarian to proletarian, bourgeois to bourgeois."[1] According to Peter Burra, Munoo of *Coolie* "is a universal kind of figure . . . the passion not only of India but of mankind."[2] And, of course, so is Bakha of *Untouchable*.[3] These two books alone give Anand the well-deserved recognition and status of a novelist who is capable of portraying something very genuine and authentic about human nature and the Indian social scene. In the famous preface, Forster is quick and forthright to admit that Anand has been able to accomplish that which he himself could not do in his *A Passage to India*. Stephen Spender in his review of *Two Leaves and a Bud* candidly recognizes that Anand occupies "a leading position amongst contemporary, revolutionary novelists in England."[4]

Needless to say that Anand returned to India in 1945 as a successful novelist and a pioneer experimentalist, but the other Anand, the Anand of the post-1945 years, is also recognized for his significant achievements in various fields. It can hardly be denied that soon after his arrival in India and following the independence Anand found his interests and commitments in several fields other than fiction, and yet keeping his prolific mind constantly engaged in writing fiction. Anand has been busy with the unusually ambitious series *The Seven Ages of Man:* the first four volumes, *Seven Summers* (vol. 1), *Morning Face* (vol. 2), *Confession of a Lover* (vol. 3) and *The Bubble* (vol. 4) have already appeared, and Anand is currently busy with the remaining three volumes, *The World Too Large* (vol. 5), *A World Too Wide* (vol. 6) and *Last Scene* (vol. 7). *Morning Face,* vol. 2 of the series, it should be noted, has earned Anand the prestigious Sahitya Akademi Award. Since his initial work as an essayist, his editorship of *Marg* shows that Anand has become an impassioned interpreter of Indian thought and art.

A cursory perusal of *Apology for Heroism* shows that there is hardly any secret about Anand's social, political and philosophical thought. Anand like Eliot has come to literature from philosophy. Deeply rooted in the European intellectual tradition, his social and political thought is traceable to the eighteenth-century philosophy, especially the ideas of Locke, Rousseau, Hume and Kant, the Romantic movement, the British socialist tradition, modern political and economic ideologies and the overwhelming responses to the two world wars. Anand like other Indian intellectuals couldn't have been expected to endorse the British governance of India and the ideologies of colonialism and imperialism. Anand may be accused of sentimentalism, but his libertarianism, egalitarianism, anti-imperialism, anti-colonialism, cosmopolitanism and universalism have a much broader philosophical base. That Anand is a serious student of history, that he has extensive knowledge of European and Indian thought and that he has been able to strike a synthesis between various traditions should be quite evident. But the most important question in Anand's fiction, as one might argue, is his vision of life and humanity at large, the ability of his imagination to interfuse historicity, ideology and value into a structure of fictional narrative, that is representation of life.

II

In "Mulk Raj Anand and Autobiography" Marlene Fisher deals with *Apology for Heroism* and *Conversations in Bloomsbury,* the two seminal works in understanding Anand's mind, as narratives of the various selves of Anand.[5] *Apology* is admittedly a reflective essay, much in the tradition of Wordsworth's *Prelude* and Coleridge's *Biographia Literaria,* but *Conversations* is a fictional reconstruction of biography, history, ideology and aesthetic, perhaps modeled after the dialogical discourse of the *Mahabharata,* Plato's *Dialogues* and Landor's *Imaginary Dialogues. Conversations,* a loosely structured narrative, is an examination of the movements of the twenties and the thirties, the reminiscence and recreation of which entails self-valuation and self-examination in a framework of objectivity, fairness and truth, especially since Anand has been a witness to the emergence of the new face of India. But the two works together show the continuous emergence of a structure of consciousness in Anand, a psychological and mental process of the discovery of truth, and a gradual synthesis of the two traditions. It must be noted that Anand has continued this technique of constructing a biographical narrative in the series *The Seven Ages of Man.* In *Apology,* Anand states some of the major hypotheses underlying his self-examination:

> What was the aim I was to set [for] myself in my work? What was my relation to writers, in India and Britain, to my own Indian cultural heritage and to the heritage of Europe which I had come to acquire? Was I to be a pure artist or would I have to play some part in the political life of the day?[6]

Earlier, of course, people like Tagore, Aurobindo, Gandhi and Nehru, and several others had faced a similar problem of achieving intellectual synthesis. In his relentless search for truth Anand seems to be fighting mental wars with his various ego-selves or projections, and the answers to his preliminary hypotheses, achieved through a continuous process of acceptance and rejection, are only illusions of truth, to ascertain which one needs what Nietzsche calls "extra-moral" sense.[7] The first edition of *Apology* is dedicated to Olaf Stapledon whose works focus on the development of man and the "deepening of consciousness";[8] and Anand has continued his mental wars. The postscript to the third edition, entitled "There Is No Higher Thing Than Truth," concludes with the following passage from the *Mahabharata:*

> *Truth is always natural with the good. Truth is eternal duty. One should reverentially bow unto truth. Truth is the highest refuge. Truth is duty. Truth is penance. Truth is Yoga. Truth is the eternal Brahman. Truth is said to be sacrifice of a high order. Everything rests on TRUTH.*[9]

Anand exhorts that these words "may be daily remembered like a prayer, even if our realization of this basic value remains always relative. . . ." If the discovery of truth "at the deepest level" means the expansion of consciousness, can history, ideology and art communicate that experience? Psychologically, the process of discovering truth is a process of internalizing the quest; whatever the nature of meditation or contemplation, it implies simultaneously a subjective recognition of the ego-self and psychic growth.[10] In the discourse of the *Bhagavadgita,* the discovery of truth presupposes annihilation of ignorance and fear. When Anand says that "the creative life" is the discovery of truth that in return is a commitment and dedication to humanism, he comes awfully close to the famous enunciations of Wordsworth—and of Shelley—about the function of art. In the preface to the *Lyrical Ballads*, Wordsworth defines poetry as "the first and last of all knowledge."[11] The poet, maintains Wordsworth, "binds together by passion and knowledge the vast empire of human society, as it is spread over the whole earth, and over all time." The Shelleyan echo of the moral nature of the imagination as going out of one's nature is not dissimilar.[12] Anand, it must be understood, assumes congruence of art, truth and life, and in doing so demolishes all exclusionary boundaries of the narrative. *Apology, Conversations* and the four novels in the series *The Seven Ages of Man*, like most biographical writings, essentially raise the critical question of transformation of biography, history, culture and tradition into an objective and autonomous verbal structure.

Whereas the narrative as social history presupposes such transformation, any progress made by the hero in the recovery of his consciousness tantamounts to the denial or reversal of the course of history through a continuous process of confrontation with social reality. Any evolution of consciousness in Bakha, Munoo and Krishan Chander demands a corresponding evolution in the narrative structure and confrontation with the thick walls of history, culture and tradition. The use of biography and history not only raises the questions of the theoretical basis of creativity but also focuses on the theoretical basis of criticism—intentional criticism, psychoanalytical criticism and sociohistorical criticism.[13] Herbert Read, for example, refers to "ontogenetic criticism . . . criticism which traces the origins of the work of art in the psychology of the individual and in the economic structure of society."[14] For students of Anand, however, there is a long string of other related issues, especially those pertaining to the complicated relationship between history, ideology and discourse. Can a writer demolish history since its very course may have been believed to function as an antithesis to sociohistorical and moral foundations of discourse?[15] Does Anand's commitment to ideology redefine or override the course of history? The English Romantic poets, for example, cast off old mythology and tradition by a process of subversion and displacement and reconstructed a new poetic mythology of liberty and equality.[16] Does Anand's humanism provide a paradigmatic structure of narrative that insures a forward movement of human progress?

III

It is utterly erroneous to suggest that Anand is a Marxist or a communist who has lost his faith in the capacity of social organism to bring about change. Anand's sympathy for and commitment to the cause of the unfortunate poor, the disinherited and the victimized—the Bakhas and the Munoos—is rooted in the tradition of liberalism and the gradual development of the English socialist thought. The history of Anand's formative years in England, especially his active encounter with the thirties movement, is vital to the understanding of Anand's mind.[17] In his astute examination of the intellectual climate of the twenties and the thirties, following the 1914–18 War, Orwell refers to the anxiety and interest shown by thirties writers in various ideological alternatives and in the "prophetic side of Marxism" as new materials for poetry.[18] The American scene had simultaneously responded to the developments in Europe with fear, anxiety and concern: undoubtedly, the works of Pound, Eliot, Dos Passos, Hemingway and others are ideological responses to the phase of history that had threatened the extinction of progress.[19] The symbolism of *The Waste Land* is the symbolism of a culture that suffers from infertility, incapacity, morbidity and despair—especially the moral and psychological problems of discontinuity and fragmentation. In addition to the optimism held out by socialism and Marxism, the ideas of people like Russell, Whitehead, Haldane, Wells and Stapledon had provided a different direction for human progress. The humanitarianism and democratic idealism of the English Romantic writers were directed at the larger issues of justice, liberty and equality. The idealism in Robert Owen's palpable and lucid treatment of the misery and suffering of the working class and the poor and in William Cobett's radical advocacy of the rights of workers and peasants had gradually found its way into the works of Dickens, and was systematically developed in the philosophies of Fabianism and modern socialism. It is important not to forget Morris's disillusionment with the English industrial culture and the role played by the Chartist movement.

Dickens's *Hard Times* and Gaskell's *Mary Barton,* the two key examples of "realism" in the English novel, portray the inhuman plight of the working class and the convoluted moral fabric of the bourgeoisie. In his introduction to *Mary Barton,* Stephen Gill quotes the following lines from *Fraser's Magazine* of January 1848: "People on Turkey carpets, with their three meat meals a day, are wondering, forsooth, why working men turn Chartists and Communists."[20] Indeed, there is a magical and spontaneous congruence between the pathology of the reader and the pathology of the character. Dickens had admired *Mary Barton,* and his own characterization of Stephen Blackpool in *Hard Times* is overwhelmingly and unsurpassingly tragic, showing the degrading morality of the philistines. It should be noted that the young Aurobindo during his Cambridge days had leaned toward Marxism and that Nehru was deeply committed to the principles of Fabianism. From amongst the various political ideologies of revolution, change and progress, Indian intellectuals like Anand had been confronted by some of the most bewildering choices: does India need a violent revolution like the French Revolution and the Russian Revolution, or a non-violent revolution like that of Gandhi? Both *Apology* and *Conversations* show Anand's deep immersion in this intellectual debate, not as an outsider or an abstract theorist but as one who became an active participant in the historical and ideological processes of revolutionary change.

Significantly, however, the issue of India's freedom from Great Britain remained the foremost emotional and political issue, even as a prerequisite for any conceptual model of India's progress.[21] While *Apology, Conversations, Untouchable, Coolie, Two Leaves and a Bud, The Village, Across the Black Waters* and *The Big Heart* deal with colonialism as a significant historical and political phenomenon, the works of the post-independence era must be considered in the light of the postcolonial rediscovery and progress of India. In "Cultural Self-Comprehension of Nations," Anand talks about the "three waves of self-consciousness," namely rejection, revolution and as-similation or synthesis, in the emergence of modern Indian thought, art and literature.[22] While colonialism as an ideological and historical phe-nomenon explains the psychological crisis of identity in the Indian mind, it also accounts for the wide gap between the level of European progress and that of the subjugated. Ideologically, colonialism as a historically situ-ated phenomenon and as a form of political governance has been variously considered synonymous with imperialism, racism, mercantilism and subju-gation. Historically, what became possible for America as a British colony was not politically achievable for other colonies in the empire. Although Blake categorically declares that "Empire is no more,"[23] Coleridge consid-ers the validity and justifiability of colonization in moral and religious terms.[24] Ironically, however, the conception of colonization as a divine dic-tate and as white man's burden remains an intriguing puzzle to the mod-ern mind. Some of the modern readings of *The Tempest* have focused on the symbolic relationship between Prospero and Caliban: the Prospero-Caliban relationship is an expression of the master-slave relationship, one of subjugation and imperial authority. Conrad's discourse in *Heart of Dark-ness* must be considered in terms of the historicity and ideology of colo-nialism.[25] In Joyce's reading of *Robinson Crusoe*, Crusoe is the "true symbol of the British conquest . . . the true prototype of the British colonist," and Friday "the symbol of the subject races."[26] Even in *A Portrait of the Artist,* Dedalus reminds the English Dean that English is not his but their lan-guage.[27] Conrad's *Heart of Darkness,* E. M. Forster's *A Passage to India* and the writings of George Orwell and other liberals are an expression of a sort of collective moral guilt about the British colonial rule. Whereas Caliban, according to Coleridge, is "all earth" and lacks "the moral sense"[28] the problem, as Auden sees, is with Prospero's failure "to impose order on his world."[29] In *Conversations,* Anand during his conversation with Leonard Woolf and E. M. Forster makes an extended use of the Prospero-Caliban analogy: "Both Caliban and Gandhi, the rebels, have yet to grow, beyond king worship—to become genuine rebels. . . ."[30] The perception of Gandhi as Caliban is a bold and overwhelming metaphor—in fact, too bold to go unnoticed in terms of the overabundance of its meaning. While the indirect irony refers to the moral basis of Gandhi's pacifism and his struggle against the British colonial rule, one can hardly miss the reference to Anand's own philosophical position on the nature of Gandhi's policies. Many Indians like Aurobindo had expressed their sharp disagreement with Gandhi's policies of appeasement and mendacity. Anand further develops this compound irony in Forster's observation, "Caliban, sulking, despairing, and yet dependent." In this notable triumph, Anand makes Forster define the philosophy and psychology of the subaltern. In the crisis of identity, can a subaltern respond to an evolving consciousness of liberty and equality and the linguistic structure emerging from such an evolution?[31]

Beyond the obvious facts of history, of course, the relationship between Anand and Forster and the latter's attitude towards India, including an objective assessment of *A Passage to India,* still remain an important subject of serious and detailed study. But Forster was knowledgeable of the misdeeds of the empire and the conduct of the Anglo-Indian community in India. Mr. England in *Coolie* can be seen in Forster's terms, as "the Jingoistic public-school-and-business type of Englishman," but regrettably enough he and other liberals, as Furbank points out, "scarcely envisaged independence for India" and "did not think of the home-rule movement as a serious force."[32] Anand and other Indian intellectuals were unable to understand the reservations of the English and European liberals in insuring the same freedom and equality and the same rights to their colonial subject as they thought were well deserved by them. What would be the referentiality of such ethics as would justify the subjugation and subservience of the Calibans? The critical argument, as Spivak points out, may finally rest on the tenacity of two divergent viewpoints, the British self-representation and the Indian self-valuation.[33] In *East and West,* Parkinson's avid defense of British colonization of India as a means of advancing modernity and progress and his criticism of American naivete in promoting democratic idealism in the East is an example of British self-representation.[34] Contrary to this type of assertive logic are the characteristic representations of the empire that Thackeray had tried to reveal in his uncompromising zeal for truth: in satirizing the empire-building mentality and in defining mercantilism and evangelicalism as the pillars of the empire, Thackeray destroyed the Victorian reverence for the aristocracy and the bourgeoisie. That India was looted and that educational and economic developments and other general problems of social progress were ignored are only historical facts. In *The Discovery of India,* Nehru mentions two sides of the English mind with respect to the relationship between England and India, one that gave India Shakespeare and Milton, and the other that manifesting itself as commercial imperialism virtually looted India.[35] History bears witness to the phenomenal amount of wealth of the "nabobs" of the East India Company and the plantation-owners of the West Indies, that had successfully made its way into England, enabling the "nabobs" in creating the "English Hindoostan" and in buying their way into the House of Commons. It should be noted that both Cowper and Goldsmith complain about the unchecked flow of this tainted wealth from the colonies.[36]

While the colonial rule may well claim to have introduced rationalism, progress and elements of modernity in India, the despotic and barbaric character of imperialism can hardly be denied. It is indeed true that the encounter between tradition and modernity and the emphasis on modernity define the structure of mythos in most of Anand's fiction, but Anand is also frightfully aware of Rousseau's fear of the impact of industrial progress on human consciousness—and, hence, on Western civilization. According to Thomas, the narrative of *Heart of Darkness* "is one of the most effective expressions of the encounter between self and 'Other,' between the European and non-European. . . . Understanding of the non-Western, can occur, therefore, only when the West is conquered by the very people it feels it is conquering."[37] If Conrad's narrative aims at revealing the truth of "the European and non-European," can this truth become accessible without any reference to the ideological structure of the imperial center? It remains to be argued if the reversal of metaphors in the paradigmatic structure of self and "Other" will enable Europe to become a part of the African consciousness. The question in Kipling's case—and also in Forster's case—is more direct: will Kipling's self, the European self, seek to discover and assimilate India as "Other"? It is important to note that Orwell's judgment of Kipling, that he is "a jingo imperialist" and that he is "morally insensitive and aesthetically disgusting,"[38] is sharply in contrast to Eliot's judgment of Kipling. Forster's own attitude toward the "Other" is governed by sympathetic identity and by the assumption that people should discover each other in mutual relationships by responding to basic human emotions. In Anand's own case, however, the "Other" is Europe, especially the British intellectual tradition: in *Apology* and *Conversations,* both Anand and his persona have persistently sought to know the "Other." But for Bakha, Munoo and Lalu Singh the image of Europe or England as "Other" is one of exotic material progress, somewhat like the femme fatale. Undoubtedly, Bakha, Munoo and Lalu are the victim-subjects. And yet there is, as Figuiera points out, the exotic picture of Europe, the "Other" just as there is the exotic image of India in the European mind.[39] The exotic image of India in the minds of people like William Jones and the English Romantic writers and also in Hermann Hesse as the subject of European discourse is comparable to the one in Macaulay, Kipling and other comfortable dreamers of the interminable glory of imperialism.

Although the early Kurtz in Conrad's *Heart of Darkness* is a staunch advocate of progress, the Marlowe-Kurtz conception of progress undeniably falls within the ideological framework of commercial imperialism. In an extended analogue, one might argue that the two discourses on India represent the involuted aspects of imperialism, one in which India is perceived as the citadel of wisdom, the exotic symbol of the spiritual East, and the other in which India is the savage and backward place to be redeemed by various European ideologies of progress and by evangelicalism. The ideas of trusteeship and limited home rule for India and the emergence of Anglo-Indian bureaucracy as paradigms of political governance can only be considered in the context of imperialism, the context that defines and sanctions the titles "possession" and "colony." It must be recognized that the voluntary acceptance of progress as an expression of the will of people is distinctly different from its selective and expedient enforcement.

In a sense, the morality of the twentieth-century war theater is not drastically different from that of colonialism, since both phenomena are an expression of collective hubris, the regressive supremacy of a group of people achieved by power, greed and sensuality. That war translates the sociology and psychology of industrial progress and the political ambitions of powerful nations should probably answer Pound's question, at least in a certain limited sense: why do men fight wars? A Dos Passos may be able to maintain the inveterate sanctity of his convictions, that war is absurd and that it characterizes the defeat of art and civilization. And yet war, one might argue, is a bold expression of the advancement of civilization.[40] In his review of *Across the Black Waters,* Bonamy Dobrée remarks that Anand's book is the only war book with "the Indian troops in France" and that "it is not as a description of war that the book achieves its great interest . . . but as a revelation of what the average Sepoy felt and thought during that strange adventure."[41] It is precisely the process of awakening in Lalu Singh, Uncle Kirpu, Lachman Singh and Dhanoo a consciousness that makes them see the absurdity of war, violence and death, and its indiscriminate savagery and brutality far beyond the imaginable scope of human values. Anand, as Figuiera observes, "levels an indictment at the British High Command's incompetence and questions the morality of using Indian troops to fight a British war."[42] The matter of India's involvement in the two world wars touches one of the highly sensitive controversies in Indian history, and

Anand treats this issue skillfully and tenaciously, implying that the Indian participation should have been decided by India as a free nation. The turgid argument that these wars were crucial for securing universal peace and order in the world is only relevant to the political conviction of insuring the stability of the empire and India's place in it as a protected territory. Indeed, there should not be any moral ambiguity in the assertion that the creation of the Indian army was one of the boastful achievements of the empire.

IV

I believe that Anand's most monumental work is *Untouchable* in the same sense as Daniel Defoe's most important work is *Robinson Crusoe*. Both *Robinson Crusoe* and *Untouchable* are canonized discourses. Ian Watt speaks about the canonization of *Robinson Crusoe*: the mythic allegory of Crusoe carries multiple meaning—social, economic, political, moral and philosophical—to the point that the narrative has become the subject of provocative commentaries by important figures like Rousseau, Marx and Joyce. Crusoe, as Watt maintains, is a culture-hero, an embodiment of a synthetic structure of history and ideology.[43] But the parallel with *Untouchable*, it must be noted, extends only to the art of restructuring a new myth that integrates in its fabric, culture, history, value and ideology. Bakha, the "hero-anti-hero" (Anand's term) is a comprehensive symbol of the evil of untouchability that Gandhi calls the greatest blot on Hinduism. Born "unclean" and untouchable in the lowest caste, Bakha will remain permanently in this fixed social state, even though he helps the high-caste Hindus to "clean" themselves. Bakha is a helpless victim of social and religious determinism and of a system from which he cannot escape. Nor can he rebel against the combined forces of religion and society. Defoe, as Joyce remarks, was the first author to portray the "lowest dregs of the population—the foundling, the pickpocket, the go-between, the prostitute, the witch, the robber, the castaway. . . ."[44] The cruel irony is that whereas the "lowest dregs" in Defoe, Dostoevsky and Gorky can rebel against the social order and can entitle themselves to some form of escape and even redemption, Anand's Bakha is helplessly and mercilessly locked into the tyrannical system that derives its authority from the religious tradition of *varanashram* in Hinduism. The philosophy of work as public and private good has an important place in Plato's plan for the development of soul, and it carries important philosophical valuations in Christian ethics and in Marxism. But surprisingly there cannot be any valuation of Bakha's work in either the Rousseauistic or Marxist terms. The Marxist theory of value is as dysfunctional as the Rousseauistic philosophy of the idealization of work. While the only way to understand the value of Bakha's work, if there is any significance at all, is to see Bakha's destiny in the context of the theories of casteism and karma, there is no possible plan for Bakha's liberation, unless of course, he, after Rousseau's ideal plan, is placed outside the social order. But despite the best possible expositions of the philosophy of karma one would find it rationally indefensible to believe that Bakha's ignominious existence and his pain and suffering should be the result of the ignobleness of his caste, the *dalit,* the *Harijan,* into which Bakha is born. Significantly, Anand has tried to show that none of the Western theoretical models, including the Hegelian and the Marxian models, is appropriate to theorizing the tragedy of Bakha's deterministic existence and the stubborn order that is responsible for the creation of the Bakhas of society.

Although Bakha has been led to believe that his business of cleaning human excrement is a form of retribution, he must discover on his own the poignant truth of his permanent subjugation and degradation, the very referentiality of the power and the system that would legitimize such suffering. Anand's ironic vision of man's inhumanity to man and of evil, as Forster seems to understand in his preface, is far more comprehensive. Bakha has three possible alternatives: the Gandhian path of pacifism, the teachings of Christianity, and the notions of modern technological progress. In seeing the futility of all three, Bakha leaves the reader in the midst of an intricate intellectual debate about the eradication of the evil of untouchability. One might wonder if even after the possible restructuring of the social organism there will be a permanent end to the exploitation and victimization of those who are less fortunate. Forster understands that while the three possible alternatives confronted by Bakha synthesize history, tradition and ideology as a basis for the structure of discourse and for the evolution of Bakha's consciousness, Bakha is after all a hero-anti-hero and not a rebel, nor is he a nihilist. Ironically, even the ideas of Gandhi, most of which were undeniably concerned with the liberation of untouchables, are irrelevant to the fate of Bakha. Untouchability, as Anand tries to stretch the metaphor, is a universal global problem: in a sense, we all are untouchables and coolies. Not only are untouchables like Bakha denied social discourse by all rungs of society, but also they are willfully and intentionally created as a permanent category in fulfillment of the self-indulgent egotism of the aristocracy and the bourgeoisie.

In a lecture delivered in 1972, Anand dwells on the function of history and ideology in the structure of discourse and the role of Indian intellectuals like himself and Raja Rao in justifiably embracing a "political cause" as had been done by Tolstoy and Stendhal.[45] Indeed, it is only logical to assume congruity of discourse and history and ideology. But now that the immediate ramifications of colonialism and imperialism are nonexistent, the decolonized imagination of Indian intellectuals must have appropriated to it a new cause or causes of social and moral progress. In calling attention to the difference, if there is one, between works written during the pre-independence era and those written during the post-independence period, I am urging consideration of such criteria as will lend universality and permanence to a work of art. Shelley's treatment of the myth of Prometheus in his *Prometheus Unbound* shows that while art responds to an immediate context, a historical and social context, it also has a broader and larger context. Anand's reference to Nehru's valuation of history and the broader context provided by the French Revolution, the Russian Revolution, the Gandhian Revolution—and let us include the Promethean Revolution and Aurobindo's theory of evolutionary consciousness—call for a universal vision of humanity, one of unremitting change and progress, and of evolution of human consciousness. One can hardly ignore the fact that the works of Dante, Milton and Coleridge provide a large body of social and political causes. In many respects, the Gandhian model of revolution is much closer to Shelley's vision of progress of mankind in *Prometheus Unbound:* mankind, if it wills, can fight against moral evil.[46] Anand views subjugation, colonialism, imperialism, including intellectual and cultural colonialism, as moral evil. While *Untouchable, Coolie* and *Two Leaves and a Bud* are commentaries on sociohistorical structure of Indian society, they are essentially studies in the sociology, psychology and metaphysics of moral evil. Rousseau and later Marx attributed evil to the social process that, as history reminds us somewhat laughingly, will always have its Bakhas and Munoos. Indeed, it is this quality of creating universal types in Bakha, Munoo, Gangu, Lalu and Ananta by a process of transformation of history, value and ideology, that puts Anand on a different pedestal among Indian writers and in the company of those great souls who have sung about evil and human suffering.

V

In all fairness to Anand, one must refer to the controversy pertaining to his post-independence achievement as a novelist. Naik, for example, asks: "Why was Anand's art unable to develop new dimensions after Independence?" But at the same time Naik has graciously compared him to an "august and many-branched" banyan tree,[47] admiring his humanistic vision and compassion. Cowasjee, a sympathetic critic of Anand, refers to Haydn Moore Williams's observation somewhat condescendingly "that with the disappearance of the British 'enemy' Anand appears to have been left without a subject."[48] Cowasjee argues that Anand, a Marxist, instead of fighting against the political bourgeois government accepted the patronage of Congress and the Congress government, thus making a dramatic shift from a well established "political novelist" to a critic of culture. Undoubtedly, this controversy is premised by a critical expectation that Anand, following his return to India, should have shown significant progress in his vision and work. Underlying this type of critical formulation is of course the presumptive fallacy of a linear and autonomous growth of an artist's consciousness. In examining the nature of ideological and aesthetic development of Anand's work as a novelist, it is important to remember that Anand had returned to India from a highly complex intellectual atmosphere of Europe that was befuddled on the one hand by an aesthetic debate on modernism, anticipating an onslaught of antimodernism and postmodernism, and by the moral and philosophical unresolvabilities, resulting from the barbarity of the two world wars, on the other. While the metropolises were actively engaged in revamping ideological strategies for redeeming a fractured civilization of the European nation-state, the impending fate of the rural constituencies—and of colonialism and imperialism—was also being rewritten, mainly by the historical process. It was important for Anand to relate his intellectual sagaciousness to the state of things in India and later to the concurrent events of 1947— the dawn of independence and the partition of the country.

Significantly, Anand never made any departure from his uncompromising war against colonialism, imperialism and other similar sociopolitical structures of human oppression and subjugation. Anand's concerns have persistently remained focused on the ideals of humanism and on the universal values of freedom, equality, justice and truth. In an interview, Anand talks about the literary virtues of love and compassion, categorically declaring:

> The search for freedom by each individual is the only way by which the struggle to live a possible existence of calmness may fructify. Compassion for the suffering may heal pain somewhat, and love for others may save the individual from self-torment. The struggle for higher consciousness is the only possible way for the good life.[49]

This is the more mature Anand, the philosopher and historian of culture, whose fundamental value structure seems to have moved closer to Indian spiritual thought. Anand has repeatedly expressed his strong belief in the universal ideals of *karuna* and bhakti: indeed, one would naturally wonder about the psychology and metaphysics of these and other such values as advocated by Anand, especially the possible sources of their development in man. In her illuminating discussion of Anand's humanism, Margaret Berry focuses on Anand's ability to synthesize the religio-philosophical position as it emerges from the Samkhya, and Western ideologies, including Marxist and Christian socialism.[50] As a student of European intellectual thought, Anand is certainly familiar with other forms of humanism—the Greek ideal of humanism, the eighteenth-century notions of humanism, Arnold's humanism, Marx's humanism and Forster's humanism. Anand's liberal humanism emphasizes both individual freedom and a progressive reconstruction of a new social order. In enunciating the fundamental premises of "comprehensive humanism," Anand "places man in the centre of all things," emphasizing his total organic growth as "a whole man."[51] This evolutionary growth of man, following perhaps Hegel, must result in the expansion of human consciousness.

The case of Anand's return to India, unlike that of an Auden coming back to England, is one of the most complicated psychological cases of an exile, an expatriate, who has confronted numerous bumpy rides in his life: initial displacement from India and alienation, problems of economic insecurity and social dysfunctionality or maladjustment in England and then the process of readaptation or resettlement. Indeed, this odyssey is certainly not uneventful and fruitless, for it gave him a heroic frame of mind and the firsthand experience of being a social outcast. And yet the self-banishment and the resultant social alienation that Anand suffered as a castoff may be deemed to have its own psychological validity, especially in terms of the objectives of self-fulfillment or self-actualization. It can be argued that Anand by removing himself from the immediate environments to the empire's metropolis provided himself with a unique opportunity to examine objectively not only the ideologies of colonialism and imperialism in the context of the universal ideals of liberty, equality, justice and truth but also the fundamental basis of India as a nation-state. But Anand's exile is not the same as the self-banishment of modern literary exiles like Henry James, T. S. Eliot, Ezra Pound and James Joyce, nor is it comparable to the exiles of Percy Bysshe Shelley and Lord Byron. While Henry James, "the archetypal exile in American literature," escaped the American cultural environment in order to nurture his cosmopolitanism, James Joyce, according to Leon Edel, escaped "the immediate world" to avoid "mediocratisation."[52] Anand's situation is not distinctly different, at least in certain respects, from that of a contemporary intellectual of the Indian diaspora. However, the greatest benefit that Anand reaped, especially following his decision to become a writer, was his participation in the common language and in the fraternal order of artists and intellectuals. Anand seems to have nourished two antithetical images of England: the England as the biggest colonial empire of which he was merely a colonized subject, a Caliban; and the England as the exotic other that had given him, among other things, the gratuitous but unfulfilled love of Irene Rhys, the marriage to Kathleen van

Gelder, the birth of a daughter and a prolonged intellectual engagement with some of the noblest minds. Anand's divisive relationship with England is redolent of the thrust of history that became instrumental in nurturing in him a profound moral and intellectual consciousness. Thus Anand's self combines the unextinguished fire of a radical idealist and the humanness of an ordinary human being: it is this fragmented and alienated Anand who has now returned to his native space for a search of his undiscovered self and identity. One would perhaps be justified in characterizing him as a Joycean "spiritual exile."[53]

But Anand's volcanic radicalism, somewhat of the nature of Blake's Orc, never died, nor was it ever compromised, despite of course the sardonic reality of stubborn tradition and colonial bureaucracy. Blake and Shelley both dramatize the philosophical and poetic principles of the functioning of revolutionary energy in their respective paradigms: the Orc cycle in Blake and the Prometheus-Jupiter struggle in Shelley. In Shelley's model, once Jupiter is dethroned, the task before Prometheus is to redeem the structure of human civilization. Since the end of the colonial era was reasonably predicted as a matter of political certainty, the progressive restructuring of tradition, of a newly emerging social order, meant a transformation of revolutionary energy into the voice of higher consciousness—Promethean consciousness. Anand clearly understood that it is through continuous and persistent struggles that one reaches a higher stage of consciousness; Hegel's theory of consciousness, Bergson's notion of the élan vital, the creative evolution of vital energy, and later Aurobindo's view of evolutionary progress are paradigmatic expressions of human progress. "We accept this civilization," maintains Anand, "but with the will to change it so that the qualities may arise above quantities and men may evolve higher consciousness." But it "is the creative imagination," argues Anand with Shelleyan vocabulary and emphasis, "which itself is the instrument of creative evolution, of the possible perfection of man."[54]

Private Life of an Indian Prince, according to Cowasjee, is "Anand's most impressive work."[55] But it is Anand's most innovative *The Seven Ages of Man* series that have lent Anand's vision and art a unique dimension and authenticity. In *Seven Summers, Morning Face, Confession of a Lover* and *The Bubble*, Anand has exhibited a keen sense of history, truth and reality. Whereas *Seven Summers* and *Morning Face* deal with the first phase of Krishan Chander's life and the struggle for Indian independence, *The Bubble* deals with his stay in England. Undoubtedly, the matter of Anand's exile in England is as significant as is the matter of his earlier growth in India. In fact, an authentic and definitive biography can immensely aid not only in the critical examination of such biographical works as *Conversations in Bloomsbury, Morning Face* and *The Bubble* but also in understanding the

whole man, Anand the artist and the man. Anand himself mentions that his
decision to explore his relationship with his family, especially his father,
was influenced by Butler and Shaw.[56] Anand's suggestion, if pursued
earnestly, would lead us into the heart of Victorian intellectual debate on
family life. The assumption that the Butlerian hypotheses in *The Way of All
Flesh*—the Lamarckian-Darwinian conception of evolution, the role of
heredity and environment and the Freudian-Butlerian controversy concerning unconscious memory—should help us to understand *Morning
Face;* its hero Krishan Chander certainly calls for a broader and more comprehensive critical approach that would combine, among other things, intellectual history, psychobiography and psychoanalysis. The most
significant issue in this debate is of course the role of family life, especially
of unconscious memory, in the process of individuation, in the making of
a creative individual and in ensuring wholesomeness. *Morning Face* got
Anand the Sahitya Akademi Award, but it is *The Bubble* that, with its "loose
narrative" of different genres and narratological techniques, is, as Riemenschneider maintains, "perhaps, the most ambitious book Anand has written so far because it tells us so much about the author himself."[57]
Considering some of the fundamental assumptions of intertextuality and
sociohistoricism, one would readily accept the presumptive hypothesis that
biography, history and other recorded materials are an integral part of the
primary text. While the Butlerian-Freudian focus reveals the psychic structure of the fragmented self, the psychology and sociology of exile help in
the critical examination of the problems of alienation and of the latent discontinuities and gaps in Anand's works of the post-independence era.

Indeed, the creation of Krishan Chander, whom Fisher calls "a
metaphor for the stages in the lives of human beings,"[58] is Anand's greatest triumph. One of the most intricate artistic problems in the creation of
psychobiographical narrative and the character of Krishan Chander is undoubtedly Anand's ability to fictionalize the history of the colonial period:
can a decolonized mind perceive objectively the neuroses of the colonized
mind and the barbaric hubris and narcissism of imperialism? Has Anand
given an independent and objective identity to Krishan Chander? In the
Freudian sense, Krishan Chander has a special affinity with Butler's Ernest
Pontifex, Joyce's Stephen Dedalus and Lawrence's Paul Morel, for they all
are ego-projections of their creators. In the case of Paul Morel, the identification between biography and fiction is more direct: Lawrence is said to
have reverted somewhat liberally into the innermost world of his own
neurosis,[59] but Joyce seems to have exercised more control and objectivity
in the creation of Stephen. Presumably, art or the creative process provides
the artist with a medium for the identification and hence for the dissolution of the ego-projections. The past, history or memory—they all enable

the artist to connect with the unconscious. Anand himself recognizes the therapeutic function of art: "My main impulse was to rely on my imagination as the only way to integrate myself as a human being in the midst of great unhappiness, confusion . . . Perhaps, by the use of the creative imagination, the author tries to perfect his own personality."[60]

Thus it can be safely assumed that Dickens's Pip, Joyce's Stephen Dedalus, Lawrence's Paul Morel and Anand's Krishan Chander cannot be understood without an authentic knowledge of their creators and precursors. This is essentially a problem of defining parameters of contextuality and intertexuality and of criticism as a structure of knowledge. In Anand's case especially, all the four volumes in *The Seven Ages* series are exclusively focused on Krishan Chander. In fact, the dedication to *Morning Face*, addressed to Krishan Chander, is Anand's definitive statement on the nature and function of his fictional hero. "The struggle of rebels like you [Krishan]," reiterates Anand somewhat emphatically, "cannot be in vain."[61] One might ask in all seriousness: Is Krishan Chander the prototype of a Byronic hero, a Promethean rebel, or a Gandhian pacifist? But he is most certainly not, as Anand reminds us in the dedication, the prototype of the mythical Krishna, nor is he "an abstraction from the Upanishads, Puranas, or the Logicus Tractus of Wittgenstein." Undoubtedly, there is a kind of Dickensian sentimentality in Anand's characters, especially Krishan Chander, and in the plethora of sociohistorical details. The intimate, tenacious and deeply personal knowledge that Anand has artistically brought to bear upon his fictional materials, particularly his characters, lends verisimilitude and plausibility to sociohistorical reality. One must also note Anand's ability to transmute the most commonplace and ordinary details and situations of life into significant fictional structures, an ability that Jessie Chambers admires in D. H. Lawrence.[62] But what is quite significant is the genuine directness, depth and simplicity with which Anand represents the most naked form of commonality. E. M. Forster fondly admires Anand's power of observation, of going where probably he himself was unable to reach in *A Passage to India*.[63] One cannot help remarking that Anand in envisioning *The Seven Ages* series has after all created *Mulk Raj Anand*, a diffused and continuous narrative, a story of dauntless search for truth.

It must be remembered that Anand did not subscribe to the "Art for Art's Sake" creed, nor did Anand abandon his commitment to the cause of sociohistorical structure of reality. The case of Gauri in *The Old Woman and the Cow*, the novel that later appeared under the title *Gauri*, contains one of the boldest expositions of the status of the emerging woman in modern Indian history. By deconstructing the tradition of the Sita myth, Anand directly jumps into the contemporary sociohistorical and feminist discourse on the identity of woman. The demystification and the subversion of the Sita myth clearly brings out the difference between R. K. Narayan and Mulk Raj Anand: while R. K. Narayan is deeply interested in the continuity of the classical and mythical tradition, Anand remains a champion of progress, persistently fighting for modernity, for the reconstruction of myth, history and tradition. But Anand is not antitradition; Anand's notion of humanism and of post-postmodernism gives him a unique position as a reconstructionist of civilization. Ironically, however, Anand, an ardent advocate of progress, does not always think that machine or industrial culture is necessarily the alternative to dogmatic tradition.

Gauri is an existential character whose value system is being continually defined by her own existence. But Anand does not portray her as an abstraction, a hypothetical personification or allegorization of a philosophical or sociological concept. In his preface to *Untouchable*, Forster makes a special note of Anand's art of characterization: "He [Anand] has just the right mixture of insight and detachment, and the fact that he has come to fiction through philosophy has given him depth. It might have given him vagueness—that curse of the generalising mind—but his hero is no suffering abstraction."[64] This observation about Bakha is also very much true of Gauri; she is a "real individual" who has been perpetually victimized because of her gender. But Gauri, as Kher explains, "refuses to accept the hypocritical values of her society and its double standards of sexual morality."[65] In a certain special sense, Gauri is very much like Hardy's Tess, an innocent and helpless victim: in either case, the stubborn structure of society, with its dogmatic glorification of obsolescent tradition, allows no room for the emerging woman and her sexuality. One must also not forget the struggles of Emily Bronte's Catherine Earnshaw, Charlotte Bronte's Jane Eyre and George Eliot's Hetty Sorrel. In terms of the precipitous politics of sexuality, the male power brokers of society define and govern Gauri's identity and sexuality, for they are immensely afraid of her freedom.

Gauri is not guilty of illicit or lecherous passion, but one certainly notes a persistent pattern of a threatened desexualization and otherization of Gauri, her femaleness, by the phallagocentric value structure whereby a patriarchal order appropriates for itself language and meaning centered on the phallus, the male pleasure principle in the *ars erotica* tradition of ancient cultures.[66] While Panchi and his family are overly concerned with Gauri's chastity and fidelity, another segment of society takes her as nothing more than a soulless female body, an instrument of sexual pleasure. Apparently, this pleasure or *jouissance*[67] is the sole privilege of male desire, and woman, having been denied any consciousness or identity of her own, becomes the otherized figure, one who is merely sexually useful and available. Ironically, the contemporary debate on the ethics of *jouissance* has remained heavily tilted toward the center, and the very basis of liberty of a Gauri is conditionally defined by this center. That Gauri can be otherized, victimized and sold is only allegorical of the values and practices of a phallocratic structure of culture where woman and sex are bartered as commodities. In fact, the language used for Gauri and the underlying intent and meaning are characteristic of pornoglossia, showing that woman is nothing more than man's sexual servant. Traditionally, institutionalized forms of human sexuality, even those evoked by *scientia sexualis*, are directed by repression and the fierce sternness of rectitudinous morality. This collusive union of power, sexuality and pleasure makes one wonder if sexuality will ever be placed in a humanist context. One must sympathize with Gauri's mutinous recusancy, wondering at the same time if her decolonized mind has made an intelligent choice between vulgarity and freedom. To the overbearing ethical question of fidelity Gauri's response is rather categorical: "I am not Sita that the earth will open up and swallow me."[68] It is indeed ironic that Gauri remains unrelated to any of the significant figures of classical Indian mythology—Sita, Draupadi, Savitri or a Shakti. And yet, paradoxically, one senses the indirection of metaphorical representation of an aspect of Kali in Gauri's determination to cast off the veil of tradition. Can a contemporary Gauri redefine parameters of sexuality and hence of individuality, freedom, consciousness and truth? "The road she has chosen, if followed with diligence," remarks Kher, "leads to self-determination, self-esteem, and self-fulfillment or self-actualization."[69] Does Gauri's existential struggle as a rebel place her in the non–Indian tradition and does Anand create in Gauri a dissociative entity, a permanently estranged figure whose intransigence will be looked upon by society as an incendiary threat to the center?[70]

VI

That Anand is one of the most versatile geniuses in the contemporary history of Indian art and literature cannot be doubted. His work as a critic of the arts, especially Indian sculpture and painting, has not drawn the attention it deserves. Anand had already published *The Hindu View of Art, Persian Painting* and *Kama Kala,* and was, as Marlene Fisher points out, under the influence of such eminent authorities as Ananda Coomaraswamy, Eric Gill and Herbert Read.[71] His work as the founding editor of the art journal *Marg* and as chairman of the Lalit Kala Akademi must have been guided by a carefully defined philosophy of art. In the early work *The Hindu View of Art,* Anand focuses on the visual arts, realizing fully "that Indian art is fundamentally religious and philosophical, rendered by craftsmen into a language of form, [and] that classical Indian art, in its many forms, flourished precisely because of its wholeness, because of its integration into and reflection of the culture which produced it."[72] This type of aesthetic formulation, as Fisher notes, is characteristic of young Anand's sensibility, but the Anand of the time period of *Marg* is much different. There is little doubt that Anand in his aesthetic formulation went directly and unreservedly to his own ancestors' occupation as *thathiars*—coppersmiths and silversmiths—and to other craftsmen who had both the natural skill and the purity of passion. In fact, Anand relied on folk art not only for its uncorrupted innocence but also for its being a representative expression of creativity and dynamism of collectivity. Anand has tried to place art and architecture in the humanist context, very much like Morris or Ruskin to an extent. In his revolutionary zeal, Morris envisions a machineless age, one of universal hope and peace.[73] Morris, as Northrop Frye notes, had believed that art belonged to the common man, the masses, in the sense that work as opposed to the enforced mechanization of life was a "creative act"; this revolutionary conception of work and art is intended to create a healthy social context that will in return "help to break down the drudgery and exploitation of factory and machine production and transform society into a community of brains and hands."[74]

Anand as an artist and critic reaffirms the social and moral function of art; the artist, recognizing the sinister mechanizing of humanity at large by Urizen's "dark Satanic mills,"[75] is fully charged with the responsibility of preventing social and moral decay by awakening social consciousness. Over the years Anand has come to recognize the centrality of the creative imagination as an instrument of change in the individual and the collectivity— its power to liberate people of their fears and neuroses and its timely and fearless release like the creative power of Brahma that liberates humanity. During all these years, Anand's search for a philosophy of art has enabled him to arrive at a closer synthesis between the Indian aesthetic of *rasa, bhava* and *ananda,* the neo-Kantian notion of beauty and truth and Marxist aesthetic.[76] In his study of Indian art and architecture, Anand is now known to be an interpreter of the central icons and major attitudes in Indian art, especially in the temple art of Khajuraho, Konark, Puri and Bhuvaneshwar. In "Some Notes on the Philosophical Basis of Hindu Erotic Sculpture," Anand notes the triumph of Macaulay's policies in keeping the minds of Indians impoverished. "To be sure, the mental imperialism of the West," remarks Anand, "seems to have succeeded in corrupting and perverting the outlook of the conquered. . . ."[77] It is significant to note that Anand has supported his exposition of some of the key issues by extensive references to Indian religious works, but this piece must be read in conjunction with the more generic essay in three parts in *The Hindu View of Art.* Part I, "The Religio-Philosophical Hypothesis" and part II, "The Aesthetic Hypothesis" fall in line with the main argument of Coomaraswamy's essay "The Philosophy of Ancient Asiatic Art."[78] Of significant interest for

a student of philosophy or of art, literature and aesthetic are lucid expositions of the major symbolic constructs in Indian metaphysics: *Brahman,*
Atman, Maya or *Prakriti, rasa, bhava, ananda* and the three *gunas.* As Anand
remarks: "Our consciousness [as Indians] was nourished on symbols, myths
and legends for generations, enabling us to recognize which images were
to be worshipped for well-being or alliance of the body-soul with god-
hood. . . . Such images lift us beyond ritualistic worship to the realm of
Ananda, the highest aesthetic value."[79]

Whether one considers the issue from a Freudian or Jungian perspective, this consciousness is actually the constitutive part of the unconscious
that manifests itself in archetypal images and symbols.[80] By responding to
various symbols, the mind of the *rasika* connects itself with its own source
of creation for a possible regeneration, expansion and translucence. The
central objective of art experience for the *rasika,* the participant or the
reader is, as Anand defines, *"darshana,* total imaginative experience."[81] It
should not be difficult to see why Anand, both as a writer and critic, has believed in the form of reality identified with *Prakriti* or Maya or "universal
matter" which is also identifiable with materialism. In Indian metaphysics,
Prakriti is at once the principle and the source of all life, of the created finite form. But this conception of *Prakriti* as the created material universe
can only be envisioned in the total context of the *purusha-prakriti* construct
that Anand seems to have taken from Samkhya Darshana. Anand transliterates this *purusha-prakriti* construct as "psychophysical interactionism,"[82]
clearly implying that for a unity of self and for evolutionary growth of consciousness mind and body are not exclusionary and dichotomous entities.

While Anand has been an advocate of progress and modernism, he has
been categorically opposed to any blind imitation of the West and to a
possible revivalism. Admittedly, Indian modernism in the arts is different
from various forms of European modernism.[83] But what about postmodernism and post-postmodernism—and postcoloniality and post-postcolo-
niality? Since tradition cannot be revived blindly, modern Indian art must
be a healthy synthesis of tradition and modernity. The blind adherence to
tradition is in sharp contrast to the philosophy of universalism to which
Anand remains deeply committed. At the same time, Anand has persistently advocated the principles of naturalness, spontaneity and "indigenousness" in defining originality, authenticity and individuality.
Coomaraswamy seems to argue emphatically that authenticity and individuality have their relevance only in the total context of a structure of
civilization.[84] Undoubtedly, Anand would add that an artist, in addition to
his indebtedness to tradition and modernity, must also show the deepest
awareness of the contemporary human condition and the reality of the
circumambient universe.[85]

Chapter 6 ⟨⟩

Ideological Confrontation and Synthesis in Mulk Raj Anand's *Conversations in Bloomsbury*

I

Mulk Raj Anand (1905–) is an eminent Indian novelist, essayist, critic and thinker. *Conversations in Bloomsbury*, a work of Anand's mature years, is an important contribution to the understanding of the English literary history of the Bloomsbury period and of Anand's own formative years in England. Anand returned to India in 1945 after 25 years of stay in England. As the author of *Untouchable, Coolie*, the Lalu Trilogy and other works, Anand's reputation as a successful novelist had been well established: *Untouchable* carries a preface by E. M. Forster; *Letters on India*, written on the model of Gandhi's *Hind Swaraj*, carries a foreword by Leonard Woolf, and his other works had drawn warm reviews from critics like Bonamy Dobrée, Stephen Spender and George Orwell. While in London, Anand had completed his Ph.D. at the University of London under the supervision of the famous Kantian scholar Professor Dawes Hicks and had come into contact with several prominent literary figures, writers and critics of the twenties and the thirties movements. In *Conversations*, Mulk Raj Anand fictionalizes his reminiscences of some of the major personalities of the Bloomsbury group and other literary geniuses of the period— T. S. Eliot, D. H. Lawrence, E. M. Forster, Aldous Huxley, Bonamy Dobrée, Leonard Woolf and Virginia Woolf.[1] Written perhaps after Plato's *Dialogues* and possibly Hume's *Dialogues*, the dialogical discourse in *Conversations* centers on a highly complicated structure of confrontations, valuations and representations of the issues of ideology, culture, art and history. In creating the personae of various prominent figures and in situating the setting back in history by more than 50 years, Anand heavily relies on memory of his experiences in England. In all these dialogues, Anand himself is the presenter, interviewer, reporter and commentator: in the creation of a portrait, Anand apportions to each person topical subjects that are supposed to be a true and accurate representation of that personality. Plato's *Dialogues* as an art form includes an "infinity of responses,"[2] but they are the product of one mind. Likewise, *Conversations* as an art form contains a multiplicity of divergent voices, some even jarring and cacophonous like Blake's warring factions, but nevertheless they are held together as a unified order by the controlling vision of the fictional persona of Anand. *Conversations* is a fictional biography, and has no conventional plot. The various dialogues are carefully structured dramatizations of some of the major ideological issues. In a sense, therefore, the fictional discourse of *Conversations* is a discourse in the history of ideas—the ideas that were at the center of the twenties and thirties movements and that were central in the evolution of Anand's own consciousness. This discussion focuses on certain selected issues and Anand's methodology, especially the nature and the degree of confrontation and synthesis in a broad historical and philosophical context, with a special focus on Bloomsbury, E. M. Forster and T. S. Eliot.

The process of recovering truth by evoking memory and history after a prolonged period of 50 some years and by examining it from two perspectives, the perspectives of the thirties and the perspective of the eighties, defines the structural principle of *Conversations*.[3] In recreating the figure of T. S. Eliot and directly ascribing him his ideas and positions on various matters requires an active and vigorous recall of the thirties memory but in the process there would undoubtedly occur an intercession of the eighties and the thirties intellectual perspectives. Thus the method of discovery of truth in history, as Heidegger would have us believe, becomes an irreversible concealment of truth.[4] The knowledge of truth and its imaginative representation essentially define the artistic principle of creating a verbal structure, a discourse, which then necessitates critical interpretation of the very meaning of the truth that initially got concealed in the process of its representation. One may consider Blake's recreation of Milton in his poem *Milton*, Shelley's portrayal of Rousseau in *The Triumph of Life* and Wordsworth's and Shelley's portraits of Napoleon only to conclude that each of these poets has combined his critical judgment with poetical perception of reality. And yet at another level where only critical judgment is involved one may get an entirely different picture: for example, Goethe's Byron stands in sharp contrast to Arnold's Byron and Eliot's Shelley is different from C. S. Lewis's Shelley. Interestingly, in his judgment of great works Eliot ranks the *Divine Comedy* as superior to the *Bhagavadgita*.[5] Since the structure and methodology call for reenactment of intellectual encounters and highly sophisticated discussion sessions in which the participants raise volatile issues, historical, moral, social and aesthetic, Anand as presenter carefully controls the selection of subject matter and the scope of discussion in each session. But this omniscient control and selectivity do not take the form of conscious manipulation that could have impinged upon his objectivity and integrity in the creation of a portrait. In this process, however, there emerges a picture of Anand as a poet-in-the-making, a young Indian intellectual who is anxiously probing Western intellectual thought, and a keen, quick and sensitive inquiring mind who in his search for truth attempts to relate the two traditions; his own that he thinks he knows enough about, and the other with which he is brought into contact. The whole exercise, it may therefore be construed, is epistemological: ironically, looking back at the thirties intellectual climate Anand now sees more self-assuredly the difference between knowledge and ignorance, truth and non-truth, vanity and true consciousness. Fully recognizing the critical issues of intentionality and orientation, one can hardly deny the fact that the personae created by Anand are reproductions of his own imaginations: the Eliot of history whom Anand had known is now an imaginatively created Eliot.

II

During his discussion with Huxley Anand asks: "Can one introduce a personal diary into a novel?" Huxley replies somewhat condescendingly: "Why not? I am doing so myself in a novel I am writing. André Gide has interspersed his narrative with the Journal of Eduard . . ."(35).[6] The artistic process of interfusing the diarized notes and history and fictional narrative should resolve, at least to an extent, the problems of intertextuality and contextuality, of defining the primary and final text. It can be safely assumed that for a critic diaries, notebooks, letters and journal entries or whatever else the writer may have written and what would have simply been characterized as secondary texts or "paratexts" cumulatively make one text. Jerome McGann variously describes this critical effort as the process of "socializing" and "historicizing" the text—of "historiciz[ing] the *logoi.*"[7] It is only logical to suggest that since *Conversations* is both a literary history and history of ideas, its prodigious narrative is a continuation of the discourse of *Apology for Heroism: An Essay in Search of Faith,* written in 1945, and the basis of Krishan's "struggle to fuse the novel of confrontation of reality with the novel of pleasure, which was to become the series *Seven Ages of Man*" (6). Evidently, therefore, in the proposed conflation not only does one encounter a world within a world but also one finds a sense of sustained unity, objectivity and continuity.

Apology, Conversations and *Seven Ages* are experiments in creating a unified structure of psychological, sociological and imaginative realities. For one thing, Anand has amassed in *Conversations* an unusually large body of extremely complex issues, some of which probably defy the scope of the narrative. It is in the midst of these overwhelmingly diverse ruminations and confrontations that one finds the recreation of the fictional "I" extremely challenging, both historically and psychologically. The artistic process of recreating the fictional "I" is a simultaneous process of "depersonalizing" and "personalizing" emotions against the objective correlative of sociohistorical reality. The complicated task of appropriating identity to the fictional Anand and to other personae entails the creation of manifold egos, private worlds of various selves, that in the artistic process of creating a unified structure of fictional narrative become engaged in sharp confrontation with one another. It is this transformational process of confrontation between the "various selves" that creates the quality of discourse, with its nostalgic reverberations of various voices from the distant past and especially the dramatic character of Anand's own youthful vigor and exuberance.

In the reconstruction of the literary map of the twenties and thirties Anand is painfully aware of "the prejudices of the literary coteries" (27) of the period and their exclusionary politics. At the Harold Monro Poetry gathering (chapter 2), Lawrence and Huxley are separated from the rest of the group, and Eliot pitifully stands alone. In the dramatic meeting between "the two lions," their attitudes and feelings come out clearly, leading the reader straight into the complex entanglements between Eliot and Lawrence on the one hand and between Bloomsbury and Eliot and Lawrence on the other. Historically, any assessment of the Bloomsbury Circle must call for two basic questions. Does Bloomsbury have a well-defined, cohesive and unified moral and aesthetic philosophy? How does Bloomsbury relate itself to other major movements and figures of the period? In his study of the Bloomsbury group, Johnstone, focusing on Forster, Strachey and Virginia Woolf, maintains that the Bloomsbury values and aesthetics were essentially shaped by the moral philosophy of G. E. Moore's *Principia Ethica* and Cambridge Humanism.[8] However, the group, as Quentin Bell argues, "was less organized, less ideologically homogeneous than the Pre-Raphaelite Brotherhood, the 'Souls' or even the Impressionists."[9] The group's embittered relationship with Lawrence, Eliot and Lewis was the result of various divergent ideological positions. For the most part, Lawrence remained an outsider, and especially during the war his relationship with the "Cambridge-Bloomsbury milieu" had deteriorated into an open confrontation.[10] But the matter of Eliot's relationship with Bloomsbury is somewhat more paradoxical and complex: "T. S. Eliot, the great opponent in literature of Bloomsbury and of all that Bloomsbury stood for," remarks Bell, "found in Leonard and Virginia Woolf publishers and friends."[11] For obvious reasons, of course, Eliot had developed a strong dislike for Lawrence. In the Eliot-Lawrence relationship one sees an unsavory confrontation between Eliot's conservative ideology and orthodoxy and Lawrence's post-Romantic idealism. But this picture of the relationship between the two major figures remains incomplete without an extended reference to the relationship between Forster and Lawrence and Forster and Eliot. It remains a fact that despite Bloomsbury's maltreatment of Lawrence, Forster remained a steadfast supporter of Lawrence. Forster considered Lawrence "the greatest imaginative novelist of our generation,"[12] a judgment that had evoked a sharp disagreement from Eliot. One might say that Forster's own reading of Eliot is a sort of tangential expression of the "Bloomsbury-Cambridge milieu." In his essay on Eliot, Forster maintains that *The Waste Land* "has nothing to do with the English tradition in literature," that Eliot's "approval of institutions [is] deeply rooted in the State," and that "Mr. Eliot does not want us in."[13] Forster classifies men into three categories: "In the first class are those who have not suffered often or acutely; in the second, those who have escaped through horror into a further vision; in the third, those who continue to suffer." Whereas Blake and Dostoevsky, maintains Forster, belong to the second category, Mr. Eliot "belongs to the third." Mr. Eliot, asserts Forster, "is not a mystic," nor is there any "religious emotion" in him: "what he seeks is not revelation, but stability."[14] Of course, the full force of this argument comes from Forster's liberalism and humanism, and indeed this is precisely where one must immediately recognize the genesis of persistent ideological confrontation between tradition and modernity—and quite certainly the very basis of Anand's own sympathy with Forster, Lawrence, Huxley and the Woolfs. Significantly, however, Anand's critical interpretation of history reads like philosophy of history in which biographical and experiential reality is reshaped into an art form of fictional dialogues.

This protrusive discussion helps clarify Anand's intent and meaning: in fact, the structure of *Conversations* presupposes reader's critical understanding of the literary and cultural developments of the period under reference. In a larger context, however, *Conversations* as a work of literary history exhibits the emergence of a moral and social consciousness that unequivocally defines the role and place of writers like Anand in a sociohistorical process. The past, the otherness, that Anand creates as a function of literary history is the deep reservoir of cultural commingling, of diffusion and discovery of identity. One no doubt witnesses in the intricate psychology and epistemology of this process the simultaneous declaration of identity and its dramatic loss and recovery, but ironically the controlling principle of the narrative—and of self-discovery—remains one of continuous confrontation and recognition, inflation and deflation of ego. Anand directs his profound irony at revealing the nature of otherness, its blatant incongruities and obliquities, by characterizing it and by submerging his "I" in it, but only to experience distanced separateness. The psychological and sociohistorical process in which the "I" is divested of the ego-self and then reconstructed by an emerging level of consciousness defines Anand's art of transforming biography into fiction and of relating fiction to truth. The diffusion, dissipation and submergence of the "I" of the initial experience and the recovery and reconstruction of the fictional "I" are inseparable aspects of the creative process, one characterized by the literal and historical "I" and the other by the fictional and metaphoric "I." In a sense, therefore, the imaginative rendering of biographical experience into an artistic experience is the unconscious process of illuminating and intellectualizing the initial experience, and not of simple recording and factual reproduction.[15]

In depicting various ideological "coteries," in characterizing each persona, and in selecting suitable subject matter for dialogical confrontation, Anand seems to have been governed by one central motif—his own intense struggle, emotional and mental, with the ideology of each movement, group or person. The two fundamental elements in Anand's strategy are: (1) his ego self that is frequently, and sometimes mistakenly, translated into his identity as an Indian who has professedly superior knowledge of India; and (2) the English intellectual thought, especially in its inescapable relationship to Indian thought, inasmuch as it successfully colored the English perception of India.

III

One might wonder why Anand has devoted the most space—four chapters—to one single poet, T. S. Eliot, in preference to Lawrence, Huxley and Forster, and why most of the dominant issues in art, literature and philosophy have been collocated around Eliot. Surprisingly, Anand has allocated only one chapter to Forster who had written a preface to *Untouchable*. Anand perhaps graciously recognizes that Eliot is the greatest poet of the century, who, after the English Romantic poets and Yeats in the twentieth century, has evinced significant interest in Indian philosophical thought. There also appears to be a certain amount of empathy for Eliot, since the poet had been lonely in the country of his adoption and struck with despair and pessimism as Anand probably was himself. In an ironic sense, however, the attitudes of Huxley, Lawrence and Forster show Eliot's rejection of the tradition to which he had desperately wanted to belong.

It must also be recognized that since both Eliot and Anand had come to literature from philosophy they shared the same common interest in philosophical thought, especially in the relationship between literature and philosophy much in the tradition of Coleridge and Sri Aurobindo. Anand had worked for *The Criterion,* and also for BBC along with T. S. Eliot, Stephen Spender, George Orwell and others. And we understand that Krishan of *Confession of a Lover* and *Seven Summers* is under the magical influence of Eliot the poet. In view of our earlier discussion of Anand's methodology, it is appropriate to ask a few questions, even at the risk of being repetitive. In the dialogical confrontation with Eliot, will Anand be fair, objective and impartial to Eliot? How far are the selections of ideas from T. S. Eliot representative of the poet? How far does Anand understand Eliot? Yet there is another puzzling issue: does Anand, an Indian intellectual, presume somewhat pretentiously that T. S. Eliot shows an adequate understanding of Indian religious thought and metaphysics? And conversely one must ask if Eliot suspects Anand's understanding of Christianity and the Western intellectual thought. The analogy in the dialogues is clear: as Anand tries to clarify his understanding of Christianity and the Western mind, so does Eliot attempt to depict his grasp of the Indian mind and the Indian religious thought. In following the comparativist methodology, Anand shows a concerted effort to establish analogues and parallels, to draw comparisons and contrasts, to achieve unvitiated clarity, and to remove problems of obvious misreadings, pedantry, obscurantism and oversimplification.

In a reverential mood, Anand repeatedly asks Eliot the meaning of *The Waste Land,* and the exuberant exchange focuses on some of the major aspects of the poem and Eliot's philosophy. Their reflective arguments freely oscillate between several philosophical views of appearance and reality and good and evil in the contexts of social and moral philosophy and the sociology and psychology of religion. Anand finally sharpens his rhetoric by asking Eliot if the main idea of *The Waste Land,* especially its mythology of infertility and despair, is Spenglerian or Schopenhauerian. Characterizing Spengler as a pessimist and Schopenhauer as an utterly destructive mind, Eliot vehemently denounces both and advises Anand that for a better understanding of the poem he should read not Spengler but the Buddha's philosophy of pain and suffering. This conception of life, Eliot emphasizes, explains the symbology of Christ as the "penal cross." Surprisingly, Bonamy Dobrée who is described as "pro-Kipling and fundamentally a Tory" and who is almost a passive auditor in the dialogues, interjects wittily suggesting that Anand should better read Frazer's *The Golden Bough* "for some of the things [he] can't understand in *The Waste Land.*" One must hasten to ask here if Anand's reading of Eliot, especially the extended comparisons between Jesus and the Buddha and the penetrating references to Shankara and Schopenhauer, can be sustained in the light of Eliot scholarship. Interestingly, Anand's exegetical exposition of Shankara's concept of Reality or the "true Self" as *sat* (Truth), *cit* (Mind) and *ananda* (Bliss)[16] compels Eliot to consider it in the context of Christian thought and the European intellectual tradition.

It is Anand's exposition of Shankara's conception of *ananda* that animates the discussion between Anand and Eliot. Plato's view of good and harmony is considered closer to the conception of *sat, cit* and *ananda* as the highest consciousness. The ideas of evil, sin and despair are openly tossed around to establish analogues to the ideas of St. Augustine, St. Thomas, St. Paul and Kierkegaard. While Anand shows his persistence in the understanding of sin in Christian thought, Eliot tries to absorb the conception of *ananda* in Indian spiritual thought. When Anand compares the child-god Krishna with baby Jesus, Eliot immediately characterizes it as the idyllic view of Jesus and categorically asserts that the meaning of Jesus is the cross. In the metaphysics of sin, the identity with the Absolute is an impossibility except in the framework of a mystical experience.

While Eliot forthrightly rejects Romanticism in preference to classicism, Anand considers the two movements as a unity. In his exposition of the Absolutist epistemology, Anand alludes to Kant and Coleridge, but he does not mention the struggle of other Romantics except, of course, Goethe. In the Romantic epistemology and aesthetic it is not Kant but Schelling who paved the way for the realization of the Absolute. Schelling solved the difficult problems of impenetrability and incertitude in one's search of the Idea.

It is commonly believed that Eliot's decision to transfer his allegiance to Anglo-Catholicism in religion, royalism in politics and classicism in literature is expressive of his strong belief in T. E. Hulme's philosophy of man's limitations and imperfections that was fundamentally rooted in the idea of Original Sin.[17] Matthiessen explains that Eliot's disenchantment with the position of Emerson and other Emersonians had led him to the election of Hulme's philosophy and to leave the country of his birth for "a living tradition."[18] But Eliot, as is commonly acknowledged, was equally disenchanted with Arnold because of his exclusion of religion in *Culture and Anarchy*. Admittedly, Eliot's widely debated conversion was essentially an expression of his poignant revolt against Romanticism, Protestantism and liberalism, but nevertheless it was supposed to have created a more congenial climate for achieving an intellectually coherent structure of religion, art and ideology.[19] In his discussion with Eliot, Anand assiduously concentrates on the categories of his new faith, distinctly focusing on the philosophies of pain and *ananda*. While Eliot seeks validity of Shankara's theory of *ananda* in the context of the Christian ideas of sin and suffering, Anand as Humean skeptic can only explicate the conception of *ananda* in terms of analogues but without affirming it either in its abstract metaphysical structure or in the context of a mystical experience. For obvious reasons brought out in the discussion, Anand does not accept the theory of original sin, especially because evil, as Anand seems to believe with Rousseau and Hegel, results from the social process. Although Anand himself does not subscribe to Shankara's thesis of *ananda,* he makes use of the philosophical idea intrepidly and effectively to elevate the level of discourse.

The two significant aspects of Anand's exegesis of Shankara's conception of illusionism and *ananda* are the Shankara-Schopenhauer and the Shankara-Jesus-St. Thomas relationships. But there is the third relationship that is not directly brought out by Anand but which is implied, and that is the Bradley-Shankara relationship, especially since Bradley's philosophy is said to have left an indelible mark on Eliot and since the philosophies of Shankara and Nagarjuna have been compared with Bradley's metaphysics of appearance and reality. Anand is very quick in pointing out that Schopenhauer's estimate of Shankara as a pessimist is incorrect, for Shankara's Vedantic monism and his metaphysics of *ananda* are essentially affirmative. In his exposition of the metaphysics and aesthetic of *ananda* in Shankara, Anand focuses on the symbology of the feminine principle in *Sundralahiri* and the general idea of shakti in Indian thought, especially the Tantric conception of shakti as expounded by Sir John Woodroff in *Shakti-Shakta.*

Eliot's asseverative allusion to the symbol of the Virgin Mother in Christian thought as an analogue to Shankara's idea of woman being the embodiment of pure harmony is somewhat ironic, for he suspects that Shankara may have gotten the idea from Christianity. It should be noted that the symbology of shakti in Indian thought has its analogues to Jacob Boehme's perception of woman as Idea, Jerusalem as the total emanation of Albion in Blake, Shelley's conception of Asia in *Prometheus Unbound* and recently Savitri in Aurobindo's epic poem *Savitri.*[20] Eliot's most revered poet is Dante, and some modern studies of Eliot have focused on Eliot's anxiety to create a symbolic structure of reality in the figure of woman after Dante's model of Beatrice. As Skaff remarks: "Rather than a translation of religion into a function of unhealthy sexuality, Eliot was seeking an integration of sexual love and religious feeling, a union of sexual desire with religious experience similar to that achieved by Dante in the *Divine Comedy* and *Vita Nuova* through his Beatrice."[21] Indeed, the two dimensions of *ananda,* the philosophical dimension and the psychological dimension, are not mutually exclusive. Whether it is Shankara's Absolute, Dante's Reality, Hegel's Idea or Bradley's Absolute, the larger issue of the realization of the Absolute finally rests on the possible limits of knowledge—the expansion of consciousness, the discovery of truth and elimination of gaps between truth and Reality. For example, Bradley's Absolute cannot be confirmed on any scale of analytic philosophy, but it can be confirmed, as Eliot suggests, "through mysticism."[22] The genesis of Bradley's Absolute, Richard Wollheim explains, lies in "Immediate Experience," the two significant characteristics of which are "sensuous infinitude, and immediacy." "The notion of Individuality, with its twin aspects of comprehensiveness and harmony," adds Wollheim, "is unmistakably Spinozistic."[23] Surely, it is the experience of seeing unity, the Idea, in the symbol of woman that Anand thinks addresses some of the fundamental issues in Eliot's philosophy and aesthetic, the chief among those being knowledge, religion and sexuality. Presumably, Eliot's acceptance of Anglo-Catholicism and the dogma sufficiently supports Anand's reading of some of the major philosophical and psychological conflicts in the poet's mind.

Anand's strategy of introducing Shankara in the dialogues is to present the major ideas of Indian metaphysical thought alongside the major ideas of Christian thought and the European intellectual tradition not only to ascertain the fundamental patterns of the unity of the human mind and produce an integrated body of collective wisdom but also to verify distinguishable modes of truth so often identified with mythic consciousness of humanity. Frazer's method in *The Golden Bough,* as Marc Manganaro explains, is the comparativist method of creating "a 'stupendous compendium' of multiple sources and voices"[24] that essentially remain non-interpretative as a part of the design and strategy. In *The Waste Land,* Eliot himself has followed Frazer's comparativist technique of profusing "sources and voices" and his "rhetorical tactics of encyclopedic inclusion." Likewise, Anand also seems to have employed the comparativist rhetoric of Frazer and Jung—of accumulating encyclopedic knowledge and of seeing similarities in the icons and the concrete universals of human consciousness. Significantly, Frazer, as Skaff maintains, has "supplied the early twentieth century with historical evidence that the fundamental pattern governing Christianity has been shared by other religions and existed long before the founding of that religion. . . ."[25] Although one may assume that by using the Frazerian comparativist strategy Anand should be able to construct a syncretic and synthetic structure of *Conversations* and that Anand's rhetoric will not be dichotomous and divisive, both Anand and Eliot, it must be noted, do not believe in confounding issues. One must not lose sight of the fact that both Eliot and Anand, two professionally trained philosophers, must be fully conversant with the difference between the philosophical method and the poetical method, especially with the superiority of the latter in seeking unity of consciousness and form. It should be noted that Coleridge, as Christensen points out, has successfully attempted to relate philosophy to poetry and criticism, but without giving it the upper hand.[26] In fact, Anand very much like Eliot expresses his "grave doubts about the capacity of academic systems for solving insoluble problems of metaphysics." Anand's startling and enthusiastic complements to Goethe's poetic genius are fairly definitive of the boundaries: "I felt that Goethe had pointed to possibilities beyond Shankara and the Christians, to the struggle for awareness from bits of knowledge to the unity of being. . . . Not dry, and dust[y] logic, but in poetical intuition as Eliot himself believed . . ." (132). That "poetical intuition" or art could possibly help in the search for a resolution of skepticism and despair, which philosophy and theology could not provide, is a significant point scored by Anand, but its full implications cannot be understood without taking into account the genesis of the Romantic aesthetic, especially the problems faced by Goethe in his encounter with the Kantian philosophy. Goethe was not an academic philosopher like Kant, but Goethe as a poet could contemplate on truth and resolve the "philosophical unresolvabilities" hitherto unresolved by the Kantian "logico-analytic."[27] Although Anand compares Goethe with Eliot, ironically, however, Eliot does not share Goethe's poetic vision of unity, identity and harmony. "Eliot as an artist," maintains Ricks, "came to rest in religious comprehensions of philosophical unresolvabilities."[28]

There is another significant aspect of Anand's rhetoric. Eliot's profound interest in Indian metaphysics and its use in his poetry have been the subject of several studies.[29] The formative influences of Lanman, Royce and Babbit, the ideas of the *Bhagavadgita* and the *Upanishads,* and the thought of Shankara and Nagarjuna and its relationship to Bradley have been instrumental in Eliot's growth as a poet. There is hardly any doubt about Eliot's familiarity with Indian thought in the works of American and European Orientalists, particularly the Brahmin and the Buddhist thought in Schopenhauer, Hartman and Deussen. But while Emerson, Whitman and Yeats, as Kearns remarks, embraced the main ideas in Eastern thought, Eliot "for reasons 'practical' as well as 'sentimental' . . . chose not to pursue the Eastern path."[30] Evidently, the practical and sentimental reasons are contained in Eliot's own admission that he wanted to think like an American and a European. From amongst the long list of modern users of Indian thought—Yeats, Huxley, Isherwood, Jung and Hermann Hesse—Eliot happens to be one of the most prominent and effective users—and interpreters. But it must be admitted that the role and function of Indian metaphysics in Eliot's poetical and philosophical thought still remains a dominant critical issue in Eliot scholarship and that it cannot be answered by the theory of exoticism. Anand has attempted to deal with this issue as an important part of the thematic structure of the novel by positing for himself a serious and definitive purpose: "I wanted immediately to ask him [Eliot] about the myths from India he had referred to in his poem, *The Waste Land*" (19). It is somewhat intriguing to note that whereas a critic like Rajan thinks that "Mr. Eliot is never happy in 'the maze of Oriental metaphysics,'"[31] critics like Cleanth Brooks and Philip Wheelwright emphasize the positive and integrative value of Indian myths and philosophy in Eliot's poetry. Referring to Eliot's method of linking up the Christian doctrine with the beliefs of other cultures, Cleanth Brooks remarks that Eliot "goes back to the very beginnings of Aryan culture, and tells the rest of the story of the rain's coming. . . ."[32] But in order to examine the issue of the use of Indian thought one must not misconstrue and misdirect the critical question stated above. For one thing, Anand does not get sidetracked by an anxiety of influence or other extraneous considerations merely to show that Eliot's poetry is a commentary on Vedantic and Buddhistic thought. In fact, in the dialogues Anand is forthrightly critical of Eliot's reading of Shankara and Schopenhauer as he himself turns out to be a staunch critic of certain aspects of Hinduism, Buddhism and Christianity. Anand disapproves Shankara's idea of Maya and personal salvation, but at the same time thinks that new knowledge has affirmed his conception of the unity of consciousness. While Eliot is examining all issues from the standpoint of his newly found faith in Christianity, especially in tradition and orthodoxy, Anand's views are colored by progressive liberalism and secular humanism. For Anand, the penal cross of Christianity and the *ananda* of Vedanta are icons of the human imagination.

IV

In his discussion of the American Left literary criticism, Edward Said raises some very pertinent questions:

> What we must ask is why so few "great" novelists deal directly with the major social and economic outside facts of their existence—colonialism and imperialism—and why, too, critics of the novel have continued to honor this remarkable silence. With what is the novel, and for that matter most modern cultural discourse, affiliated, whether in the language of affirmation or in the structure of accumulation, denial, repression, and mediation that characterizes major aesthetic form? How is the cultural edifice constructed so as to limit the imagination in some ways, enlarge it in others? How is imagination connected with the dreams, constructions, and ambitions of official knowledge, with executive knowledge, with administrative knowledge? What is the community of interests that produces Conrad and C. L. Tem-

ple's *The Native Races and Their Rulers?* To what degree has culture collabo-
rated in the worst excesses of the State, from its imperial wars and colonial
settlements to its self-justifying institutions of antihuman repression, racial
hatred, economic and behavioral manipulation?[33]

Whether one agrees with the philosophy and critical orientation of the
American Left writers and critics, Said's questions define larger issues of the
scope of the novel and criticism. It may, however, be argued that if the novel
is a cultural discourse and if in the context of literary and critical theories
the novel, whose critical reading is expected to create a body of such a discourse, must include in its total structure a broader and more comprehensive vision of culture. As a writer, E. M. Forster had developed a strong
dislike for politics, but his discerning comment on the nature of English
freedom is hardly apolitical or nonpolitical. Forster boldly states that English
liberty is "race-bound" and "class-bound" and that "it means freedom for
the Englishman, but not for the subject-races of his Empire." "If you invite
the average Englishman to share his liberties with the inhabitants of India
or Kenya," adds Forster, "he will reply, 'Never,' if he is a Tory, and 'Not until
I consider them worthy,' if he is a Liberal."[34] Can we attempt a reading of
A Passage to India in terms of some of these bold ideological beliefs and assumptions? "And if we writers today could carry this tradition on," exhorts
Forster, "if we could assert, under modern conditions, what has been as-
serted by Milton in his century and by Shelley and by Dickens in theirs, we
should have no fear of our liberties."[35] It is significant to note that in *A Passage to India* Forster's iconoclastic experiment with sociohistorical problems
of a newly emerging culture defies all limits and expectations of a conventional model in dramatizing and affirming the psychological need of liberty
and other humanistic values in human relationships.

One would hardly contest that the question of India's freedom from
Great Britain should, for obvious reasons, remain one of the major issues
of ideological confrontation between Anand and the British intellectuals,
including Forster and Eliot. The political ideologies of colonialism and imperialism and other forms of human subjugation can only be considered
in a broader context of the European intellectual thought. Indeed, it is the
narrative of *Heart of Darkness* that has proved to be a revolutionary literary
document in opening a modern ideological debate on racism, colonialism
and imperialism and the relationship between cultural and sociohistorical
issues and fictional narrative. I have dealt with this subject elsewhere.[36] The
matter of India's freedom must have remained very crucial to the evolution of psychological, political and cultural identity of the young Anand
who could not see any justification whatever in the British imperialist
colonialism.

"Culture," "State" and "Power" are mutually inclusive and interdependent conceptual terms in the vocabulary of modern political and sociological thought. In such polymorphological structures as *Heart of Darkness* or *Conversations,* these terms become much too convoluted, complex and fluid—at times, in fact, morally assertive and ambiguous—to be understood clearly and precisely as truthful expressions of the ideologies they represent. In fact, what, one must ask, is the referentiality of colonialism and imperialism in the history of social and political thought, especially in contemporary literary theory? J. S. Mill had opposed self-governance for India, and, of course, Macaulay's controversial position on India is too well known to call for any further attention. Vincent Pecora maintains that the English discourse on imperialism at the end of the nineteenth century "is in many ways structurally determined by the very conjunction of Enlightenment rationality and monopoly capitalist economic power—a discourse in which Conrad's work participates." "No matter what form rational European discussion of the abuses of imperialist 'monopolization' takes at this time . . . the power of a Europocentrically administrated civilization over the globe," adds Pecora, "would still be capable of appropriating the rhetoric of free trade, or technological mastery, or even political justice for its own purposes."[37] Pecora's analysis should help us to understand the magnitude of the political and economic dimensions of imperialism and Conrad's inestimable moral anxiety in the creation of Kurtz as the representative of entire Europe. Strangely, Conrad participates in the elaborately politicized discourse, persistently seeking some form of moral validity of his strong personal feelings of "criminality" in the repressive deeds of Kurtz who collectively symbolizes all of Europe. On the other hand, Anand participates in this discourse as an oppressed victim from the "subject," "lower race" in an attempt to seek moral and psychological validity of his own personal experiences in the light of the fundamental principles of liberty, equality and justice. While in Conrad's case it is what Ian Watt calls "delayed decoding"[38] of his raw, personal experiences, somewhat of the type of Wordsworthian distancing of the initial experience from its conceptualization, Anand's experiences have been "decoded" by a historical distancing of the colonial period, the time of Anand's active involvement in the revolutionary struggle, to the postcolonial era when his experiences have now been reorganized. The psychological significance for Anand is that in this process of "decoding" he must analyze the volatility and magnitude of his feelings and thoughts, remove any possibilities of conscious manipulation, and formulate some humanistic conceptions for the restructuring of the narrative. Significantly, while Conrad in this process of "decoding" reaffirms collective guilt and self-indictment, Anand focuses on the philosophy of human subjugation, repression and suffering. But one might ask if

Anand's own experiences—and also of several other compatriots—should be decoded by Western ideologies and assumptions.

It should be evident from history that colonialism and imperialism were an expression of the self-aggrandizing ambition of powerful nations for economic and political dominance of the less powerful nations. How would these economically and politically monopolized structures bear a morally defensible scrutiny by idealistic entities of culture and religion? In *The Idea of a Christian Society,* Eliot maintains that the ideal Christian society must consist of the following three elements: "the Christian State, the Christian Community, and the Community of Christians,"[39] and that Christianity plays the most crucial role in directing and unifying these elements. In fact, in *Notes towards the Definition of Culture* Eliot categorically declares that "no culture can appear or develop except in relation to a religion."[40] If religion alone were to provide a total and ultimate sense of direction of what is *"morally* wrong" (Eliot's emphasis), colonialism and imperialism as forms of commercial and industrial expansionism will be deemed as expressions of avarice—a Dantesque judgment, indeed—unless the oppositional argument for colonization is invoked and justified by benevolent paternalism and a divine authority vested in religion. Coleridge's support of colonialism, for example, is basically derived from his strong religious conviction in the need to spread divine light. Now one must ask if such a view of creating an imperialist and ideological umbrella of political power was advanced by the Church in conjunction with the State and if the pagan and heathen nations within the British Empire were to be converted to Christianity before deserving any considerations of commonalty and the basic sense of social and political justice. And, more importantly, one must ask if there are universal principles of human civilization that recognize the values of liberty, equality and truth—fundamental values of human dignity—irrespective of any religious, cultural and geographical restraints and affiliations. The answer to this question in Eliot's political ideology has been the subject of much critical scrutiny, and undoubtedly it must finally rest in the threefold creed of the poet—royalism, classicism and Anglo-Catholicism. It is important to note that Eliot did not accept Babbit's humanism as a possible alternative to religion; and that the term "classicism" ultimately meant belief in antidemocratic and antiegalitarian convictions and the fear of the middle class and masses. In a way, the attitude of the humanists and liberal critics toward Eliot—Daiches, Laski, Leavis, Forster and others[41]—is probably spurred by Eliot's belief in conservatism and orthodoxy whose essential context is defined by the poet's utopian ideals of Christian society and culture. Anand does not refer to these two essays directly in *Conversations,* but his repeated reference to Eliot's conversion unfolds the circumambient world of Eliot's political ideology and identity. Anand seems to be fully cognizant of Eliot's attempt to place himself in the Burke-Coleridge-Arnold debate on the theories of state, culture and religion.

In *Notes towards the Definition of Culture,* Eliot maintains that the failure of the British colonial rule in India in achieving "a complete cultural assimilation" is attributable to "a religious failure," for "[t]o offer another people your culture first, and your religion second, is a reversal of values. . . ."[42] Eliot notes that the British rulers of India were not only professedly ignorant of the relationship between religion and culture but also were poor representatives of their own culture and religion. The argument that the introduction of Christianity instead of westernization of India would have been a better alternative is utterly contentious, unless, of course, Eliot means to suggest that the dialogue among various religions will define some universal humanistic ethics for all humanity. Although Eliot deplores the disruption of Indian culture by the very nature and design of British imperialism, his argument remains unquestionably defensive of the empire: "To point to the damage that has been done to native cultures in the process of imperial expansion is by no means an indictment of empire itself, as the advocates of imperial dissolution are only too apt to infer."[43] In the same overly defensive vein Eliot also notes the apparent contradiction in the anti-imperialist protestations of the British liberals who are quick to affirm the superiority of Western civilization.

In *Conversations,* Eliot asks Anand somewhat chidingly the justification for the use of violence by Indians against the empire, especially since Britain has done so much for India and since Gandhi himself is committed to the philosophy of nonviolence. Eliot further suggests that Gandhi's philosophy of nonviolence may have come from the teachings of Jesus, although one can hardly miss the cruel irony in the observation. What about the repression, brutality and violence used by the British government? Speaking about the disintegration of native culture, Eliot points out that "the cause of this disintegration is not corruption, brutality or maladministration."[44] In direct contrast, of course, one cannot help noting that E. M. Forster had rigorously and persistently followed the story of the Amritsar massacre and of the O'Dwyer trial in England and that to Forster's horrible surprise and degrading shame General Dyre was vindicated by the jury.[45] Eliot admires Kipling, and had edited and published Kipling's works. Ironically, most people outside India had known about the country from Kipling's works as the land of wandering lamas and the orphan Kim O'Hara.[46] But could one move, as Nikhil Sen wonders, from Kipling's *Kim* to Forster's *A Passage to India?* "Eliot," remarks Northrop Frye, "stresses the feeling for soil and local community in his essays on Virgil and Kipling, the two poets who have little in common except a popular reputation for being imperialists."[47] At least, Conrad, Forster and Orwell had shared the collective guilt of empire-building, of human subjugation. In a rare stroke of irony, Eliot asks Anand why India cannot stay within the empire because that way "we" will be able to learn more from India. Indeed, it is not un-true that within the framework of the European Christian society con-ceived by Eliot, possessions and dependencies like India have little or no place. Generally speaking, commerce, evangelicalism and imperialistic ego are considered to be the pillars of the empire-building philosophy, and surely Anand would hope that these three elements do not define the words "culture" and "progress," nor are they expressive of Eliot's politics of royalism and classicism. If tradition in royalism must guarantee continuity and status quo, colonialism and commercial imperialism will continue to be recognized as touchstones of progress and culture.

In the dialogue with E. M. Forster and Leonard Woolf, Anand's ex-tended reference to Gandhi's philosophy of nonviolent struggle is marked by dramatic irony and exacerbated sense of puzzlement and ambivalence:

> 'Perhaps,' I began, 'Shakespeare stated the problem in *The Tempest*. I saw the play in the Old Vic. Both Caliban and Gandhi, the rebels, have yet to grow, beyond king worship—to become genuine rebels . . .' I was surprised at my eloquence after I had said this. I felt my cheeks warming and my eyes burning, from the feeling that I was dramatising my own inner hates with a bright metaphor.
> 'Caliban and Gandhi!' Leonard said looking from the corners of his eyes at Morgan. 'I never thought of that equation! . . . Clever boy!—Come to think of it, he is right, Morgan?'
> 'Caliban sulking, despairing, and yet dependent,' said Morgan, with an amused smile. 'And yet possessed of the desire for revenge.' (74)

Are there any rational causes of Gandhi's revolt? Can a Gandhi-Caliban re-lationship problematize—and thematize—the empire-nation allegorical relationship? What would it take for Caliban and Gandhi to become "gen-uine rebels"? What about the "inner hates" of a Caliban? Are Christ, Shel-ley's Prometheus, Napoleon and Nietzsche's Superman "genuine rebels"? Evidently, Forster's and Anand's readings of *The Tempest* are combined at-tempts to produce a structure of irony that must reveal the moral parame-ters of Gandhi's philosophy. In a sense, Gandhi the anarchist and Gandhi as Caliban are self-contradictory, meiotic images, because they reveal the bla-tant incongruence between historical truth and moral truth. Historically, the metaphor of Caliban suggests a denuded self-indictment of the Indian mind that had accepted slavery and subjugation as conditions of disen-franchised existence. The Prospero-Caliban analogy clearly defines the so-ciohistorical context of the Indian struggle for independence, sharpening the sensibility of the reader toward the disproportionate and imbalanced use of "crude power" in human relationships. After all, the analogy is a commentary on Prospero's vision of the exclusionary politics of subjugation. However, it must not be forgotten that the analogy also sheds light on Anand's own differences with Gandhi's policy of appeasement and mendacity, and it can be argued that Anand's preferential choice of the ideal hero from amongst several archetypes—the Shelleyan Prometheus, the Napoleonic hero, or the Arjuna of the *Bhagavadgita*—remains a masked ambiguity. Indeed, the analogy and the metaphor derive their basic strength from the inherent parody of Prospero's magical power: Prospero's vision and art do not include the Calibans of the world. And yet in another sense the parody justifies the Gandhi-Caliban anarchism as a moral necessity.

One can hardly ignore Mannoni's Adlerian psychoanalytical interpretation of the Prospero-Caliban and Crusoe-Friday analogies. Mannoni brings out two important characteristics of the relationship between the colonized and the colonist, dependency complex and inferiority complex. While the colonist of the Prospero type would be regarded as misanthrope, escapist, individualist and aggressor, the colonized individual of the Caliban type is essentially a self-defeated weakling who has been tamed into a psychological dependent type. Thus the inevitable conclusion that one essentially draws from the Prospero-Caliban and Crusoe-Friday analogies is that there exists an unmitigable conflict between the psychology of dependence and the principles of egalitarianism, democracy and republicanism. Thus one can probably understand Forster's deep consternation at the illogicality of Caliban's "sulking, despairing, and yet dependent" personality and his "desire for revenge" (74). The complexity of Anand's irony is that while such reading of the Prospero-Caliban relationship as that of Forster and Woolf shares the European perception of the use of power in political governance and the resultant dependency of a Caliban or a Prospero, the true meaning of Gandhi's moral philosophy of nonviolence, especially the disuse of power, as a method has been sadly misunderstood as a weakness. In *The Tempest,* as Mannoni points out, Caliban "does not complain of being exploited; he complains rather of being betrayed. . . ."[48] Indeed, betrayal is essentially a grievous moral issue that in Dante's theology constitutes one of the most heinous crimes of malice and fraud. After all, the British imperial governance of India, marked by India's historic place in Queen Victoria's empire, had its origin in the commercial enterprise of the East India Company. Ironically, the dialectical confrontation implied in the metaphor trenchantly focuses on the moral creed of the disuse of "crude power" as a political strategy as advanced by Gandhi, a Caliban, whose startling progress far exceeds, even by any modern standards of evolutionary anthropology and ethics of political governance, the legitimatizations of the Prospero complex. Mannoni's psychological analysis has shown that "what the colonial in common with Prospero lacks, is awareness of the world of Others, a world in which Others have to be respected."[49]

"Eliot," remarks Northrop Frye, "is uniformly opposed to theories of progress that invoke the authority of evolution and contemptuous of writers who popularize a progressive view, like H. G. Wells."[50] Although this view may undoubtedly be characterized as the Romantic-liberal assessment of Eliot, it cannot be denied that confrontation between the proponents of tradition and modernity is creative and progressive. Anand is a romanticist who shares the ameliorative vision of human progress. While Eliot is "clearly on the political right,"[51] Anand is a left writer who is committed to "the more comprehensive ideology"[52] of humanism. In a recent interview, Anand reaffirms his assessment of Eliot: "All his [Eliot's] brilliant insights into the age were, however, compromised by his dogmatic revivalism."[53] In the postscript "There Is No Higher Thing Than Truth" appended to *Apology*, Anand has reexamined his ideals and commitments candidly and forthrightly. Anand's liberalism, egalitarianism, globalism, cosmopolitanism and multiculturalism fall under one term: "Humanism."

Can art, ideology and consciousness be unequivocally unified to create the larger vision of one humanity? Anand has persistently subscribed to Shelley's conception of the poet as an "unacknowledged legislator," and yet it is ironic that despite his firm convictions he should call himself eclectic in dealing with the Bloomsbury elite. Even though the parameters of ideological confrontation couldn't have been clearer, and at times even more sharply pronounced, Anand creates a very urbane and civilized poetic discourse, one in which he himself participates as a bold inquirer of truth. He often wonders in his own innermost consciousness about the engaging agenda of the left and the right writers, the protrusive commitments of the humanists, socialists, liberals and religious thinkers. It is abundantly clear that Anand's rhetoric in *Conversations* is not vitiated and imbalanced, nor does it smack of complicity, collusion and misrepresentation. The dialogues do not reveal any surreptitious agenda or motive on Anand's part. Anand's tone, mood and idiom are highly civil and polite. There is no inexorableness, arrogance and violence in Anand's rhetoric, nor is he overassertive, elliptical and hyperbolic. Anand is by no means pliant, nor is he submissive and condescending. He understands Eliot's demeanor, his sternness, placidity and coldness, but he also knows that beneath the mysterious and stony mask of sternness there is the wounded heart of a kind and gentle soul. Anand would fully and readily share the epistemological predicament loudly echoed in the line: "I sometimes wonder if that is what Krishna meant—."[54]

Does Anand achieve in *Conversations* something that is serious, substantive and significant? Although the dedication to Cowasjee reads like a light self-parody, *Conversations* remains a serious achievement of Anand. Needless to say that without extensive treatment of some of the major ideological issues and the penetrating psychological and sociohistorical analysis of his personal experiences the narrative will have lost its vitality, seriousness and significance. It is Anand's ability to examine his experiences carefully and comprehensively and to reflect upon these more deeply and intensely in a broader context of the history and philosophy of ideas that lends force to the narrative. But one cannot help feeling that it is Anand's poetic perception of Eliot—his successful creation of the figure of Eliot—and the image of Bloomsbury that determine the success of *Conversations*. Anand's confrontations with the great minds are what Blake calls "mental wars," spiritual ruminations of the Kierkegaardian type, in which the search for truth is a process of discovery of the self and a means of developing communal discourse. A close reading of *Apology* undoubtedly suggests that Anand has been seeking a progressive synthesis of East and West in the hope that human civilization can be saved, that a new world order will not be merely a utopia but a practicality and that fundamental values of human existence can be realized for the emergence of a progressive humanistic culture.

Chapter 7

Balachandra Rajan's
The Dark Dancer:
A Critical Reading

While Rajan's fame as a critic and scholar has been well established, the debate about his vision and art as a novelist is still
going on, both in India and abroad.[1] *The Dark Dancer*, his first
novel, is a bright and sensitive work; it is much too deep and subtly allusive for a commoner's zeal to categorize and label it only as a portrayal of
a sociological confrontation between two cultures, in which convenient
and facetious judgments are made of winners and losers. It is no doubt true
that after Kipling, E. M. Forster's *A Passage to India* is the pioneer work that
dramatizes with the greatest intrepidity the East-West conflict, and in a
sense the Forsterian theme is present in Rajan's work and in the works of
other contemporaries of Rajan.[2] But *The Dark Dancer*, it appears to me, is
a much more comprehensive, illuminating and ripe work, both in breadth
and scope: it portrays the quest of the Cambridge-educated Krishnan for
identity and enlightenment; and it deals with the myth of the dark dancer,
Shiva, the central symbol of the story. In his review of the book Monroe
Spears remarks: "*The Dark Dancer* is an extremely ambitious work, in that
it deals explicitly with the greatest issues, political, moral, and religious; it
presents a wide range of characters and shows them in crucial years of recent Indian history; it takes the greatest risks possible."[3] V. S. Krishnan's
alienation, resulting from his prolonged stay in England, is a historical and
social phenomenon, but the unostentatious confrontation with the matter-
of-factness of the situation and the evolutionary process of awakening to
various phases of reality and of expanding consciousness define the mythos
and *dianoia* of the work. The case of *Too Long in the West* is, however, quite

different: it is a witty, sarcastic and hilarious parody—much in the tradition of the eighteenth century satirical writing and to an extent of Jane Austen—of the process of adjustment or maladjustment of the Columbia-educated Nalini who has returned to India after four years and is now confronted with the oddities of custom and tradition of her country. In a way, it is a comedy of manners in which the young heroine needs to know much more about life than the academic education she has received. But the two novels have some common hypotheses: the East-West confrontation in which the investiture of ego is followed by a process of divestiture and finally by a search for true identity; the conflict between conformity and freedom and tradition and modernity, in which Krishnan and Nalini test their true mettle, thereby discovering truth by living it; and the crystallization of experience, a stage in which determination is made of the nature and quality of self-discovery.

The Dark Dancer seems to have been patterned after the *Mahabharata* model: while its structure reverberates direct and indirect allusions to Kurukshetra as a battlefield of life and history and the convoluted allegory of Karna, the son of Kunti, its cohesive unity is controlled by the central symbol of the Nataraja, the cosmic dancer. In fact, the myth of the Nataraja encompasses two integrative phantasmagorias, the myth of restoration and progress and the myth of destruction—not as two oppositional or counterproductive forces but as complementarities in the evolutionary structure of civilization. Thus in the aestheticization and mythicization of history, civilization and barbarity, creation and destruction together define a paradigmatic structure that has a cohesive but paradoxical unity of its own. The agglomeration of a large number of sociohistorical events and a specific periodization of history—the picture of colonial India, the echoes of national struggle for freedom, the dawn of Indian independence, the partition of India, the creation of Pakistan, the mass migration of people and communal riots—are reshaped into a unified structure of mythos, showing Rajan's distinct and skillful achievement as a novelist. No doubt, the historical narratives of Tolstoy and Scott, as one must argue, are enviable models,[4] but it appears that Dostoevsky, if one were looking for a model, would more likely be appropriate. From amongst the various strands of sociohistoricity it is finally Krishnan's and Kamala's consciousness that constitutes the thematic center of the narrative. Looking at the inextricableness and complexity of various issues during the period of Indian history under reference, one must ask if a postcolonial text can legitimately and objectively retextualize the history of colonial India without falling into a trap of derivative discourse of Orientalism.

Rajan as a critic is also a student of Milton, Eliot and Yeats; although one must inevitably assume that *The Dark Dancer* contains echoes of Milton's epic, or of Eliot's wasteland mythology or even of Yeats's search for his roots and identity,[5] the fact remains that Rajan's imagination as a novelist and a critic grapples with the universal problems of an individual's struggle with society and history in the colonial and postcolonial contexts and the unresolvable complexities of a newly emerging social order. While the study of Milton may have helped Rajan in his search for order and a sense of form, his study of Eliot undoubtedly brings him closer to the Indian religio-philosophic tradition. But it is Yeats in whom he finds the dramatic poetization of a conflict between alienation and identity and an incessant search for the unity of being.[6] An astute critic like Rajan must be fully aware of the Romantic and post-Romantic interest in Milton and of Eliot's devaluation of Milton. In *The Dark Dancer* Rajan has attempted a universalization and transvaluation of various traditions and value structures, showing that a transformative synthesis—and here one must remember such techniques as subversion in English Romantic literature and the Frazerian composite in Eliot's *The Waste Land*—can contain history, coloniality, postcoloniality, modernity and postmodernity and the psychoanalysis of the individual mind and collectivity in a single form. Is Krishnan a Karna, an Adam, an Oedipus or simply an emaciated inhabitant of Eliot's *The Waste Land*? Is Krishnan's rootlessness or the apparent lack of definable identity traceable to the gross incongruities and obliquities of a new social order, or to the uncharitableness and ignominiousness of a past, or perhaps to the psychoanalysis of his self-representation? In his search for form Rajan does not debunk myth and tradition, but he attempts to establish continuity by a transformative synthesis of the multiplicity of voices, while seeking at the same time some sort of order in the indomitableness of chaos of history, the destructive phase in the symbology of the cosmic dancer. Rajan firmly believes that Indian literature "inherits a rich past, a classical world which has both its Mycenae and its Athens and a religio-philosophical tradition unequalled in its power of radical thought," hoping that "the writer of integrity will continue to pursue integration." And yet the affirmation and hope are qualified by a note of caution: "The novel that will come to terms with modern India in its unique blend of quietism and turbulence and in those agonizing confrontations that are forced upon it by the pressures of change, has yet to be written."[7]

The organizing principle followed by Rajan in the structure of the mythos of *The Dark Dancer* takes its cue from the dialectical method: to present manifold conflicts and polarities in the life of the hero, mostly occasioned by social conditions; to choose for setting a period of Indian history that happens to be the most fertile soil for developing such conflicts; and to use the tension arising from these complex conflicts as a means of furthering the movement and bringing it to a climactic point in the hero's quest for identity and truth. The East-West confrontation is one of the most obvious modern conflicts in the novel, and it happens to take place first in England during Krishnan's education at Cambridge, and then upon his return to the India of 1947. What is the theoretical genesis, if any, of a presumptive motif such as East-West conflict? Is it merely a matter of "deceptive stylization," a rhetorical and linguistic camouflage, or does it have an intellectual validity and moral authenticity beyond the obtrusive limits of sociological indeterminacy? "The clash," reminds Rajan, "is not simply between East and West (a conventional but deceptive stylization) but between the mores of a pre-urban civilization and one committed to drastic industrial growth."[8] Can these mores be further problematized into substantive theoretical categories that have persistently defined hegemonic relationships in the history of politico-economic and sociological thought? If the conflict is centrally situated between tradition and modernity, should one hope that "the Indian tradition, with its capacity for assimilation and its unique power of synthesis," can successfully deal with progress without disrupting its own true indigenousness? The inchoate image of the Indian society at this time resembles a leviathan whose hideous monstrosity is out to devour individualism, personal freedom and creativity and yet to whose determinism Krishnan must submit. Fresh from the liberal and intellectual climate of England, Krishnan finds himself in direct confrontation with traditional India—its religion, its caste system, its social structure, its economic backwardness, and, above all, its colonial politics and the emergent postcolonial temper. But as the multidimensional conflict between traditional India and Western ideals intensifies, we see that the assiduous logicality of the dialectical approach, rooted in Krishnan's own ego, gradually vanishes, enabling him to hear through Kamala's intuitive vision the echo of his own unconscious self.

V. S. Krishnan, Kamala and Cynthia Bainbridge—all three are battling the leviathan of history, the invincible and omnipotent monster of social determinism, fed variously and jointly by social, economic, political and religious forces. Cynthia Bainbridge's resuscitated dream collapses, and she is advised to make a graceful exit from the scene; Kamala is literally devoured by the monster; and Krishnan, through Kamala's death, finally sees the meaning of Krishna's advice given to Arjuna in the *Bhagavadgita*. Hitherto, he had been aspiring for the vision of the Nataraja, the cosmic dancer (the paradoxical meaning of the Dark Dancer of the title), who holds, with equanimity, the inexplicable equilibrium and unity between good and evil. One Kurukshetra, the symbol of the battle that we all wage in life, has concluded, but the war is hardly won. There is another Kurukshetra out there, the Kurukshetra of history, where humans are pitted against fellow humans in a fratricidal conflict of self-destruction. Hegel's theory of tragedy, it must be remembered, is an aesthetic formulation of the idea of evolutionary progress in history: hence, tragic events or violent revolutions in history finally define the principle of liberty in human consciousness. Life is an endless series of Kurukshetras, and Krishnan must continue his karmic struggle, his ascent to a vision of unity. Indeed, this pattern of Krishnan's quest is the pattern of myth in which the Nataraja is the anagogic symbol of unity, totality and simultaneity. In this sense, the identity realized by Krishnan is the identity with the work of art and with the anagogic symbol itself.

The question of identity, both in literature and philosophy, has been an engaging one.[9] The Romantic notion of unity between the subject and the object presupposes the capacity of the self to achieve such relationship as will annihilate illusion. While the Romanticist's self-projection of reality gives concrete form to the fabulous, the miraculous or the fantastic, it does not preclude reality. The fabulators, mythmakers and projectionists all use imaginary and fictional structures and constructs to communicate various forms of reality. The identity usually sought in a mythic framework is with the essence, the higher self or truth by mitigating differences in time and space; it stipulates the ability of the self to perceive the object-world as integrally related to the self. But the literature of social realism is usually concerned with the images of temporal-spatial reality, such as the one Bradley has expounded in *Appearance and Reality*.[10] While the Freudian "I-ego" patterns of identity deal with the limits to which the self can be extended unto the id, they finally focus upon the sources of discontentment of modern civilization—conflict between ego and id, the alienation of man, and the problems of man's loneliness, fear, anxiety and neuroses, to name only a few. Sociological theories of roles or masks are basically concerned with patterns or models of values and relationships that progressive and civilized societies use to measure an individual's growth and refinement. These and various other forms of identity are possible to be realized only if man is able to see the source of his own potential vitality in his own self. The Romantic self and the Upanishadic self allow an uninhibited and infinite freedom of expression to the spirit of man. However, modern man has lost his vitality, humanity and confidence—the will to leap forward and the urge to create. As Langbaum sums up the problem:

> The declining vitality of the self in literature has accompanied a declining confidence in society, in the spiritual power of nature, and in the organic connection of the self with nature. It has accompanied a loss of confidence in the individual and individual effort due to mass production, mass markets, mass media, to increasing urbanization, industrialization, specialization and to the increasing alienation of the self, according to Marx's analysis, from all its specialized functions.[11]

To these forces that have led to the gradual emaciation of man we must add colonialism, imperialism and other forms of tyrannous subjugation of man. Although one may object that some of these ideas are relevant more to Western societies than to India, it must be emphasized that all these different conceptual approaches—philosophical, psychological, Freudian and Marxian—address the fundamental questions of man's disintegration and the possibilities of his moral and intellectual improvement, and thus their value, both intrinsic and aesthetic, cannot be minimized by national labels. After all, Krishnan is a product of the environment referred to by Marx in his analysis. It should also be noted that the entire question of identity and relationship is crucial in estimating the nature of sincerity, authenticity and integrity not only in relationships amongst people and their values in the fictional universe but also in the special bond that exists between the artist and the work itself.[12]

For a very significant theme, let us look into the opening pages of *The Dark Dancer:*

> He was coming back, but not to an identity, a sense of being rooted, not even to an enmity like that of sun and earth, a struggle against circumstance, a creative confronting, which would open his mind to its depths of repossession. He was coming back to an indifferent sky, an anonymous teeming of houses, the road striking forever into a distance which not even the clenched thrust of the temple could make real.[13]

Rajan, unlike Henry James, comes immediately and directly to the point of the story without taxing the reader's patience. The novel opens with a well-defined thesis: the ten-year stay in England has alienated Krishnan from his home, country and people, and the place to which he is returning is a wasteland. On the face value of it, one gets an impression that Krishnan has already formulated some preconceived notions of his emotional and intellectual aloofness. From this point on in the story, the reader can safely surmise without much difficulty that the hero is going to be introduced to the society to which he thinks he cannot belong. The blatant irony and paradox in the sentence, "He was coming back, but not to an identity, a sense of being rooted," subtly but strikingly define one of the central issues in the book. The paradox is that he does try to establish identities in terms of relationships, perceptions and values: the several masks that he wears as a son, a husband, a lover, a government officer, a nationalist all point to an unconscious urge in him to bestow some form and meaning on his environment, to strike a synthesis between his Western ideas and the emotional and instinctive self that is rooted in the East. Krishnan went through a "conditioning" process in one structure, and now he has been introduced to another structure: in both cases, the predicament at the beginning is, if we go along with the ideas of Freud, Darwin, Marx and Frazer, that the subject, like a writer, does not know what he is doing. It is important to note that since Krishnan does not have the urge to rebel, the psychological feelings of aloofness and incongruity appear to result from a temporary self-immurement. Of course, Krishnan's dilemma recalls the predicament of Victorians who lived double personalities because they failed to reconcile the scientific view of progress and the religious view of life, not fully comprehending the meaning of either of the two. But Krishnan's problem brings him face to face with existential reality, such that he can forge a relationship or identity between existence and perception and existence and reality, even though in the early stages he has been quite skeptical about the possibility of entering into a relationship. Whether it is social reality or existential reality or even the reality of Being, Krishnan must mediate, through his karma, between perception and existence in order to establish an identity.

As a character in Indo-Anglian fiction, the Western-educated Indian is a type, and a distinct category. The origin of this type is, of course, traceable to the colonial period of history when Indians sought English education in England for social, economic and political reasons. In the history of British colonial governance the political strategies of establishing a subordinate tier, a collaborative structure of administration, in the colonies like India had principally determined the policies and programs of educational and social development. One must remember that insofar as India is concerned Macaulay and his associates had emerged triumphant in the stormy Anglicist-Orientalist controversy. But gradually, as students of Indian colonial history know, there had grown a genuine interest in English and European thought. Historically, therefore, the Western-educated Indian represented, in a more positive sense, the voice of progress, modernity and intellectualism of the European tradition. It will not be an exaggeration to say that colonial India, including its educational system, was virtually run by these westernized intellectuals, the progeny of English schools and universities.[14] On a more positive note, of course, the Indian intelligentsia, starting from the time of the early Anglicists like Rammohan Roy, became much more conscious of the need to understand Western thought and to explore common grounds for a progressive synthesis. Although Kipling had divined that the twain shall never meet, writers like Forster, Anand and others have presented the theme of East-West relationship boldly in order to open an intellectual dialogue between the two sides, if there are sides at all. While advocating Indian independence from Great Britain, Aurobindo, Gandhi, Nehru and others believed that there could be a harmonious marriage between Eastern ideas and Western scientific thought. Hence, it is from this colonial India that we can objectively trace the social and political structure of the Indian society and the emotional and intellectual character of the Western-educated type. Considered in this context, one wonders if Krishnan has been truly subjected to a process of psychosociological estrangement from family, society and country. If Krishnan had been overwhelmed by the superiority of Western thought, we could not raise any questions about his delusiveness but instead affirm his situation as authentic. If the English environment has been as powerful an influence on his disorientation as can possibly be attributed to one single factor, his condition bespeaks of the triumph of environment over individuality. We may also wonder if Krishnan, the fictional hero, bears any credible resemblance to a Gandhi, an Aurobindo or a Nehru or even to his own creator. Krishnan, we might be compelled to say, belongs to another category!

The British Empire, to use Thackeray's satiric characterization of it, has its foundations firmly rooted in three values; colonialism, mercantilism and evangelicalism. The fact remains that whether we take hatred and viciousness or paternalistic benevolence as a directional force in our relationship with others, the politics of the ruler-and-the-ruled and the image of the governed as Caliban, especially the one entertained by Macaulay and his supporters, had given a special status to the Indian who was educated in England and selected as a member of the Indian Civil Service. This distinct brand of Indian is the privileged, upper-class Indian upon whom history and chance have bestowed cultural and socioeconomic advantages totally inaccessible to an average Indian. Krishnan as a type does not represent a commoner, nor are his problems and predicaments representative of the realities of Indian life in general.[15] Nevertheless, it is not difficult to see how in a sustained historical process the configuration of the fable of Caliban has undergone a dramatic reversal. The special socioeconomic status, the superficial consciousness of dignity, the so-called intellectual superiority—they all contribute to his hubris. Ironically, the colonized, civilized Caliban becomes an arrogant, puffed-up snob. At places in the story, one suspects rather quite strongly that Rajan, through Vijayaraghavan's wit, is persistently parodying Krishnan in an attempt to make him see his own narcissistic-solipsistic picture. Krishnan is quick to recognize this psycho-pathological symptom when he tries to analyze Karna's paradoxical condition: in the analogy[16] thus developed Krishnan seems to suffer from the same hubris that he sees in Karna, one of the sons of Kunti in the *Mahabharata*. "If you want the moon," explains Krishnan, "you must be tamed to accept the earth" (131). Karna's imaginative protrusion of reality seems to have prevented him from making some sense of his life and from being able to belong to either of the two sides in the conflict. Krishnan further extends this analogy to Oedipus: "He [Karna] made his mistake the same way Oedipus did, and the retribution was greater than the flaw. It's the nature of tragedy and you [Cynthia] mustn't confuse it with justice" (131). But Krishnan soon discovers that he cannot separate tragedy from justice and explains that Karna's problem "is not that he didn't belong but that he insisted on belonging somewhere else" (132). Of course, that "somewhere else" explains the irony and paradox of the perplexing dilemma. Apparently, he does not consider the image of Karna, and by implication, of himself, complete without taking into account the other side, "the shiny side of the coin," which, as exemplified in the story of Nanda, is "the face of conscience and enlightenment" (131–132). According to the legend, a pariah was disallowed by the priests on the steps of the temple but by the strength of his incessant prayers he was able to make "the statue of Nandi, the great bull, [move] aside, so that he could see the dancing image of Shiva" (131). Cynthia regards these two sides of the coin as polarities, but actually these are "complementarities."[17] This design of providing "complementarities" defines the structural principle of the narrative, the direction of Krishnan's movement toward a higher synthesis in which the two conditions are held together.

Krishnan no doubt knows that both Karna and Nanda are complementary sides of the same self, but as yet his perception of reality is rational and analytical. Evidently, Krishnan's excessive rationalism is symptomatic of his egotism. In the Freudian sense, it would seem that his personality has several ego-clusters, each having a divergent point of reference rooted in his ego and superego. These divergences or conflicts not only keep Krishnan away from his roots, both the individual id and the collective id (more in the sense of Jung's racial memory), but also make him an overly self-defensive, excessive "brooder." This kind of conflict between his manifold "egos" or ego-clusters creates multiple personalities. Blake's image, it may be noted, for this neurotic, spectrous self without the other side of the coin, is the "Human Abstract." Both Krishnan and Cynthia, as we understand from the reflective analysis of their respective situations, are "half and halfers," "in-betweeners"; and they possess "the Hamlet mentality" of being unable to belong. Krishnan, whose ego defines the nature of his commitment to Kamala, can respond to the pleasure principle, and have an adulterous affair with Cynthia. On the other hand, Cynthia's ego—she calls herself a "half and halfer" (97) and an in-betweener—drives her to possess Krishnan totally and entirely. Love has no meaning for her, but commitment is what she wants and it is that which Krishnan is unable to make. They both are playing the field with their ego-projections and regressions. In a very intimidating and abrupt manner, Cynthia comes out with a Freudian cure for the neurosis of the Hamlet-like Krishnan: "You ought to write. . . . It's the solution for people who don't belong. All

writers are children who gaze at their dreams through brilliant plate-glass
windows and go home sadly, not daring to throw the stone" (161).

Cynthia's sarcastic retort alludes to the therapeutic value of art. Since
she views the Hamletian condition as an abnormality, an imbalance or disorder, one wonders if she fully understands the far-reaching implications
of her observation. It is directly related to Freud's conception of art as an
expression of neurosis.[18] An artist, according to Freud and Jung, discovers
the chaos and disorderly structure of his psyche by his works. "It is not
Goethe who creates *Faust*," maintains Jung, "but *Faust* which creates
Goethe."[19] Indeed, one could make a similar case about Dante and the *Divine Comedy*. The view that art has its origin in neurosis also implies that
what is created by an artist is a prototype of that which existed in the mind
but which had otherwise become inaccessible. The work of art is thus both
a medium and a reality. That a work of art could have given him a more
wholesome structure of his psyche has perhaps been known to Krishnan
all along as he debates about choosing writing as an alternative to the ex-
asperating and deadly boredom of a government job.

Krishnan's relationship with his parents and his uncle Kruger, his marriage to Kamala, his short-lived affair with Cynthia and his friendship with
Vijayaraghavan are a story of manners, morals and attitudes. In a true sense,
relationships are a means of figuring out the nature of man, not just the
outward man who is a product of certain social processes, but the inward
man, his psychic structure that responds to the illusion somewhat differently. Our perception of reality no doubt takes us closer to the manifest
form, but it may very well turn out to be an illusion. We create illusions—
and all relationships in this sense are illusions—and readily respond to these
with spontaneity, naturalness and exuberance. But when the illusion is
shattered, we are left bewildered by the cleavage it has created in our perception of reality. That Krishnan does not experience any "tide of emotion" in coming home and that he considers home a cave and the family
and marriage cages should remind us of a Kafka hero who cannot cope
with the expectations of an industrial and bourgeois civilization and has
consequently lost his individuality, sense of identity and faith in humanity.
Although this is not the direction and extent to which Krishnan goes, the
initial parallel is rather aptly drawn. Krishnan unwillingly and begrudg-
ingly accepts the yoke of tradition and authority, but at the same time he
reexamines analytically and critically with the sharp eyes of a rationalist
and empiricist all that he is made to accept. Krishnan's English education
has given him a method of perceiving reality, which is totally different
from that of his family and friends. Krishnan considers himself a progressive, modern and liberated intellectual and the rest of the Indian society a
follower of the Hanuman tradition. It is a conflict between two percep-

tions of reality, a conflict in which "Tarzan the ape man and Hanuman the monkey, servant of God and savior of Sita, would grapple together in the coexistence of cultures" (5). There is little doubt that Krishan's sensibility remains frozen either because of his excessive rationalism or because of the impending confrontation, the fear and unwholesomeness of the situation. On the contrary, the parents suspect that after the hard life he led in England their son needs to be rejuvenated, and apparently, the two most obvious rewards that they think will reanimate their son are a well-placed marriage and a prestigious government job. This section of the story, that reads like a chapter from Jane Austen, reveals those manners and attitudes that merely add to the emptiness, grossness and ugliness of life. "The great novelists," remarks Trilling, "knew that manners indicate the largest intentions of men's souls as well as the smallest and they are perpetually concerned to catch the meaning of every dim implicit hint."[20] Krishnan's mother reminds one of Mrs. Bennett of *Pride and Prejudice,* who is busy shopping, with calculated and cunning manipulations, for husbands for her daughters.[21] Marriage, as it seems, is a cleverly negotiated commercial enterprise in which the language of barter is money and status. Incidentally, the legal conception of marriage as a social contract is only a slight variation of this notion.

Fortunately or unfortunately, money has been one of the greatest symbols of social reality in history: in most cultures, moral and spiritual concerns have been replaced by a pantheon of materialistic gods. The center of reality is located in material objects, and these constitute monads of living reality in the world of Mammon. The very nomenclature of this reality is so differently colored that every aspect of human dream and aspiration is measured by one's identification with the reality of money. Krishnan's wife will be chosen from amongst those who have the capacity to give respectable dowry: that is, the indices of material acquisition will determine the value of a wife, perhaps, in accordance with the price theory in economics. Krishnan cannot go into teaching, the ancient calling of a Brahmin, because it will not be financially rewarding. Of course, without his father's wealth, Krishnan couldn't have possibly gone to England for his education. But what about status? Snobbery, as Thackeray seems to tell us in *The Book of Snobs,* is a vanity, a conceit, and results from a superficial feeling of self-consciousness, but not from action, or something tangible. Most certainly, the feeling is not genuine and authentic: in fact, it is merely another form of thwarted or repressed inferiority. Money and status are expressive of that grand illusion that is often mistaken for reality, and of that repelling and unholy world that measures human dignity by self-defeating and falsifying standards. Indeed, such are the hearts and minds of Krishnan's parents as will barter their only son's happiness for money and

status. Their expedient and compromising morality allows for the manipulation of laws to get Krishnan into government service, since nepotism,
favoritism and bribery speak the language of pragmatic compromise. The
whole society, it appears to Krishnan, is a wasteland, a dissipated mass of
hollow men whose conscience and creativity have been throttled by time.

The marriage to Kamala is the enactment of a ritual, not of love and
romance but of a humiliated submission to a choiceless situation. Helplessly sandwiched between the urge to rebel and the coercive expectation
to conform to the deterministic collective will, Krishnan is forced to put
on the masks of a Yeatsian dancer who will now participate in the dance
of life. All masks, it should be noted, are contrived and negotiated roles
that, lacking in creative energy of the soul, are basically insincere and flippant, especially when the point of reference is situated somewhere outside
the human context. It seems that the whole society is a body of dancers
and life one continuous dance of playing roles, establishing relationships
and creating identities. When Krishnan finally becomes a dancer rather
helplessly, he too starts making compromises. In examining his odds with
Kamala as a prospective wife, Krishnan thinks that "her body would serve
its purpose . . . [and that] she would lead him to the precipice of belonging, the point of no return and no escape" (19). Thus, Kamala is perceived
to be a "functional" wife whose physicality, womanliness, Indianness, socioeconomic status of her family, caste and education seem to satisfy the
utilitarian calculus of a social criteria for matrimony. Krishnan's assumption that Kamala will awaken in him the desire to love and to identify is
no doubt ironic, but it is the only safe rationalization that will give some
validity to the situation: in an arranged marriage love is supposed to start
in a moral context already established, in which *dharma* and karma act as
extensions of a pattern of unification and identity. The notion of his initial
relationship with Kamala, especially her functionality as a wife, is centered
on the female body: that the gratification of his sensual desire will awaken
him to a higher world is a pattern of the working of Eros. But the assumption that the gratification of the world of sense will lead to the world
of ideas is indeed suggestive of the pattern of Lockean epistemology. It is
a debatable point whether the union of two people in marriage needs to
be so carefully defined and predicated by a series of rational hypotheses,
but the fact remains that Krishnan and Cynthia view this type of marriage
as a pseudomarriage. If we consider that all relationships—father, mother,
son, husband and wife—are verbalizations of socioeconomic necessities
and functions, we cannot have any identity in the ideal sense. The Marxist
position, for example, defines identity purely in socioeconomic terms: concrete, temporal socioeconomic locations are provided to individuals, so
that they can freely respond to these symbols of socioeconomic reality. On

the other hand, one might argue that identity is a form that one gives to one's feelings for, and intellectual perception of, another: in this sense, love as a passionate desire to identify oneself in another who is distinct and unique defines a pattern of identity that we do not see in Krishnan's relationship with Kamala. We keep hearing the ironic expression that Kamala is a "Hindu wife," but we do not see any fire having been lit in their hearts.

In contrast, Krishnan does seem to have a passion for Cynthia Bainbridge, which would compel him to decide that he can no longer live with Kamala. Cynthia, who seems to have renewed her feelings for Krishnan, dramatically finds herself at the right place and time to remind Krishnan of his weakness of not being able to belong. She has read Krishnan correctly, and is quick to remind him firmly but coercively that he cannot have both Kamala and her. While she will not let Krishnan know her "two selves," she wants all of Krishnan as a precondition for an enduring relationship. Her fierce and strong-willed determination to "own" all of Krishnan smacks of jealously and possessiveness: she does not believe in any such thing as selfless love by which she will give herself totally and completely unto a true union of the two souls. Like Blake's Female Will, Cynthia plans to establish complete dominion over Krishnan. Ironically, she is unwilling to grant to Krishnan the same freedom and individuality that she must appropriate for herself. No wonder, Krishnan is suddenly awakened to the truth of the situation, and categorically tells Cynthia that he does not love her, since only "death can make that kind of claim" of total possession. One might argue that Cynthia's English background amidst nationalistic feelings and the seething turmoil of 1947 has contributed to the cleavage in her relationship with Krishnan. On the contrary, Krishnan, in moments of self-pity for his either/or predicament, thinks that deep underneath her skin Cynthia is Indian. And Cynthia has told Krishnan that her grandmother was Indian: in a sense, this may explain the literal meaning of "half and halfer," the expression she uses for herself. In any case, it is abundantly clear that Cynthia's failure to establish identity with Krishnan results from her subjugation of Krishnan to a set of conditions in which love remains "a four-letter word" and belonging a "high-class fib." In fact, the alternative provided by Cynthia is not any different from the one afforded by the authoritarian Indian social tradition: both designs will cripple Krishnan's freedom and individuality.

While Cynthia, protrusively acting out her will and sensuality, would divest Krishnan of his freedom of creativity, Kamala honestly recognizes his freedom to do what he thinks is right. Since Krishnan and Kamala have been brought together by the same set of circumstances in the Indian tradition, Krishnan cannot blame Kamala for their marriage. A scholar of Sanskrit, Kamala understands her position as a woman and as a wife in the

Indian religious tradition: Krishnan had known right from the very beginning that in accepting him "she would leave him nothing but himself, no mask, no pretense, no illusion" (19). But the problem is that Krishnan has not as yet tried to understand Kamala, her enviable purity and devotion, her infinite capacity to suffer and endure, her overwhelming sense of *dharma* and karma and her calm disposition. Kamala understands the metaphysical and spiritual contexts of marriage and indeed her sense of identity is not derived from gratuitous altruism and utilitarian perfunctoriness. Variously described as a "female Gandhi,"[22] a saint, a martyr, a Joan of Arc, she is killed by the society she is committed to serve. It is only after the break with Cynthia that Krishnan gets actively involved with history and Kamala. It must be noted that Kamala is forced to move to the highly inflammable situation in Shantihpur by Krishnan's behavior and that Krishnan would now encounter history and Kamala together. Apparently, the train journey to Shantihpur is an important image of Krishnan's speedy thrust into the body of history, of which Kamala is a symbol. The logic of the metaphor is fully sustained if we understand the inference: to discover Kamala, Krishnan must experience historical reality in which Kamala's own personality is submerged. The map of Krishnan's movements explains the pattern of his growth. There are three major phases in Krishnan's growth: the first phase in which Krishnan returns to Indian society and encounters a multiplicity of conflicts; the second phase where the nature and scope of his confrontation are extended to a wider canvas of history, the battlefield of Kurukshetra, in which he becomes directly involved; and the third phase in which Krishnan moves to a higher spiritual plane of imaginative awakening and synthesis. Of course, there is the earlier phase of his education in England, which is supposed to be a part of the first phase. Indeed, we are beginning to see a dramatic change in Krishnan's early delusions:

> Complementing her power of acceptance, he felt in himself a capacity for commitment, a compulsion to the irrevocable act, a will to burn bridges and create his island. In infinity what is belonging? Indus or Kistna? Creek of Cochin or the ice-blue waters of the Ganges tumbling through the northern gorges? Belonging is a body, a place, a problem, a responsibility; acquire them as you can, endure them as you must, and with the passion of your attachment change them. A man creates when he is unable to escape. When what one is is taken and thrust and hunted into a meaning. When a barrier is thrown across the flood of one's loneliness, controlling it to patience while the green acres grow. (19)

This ironic brooding belongs to the first phase, but now his image of Kamala is much different, one of optimism, dynamism and self-assuredness.

Undoubtedly, the relationship with Kamala, an authentic and creative identity with her, especially as it is intensely sought in the last two phases, constitutes the thematic center of the novel. Structurally, however, there are two main difficulties. The last two phases focus heavily on the theme of Kamala; and since her undeserved suffering and death define her tragedy, the novel, one might argue, is predominantly the tragedy of Kamala. Undoubtedly, Kamala is a martyred victim of the collusive forces of an estranged social order, phallocentrism and history. Her marriage to Krishnan turns out to be nothing more than a farce and she finally becomes a sacrificial lamb on the altar of history—the 1947 communal riots in Shantihpur (literally meaning the city of peace) in the Punjab. It is true that she is a staunch Gandhian moralist, but should she have been assigned a tragic life of improbable weight and magnitude? Does Kamala's tragedy approximate any of the classical models, or is it even consistent with the thematic center of the novel? Surely, it could also be argued that Krishnan's own tragic loss and suffering are much more intense; but then, Krishnan's loss must be determined in terms of the nature of the relationship that Krishnan is able to establish with Kamala. The irony of Krishnan's situation, especially when, soon after the final rites, his parents are talking about his second marriage, can hardly go unnoticed. The second difficulty comes from Rajan's preoccupation with the details of events pertaining to the partition of India.[23] I admire Rajan's objectivity and discriminating taste in having covered a wide range of sensitive and difficult material, although one may feel that there is a sort of bulkiness, a protuberance that needs to be carefully controlled. The question of the voluminous social and historical detail as an intrusive interference in the compactness and unity of the plot has been often raised in the case of Dickens and Thackeray in the English novel and also in the case of Tolstoy's *War and Peace*. After all, the novel as a genre is a commentary on society; it deals with man in relation to time, that is, history;[24] and it can justifiably define the time period of history and its content. But the question of setting limits of social and historical details pertains to the artist's sense of economy and austerity by which he can create an illusion and transform fact into fiction with such verisimilitude as will unquestionably sustain the illusion. In Rajan's case, the historicity of 1947 and 1948, with all the attendant detail and drama, including the background of the British colonial rule, is significant for understanding Kamala, the East-West confrontation, the structure of postcolonial consciousness and the problem of social evil.

The French Revolution is a major political phenomenon that engaged the attention of most English and French writers. The Russian Revolution has been a dominant theme in the works of Russian writers like Tolstoy. The importance of the American War of Independence as a literary phenomenon has never been minimized. For modern Indian writers, the British colonial rule in India, the partition of India in 1947 and the independence of India in 1948 have the same significance as most revolutions have for Europe. The emergence of a free nation and the recovery of the lost human dignity had been at the center of the dream and the sensibility of writers like Tagore, Ghose and Anand and the younger writers, including Rajan. Krishnan, Kamala, Kruger and Vijayaraghavan are a product of this period of Indian history and they share the sensibility of their creator. Furthermore, both Krishnan and Cynthia are a product of the British liberal tradition that fully shared the collective guilt of colonization. During his Cambridge days, Krishnan, like most Indians residing abroad, had been actively engaged in the struggle for Indian freedom. Cynthia, we are told, is anticolonial and a strong advocate of Indian freedom. A firm believer in Social Darwinism and in the Nietzschean idea of the eternal repetition, she, unlike Kamala, does not subscribe to the Gandhian philosophy of nonviolence. During her heated exchange with Krishnan, she concedes that the British rule in India was virtually a 300 year "occupation." Krishnan's view of the role of the British colonial regime is rather sharply pronounced: "For a whole generation you British have stirred up the trouble. It's you that made the religious divisions take priority over our common political interests. Communal electorates, communal representation in the civil service. Communal this and communal that. Even the cricket matches were communally organized" (159–60). Earlier, the speaker at the rally observes that "the British . . . had ruined India politically, economically, physically, psychologically, socially and morally" (35). Most Indians and English liberals shared this view, and surprisingly enough Cynthia is quick to reproach her country.

While the colonial era was coming to a close, the fulfillment of the dream of Independent India was threatened by the principle of partition that the Indian leaders were forced to accept as an ineluctable destiny. The British plan, according to this principle, proposed two successors. India did gain freedom, but it was not the unified India that became the successor. Freedom came along with the tragedy of partition, and this tragicomedy of politics has since then preoccupied politicians and thinkers with soul-searching.[25] It is somewhat surprising to note that Rajan has presented us with four different viewpoints on the perplexing subject of partition: significantly, these viewpoints are fairly representative of various political positions in the history of India's struggle for independence. Krishnan clearly and unequivocally holds the British responsible for the fragmentation of the dream. Cynthia unreservedly supports the cause of freedom but, subscribing to the official position of the British government, justifies the partition of the country along communal lines. Pratap Singh looks at the indistinguishableness of the situation from a different point of view: "The Hindus want independence. The Moslems want their theological state. We'll have to pay the price between the millstones" (89). But the most significant, rather hard-hitting case is made by Kamala:

> It isn't really in anything that your people did. You couldn't have brought it out if it wasn't in us. It's all in us, in the many, many years of occupation, submission to the State, obedience to the family, every inch of our lives completely calculated, every step, down to the relief of the grave. And if we wanted to protest, there was only the pitiless discipline of nonviolence. Then all of a sudden the garden belongs to us, and we reach up into the blossoming tree to pluck the ashes. (74–75)

It is not surprising that Vijayaraghavan shares this view: "Frightful rotters the British. Absolutely satanic. Don't know what we would do without them. Who are we going to blame after they leave?" (35) While Kamala and Vijayaraghavan hold Indians responsible for their decline in history and for having reduced fruit to "ashes," Krishnan blames historical forces. Kamala's analysis, it must be noted, is much too deep and subtle and it represents the moral and philosophical positions of many Indians, including Gandhi. What Kamala is essentially saying is that India's social and political degradation is traceable to the moral and spiritual deterioration of its people.

"Old Delhi," we are told in an acerbic observation on the philosophy of history, "was a city made for burning" (159). Evidently, the story of Old Delhi is an allegorical extension of the story of Kurukshetra, echoing the unsavory and rapacious rage of time and the periodic tandav dance of Shiva. Old Delhi, once the seat of the Mogul Empire, is a representation of the glory of one empire, but later it was conquered by another empire and replaced by the modernist monument known as New Delhi. Conrad in the beginning of *Heart of Darkness* refers to such an ironic displacement in history and especially to the difference between conquest and colonization. But the year 1947, with a crowded and unwieldy concentration of some of the most difficult and embarrassing events of history, marks another type of displacement in the evolution of a new society: the transfer of political power is accompanied not only by the division of country but also by an unusually gross outburst of racial and communal psychosis. It must be remembered that Rajan has devoted two complete chapters to the subject of communal riots and that Kamala finally becomes a sacrificial victim of the psychosis of collectivity. In the discourse on British colonial governance it still remains a matter of intellectual debate whether communalism and the nurturing of local and regional identities were deemed to be the direct consequence of the divide-and-rule policy of the colonial regime. The protrusive history of communal and racial strife in India and elsewhere in the world shows that it stands in utter defiance of the moral postulates of a civil society; and yet, ironically, it is evident that political and social structures have benefited from communal and social disturbances that otherwise stand to be condemned morally and socially. If communalism and the creation of local and regional identities unwittingly aided nationalist interests, then it was certainly, as Ray points out, an error of judgment on the part of the British administration, an error that probably cost the British the empire.[26] Indeed, in theorizing a civil society we must distinguish true religion from communalism and fanaticism, remembering at the same time that religion as a humanist discourse has been instrumental in shaping the social and political vision of the world's greatest thinkers, philosophers and poets.[27]

Krishnan sees the partition of India as the reenactment in history of the senseless Kurukshetra fratricide in which the blood of thousands of innocent people was spilt for a cause that did not have any moral justification. The racial riots between the Hindus and the Moslems—violence, rape, massacre, looting and destruction—were an expression of human depravity and ugliness in their most perverse form. Racial and religious fanaticism simply fanned the uncontrollable fire of hatred and revenge that subsumed all human reason: it was a naked dance of bestiality in man. The whole nation was driven into a state of insecurity, instability and chaos. Krishnan witnesses this sad debacle of degradation and wonders about the character and content of human civilization. Was it morally justifiable to pay such a heavy price for freedom? Between nationalism and racism, which of the two must take precedence? Between the pride of being an Indian and the pride of being a Hindu, a Moslem, a Christian, or a Jew, what must be the directional force? Should racism, nationalism, patriotism, religion and any other "ism" or label hinder the expression of man's humanity to man? Can modern man conquer his bigotry, prejudice, anger, hatred and other forms of psychosis? These are some of the fundamental issues that have confronted India and other pluralistic societies that keep continually searching for patterns of coexistence and synthesis.

Kamala's answers to all these questions lie in the moral and spiritual discipline of nonviolence, the most fundamental doctrine of Gandhian philosophy. Krishnan's understanding of the history and philosophy of nonviolence, with which he has been grappling from the very beginning, brings him much closer to Kamala: this movement marks the third phase of Krishnan's self-realization. Indeed, Kamala understands the meaning of nonviolence as well as its logic and morality. Nonviolence, as Krishnan seems to gather from Kamala's sense of sympathetic identity with Gand-

hian ideology, is "not simply a technique but an invoking of qualities instinctive in her nature." However, when Cynthia cleverly differentiates between nonviolence and pacifism, maintaining that "nonviolence takes
resignation and transmutes into resistance," Krishnan dubs it as a pedantic
"juggling with abstractions." "Nonviolence," we are told by the speaker at
a meeting, "is a force and not an attitude" and noncooperation is "the statement of freedom despite subjugation, the moral challenge like a lens focusing injustice" (37). Gandhi's war against British colonialism was
essentially a moral war: it was a war not against England but against the
mentality of enslavement, dehumanization, repression and injustice. For a
better understanding of Kamala's position and of Gandhi's philosophy of
nonviolence, I am tempted to refer to Mulk Raj Anand's lucid exposition:

> In Gandhi's ethics, dissociation with hatred and evil means the dissolution
> of the brute in man. He felt that, by eschewing revenge, one can change the
> heart of the opponent. Non-violence thus becomes a positive force. The
> means of non-violence was conceived as non-cooperation. This was not to
> be interpreted as a coercion of the oppressor. It is a kind of suffering on the
> part of the passive resister. To be sure, this resistance involves suffering for the
> person who undertakes it. But the sacrifice for the common good is a kind
> of expiation. *Swaraj*, or freedom, attained through non-violent non-cooper-
> ation, was to be more than political freedom. *Swaraj* was conceived by
> Gandhi as a state of becoming, in which people would learn, through the
> practice of non-violence, to live in harmony with other people.[28]

If we understand the genesis of Gandhi's complex philosophy of nonviolence, we find that it is somewhat closer to Christ's teachings and to Shelley's thought as contained in *Prometheus Unbound*, although it is derived
from the *Bhagavadgita*. Once man builds strong moral will and is prepared
to say with Prometheus, "I wish no living thing to suffer pain,"[29] the repressive tyranny and vicious omnipotence of Jupiter will cease. In the history of civilization, man has been continuously searching for a philosophy
of peaceful change, knowing fully well that most theories of change sanction the use of force as well as the total destruction of the stubborn structure, if that is what it would take to affect the desired change. In fact, we
know well that most revolutions in history, such as the French Revolution
and the Russian Revolution, were violent and bloody events. In a different context, however, World War I and World War II and all other national
and international conflicts in modern history have not shown any restraint
in the savage use of force. Following the events of the 1857 mutiny in India
and the upsurge of a strong national consciousness as well as the confrontation in Africa, Gandhi had no difficulty in foreseeing the possibility
of the Indian discontent developing into a violent rebellion. In fact,

Gandhi had vehemently and uncompromisingly opposed the idea of a violent revolt in India. Krishnan still remembers the tragedy of Jallianwalla and at times, in spite of his being an avowed pacifist, he has participated in violence. It has taken a long time for Krishnan to learn from Kamala that suffering makes one not bent and broken, but stronger and wiser, both morally and spiritually, and that self-purification by a process of continuous self-annihilation—extinction of the non-self or ego in the Buddhist sense—will expand one's moral consciousness. This is the moral of the fable of Oedipus that Cynthia could not understand but that Kamala has understood all along.

The central symbol in the novel, as mentioned earlier, is the Nataraja. There are repeated references in the narrative to the symbolic myth of Shiva, the cosmic dancer who holds in unison creation and destruction and good and evil. This mythic perception of unity in diversity and multeity is characteristic of the Indian mind in much the same manner as the Faust myth is characteristic of the German mind. Earlier in the story, Krishnan hears the myth of the Dancer sung at his wedding feast:

> She sang of Shiva dancing in the great temple of Chidambaram, the timeless dance in which each gesture is eternity with every movement of that mighty form expressing and exhausting the history of a universe. "You who danced with your limbs held high, the moon in your forehead and the river Ganga in your matted locks, lift me great Shiva as your limbs are lifted." In the beginning was rhythm, not the word. Not darkness, but moonlight and the radiance of creation. There had never been nothing without form and void but always form in its essence, everlastingly changing. He heard, half heard, the drums and the *tamboura* accompanying the voice—throbbing, civilized, sophisticated frenzy. He saw the great figure of the Nataraja, one leg arched in that supreme expression of energy, the dying smile of the demon beneath the other's lightness, all that infinite power of destruction drawn back into the bronze circle of repose . . . Creation, Destruction. Two concepts but one dance, the trampling leg, the outthrust arms asserting the law invincibly, ecstatically, the drums beating, the strings plucked in supplicating monotony, raise me, raise me into the mystery's center; for something to be born something must die. (27–28)

These lines are punctuated by a quotation from Eliot's *Burnt Norton:* "*neither flesh nor fleshless / Neither from nor toward, at the still point there the dance is*" (28). Krishnan is wondering rather skeptically about the metaphysics of the unifying principle and its relevance to the problems of time and existence. Later, when he joins Kamala in Shantihpur, he sees in the anteroom the bronze image that Kamala has carried with her. This time Krishnan's mind experiences the image aesthetically as a work of art:

But the god itself was still, as if the quintessence of motion were repose, as if only the reflections moved and maimed, and as if, beyond them, shaping them, discarding them, one could reach the source of change and its serenity. The mind went over the exultant, lusting body and was tranquil, as if ambiguously blessed, as if no matter how deep the emptiness or obsessive the violence, the infinite arms reached out, the great foot trampled, the desperations came back to a meaning, which conferred truth because it was beyond desire. It was not the catharsis of art—there was no purgation, no refinement, no transmutation of the strength of darkness. It was as if one were raised into the mystery's center, into the transformation of the god's eye, as if the destruction shimmering on the leaping muscles, sucking down the thin wail of the dying man, was not a barbarism to be subdued, a violence to be disciplined, but a jubilation that absorbed the flesh, the rivers and the peaks of comprehension being but one hair of the unanswered stillness. (225)

I believe that for a better understanding of the symbol of Nataraja the two interpretations, philosophical and aesthetic, should be read together.[30] One can recall Keats's response to the Grecian Urn, Shelley's response to da Vinci's Medusa's head and Botticelli's Venus and of course Byron's response to the Apollo Belvedere.[31] In Rajan's own response to the molten image, the focus remains on the paradox of the mystery of the still center: while the stillness of the image merely refers to physical reality as defined by temporal time, motion, spontaneity, balance, symmetry, rhythm and harmony are mentally perceived. But in another sense the still center refers to the very source of consciousness, the point of intersection of time and eternity. The iconography and the statuesque, rather sculpturesque, form of the molten image convey not only harmonious transmutation of power, the spontaneity, symmetry and balance in its visual expressiveness but also the ontological unity of Becoming and Being and the ecstasy in the inexplicableness of order. The presiding idea of the image, including the meaning of the dance, is recreated in the song; the singer communicates the rhythmic structure of the dance and the otherwise incommunicable ecstasy. Paradoxically, "the pure circle of form" is the all-inclusive circle, exhibiting various aspects of Shiva—Kāla as time, Agni as consecrator and Vishnu as restorer and preserver. At the cosmic level, "the pure circle" as the circle of destiny contains the cesspool of history and yet it portrays a state of serenity and a condition of truth that are beyond desire—and hence beyond the "catharsis of art." The "ekphrastic"[32] image of "the pure circle" directs not only the movement of the text but also the reader's response to issues of intertexuality and contextuality. Can a myth articulate in a single cosmogonal image such diverse and radical questions of philosophy, theology, psychology and history as are boldly postulated in *The Dark*

Dancer? What is the nature of "the intuitive experience" of a poet who initially conceived such an anagogic symbol of the unity of consciousness, the
kind of unity contemplated by Schelling and Coleridge?[33] Is the circular-
ity of "the pure form" supposed to represent a pattern of evolutionary
growth and cosmic integration, somewhat like the Romantic metaphor of
history as "circuitous journey"? Does it combine the Nietzschean conception of the Dionysian and the Apollonian principles? Is the very contemplation of the image of the Nataraja some sort of anamnesis, a
"progressive return" through time or memory to the "origin"[34] of consciousness, "mystery's center"? Can a sense of indeterminate incongruity
between appearance and reality be overcome? The center of pure consciousness is not the zero hour of chronometric time but the center of
original harmony, for in the beginning was rhythm. Is this reversal or passage of time a form of anamnesis, a complete annihilation of ego, the extinction of the non-self, or the recovery of innocence?

Creation and destruction are two aspects of the same power, the two
world cycles combined in one dance. Shiva's dance is, therefore, both the
dance of creation and the dance of dissolution. In the dance of dissolution,
the Nataraja as destroyer releases man's spirit from its bondage, the fetters
of illusion. No wonder, Kamala in reply to Krishnan's observation remarks
with intuitive spontaneity: "Nothing ever dies. It says so in the *Gita*" (29).
It is not until we reach the eschatological section of the novel that Krishnan during the discussion on the metaphysics of death accepts Kamala's interpretation. He tells Cynthia that he has not lost anything and that Kamala
did not die for any cause, social or moral. In the cycle of creation, Shiva
brings inert matter to life, while in the cycle of destruction the soul is freed
from karmic illusion. As Coomaraswamy sums up his interpretation of
Shiva's dance:

> *The Essential Significance of Shiva's Dance is threefold: First, it is the image of his
> Rhythmic Play as the Source of all Movement within the Cosmos, which is Repre-
> sented by the Arch: Secondly, the Purpose of his Dance is to Release the countless
> souls of men from the Snare of Illusion: Thirdly the Place of the Dance, Chi-
> dambaram, the Centre of the Universe, is within the Heart.*[35]

It is important to note that Chidambaram, the place of dance, is the inside
of man. Krishnan has often expressed his anxiety to see the ecstatic dance
of Shiva and has wondered all along about its meaning that he now finds
in Kamala's death. Marriage as the symbolic union, the creative act, belongs
to the cycle of creation, while death, the deliverer, belongs to the cycle of
dissolution. Thus, birth, marriage and death are combined in one art form,
the dance. He further realizes that the portion of history that has taken a

heavy toll of life characterizes the cycle of destruction that will soon yield to a restorative phase of creation. Shiva, as Kramrisch explains, has two fundamental integrative aspects: "Śiva, the Lord of Yoga, dwells in timeless eternity, while Śiva, the dancer, performs his aeviternal dance at the end of each aeon across which Kāla speeds."[36] Thus Time as Kāla "the antagonist and alter ego of Śiva"[37]; in the phase of dissolution it must also simultaneously act as an agent of restorative change. It should be noted that Agni to whom the invocation is made at the final rites is also an aspect of Shiva. Coomaraswamy explains that Shiva the destroyer dissolves not only the cosmic illusion at the end of a cycle of history but also the intricate web of individual egos. However, the paradox is that Shiva the destroyer is actually the deliverer of freedom from bondage: this is the symbolic significance of "the pure circle of form."

Kamala's understanding of the meaning of the symbol has freed her from the bondage of fear, desire and attachment. Krishnan now sees the relevance of these verses from the *Bhagavadgita:*

> *He who seeks freedom*
> *Thrusts fear aside,*
> *Thrusts aside anger*
> *And puts off desire:*
> *Truly that man*
> *Is made free forever. (308)*

Speaking of Conrad's ambivalence and elusiveness in defining philosophical and aesthetic positions, Forster says: "What is so elusive about him that he is always promising to make some general philosophic statement about the universe, and then refraining with a gruff disclaimer."[38] Surely, we have no such feeling about Rajan's position as a novelist. In an open confrontation with Vijayaraghavan about Kamala's death, Krishnan, overwhelmed by his sagacious recognition, reminds him somewhat confidently that his life with Kamala did not give him just happiness but also "a sense of order" that "hasn't gone entirely with the ashes" (306). The clarity of his understanding of the symbology of the Dancer and the Dance and the range of his own self-realization are reflected in his firm convictions which are indeed supported by his references to the *Gita:* Kamala "didn't die for anything," not even to protect a Moslem prostitute, but she died in the call of duty—"to do what was right" (307). Clearly, her sense of duty is not the efficacious acquiescence to social or moral law but the call of her conscience, her inner self. Identity for Krishnan becomes a matter of individual consciousness, far surpassing the Hegelian view of consciousness and the Marxian view of identity. The moral imperative of duty, freed from attachment and fear, is only a transliteration of his own consciousness. This awakening in Krishnan, which cannot be comprehended by Vijayaraghavan's witticism and Kruger's fanaticism, enables him to see clearly the relationship between the myth of creation and dissolution and the paradoxical postulate of the *Gita,* averring that "nothing dies." Krishnan understands that conquering fear, anger and desire, the three elements that define the abrasive world of karma, of desire and attachment, is a precondition for an authentic search for truth and freedom. Is the freedom so hypothesized— in fact, guaranteed to the seeker—the freedom from the world of desire? Will the cessation of desire also mean cessation of all action? The paradox is that this higher level of consciousness is the precipitous condition in which the mind becomes infinitely and uninhibitedly free to seek truth. By so doing Krishnan contemplates upon the unity of the self that only he himself can achieve. Can Krishnan now face reality and say with Arjuna that that is what Krishna meant?

Chapter 8

Myth and Imagery in Nissim Ezekiel's *The Unfinished Man:* A Critical Reading

Although *The Unfinished Man* marks a positive advance over the early poems in terms of quality of perception and poetic image,[1] this volume essentially exhibits Ezekiel's continued and keen concern with life, especially the image of man. This concern with existence, which springs from ethical anxiety and commitment and which is based on a conception of correspondence between life and art, takes the form of an ironic myth in which the central images are those of his hero, the city and the woman. As man strives to exist in a modern urban society, to search for truth and to realize identity with the self and the community, his struggles, failures and frustrations reveal not only his own inward nature, but also the insufficiency and frailty of the fallen city, an image of which appears in both Eliot and Auden. Deeply rooted in Ezekiel's ironic perception of existence and the polis, the mythic concern, however, centers on the image of man, which, as the title of the work as well as the epigraph from Yeats suggest, remains unfinished. The evolutionary view of human nature, which in one sense is Romantic, and even Darwinian and Freudian, and in another existential and classical, allows Ezekiel to view life and art as a continuous journey of the self. But the metaphor of the journey is ironic, though very apt, in the context of Ezekiel's myth.[2] The problem raised here directly pertains to the dimensions of the myth and the reality that it encompasses.

The imaginative cosmos of the Romantics presupposes the capacity of the mind to experience infinitude and consists of both the worlds of experience and reality. It is a world in which the heroic spirit of man projects his totality of being, thereby achieving fulfillment, self-realization and identity. Although the world of experience, the fallen world, stands in an ironic contrast to the ideal world, the two worlds together offer a full and comprehensive canvas, both in terms of form and content, to represent life and reality. Much of the modern poetry, on the contrary, subscribes to the view that the nature of man is finite and that its principal concern is the world of experience, the image of life as it is, the fallen world like that of Eliot's *The Waste Land,* or the usurious world of Pound's *The Cantos.* However, there is a significant thread of continuity running through the two sensibilities, especially in reordering and restructuring literature as a total order of experience: as the Romantic myth of freedom, equality, wholeness and happiness is a radical reconstruction of imaginative experience in which the entire hierarchy of symbols is displaced, so is the modern myth in its representation of life. The continued displacement of myth is evidence not only of the shifts in sensibility but also of the ability of art to validate and to absorb fully the historical view of life and reality. Since the modern myth like the Romantic myth is man-centered, the image of the man as hero is neither a Titan nor a Don Quixote. Thus we can attribute this picture to the modern psyche crushed and disintegrated by the pressures of the city which the hero is expected to build despite his inevitable pathetic destiny. That he, like Ezekiel's unfinished man, is a weakling and perishable creature who is easily defrauded by the tyranny of the city or by his own incapacity, is in tune with the facts of modern existence. Ideally, men strive to build a community of beings, but the city actually turns out to be a fallen city with all the symptoms of a mass culture that devours its own creators. The central power that lends order to life and the city is love, but the city is lifeless, indifferent and inhuman. As a kind and affectionate mother, nature is in harmony with man and helps to recreate his vision, but nature is neither nourishing the city nor is it preeminently hostile to it. In a sense, the modern myth is antiheroic, and this quality of the myth is in keeping with the mythos of irony and the character of the modern man.[3] However, Ezekiel's feet are in several traditions: on the one hand, *The Unfinished Man* shows in general sense a close affinity with the postwar poetry and the psychological and social determinism of the twentieth century; but on the other hand, one discerns in it a hidden and powerful yearning of the spirit, somewhat like the Romantic nostalgia, for the lost home that is the vision of the world before the fall.

This conceptual frame of reference is intended to suggest not a priori, but only such critical attitudes as will help us in understanding the nature of the myth, the structure of imagery and Ezekiel's vision in *The Unfinished*

Man. Although Ezekiel has grown mostly under the influence of the British modernist poetic, it would not be logical to ignore the impact of postmodernism, poststructuralism and postcoloniality. The world of the modernist poet is the environment of post–World War I, the era of moral and psychological fragmentation and of distrust, fear, horror and anxiety, but the postmodernist aesthetic has already absorbed the modernist history without of course any guarantees of an apocalypse. It is only logical to assume that these various shifts in the structure of civilizational landscape are largely responsible for a change in poetic sensibility. The large urban centers—Bombay, Calcutta, Madras and Delhi—of the erstwhile rural constituency of the British Empire have since then been impacted by postcolonial developments. Is Bombay, a nerve center of the imperial colony, the same as London, the polis? Once the psychoanthropological and sociohistorical contexts of a changing mythology are clearly understood, we can then respond to a structure of the verbal universe. Indeed, we know the nature of the unfinished man, but will contemporary civilization or any future structure of civilization ever be able to produce at least a poetic model of the finished man?

II

Almost all the poems in *The Unfinished Man* are epistemological in character; they are mental excursions into some specific aspect or problem of existence. The failure, frustration and self-doubt resulting from such an experience are a part of the larger irony in which discovery as self-knowledge reveals not only startling paradoxes and incongruities of life but also all its ugliness and absurdity. By this cognitive process, the mind tries to grasp the experiential reality and the ontology of existence. Thus, the perceptual process dramatized as a sort of case history—and most poems in *The Unfinished Man* are case histories[4]—is essentially introspective and psychic.

In "Urban," the persona, like most figures in other poems, represents the modern incapacitated human will that is alienated from nature and the true self and is trapped in an urban wasteland of illusion. The "hills" of vision, unity and perfection are *always* beyond his reach. The river of life has gone dry and the winds of creative energy are also dead. He is unable to apprehend the skies at dawn or "the shadows of the night"—dawn and night symbolizing the principles of light and darkness. Nor does he respond to sun and rain, the generative symbols of light and life in the cosmos. Hence, his landscape with "no depth or height" is a flattened landscape of emptiness and nothingness. And even when he "dreams of morning walks, alone, / . . . floating on a wave of sand," he quickly lapses into the "kindred clamour" of the city. But while the complex of symbols in the poem does delineate the fallen world, it strongly suggests, ironically and paradoxically, not only the ideal state from which man fell but also a structure of validity of these symbols. In the ideal sense, such images as hills, river, sun, rain, beach, tree and stone are archetypal life-symbols of man's ideal dream of the city or the Garden of Eden.[5] They project a pastoral vision of a fully refulgent and harmonious life, a pattern in which man enters into sacred communion with his cosmos, including objects of nature, as a metaphorical condition of his integrated humanity and of his desire to foster a community of beings. The stone is neither a dead object nor a meaningless idol, but a living embodiment of a communal temple, an archetypal symbol of a community of worshippers; and it has its affinity with the "hills." The river, an ancient symbol with manifold allusions, is a representation of flowing and creative life as well as communal consciousness; and "beaches" by implication suggest a point of contact with the holy and pure waters of life. The tree, an archetype of the imagination, too, is a symbol of communal sanctity, harmony and growth. Cumulatively, these images suggest a spousal relationship with nature and with what man loves and creates—his city, his cosmos. But such a context, as Ezekiel seems to imply, apparently does not have any relevance to the modern man, because his city lacks the kind of relationship, commitment and identity that are necessary to build a community.

In raising the issue of the lack of commitment and identity in "Urban" and other poems, Ezekiel seems to be ironically reflecting on man's fallen perception as well as the role of the city in conditioning such a perception. The persona cannot respond to the life-symbols, because he "knows [only] the broken roads" and moves in ritualistic "circles" of custom and dead habit deeply "tracked within his head." Instead of apprehending man's individuality and freedom, the city with its mass culture and repressive social code has subdued and conditioned his perception. Since his will or imagination is fragmented and confined to the world of ego, his responses and identifications are superficial and stereotyped, and even schizophrenic. For example, in the line, "The river which he claims he loves," the nature of love is simply ironic, lacking sincerity, integrity and commitment, especially since the river is actually dry. But while the city contributes to the weakening of the individual will, man himself is primarily responsible for this disintegration. It is because of his inability to enter into absolute relationships with the object-world that various symbols cease to become true life-symbols for him. A symbolic suggestion of this weakness occurs in the last stanza of the poem, although the image is ironic and ambiguous. The city that "like a passion burns" is the image of the bride, and in the ideal sense a complete sexual union would mark the realization of fullness and identity. But the persona dreams *alone,* and thus shies away from her: the sexual impotence of the persona significantly illustrates the impotence of his will, and his general mental structure shaped by fear and constraint. Yet, if the image of the city is taken to mean the sensual and illusive bride and the persona's evasive attitude as an expression of his moral restraint, the so-called cautiousness simply adds to the ambiguity of the image, especially when we find that the persona finally loses himself to the "kindred clamour" of city—here the key word is "kindred"—without any effectively realized union. The key to the paradoxical ambiguity is that the persona embraces illusion neither as an act of self-discovery nor as a forward thrust of the imagination, but as a habitual response. We may most certainly assume that a true unity with the world of phenomena will have dissolved, transmuted and absorbed that illusion.[6]

The image of the world of illusion to which Ezekiel repeatedly and fondly returns in his poetry is rather ambivalent: in one sense, the sympathetic portrayal of the persona, and especially the pilgrimage and its object, suggest Ezekiel's close affinity with the fallen polis, but in another sense the sardonic irony and satire reveal his strong criticism of the inhuman and mechanical environments that continue to cripple our existence. Thus, after the illusory and fretful pilgrimage in "Enterprise," the pilgrims find that "Home is where we have to gather grace." "Home" is used here only metaphorically as another image of the city, and although it is supposed to be a place for the mind to achieve a delicate balance and harmony, the image as such still refers to another plane of illusion in the stages of a mental journey. The painful discovery that the purpose and goal of the pilgrimage remain unknown is as ironic as the inference that "Home is where we have to gather grace." A somewhat similar conception of the city occurs in "A Morning Walk" where the persona wonders in his "old, recurring dream" about the condition of his cosmos:

> Why had it [the sun] given him no light,
> His native place he could not shun,
> *The marsh where things are what they seem?* ("A Morning Walk";
> emphasis added)

The metaphor of the marsh, with its associations with wetness, softness, lowliness and swampiness, suggests the dark, unformed and, hence, demonic state of nature that, generally speaking, conceals or devours the regenerative and redemptive principle. The marshy world without the creative and sustaining light, the logos, therefore, signifies the subhuman level of individual and communal existence, a condition in which man's vision and humanity are lost. With this fragmentation or perversion of vision, man perceives the object-world not as a manifestation of reality but as reality itself.

The image of the marshy world, of course, directly refers to the historical view of reality. In contrast to the ideal city of vision, the city of history is a dehumanized and infernal abode—"cold and dim / where only human hands sell cheap":

> Barbaric city sick with slums,
> Deprived of seasons, blessed with rains,
> Its hawkers, beggars, iron-lunged,
> Processions led by frantic drums,
> A million purgatorial lanes,
> And child-like masses, many-tongued,
> Whose wages are in words and crumbs. ("A Morning Walk")

The "Barbaric city," which sternly reminds one of Blake's "London,"[7] is devoid of any communal consciousness; the cacophonous chorus of haunting poverty defines the character of its mass culture. It is a city without hope and grace. Does Ezekiel's drastic condemnation of the culture of barbarism presuppose the coexistence of pain and pleasure or is it a precise and direct statement of social reality, echoed somewhat more loudly later on in the poem "In India"? Although the sun does not give the persona any light and the prophetic "morning breeze / Release[s] no secrets to his ears," the imagery strongly suggests the possible cause of dehumanization of man and his city—why things are what they seem. But while the essential concern of the persona directly centers on the fragmentation of his vision, this concern, as becomes further evident from the concluding stanza of the poem, especially raises the issue of the relationship between individual consciousness and communal consciousness:

> The garden on the hill is cool,
> Its hedges cut to look like birds
> Or mythic beasts are still asleep.
> His past is like a muddy pool
> From which he cannot hope for words.
> The city wakes, where fame is cheap,
> And he belongs, an active fool. ("A Morning Walk")

All the major symbols connected with the mythic garden on the hill—the sun, the morning breeze, the trees and the mythic beasts—have lost their original significance. What was once an integral myth and vision of man's perfect home—and the allusion here is to the Garden of Eden—is now merely a meaningless and unauthentic topography. Ironically, the paradisal garden on the hill is cool, illusory and asleep, but the "Barbaric city" of history, with its fallen humanity, is fully awake. Yet, paradoxically, it is the latter to which the persona belongs as a willing participant, "an active fool."

The ironic lament of the persona about his inability to relate himself to the archetypal world of vision no doubt portrays a familiar problem in art, but the nature of alienation should perhaps remind us of the view that as civilization progresses, man loses his innocence and humanity. Of course, such a conception of progress is obviously ironic and paradoxical, for progress in this sense simply means diversion of social energy into a superficially deterministic culture, the two polarities of which are the ostentatious barbarians and the vulgar crowd.[8] Generally speaking, the crowd or mass culture, the lowest form of social environment, is utterly indifferent, and even hostile, to individual growth and freedom. Even a society, though a slightly more organized form of environment, is mechanically structured on the principles of coercion, necessity, limited choice and constricted reason. But the true and ideal progress means the development of a community of mankind, a self-sustaining and organic order, which is based on freedom, love and the universal order of nature.[9] In the first two categories of crowd and society— Ezekiel's "Barbaric city" embodies both these—cultural progress is nothing but an organized form of anarchy where the human will degenerates and finally succumbs to the collective will as a matter of social and psychological necessity. But in a community, the individual consciousness and art flourish by participating in the communal consciousness. Thus, we can understand that the persona can recuperate his vision of unity and the fallen city can be redeemed only when the city approximates to the condition of a community and when both art and community, being analogous forms of creation, strive toward a mutually inclusive goal of grace, identity and order. Ezekiel's subtle irony pointedly focuses on the development of the individual consciousness as a necessary prerequisite for salvaging the mass culture of the city, so that all action is prompted by what is morally and spiritually possible, and not by what is naturally expedient.

III

The struggle of the artist, as we have seen, centers on the recovery of his vision, the poetic logos; the psychological process of recovery appears in two main metaphorical forms, pilgrimage to the center of life or vision and the meditation or prayer for the poetic images and the total word. In "Enterprise," a collective enterprise, apparently having an ambitious goal, goes through several phases and ends with a skeptic note:

> When, finally, we reached the place,
> We hardly knew why we were there.
> The trip had darkened every face,
> Our deeds were neither great nor rare.
> Home is where we have to gather grace. ("Enterprise")

The pilgrimage from city to nature has a good start, but with the exception of the second stage where the only notable but ironic achievement is the gathering of "copious notes," all other stages prove to be frustrating. The pilgrims find it difficult to cross a desert patch; they are "twice attacked" and are lost; some members of the group desert; and they virtually see "nothing" as they go on. In fact, all these and other experiences show no real and substantial progression in the pilgrimage. And by the time we reach the last stanza we find that the "The trip had darkened every face" and that the destination reached betrays all expectations. Actually, the extent of frustration, weariness, and dejection prevent us from considering any real anabasis.[10] We cannot even say that the projected illusion has been shattered in the end—the last line of the poem ironically points to another illusory hope. However, the paradox is that the pilgrimage, as the imagery suggests, is to the realm of nature; and it seems that this realm of the alienated pilgrims is as hostile and unappealing as perhaps is the city from which they try to escape. Although they finally consider home as a place for realizing grace, true grace lies in the identity of the self with the object-world.

The same skeptical view of pilgrimage appears in "A Morning Walk" where the persona in a sort of anxiety-dream is "lost / Upon a hill [which is] too high for him." As discussed in section II, he can identify himself not with the world of myth and vision but with the barbaric city, and Ezekiel's emphasis is on the nature of the human will or imagination:

> Returning to his dream, he knew
> That everything would be the same.
> Constricting as his formal dress
> The pain of his fragmented view.
> Too late and small his insights came,
> And now his memories oppress,
> His will is like the morning dew. ("A Morning Walk")

The morning walk is supposed to be a metaphorical journey or an awakening unto the world of unity, but what the persona painfully discovers is the ironic difference between the historical world and nature as well as his own inability to perceive these two worlds as a unity. The strong imagination will associate itself with a higher world, but the weak imagination, which is "like the morning dew," is incapable of making such a forward thrust. His insights come "Too late and small," and "His past is like a muddy pool / From which he cannot hope for words." The past as the "muddy pool" is the world of history that cannot reveal truth and the structure of language to him. This fierce indictment of history merely reinforces the notion of the barbarism of human civilization. Considered from a psychological point of view, the past as the "muddy pool" signifies the world of id from which truth of consciousness and the structure of language possibly cannot be retrieved.

But, as is evident from "Morning Prayer," there is a loftier and more ambitious goal behind these pilgrimages. "Morning Prayer" expresses a sincere and legitimate concern of the artist for perfection of his vision and art:

> God grant me privacy,
> Secretive as the mole,
> Inaccessibility,[11]
> But only of the soul.
>
> Restore my waking time
> To vital present tense,
> And dreams of lover or crime
> To primal quiescence.
>
> God grant me certainty
> In kinships with the sky,
> Air, earth, fire, sea—
> And the fresh inward eye.
>
> Whatever the enigma,
> The passion of the blood,
> Grant me the metaphor
> To make it human good. ("A Morning Prayer")

This time, there is no skeptical irony, frustration or doubt resulting from the collapse of vision; instead we have a frank, positive and definitive statement of the artist's personal faith in his art, and of his sincerity, integrity and commitment. Does Ezekiel's "Morning Prayer" remind us of Yeats's Prayer-poems, especially in terms of the intense and authentic desire to seek fulfilment?[12] The poet prays for the unity of perception and the vital power of making poetry. He seeks privacy and inaccessibility of the soul, because the world of imagination and art demands a personal and subjective realization of the self. He asks for the restoration of his "waking time / To vital present tense," because it is only by existing in *the moment, the now,* that the imagination experiences eternity and identity. He aspires to the condition of "primal quiescence," because the imagination can reconcile the so-called dualism between good and evil and experience original unity and harmony of consciousness. But the crucial part of the prayer appears in the last stanza of the poem, where Ezekiel boldly defines the moral function of art: he asks for the gift of metaphor that will transmute the "passion of the blood," man's untamed energy, into "human good."[13]

Whereas "Morning Prayer" suggests a certain specific direction and discipline for the pilgrimage of the artist, "Jamini Roy" delineates the stages in the process of maturity, and the joyous fulfillment achieved by the urban artist. The last two stanzas of the poem especially focus on the nature of fulfillment:

> He started with a different style,
> He travelled, so he found his roots.
> His rage became a quiet smile
> Prolific in its proper fruits.
>
> A people painted what it saw
> With eyes of supple innocence.
> An urban artist found the law
> To make its spirit sing and dance. ("Jamini Roy")

The three stages of travel referred to in the poem are childhood, adulthood and maturity. In childhood, Jamini Roy's "purple elephants," cats "with almond eyes" and blue aristocratic birds are symbolic of childlike simplicity, directness, vividness and literalness. Progressing from the state of childhood to that of adulthood, "His all-assenting art" successfully copes with the hostile adult world "Of sex and power-ridden lives." Upon maturity, however, his more energetic and direct concern with man and city becomes "a quiet smile / Prolific in its proper fruits." And now having discovered the "law," he can aspire to the world of myth and realize a simultaneous identity with his art and the barbaric city. The law, of course, refers to the rigorous discipline that transforms energy into a vision of primal innocence and unity and that gives art its self-sustaining and eternal character. Thus, by reintegrating his wholeness, and by creating a comprehensive myth of concern, the artist participates in the joyous art of creation and attains his freedom.

IV

Our discussion of the image of the city and the metaphor of pilgrimage has briefly referred to Ezekiel's emphasis on commitment, sincerity and integrity as essential conditions for complete fulfillment in life and art. "Commitment," "Event," "Marriage," and "Case Study" contain a more extended treatment of this theme: using commonplace but intimate and personal situations and such devices as self-parody and self-censure, Ezekiel dramatizes the too-human problem of man's pathetic failures and frustrations, primarily resulting from his lack of commitment, and the image of life turned into hell. In "Commitment," men who forsake action in preference to some illusory quietism are lost in the thick fog—they "wanted only quiet lives / And failed to count the growing cost / Of cushy jobs or unloved wives." To commit oneself is to perceive the world of things and to establish a relational identity; therefore, commitment is a total act of the will, launched in all sincerity, to unify the thinking self and the extended realm of things. Thus, with true commitment that is an ethical act, man can find true meaning in the immediate and ordinary world around him. But without commitment, his foggy perception makes him wander from one illusion to another. The failure to figure out "the growing cost / Of cushy jobs or unloved wives" is the consequence of psychosociological misperception of the barbarity of industrial culture. Of course, the ironic conclusion suggested in the poem is that if man cannot understand matters of ordinary existence or the lower world, he is equally incapable of apprehending the reality of the higher world.

Is true commitment a function of unadulterated desire and strong moral will? Without commitment, man's life and cosmos have no meaning and his actions are merely glorified, ritualistic responses. Much of the problem concerning the loss of individual identity, we have seen, arises from the devouring character of the modern urban society. In "Case Study," a diagnostic poem with a heavy moral tone, all the actions of the persona—"a foolish love affair," "useless knowledge," involvement in politics, marriage and vocation—are a part of the rigorously conformative and highly programmed social ritual that we all are expected to perform. The poet tells us in the first line of the poem that "Whatever he had done was not quite right"; and following a succession of paradoxical sketches, we encounter his decisive voice:

> He came to me and this is what I said:
> "The pattern will remain, unless you break
> It with a sudden jerk; but use your head.
> Not all returned as heroes who had fled
> In wanting both to have and eat the cake.
> Not all who fail are counted with the fake." ("Case Study")

Unlike Kierkegaard's esthetic hero who sinks in despair and sickness-unto-death and casts himself in the limbo of "either/or," Ezekiel tells his hero to make a choice and break the pattern "with a sudden jerk." He should not be wanting "both to have and eat the cake," and, in order to make his life new, he must take a "leap" from the absurd circle of ritualistic existence. But, again, the "leap" implies commitment that is an obligation arising from an inner necessity rather than from tradition and custom; and it means freedom that is a realization or discovery of the self.

Love and marriage, as Ezekiel implies in "Event" and "Marriage," are sacred commitments. But when the "ironic gift" of time destroys "the will to act or pray," love degenerates into possessive sensuality and flippant indulgence. The woman in "Event" plays this game of false love:

> She lay and waited, watching me,
> Like a child in her nakedness,
> Uncertain if it ought to be,
> Awe-inspired and motionless. ("Event")

She is completely unsure of herself, especially about her role in the affair. She merely carries the book *Wine and Bread,* but does not know the symbolic significance of wine and bread. Her interest in art and the superficial dialogue and wit explain her attitude and the ritualistic process. Ironically, this gross and empty ritual of our world stands in sharp contrast to the sacred and creative ritual of the pastoral romance, in which love, bread, wine and sexuality are considered sacred. Thus, the woman in an urban society plays the stereotypical roles: she, like her male counterpart, exists purely as an instrument and does not have personal identity.

Obviously, the image of woman as portrayed in "Event" is ironic; and the same terse irony and concern continue in "Marriage." We are, of course, reminded in "Case Study" that "A man is damned in that domestic game" of marriage. In the ironic sense, marriage as a social custom is a bondage, a state in which man and woman, though intended to be united eternally, lose freedom and identity. While Ezekiel parodies the traditional view of marriage, he raises serious issues of sin and guilt:

> The darkened room
> Roars out the joy of flesh and blood.
> The use of nakedness is good.
>
> I went through this, believing all,
> Our love denied the Primal Fall.
> Wordless, we walked among the trees,
> And felt immortal as the breeze.
> However many times we came
> Apart, we came together. The same

Thing over and over again.
Then suddenly the mark of Cain

Began to show on her and me.
Why should I ruin the mystery?
By harping on the suffering rest,
Myself a frequent wedding guest? ("Marriage")

Evidently, the phrase "wedding guest" alludes to the Mariner's tale of sin, guilt and penance in Coleridge's *The Rime of the Ancient Mariner*.[14] Does Ezekiel consider the "joy of flesh and blood" and the "use of nakedness" sinful?[15] The answer is rather ambiguously cloaked in the trenchant emphasis on the absurdity and boredom of "The same / Thing over and over again." The metaphor of "the mark of Cain" is used only lightly to suggest, not any theological implications of the guilt, but its psychological and personal nature. The nature of suffering portrays neither the Freudian *Angst* nor the Kierkegaardian anxiety. And yet, the persona, in wanting to preserve the mystery, actually wants to demolish it. Has Ezekiel portrayed the archetypal image of woman, something that Yeats, following Spenser, Blake and Shelley, tried to achieve in his love poems?[16] Is the poem concerned with the idea of love as Eros or with the psychology and sociology of man-woman relationship, with particular reference to the aesthetic of sexuality? Does Ezekiel's treatment of female sensuality and eroticism here and later in a poem like "A Woman Observed"[17] adequately converge into the aesthetic—and an ideology—of contemporary feminism? Dante, unlike Eliot, was able to reconcile sexual love and spiritual love and so were Blake and Shelley, but does Ezekiel's poetic sensibility envision sexual and spiritual aspects of love as a unity?[18]

Chapter 9 🌀

Humanity Defrauded: Notes toward a Reading of Anita Desai's *Baumgartner's Bombay*

I

Baumgartner's Bombay is undeniably Anita Desai's signal achievement as a novelist, both in terms of the magnitude of meaning and the superb artistry. As a postcolonial novel, it carries the most intricate philosophical meaning of the puzzle of human existence, its obscenity, absurdity and meaninglessness. In a more universal sense, it is a story of the sociohistoric process of man's degradation and dehumanization by fellow man: it is a discourse on the nature of evil, the structure of human consciousness and the history of fragmentation and the collapse of civilization. Hugo Baumgartner, a German Jew, is forced to flee prewar Nazi Germany to India and even after 50 years of his residence in the country of his adoption he is variously known as a *"firanghi,"* a *"melachha"* and "the Madman of the Cats, the Billéwallah Pagal"[1] and finally murdered in cold blood by a young German hippie, an Aryan. In a more specific sense, therefore, especially considering the periodization and historiography, one may think that the narrative centers on the ethics of anti-Semitism and the historical treatment of Jews in Nazi Germany. Indeed, it may be argued that *Baumgartner's Bombay,* in invoking the history of imperial governance and the disdainful obliquities of European history, fearlessly and incontestably participates in the contemporary debate on Aryanism, anti-Semitism, colonialism and postcolonialism: the narrative covers the modernist and postmodernist ideological concerns about the use and abuse of power—economic, social and political. The strategic encapsulation of a period of history and the location of the narrative at the center of a frightfully disjointed structure of world order—the pre–World War II developments in Europe and Asia, events of World War II, the breakdown of the empire and the division and independence of India—only sharpen the intellectual and moral debate about Hugo Baumgartner's exile, suffering and extermination. Hugo Baumgartner starts his journey from Berlin, supposedly an enlightened metropolis of Western civilization, to Venice, the meeting point of East and West in both E. M. Forster and Thomas Mann, to Calcutta the first metropolitan center of the imperial establishment and finally to Bombay the metropolis of postcolonial India. As compared to Berlin and Venice, Calcutta and Bombay are the empire's ambiguously conceived "rural dependencies" or "peripheral spaces."[2] The intellectual designs of the denuding of civility are conceived, debated and enacted in the prominent metropolises of Europe, and, in comparison, the colonial spaces are designated merely as satellite spaces, loosely attached secondary centers of the major European war theaters. Baumgartner's experiences of these spaces elaborately redefine the historical time plan of dismantling and restructuring civilization.

Baumgartner's Bombay in its universal and peripheral contexts can be legitimately considered a historical novel in the same definitive sense as is implied by Georg Lukács in *The Historical Novel*.[3] The structural design of the novel, somewhat resembling that of a modern Kafkaesque tragedy, recounts the story of Hugo Baumgartner's alienation, exile, suffering, loneliness and finally the ill-fated death. But all these elements of Baumgartner's life are essentially and intricately woven around one central fact of history—the fact of his racial background as a Jew. The fact of Baumgartner's ancestry cannot be considered a matter of simple coincidence, for such a consideration will demolish the structural principle of the work. Baumgartner is a victim of a monstrous collocation of blind and bigoted antagonisms—religious, economic, sociohistorical, racial and political—and the boastful pride of a diseased civilization. It may be construed that Hugo Baumgartner like Hardy's Tess is pitted against the deterministic order of history, the Schopenhauerian will, the world of phenomenal reality. The manifest structure of civilization in Europe, as one would conclude, is not that of a community of beings but that of an undifferentiated mob or that of the philistines, to use Matthew Arnold's term,[4] the bourgeoisie, whose vulgar sociology and psychology are fundamentally opposed to the ideology and practice of humanism, liberty and social justice. The cruel irony is that Hugo Baumgartner's arrival in India cannot be considered more than a temporary relief, since India's social and political engineering is basically controlled by European imperialism and commercialism. Thus one finds the dialectical conflict between the two antithetical worlds, the word of history and the world of desire

(Jameson's terminology)[5] continuously and inexorably pitted against each other: unable to withstand the struggle, Hugo Baumgartner gets crushed by the wheels of chronometric time and sociohistorical reality. In this particular sense, his death is symbolic of the defeat of the ideals of individualism and freedom by the barbarism of collectivity.

Baumgartner's Bombay as a historical narrative contains two interrelated but overlapping representations, the representation of India and the representation of Europe. Despite the polyphonic character of the narrative, both India and Europe have been reinscribed primarily by Hugo Baumgartner. Insofar as India is concerned, it remains to be argued if Desai's historicization of India is a continuation of the imperial point of view one encounters in Kipling's *Kim* and Forster's *A Passage to India.*[6] The major problem in the representation of India is not only the narratological principle but also the philosophical position of articulating the colonial past and the postcolonial present. Surely, Thackeray's representation of India in the figure of Jos Sedley in *Vanity Fair,*[7] Kipling's Kim O'Hara's picture of India in *Kim* and Forster's "carnivalesque" polyphonic chorus in *A Passage to India* must be read from a postmodernist position. Does Hugo Baumgartner join these various expatriate "circus players" or does he effectively articulate and objectify the postcolonial or postmodernist position? How would Baumgartner respond to a Rushdie or a Naipaul? Whatever the legitimacy of these different voices, it remains a fact that Forster like Conrad has applied a very uncompromising and significant modernist correction to his representation of India. The poststructuralist and the postmodernist correction in which Desai's work participates brings out the moral and psychological truth of history—collectivity's overassertive narcissism and overindulgent egotism. In the case of the European representation, however, we are told in Desai's published interviews[8] that it is drawn from her German past transmitted to her by her mother. The history of the German mind's preoccupation with India, from Goethe and other German Romantics to Hesse in the twentieth century, should help us to examine the significance of the German element in *Baumgartner's Bombay.* Ironically, Hesse's fictional treatment of India in *Siddhartha* stands in sharp contrast to most imperial representations of India in history. In terms of the use of historiography, *Baumgartner's Bombay* undoubtedly belongs to the tradition of the English historical novel, with one very important exception. Desai has skillfully combined her background in European literature, especially German language and literature, with the English tradition. In the history of the English novel, Carlyle's *Sartor Resartus* is the first protracted experiment in the liberal use of German element. One can safely speculate that the figure of the Jew in European literature and the archetypal myth of the Wandering Jew must have been helpful in Desai's plans of shaping Baumgartner's story. One would further speculate that the story of Feuchtwanger's Süss Oppenheimer who is led from the European intellectual philosophy of action to the Indian spiritual philosophy of inaction or non-action[9] may have been another possible source for the design of Baumgartner's character and story.

II

In *The Historical Novel,* Georg Lukács maintains that Walter Scott's historicism seems to have been influenced by Hegel's philosophy, of course, without Scott having read Hegel.[10] Hegel's idealistic philosophy, especially as embodied in *The Philosophy of History,* considers history as a continuous process of the emergence of human consciousness and human progress. Hegel saw in the French Revolution the fulfillment of the dream of freedom and "the complete and final truth of human history."[11] Hegel, Lukács tells us, "sees the total life of humanity as a great historical process."[12] Lukács's Marxist analysis of the Hegelian-Romantic impact on Scott's art and thought, even after one discounts his lavish praise of Scott, shows that Scott's historicism as compared to the eighteenth-century Realist tradition, has successfully developed the epic character of the novel, the philosophy of "the historical spirit" of looking at the present "historically."[13] Undoubtedly, the overwhelming opposition to the Hegelian view of progress raises the question of the role of ideology. Should the past be reminisced or recreated only from a certain ideological position? Should history—and Benjamin calls it "an even higher pile of debris"[14]—be concerned with freedom, truth or progress? In the larger debate on the meaning of history, from Hegel to Benjamin, whether one looks at history from the standpoint of Hegel's theory of infinite progress, Nietzsche's conception of eternal return or even Spengler's philosophy of pessimistic determinism, one must continue asking: can there be an objective representation of history? Can history communicate truth? Are Tolstoy's *War and Peace* and Stendhal's *Life of Napoleon* empty reinstitutions of the past in the present? Will ideology—metaphysics, religion, Marxism, Utilitarianism, political economy, Fascism and humanism—color or discolor history? Here, for example, are two statements from Lukács's *The Historical Novel:*

> The great task facing anti-Fascist humanism is to reveal those social-historical and human-moral forces whose interplay made possible the 1933 catastrophe in Germany. For only a real understanding of these forces in all their complexity and intricacy can show their present disposition and the paths which they can take towards the revolutionary throw of Fascism. (342–43)
. . . .

The classical type of historical novel can only be aesthetically renewed if writers concretely face the question: how was the Hitler régime in Germany possible? (344)

Undoubtedly, these statements provide a strong philosophical argument for an intellectual understanding and a possible reconstruction of German history, but one wonders if Lukács's logic can also be extended to our examination of Desai's representation of India as imperial possession, especially the history of political struggle for freedom from colonial subjugation.

Considering the thrust of ideological position of anti-Fascist Humanism, one would hardly have any difficulty in placing Desai and her *Baumgartner's Bombay*. Is Desai an anti-Fascist humanist who has set out to explore the moral history and philosophy of Nazism, Fascism and racism, the regression of Germany and the rise of colonialism and imperialism? *Baumgartner's Bombay* is a postmodern tragedy in which the inevitable collision of personal and sociohistorical realities determines a self-obliterative course, not of human progress, but of human intolerance, egotism and extermination. In one sense, *Baumgartner's Bombay* resembles the model of a classical tragedy, like the tragedy of Oedipus, where Baumgartner, driven out of Germany by implacable hate and the repressive tyranny of time, history and social determinism, is finally defeated by the iron hand of destiny. Moses has tried to make a fairly convincing case for the relationship between Hegel's philosophy of history and his theory of tragedy. Hegel, according to Moses, does not regard the unfortunate abuse of history as tragic but "looks back at the most violent political conflicts, turbulent religious and ethical controversies, and bloody collisions of peoples and individuals as forming a linear pattern of human development that ultimately resolves itself in a final ideal synthesis at the end of history."[15]

Can a modern man, a Baumgartner, entitle himself to freedom and hence to the Hegelian historical synthesis and "the end of history"? Must he be subjected to the fate of Sisyphus or the Nietzschean vision of the "eternal repetition"? Walter Benjamin in his "Theses on the Philosophy of History," as Wolfarth explains, calls the nineteenth-century conception of history—and also the twentieth-century conception for that matter—"vertiginous, because it seesaws between two antithetical phantasmagorias—that of infinite progress and that of infinite repetition—which coalesce in the bourgeois dictum 'Plus ca change, plus c'est la même chose.'"[16] Can modern man or collectivity or the very spirit of modernity prevent the return of Chronos, the god who devours his own children? Will empty slots of time continue to be filled by fetishized objects and reified facts as measures of the so-called cultural progress? Benjamin's statement "there is no document of civilization which is not at the same time a document of barbarism" (Thesis 7)[17] is a stern and chilling reminder of the discontinuities of historical time and the disjunctive modes of social reality. Documents of barbarism, as Löwry explains, will include materials pertaining to "class injustice, social and political oppression, inequality, repression, massacres, and civil wars."[18] But Benjamin's paradoxical equation must be understood in terms of the Hegelian-Marxian dialectic of social consciousness. The pungent intellectual irony remains deeply ingrained at the center of the questions: whose civilization and whose barbarism? Whose history and whose representation? Can there possibly be an objective representation, textualization or retextualization of history, its very truth? C. S. Lewis has tried to suggest that "*The Inferno* is not infernal poetry: *The Waste Land* is."[19] If one were to extend this analogy to include Desai's *Baumgartner's Bombay,* one would say unhesitatingly that it is more hellish than Eliot's *The Waste Land.* The fallen figures of Albion and Urizen in Blake's *The Four Zoas* and *Jerusalem* and Shelley's Jupiter in *Prometheus Unbound* are comprehensive symbolic allegories of the nightmarish tyrannies of history.[20] If history is merely a "pile of debris," to use a Benjaminian postulate, can art or another humanist discipline reconstruct or possibly resurrect a vision of hope and progress?[21] In *The Political Unconscious* Jameson has vigorously argued that history is neither a text nor a narrative and yet history and the text remain inseparable.[22] The events of history, maintains Jameson, "can recover their original urgency for us only if they are retold within the unity of a single great collective story . . . [with] a single fundamental theme"[23] of social reconstruction and progress.

III

The outline of Baumgartner's story is somewhat simple, but the reconditeness of his mental and emotional structure is much more difficult to comprehend. Born of upper-middle-class Jewish parents in Berlin, he grows up as a very timid and shy youth who has developed a strong emotional bond with his mother. Baumgartner's father has lost his successful furniture business to an Aryan who helps Baumgartner to escape from Germany to India where he is supposed to work in the timber import trade for the new owner of his father's business. The business involvement with Habibullah in Calcutta is suddenly halted by Baumgartner's imprisonment in an internment camp during World War II. With the partition of India in 1947, Baumgartner moves to Bombay where he encounters Kurt, a helpless and starving German Aryan youth, a hippie lost to the contemporary drug culture. Baumgartner gives Kurt a temporary refuge but is finally stabbed to death by him. The narrative, in powerfully dramatizing the major events of his story, focuses on the life and experiences of Hugo

Baumgartner: ironically, the racial element of Jewishness that plays a dominant role in the narrative is painfully reminisced during his exile in India.
What history and culture have essentially created is the desiccated figure
of the exiled keeper of the cats. The psychoanalytical nature of his alienation and introversion is a challenging phenomenon of our civilization,
something that Freud quite appropriately refers to in his essay *Civilization
and its Discontents*.[24] As a child, Hugo has constantly experienced the fear
and paranoia of being Jewish. At a Christmas party in school he is overwhelmed by the strange and awkward sense "that he did not belong to the
picture-book world of the fir tree, the gifts and celebrations . . . [and that]
he did not belong to the radiant, the triumphant of the world" (36). While
in Germany he is comparatively of a darker skin than the radiant Aryans,
in India he is considered fairer than native Indians. Hugo's experience in
the Jewish school merely strengthens his protracted sense of fear, alienation
and anxiety. The visit to the Freedmanns where his mother boastfully and
exuberantly recounts her Germany of Goethe, Heine and Schiller simply
elevates his estranged sense of self-consciousness as one who in utter exas-
peration sees the two dichotomous and exclusionary worlds: the world of
history that is out to punish him for no crime of his own and the world
of desire that has been crumpled.

The repetitive and tortuous violence to which the young Baumgartner's sensibilities have been subjected over the years has simply nurtured in
him the degenerate feelings of fear and self-contempt. This fear that is
both paraesthetic and paroxysmal in nature is conducive to paranoia and
neurosis. Baumgartner's demoralization is the desired consequence of the
psychologism of the powerful Nazi propaganda and the Aryan racist ideology. One can undoubtedly see the continued impact of the Nazi propaganda on Hugo's mind during his residence in India, especially in the
internment camp. The dramatic reenactment of the Nazi-Jewish conflict in
the internment camp, one of Desai's splendid achievements, is a praxeological study of the German mind during Hitler's régime. The history of
the racial division in Germany is emplotted in India in conjunction with
the British colonial governance of India and the hysteria of World War II:
in the internment camp there is the German Aryan class, "the ruling kind,"
and then there is the Jewish group that is expected to "do the menial
work." Baumgartner's constant fear of the men in khaki is a significant reminder of the violent and repressive power that persecuted the Jews. The
men in khaki, the ruthless force of history, have killed the Germany of his
childhood fantasy and the Germany of his mother. He can now say fearlessly that he is "no enemy, merely a refugee from Nazi Germany who only
wished to pursue his business interests in India . . . [and that] there are
German Jews and there are Nazi Germans and they are not exactly the

same" (106). His bold and daring recognition of the psychological truth of his own existence and identity is extremely ironic: "He wanted to tell them it was their defeat, not his, that their country might be destroyed but this meant a victory, terribly late, far too late, but at last the victory" (135). During the course of his encounter with Lotte and Kurt in Bombay, Baumgartner forthrightly affirms the truth of his deracination and depersonalization. He has been reluctant in seeking the company of other Europeans perhaps for fear of being branded, bullied and humiliated and hence for reexperiencing the unsavory European treatment of Jews. He associates with Lotte not because she is German "but because she belonged to the India of his own experience . . ." (150). The trenchant irony of his unexpected encounter with Kurt, the golden-haired Aryan youth, is that he, too, like one of his maimed cats, desperately needs food and shelter. At the same time, however, Baumgartner's quick glance at Kurt revivifies the old memories and images of the tyranny of racism:

> That fair hair, that peeled flesh and the flash on the wrist—it was a certain type that Baumgartner had escaped, forgotten. Then why had this boy to come after him, in lederhosen, in marching boots, striding over the mountains to the sound of the *Wandervogels Lied?* The *Lieder* and the campfire. The campfire and the beer. The beer and the yodelling. The yodelling and the marching. The marching and the shooting. The shooting and the killing. The killing and the killing and the killing. (21)

"The looks they had exchanged," we are told, "had been the blades of knives slid quickly and quietly between the ribs, with the silence of guilt" (21). Evidently, there is a reference to the theory of collective guilt, according to which the German mind is believed to have striven for the purity of Aryanism and hence for the mass extermination of Jews. It is the predominant emotion of fear, compounded into horror and terror of persecution and extermination, of being throttled by the brute power of Nazi fascism, that partly explains the psychoneurotic nature of Baumgartner's introversion. Baumgartner's neurosis and depression, especially his morbidity and fear, have now become a permanent part of his internalized personality, intensifying his deluded sense of alienation, intellectual timidness and claustrophobic existence.

Does Baumgartner join the contemporary debate on Jewish history— the treatment of German Jewry, the ethics of German Jewry, the facts of the Holocaust, the genesis and the rise of anti-Semitism and the role of Nazi ideology and Nazi propaganda—suggesting even demurely that the German (or European) masses were responsible for the mass extermination of Jews? Does Desai, in fictionalizing some of the most dehumanizing events of history, provide a postmodernist correction to the controversy? Goldhagen's *Hitler's Willing Executioners,* for example, maintains that the mass slaughter of Jews in Germany was the direct result not of the Nazi ideology but of the deep-seated anti-Semitism in the German mind. That is, the Nazi ideology by itself did not provide a self-sustaining operative structure to carry out the "eliminationist anti-Semitism."[25] However, it may be argued that the central thesis that most Germans wanted the mass extermination of Jews is contrary to the facts of history. Whatever the religious history and cultural roots of anti-Semitism, it has come to represent one of the ugliest and vilest of human passions—hatred of fellow man. In German history, however, the conception of Aryanism came to signify racial superiority, purity and exclusiveness. Thus Aryanism became synonymous with Germanism, and the German Jews were designated as non-Germans or non-Aryans. It is commonly believed that Hitler's ideology of German Socialism is prefaced by the German mind's renewed exuberance in Romanticism and in the writings of writers like Nietzsche and that the immediate cause of the phenomenal rise of Hitler, the pan-German expansionism and the rapid spread of anti-Semitism is the defeat of Germany in World War I.[26] The social and political programs of the Nazi party were principally focused on nationalism, socialism, Germanism and the working class, and undoubtedly they cashed in on the psychological theories of racial superiority. The Jews were publicly and officially disenfranchised of their national origin and designated as non-Germans. Having successfully exploited the supremacy of Aryanism, Hitler's propaganda machine directly targeted the total elimination of Jews from the German economic structure. Ironically, the Nazi propaganda machine in its concerted tirade against the Jews derived its support from Bolshevism. In the conventional reading of history Jews have been accused, among other things, of an unethical control of Europe's economy, cosmopolitanism, pacifism and the lack of patriotism. Of immediate relevance to our discussion is the issue of moral good, true consciousness as opposed to false consciousness, in a structure of civilization where its citizens are judged not by bigoted considerations of race, ethnicity or other prejudices but by a just and humanistic order of civil society. That in a denuding whirlwind of collective egotism people can be marginalized, branded and declassified, and then finally cast out from their legitimate homelands is one of the greatest tyrannies of civil societies. Is the conception of moral good advanced by Aryanism any better than the ethical consciousness of German Jewry? Is this a question of the emergence of ethical consciousness or of the usurpation of power by false consciousness?

In Mannoni's psychoanalysis of power, a Prospero must have a Caliban, the Other.[27] The creation of a low culture or a cluster of subcultures by a high culture as a part of its assiduously conceived politico-economic strategies is a rendition of the history of class structure, categorization of culture, in Europe or elsewhere for that matter. Thus the "Otherized" or marginalized Jew in Europe, a Baumgartner, is an analogue to a colonized subject or to a "Dalit" in the Indian caste system.[28] Whether one looks at the process of history from a Hegelian or Marxist perspective, the emergence of consciousness is the consequence of a dialectical confrontation between the consciousness of the domineering class and that of the oppressed: during the process of historical synthesis the false consciousness must be revealed and offset by true consciousness. Hugo Baumgartner, doubly marginalized and "Otherized," first as a Jew in Germany, the country of his birth, and now as a "*firanghi,*" a citizen of India, the country of his adoption, reflects on the historical developments in Germany and India in a global context, identifying centers of social, political and economic power, that define and control asseverative paradigms of universal human civility. Is he a victim of industrial capitalism or racism or of a diachronic collusion of both? Does he comprehend the criminality of the human mind in a universal context?

In the piquant strategies of power struggles and subjugation fear, hatred, violence and war are potent psychological weapons, with fear being the most central emotion in the social psychology of disorientation and regimentation. These destructive instincts are subversive forms of the same creative energy, Eros; their violent, invidious eruptions signify the destruction of the world of Eros, which in Baumgartner's case is symbolized by the death of his mother. While fear serves as the most volatile instrument of repression and subjugation of the targeted subject, it acts conversely in the minds of its perpetrators—individuals, groups and nations. The functionaries and aspirants of power are basically controlled and directed by the negative emotion of fear which is essentially fanned by a bifurcated sense of false supercilious insecurity, pride or consciousness and the irresistible impulse to control, dominate and govern. Thus in the psychoanalytic view of power the Alexanders, the Caesars, the Napoleons and the Hitlers of history have themselves been victims of fear while at the same time they have relentlessly used it as a politico-moral weapon against their adversaries. It is fear turned into jealousy and hatred that often becomes a powerful psychogenic tool of propaganda and the progenitor of violent and subversive language. Blake's Urizen and Shelley's Jupiter are cases in point whose narcissistic hubris thrives on fear of the threatened loss of usurped power and who in turn inveterately use the psychological weapon of fear to enforce acceptance and subjugation. The ungenerate rhetoric of collective demagoguery and bigotry and of mass hysteria, insanity and violence, a rhetoric that is no different from that of imperialism and colonialism, could possibly be viewed as a skeptical commentary on the failure of the theories of progress and Western humanistic philosophies. That Baumgartner must be permanently forced out of his homeland and reworlded in India, where the circuitous drama of his imprisonment in the internment camp and subsequently the treacherous murder by an Aryan youth has been reenacted with a keen sense of tragedy, proves to be an open acknowledgment of the truth of neurotic estrangement and dehumanization and hence of the failure of civilization. In this deeply fractured civilization hope and a possible apocalypse are virtually nonexistent. Undeniably, such a thesis loudly echoed in the wasteland mythology of T. S. Eliot and in the writings of Camus and Sartre only redefines modern tragedy in anti-Hegelian terms.

IV

Whereas the utopian world of Aryanism, of racial purity, presupposes a certain normative structure of political ideology, Baumgartner's dreamworld, the Germany of his wish-fulfillment, the Germany of Goethe, Schiller and Heine, is fundamentally rooted in the feminine principle that may be defined as the principle of spatial reality. It is here that one would readily see a triple configuration of the feminine principle: first, in Desai's psychobiographical relationship with her mother Toni Nime and her mother's affiliation with Germany; second, in the psychological transference of this relationship to Baumgartner's filial bond with his mother; and, third, in Baumgartner's relationship with India as the transposed female space. This matter of Baumgartner's psychological and sociohistorical identity and of the representation of Europe are incontestably centered in the symbology of the mother, the creative principle. In the death of Mutti No. J673/1, not only does the Germany of his mother—the Germany of art, music and literature, the Germany of primal innocence—vanish but also there occurs a permanent severance of physical and historical ties with Germany, followed by a simultaneous replacement by a migrant's bond with India. Yet the irony is that the world of the mother, although literally decimated by the combined power of logocentrism and phallocentrism, has been figuratively elevated to another realm, the undying realm of wish-fulfillment, dream and memory. It is the sociohistorical conflation of two spatial categories, the Germany of history and the India of the present, that not only enlarges his perception of life and reality but also provides him with some sort of psychological assuagement. Baumgartner has now started seeing history from a universalized and syncretized perspective. When Baumgartner discovers that Sushil the Marxist has been murdered, he at once perceives a symbolic analogue and a pattern of historical repetitiveness: "In his sleep, in his dreams, the blood was Mutti's, not the boy's. Yet his mother—so small, weak—could not have spilt so much blood" (179). Of course, both the analogue and repetitiveness intensify the grossly cruel and inexplicable ironies of history: the psychoses of racism, hatred, fear and violence have led to the gruesome murders of innocent human beings like Mutti, Sushil and Baumgartner. But the complex symbology suggests that his mother's blood is a universal symbol of the blood of humanity shed by the tyranny of history.

Undoubtedly, history has provided Hugo Baumgartner with a larger cultural base for the expansion of his consciousness. Desai's representation of the history of Europe, its totalization and periodization, is realistic, objective and candid and so is her representation of India: both representations are largely free from tangential and deflective rhetoric. But what essentially emerges from the juxtaposition of the two representations is the psychological character of Hugo Baumgartner whose a posteriori perception of the muddle of existence and human civilization assumes a broader cosmopolitan, universal and global meaning. Apparently, Baumgartner's arrival in India and his successful business associations with Habibullah and Chimanlal follow the standard model of a non-colonist's strategy of commerce and trade, one that is evidently devoid of any political interests and motives. The young Baumgartner had known "the pre-war Calcutta of bars, dances, soldiers, prostitutes, businessmen, fortunes and fate" (172), but with the break of World War II there is a dramatic turn in his thinking and general attitude. After his release from the internment camp, Baumgartner finds that Calcutta like other big cities has been torn by racial disturbances. Historically, of course, Calcutta has been systematically destroyed by different political interests. If the mythical image of the origin of Calcutta as the city of Kali, the consort of Shiva, is remembered, one would undoubtedly see here a collusive interplay of history and myth. The quick and successive imbrication of the facts of history—the abrupt dismantling of the empire, the dawn of Indian independence, the division of India, the mass killings and bloodshed and Habibullah's migration to Pakistan—marks the second stage of Baumgartner's awakening. His residence in Bombay, the business dealings and friendship with Chimanlal, the relationship with Lotte the cabaret dancer and Kantilal's mistress, the rediscovery of Julius and Gisela, friendship with Farrokh the owner of Café de Paris and the tragic encounter with Kurt the Aryan are some of the most crucial situations in the third stage, all of which contribute to the perspicacity of his understanding of India and of himself, especially his own spurious identity as a *firanghi*, a *melaccha* and "the Billéwallah Pagal." It is significant to note that soon after his departure from Germany he had found Venice, the meeting place of East and West, very congenial to his taste; and later on of course he admits somewhat nostalgically that if given the choice he would still go back to Venice. But the most decisive awakening in Baumgartner, especially in his relationship with Germany, fulminates with the fascist and anti-humanist historical-political developments in Europe that finally led to World War II. Although in the original plan he had prepared with his mother he was supposed to have returned to Germany on the successful conclusion of his business undertaking, he, unlike Heinrich Heine who is known to have struggled to be a German and a Jew,[29] decides to sever his relationship with Germany permanently. There is no moral ambivalence or indeterminacy in the questions: "Go back *where?* To what?" (211) Of course, Baumgartner's rejection of Germany is based on his cognitive recognition of the ideological limitations of Western humanism and democracy. But once he has dared to terminate his nationality as a German, he embarks on the broad course of humanism and globalism amidst a multireligious and multiethnic structure of a rapidly evolving postcolonial entity. This marked progression from localized identity as a German national to universalized consciousness as a world citizen enables Baumgartner to perceive cultural identities in a pluralistic, syncretic and transnational context.[30] His long and uninhibited associations with Chimanlal, a Hindu, Habibullah, a Moslem, and Farrokh, a Parsi, help him to rediscover and reascertain his identity as a Jew living in India and the nature of his own humanity as a global subject. As a child, he had formed a more parochial and ethnic image of his Jewish mother and of his own Jewishness, but now this image has been redefined by postcolonial consciousness.

It is perhaps strategic and historically and psychoanalytically tenable to remove Baumgartner outside his natural and familial affiliation in order to ascertain the objectivity and substantiality of German-Jewish identity beyond the possible limits of national and geographical boundaries. His transplantation in India thus enables him to reexamine his own emotional and intellectual commitment to Germany and subsequently to India in a universal humanistic context. The startling realization that his avulsion from Germany and his adoption of India are unalterable facts of history must redefine his "Jewishness" and "Germanness." One can argue, rather tenaciously, that Baumgartner belongs neither to Germany nor to India and that he is now submerged in the sea of universal humanity where obfuscations of history, morphology, tradition and geography are automatically washed off. One thing becomes abundantly clear in Baumgartner's predicament, especially after he has witnessed firsthand the disastrous consequences of German nationalism: the term nationality, as commonly defined in juridical terms, does not bear any relationship to the conception of identity in Locke, Hume or Hegel. For Baumgartner, Germanness as mere nationality has been found to be dispensable and the meaning of the newly acquired Indian nationality is characteristically limited only to the terms of the document known as passport. Has Baumgartner been able to retain his Jewishness? Does the deliberate renunciation of his "Germanness" carry any substantive intellectual and moral validity? Can localized identity be replaced by universal consciousness or does one simply cross over from one type of local identity to another type? In Baumgartner's case, can Germanness be abruptly substituted by Indianness? Since Baumgartner is doubly marginalized, will he ever be able to overcome the problems of alienation and marginalization? Can the history of his depersonalization and deracination ultimately enable him to invoke his authenticity and to reclaim his true identity? Hugo Baumgartner has been vacillating between the states that Sartre characterizes as the authentic Jew and the non-authentic Jew,[31] but during the psychosociological process of his affiliation with India he seems to have appropriated for himself the position of the authentic Jew, one who is neither ashamed of himself nor of his people. But this progressive change in Baumgartner's mental and emotional condition is a consequence of his open confrontation with history and with the diffused cultural landscape of India.

Although his mother's blood-stained letters do not assist him in absorbing the complete meaning of history, they nevertheless are instrumental in bringing him to an intellectual and moral decision to differentiate between "Germanness" and "Jewishness" and finally to discard his German identity. Desai has successfully used the methodology of ideological subversion and transvaluation—of looking at Europe differently—to make Baumgartner realize the truth of universal human values. Having seen the immorality of violent and repressive rhetorical structure of anti-Semitism, Baumgartner as keeper of the maimed cats now seems to subscribe to cosmopolitanism, pacifism and globalism, the values for which German and Eastern European Jews had been punished. But Desai does not follow the psychophilosophical strategies of ideological conversion as, for example, is done by Feuchtwanger in the case of Süss Oppenheimer who is converted to Indian philosophy of nonaction or by Hesse in *Siddhartha* where Siddhartha, the symbol of disillusioned European youth, finally seeks unity of consciousness, of Atman and Brahman.[32] Nor is Desai an assimilationist: there is absolutely no attempt on her part to direct the course of Baumgartner's destiny by any such stereotypical device as miscegenation or to provide him with a contrived plan for any sustained assuagement. Baumgartner understands the parody and irony of Lotte's fake marriage to Kantilal Sethia. But will Baumgartner ever realize the unity of the self, which has been questioned both by Locke and Hume.[33] An obstreperous chorus of cacophonous voices endlessly echoes the puzzling unresolvability and irreversibility of the fact of his being an exile, an uprooted stranger who, perhaps sharing his creator's own predicament,[34] will forever remain divided in his intellectual and emotional responses to the materialistic reality of new spaces. But the obstreperousness basically lies in the psychosociological confrontation between morphological assumptions and cultural materiality. The deflectional terms "resident alien," "alien," "emigration" and "immigration" in contemporary juridical vocabulary are conspicuously connotative not only of such moral and political exigencies as are implied in the sociohistorical acts of transference from familial spaces but also of the psychological truth of alienation and uprootedness.

V

That Baumgartner does not see much of a problem in his affiliation with India is not entirely surprising: "It was his country, the one he lived in with familiarity and resignation and relief" (219). But Baumgartner's identification with India is not so much a matter of logical consequence of geographical positioning as it is of psychological and sociohistorical redefinition of the reality of life itself. The three most significant associations he has established in India—Chimanlal, Habibullah and Farrokh—provide him with three distinctly different voices from India. Chimanlal's bifurcated sense of Indian colonial history combines the modernist and postmodernist applications of nationalism, but Habibullah's experience of Indian history is limited to the time of India's political division. Farrokh's postcolonial rendition of the problems of contemporary European drug culture should be read only in conjunction with Kurt's picaresque and hyperbolic narrative. But during his discussions with each one of them Baumgartner emerges as a passive and absorbent listener and an enlightened empiricist. He listens to all these and other voices in the maddening chorus cleverly and objectively, sifting through the legitimacy of each during the course of self-examination but certainly without accepting any one of these blindly and flippantly as an injunction or a doctrine.

The subtleties and unintelligibilities of India's mind have initially surfaced in Baumgartner's mind: "Was it not India's way of revealing the world that lay on the other side of the mirror? India flashed the mirror in your face . . . India was two worlds, or ten" (85). Significantly, in her latest novel *Journey to Ithaca* Desai repeats the same theme about the perceptibility of India: "I told you—to find India, to understand India, and the mystery that is at the heart of India." Undoubtedly, there is a clever allusion to the European discourse on India—the multiplicity of voices about India since the British and German Romantics to the modernists and postmodernists. Whose India? Goethe's India, Schlegel's India, Hegel's India, Jones's India, Schopenhauer's India, Macaulay's India, Burke's India, De Quincey's

India, Mill's India, Forster's India, Eliot's India, Kipling's India, Yeats's India or Hesse's India? But in the discourse on India these divergent European representations of India, especially the imperial representations, stand in sharp contrast to the picture of India in the works of such writers as Tagore, Aurobindo, Nehru, Anand, Raja Rao, Naipaul and Rushdie.[35] Can Baumgartner distinguish between the Mill-Macaulay line of thinking and the Orientalist position? While in Germany, Baumgartner had heard about Tagore, "the Sage of Bengal," the Nobel prize-winning Indian writer.[36] The picture of classical India as the home of philosophy and metaphysics that has attracted great European minds must be compared to the socio-historical reality of India, especially the inexplicable poverty, hunger and disease. Of course, any study of the second picture will essentially entail an objective and comprehensive assessment of the political and moral respon-sibility of the British colonial administration in a broader philosophical context of the empire's relationship with colonies.

Habibullah's summative expression "For us—India is finished" (168) not only explains the sentiments of a large segment of the Moslem population of the prepartition India but also, quite ironically, invokes the painful mem-ories of one of the most tragic chapters of Indian history. It is also ironic that although the event marks the creation of Pakistan as an independent republic, the intellectual debate about the moral responsibility of the divi-sion of India, the unprecedented migration of people and mass murders in history has not as yet yielded any significant results. The question still re-mains: can a postcolonial text aestheticize the ignominious brutality and monumental cruelty of this and other forms of naked human savagery in history? Actually, not many works of fiction, Indian or non-Indian, with the singular exception of Khushwant Singh's *Train to Pakistan* and Bapsi Sidhwa's *Cracking India*,[37] have treated the subject of India's partition as an intellectual idea. Desai's own continued interest in the event becomes clearly evident from her *Clear Light of Day*, but there is hardly any doubt that *Baumgartner's Bombay* contains a much stronger note on the subject.[38] The climactic turn in Baumgartner's story, the horizontal movement from the life in colonial India to that in postcolonial India, is undoubtedly de-pendent on this one major episode of Indian history. The constellatory pat-tern of events—Habibullah's dramatic exit from India and hence from the narrative, the division of India, the independence of India, the creation of Pakistan and mass murders—is allegorical of a much more complex issue in the philosophy of history, the theory of change and progress in history. Does Baumgartner's experience of postcolonial India make him somewhat nostalgic of colonial India, the Raj? Can Baumgartner now relate these ex-periences of colonial and postcolonial India to the analogous experiences of imperial Europe whose fierce power had forcibly ejected him from the place of his birth, a highly industrialized structure, to a colony, an industrially infantile rural dependency of the empire? Does Desai expect Baumgartner to sympathize with Habibullah, since they both are now uprooted refugees or migrants? Indeed, the inextricability of all these and other related issues must bring us to Desai's own views on coloniality, postcoloniality and the philosophy and history of progress. Theoretically, it is the continued interpretation, historical, philosophical or aesthetic, of the idea of India's division and independence that will give this and other such matters the centrality they deserve in the history of ideas. One must not forget that Hegel's conception of history and human progress is based on his philosophical analysis of the French Revolution and that Shelley's *Prometheus Unbound* is essentially a mythicization of the idea of the revolution. Of course, Rushdie has tried to aestheticize the intricate puzzle of this political reality of history in *Midnight's Children,* but that perhaps in itself is a response to defining the limits of the novel, something Forster attempted to achieve in *A Passage to India.*[39]

The friendship with Sushil creates another level of awareness in Baumgartner—about the role of the Indian National Army and the deflected political sympathies of certain nationalistic Indians for Germany and Japan which were supposed to have helped India in its struggle for independence. In the internment camp the dominant concern is with the war and events in Europe but not with what was happening in India: "The freedom movement, the famine, the political revolution . . ." (168). The following analogy further problematizes the issue: "But Habibullah had no more conception of Baumgartner's war, of Europe's war than Baumgartner had of affairs in Bengal, in India" (169). Evidently, Habibullah does not comprehend the moral and intellectual issues pertaining to the freedom movement and World War II as clearly as does Sushil the Marxist. The fact remains that a number of Indians had persistently raised the moral issue of India's involvement in the European war theater, arguing that it was Europe's war and not India's and that the matter of India's participation in the war could only have been decided by India as a free nation. In his novel *Across the Black Waters,* Mulk Raj Anand "questions the morality of using Indian troops to fight a British war."[40]

Both Habibullah and Sushil help Baumgartner to understand British colonial attitudes and the destruction of Calcutta during World War II and later during the prepartition riots, but it is Chimanlal who establishes him in Bombay as a naturalized citizen of free India. Ironically, Chimanlal's nationalism and patriotism could only be characterized as mercenary, for after all, Indian traders like him had benefitted financially from their business dealings with the British war machine during World War II. In that sense alone, Chimanlal and Habibullah are typical traders and so of course is Baumgartner, but none of them seems to comprehend how the West could justifiably profess to have a "civilizing mission." Baumgartner is beginning to understand the relationship between colonial political ideology, capitalistic economics and institutional religion in humanistic terms: he sees more clearly the analogues between his German and Indian experiences. He finds to his surprise a puzzling relationship between religion and economics in the mythical figure of the goddess Lakshmi who Chimanlal worships as a matter of faith. Does Chimanlal understand the true meaning of the icon in the total context of the philosophy of *dharma*, *artha*, *kama* and *moksha*? In this philosophical paradigm, the essential governing principle is *dharma* without which *moksha*, the spiritual freedom, is denied. Ironically, Chimanlal values and worships literally only the idea of economic freedom but without any comprehension of the metaphysics of the icon.

Chimanlal and Baumgartner are two different minds: whereas Chimanlal's religious beliefs are a typical representation of an average conventional Indian mind, saturated in religious thought and metaphysics, Baumgartner's mind is rational, empirical and skeptical:

> Chimanlal expressed regret that he had never been able to make any dent in Baumgartner's wary agnosticism. Baumgartner's fumbled, embarrassed replies to Chimanlal's questions about Judaism, about how a Jew could believe in the same Moses, Abraham or Jacob that the Christians did, had brought about an early end to anything like the theological discussions in which Indians revel—and he never went so far as to ask Baumgartner to accompany him to a temple or on a pilgrimage—to his profound relief. (205)

Admittedly, Chimanlal is no Godbole who argues about the Hindu view of the world as a muddle, Maya, nor is Baumgartner a Fielding or anywhere close to any of the apostolic minds of *The Longest Journey* who are engrossed with the intellectual thought of Plato, Locke and Berkeley on appearance and reality.[41] Indeed, Baumgartner's "wary agnosticism" is the key to the reading of his descent into the cave:

> But he was certain there was an object there. Trying to stand still and breathe calmly, he told himself it could be an idol. What kind of idol? Could it be that black, engorged penis he had seen in roadside shrines, or an oxen hump, placid and bovine, some swollen udder of blood? He strained his eyes to see but his eyes had never met with such total blackness. The darkness itself was a presence. (189)

The estranged meaning of the mythic *lingam* as the "engorged penis" or the phallic pillar is not any different from some of the commonplace and controversial European readings of Indian religious thought and iconography in general. If one were to interpret the descent into the cave as symbolic of the journey into the unconscious, the black "engorged penis" will mean the cosmic creative principle. Is it Hugo's skepticism or "wary agnosticism" that would prevent him from understanding the truth of religious emotion or the mythic dimension of reality? Does he find it difficult to appropriate the legitimacy of religious emotion to a structure of empirical and rational understanding? The clever interpolation of the cave experience, it may be argued, is uniquely characteristic of Desai's way, of landing Baumgartner into the intricate maze of Indian metaphysics.[42] Aesthetically, the narrativized myth in terms of the iconography and paradigm, especially in the composite sense of the meaning and the visual form, is somewhat like an "ekphrastic poem"[43] where the thrust of the meaning is directly related to the self-communicative, visual and sculpturesque form of the icon, the "engorged penis," and where the allusive form of the stony idol teasingly hints at the metaphysics of the myth and the complexity of discourse. Is Baumgartner attempting to articulate the inarticulate and the unapprehendable? Will Baumgartner's bold and daring initiatory confrontation with the closed world of myth have any impact on his empirical thinking? Will Baumgartner, a commoner, be able to pierce through the camouflage and unintelligibility, the supposed characteristics of what Eliade calls the elitist myth?[44] Now that Desai has used such a myth in the narrative, will Baumgartner's penetrability into its closedness make any substantial difference in his growth, or will such penetrability be considered fundamentally inconsistent with Baumgartner's intellectual capacity?

The idol and the intense "thick blackness" in the cave are somewhat reminiscent of Kurtz's confrontation with "impenetrable darkness" and the penultimate realization in the resounding voice "The horror! The horror!" in Conrad's *Heart of Darkness*.[45] But the Marabar Caves in Forster's *A Passage to India* are undoubtedly a more beneficial pointer to the meaning of the cave symbolism in *Baumgartner's Bombay*. "In the cave," writes Forster in a letter to Dickinson, "it is *either* a man, or the supernatural, *or* an illusion."[46] The cave for Forster means "an unexplained muddle" probably just as "India is an unexplainable muddle."[47] Undoubtedly, Desai's treatment of images includes both the implications. In a sense, the cave symbolism in Plato suggests the world of illusion and in Indian thought it comes to mean Maya in which sense then one would interpret the integrative symbol of the cave to mean cosmic egg or the womb, the snake the directive principle of wisdom, and the black stone, "the engorged penis," the *lingam*. There is no doubt that Desai has rewritten Forster but with a more comprehensive meaning and greater perspicacity, though obviously not quite so for the agnostic Baumgartner: "What did this black stone profess to be that it was so honored? Baumgartner would have liked to know. The chamber seemed to hold a secret. If Baumgartner could find out that secret—" (189). The black stone, the *lingam,* symbolizing the cosmic principle of creation, dissolution and regeneration, is the collective representation of Shiva in the Hindu Trinity as being the progenitor of the world of Maya. As an agnostic and/or skeptic, Baumgartner thinks that the nature of reality is unknown and probably unknowable. Although he does feel the presence of some unseen power in the cave, he cannot recognize or define it. Nor can he enter into any intelligible discourse with this power. It may be debated whether Baumgartner is agnostic or skeptic and whether his skepticism comes from the English tradition of Locke and Hume or from the German tradition of Kant. The epistemological dilemma ends in bitter frustration and humility, since he "would not have its no": "Indigestible, inedible Baumgartner. The god had spat him out. *Raus,* Baumgartner, out. Not fit for consumption, German or Hindu, human or divine . . . Baumgartner knew he had been expelled from some royal presence. Go, Baumgartner. Out. He had not been found fit. Shabby, dirty white man, *firanghi,* unwanted. *Raus,* Baumgartner, *raus*" (190). Is this the story of a god who became indifferent and failed or is this the case of Baumgartner's own intellectual inability to comprehend and to demythologize the classical myth of Shiva? Such violent imprecations no doubt show probable or improbable assumptions about the nature of the deity— a wrathful, revengeful and punishing god—but these reflect the psychological anxiety in Baumgartner's recalcitrant mind to configurate his own imperceptibities and projections of time and reality. Apparently, Baumgartner's sensibility, like the modernist and postmodernist sensibilities, has failed to reconcile the conflict between myth and realism on the one hand and between epistemology and morality on the other. More appropriately, perhaps, Baumgartner's struggle is reminiscent of the struggle between the Romantic world of imaginative idealism and the modernist world of cognitive, realizable imaginative reality.

It is not surprising that Chimanlal's faith cannot help Baumgartner in his perception of the muddle—the epistemological muddle of reality and existence as well as the muddle that is India. As compared to Baumgartner, Kurt's view of India, especially his perception of Hinduism, is a gross parody, a vulgar and hallucinatory picture—India as a contemporary Bohemia for young hippies and drug addicts, where social and moral values have been permanently suspended in the name of licentious freedom and indulgent hedonism. Students of contemporary civilization need to debate the subject of social disorientation and alienation among modern youth like Kurt who, having been disillusioned by their familial cultures, are desperately seeking pleasure domes outside their own geographies and lineages. Clearly, Kurt does not understand Hinduism, nor does he mean to embrace it as a faith. Whereas Kurt's rejection of Europe means the inveterate rejection of the sociohistorical process of culture and its very meaning, his social disorientation has not excluded invidious elements of hatred and prejudice. Kurt's psychopathological condition, symptomatic of acute mental disorder, social dysfunctionality and utopian escapism, may be partly attributed to his dependence on drugs. Whether he kills Baumgartner because of his psychotic Aryanism or because of the compulsive need for Baumgartner's prized collections or possibly both, his psychopathological behavior remains one of the most damning commentaries on the value of a high culture. The nature of Kurt's social tragedy is far more serious and intricate than what might be concluded from Farrokh's sentimental outbursts. In fact, the two tragedies, the social tragedy of Kurt's repugnant existence and the moral tragedy of Baumgartner eloquently echo the seriously flawed nature of our civilization. Only in such a terribly confused and vitiated structure of civilization could Baumgartner have been brutally murdered.[48]

Emil Schwarz's picture of India shares the warm and enthusiastic representation of India in the German mind from Goethe to Schopenhauer. In fact, his knowledge of India and Indian art is a continuation of the early references to Tagore and his *Gitanjli* at the Freedmanns in Germany. One wonders why Emil Schwarz's character remains undeveloped, especially as compared to other figures, such as Julius von Roth, Gisela and Lotte. It is Emil Schwarz who educates Baumgartner about the surreptitious activities of Julius von Roth and the true meaning of Indian art. According to Schwarz, von Roth does not know the iconography, symbolism and the religious context of Indian art and his interests in Indian art are dictated solely by commercial considerations. It is only ironic that wealthy patrons of Indian art and the struggling Indian artists cannot recognize von Roth's commodified view of India and Indian art. If the scrofulous lives and interests of Julius von Roth and Gisela are fundamentally directed by covetousness, the case of Lotte is much more complicated. Her pretentious marriage to Kantilal Sethia and the relationship with Baumgartner simply define the modern social trickery of survivalism. As transplants, Julius von Roth, Gisela and Lotte are hustlers. During the war period while Baumgartner must go to the internment camp, Lotte can escape the tyranny of imprisonment by a false marriage to Sethia. But such a sequestered position of miscegenic assimilation has not been made available to Baumgartner.

Desai's portrait of women in *Baumgartner's Bombay* is somewhat puzzling, especially as compared to her more clearly defined position in earlier works.[49] Despite her staunch advocacy of woman's rights, one may find her position vacillating between patriarchal and matriarchal models. For one thing, Desai has not boarded the bandwagon of contemporary Western feminism, nor does she seem to endorse the complete disintegration of patriarchy in preference to any of the matriarchal paradigms. There is hardly any doubt that the most well-developed and dominant female character is that of Baumgartner's mother, a composite image of the Jungian archetype and the Indian idea of the feminine principle, but the stereotypical portrayal of the two European women Gisela and Lotte as hustlers is intriguing, since their feminine identities are solely and expressly defined by socioeconomic and political considerations. In fact, it becomes all the more evident that the female quest for identity is bound to prove to be a miserable failure. It is however true that their presence in the narrative provides an immediate dramatic contrast to the conventional images of woman in the families of Kantilal and Chimanlal. If the function of such a contrast is to suggest some realizable possibilities of subverting the Indian patriarchal structure, that result is undoubtedly achieved, though only to a certain limited extent. Ironically, Gisela and Lotte are bold, daring and recusant, but their self-assertive roles and sexuality are undoubtedly a direct reference to the modern discourse on sexuality. Whether the nature of sexuality is biological or social still remains a major part of this debate.[50] As dancers, they are entertainers of men. The unsavory assumption that the entire existence of woman must be geared to the satisfaction of male desire is indeed a deprecation of the ideology of patriarchy. Gisela, the prototype of a Circe, sees herself socially humiliated and thus she must fight with vengeance to win back her position as controller and manipulator of man. She has already made a fool of Om Sahni but in von Roth she finds a collaborator. Lotte, the so-called liberated woman, conveniently uses her sexuality to legalize her immigrant status in a fake ("Jhoota") matrimony with the affluent tea-planter Kantilal Sethia. Her willing and efficacious acceptance of a hegemonic polygamous relationship with Kantilal as his insignificant other is an attestation of a pattern of misdirection and circumvention of the power of sexuality, an iniquitous pattern of manifestation of repressive and dominant power one must readily see in an imperial design. Lotte's body is the typical patriarchal portrait of the female body as a fleshy object that becomes the center of attraction and repulsion, combining the paradoxical interplay of pre-Oedipal and post-Oedipal impulses. In his incestuous relationship with Lotte, Baumgartner wants to stay chaste and yet in embracing her he experiences the androgynous oneness of flesh, "one comfortable whole, two halves of a large misshapen bag of flesh" (82). Although he imagines himself and Lotte "brother and sister . . . with Mutti as their mother" (208), he experiences the *"jouissance* of infantile fusion with the mother."[51] The image of the missionary Bruckner's young wife as the "Nordic type of beauty" (127) is an extension of the feminine principle, the composite image of which is Baumgartner's mother. Kurt's appearance on the Indian scene marks the reenactment of the Oedipal drama in which the son figure must now intercede and eliminate the oppositional force, the father figure, in order to safeguard his own threatened world of desire. If one considers the Indian space as a metaphor for the female body, the womb, to be conquered and possessed, Kurt's role as a possessor of the female space should explain Desai's own predicament in choosing Baumgartner's murder by Kurt as an appropriate ending. Would Baumgartner's murder be seen as a case of abrupt closure wrought by the iron hand of destiny or what Freud calls parricide in Sophocles's *Oedipus Rex,* Shakespeare's *Hamlet* and Dostoevsky's *The Brothers Karamazov?*[52]

VI

It must be quite obvious that any estimate of Baumgartner's emotional and mental state cannot be complete without taking into consideration the ineffable internalization of his alienation and suffering. There is no bitterness or renitency in him, nor is there any rebellious protest in his social disengagement. Surely, he is not a Nietzschean nihilist, nor is he a Promethean rebel pitted against a Jupiter in his fight for the deliverance of humanity from despotism and repression. And yet his values and attitudes undeniably reflect some transvaluations of the Promethean-Gandhian idealism and Tagorean humanism. The transformations of the early metaphors of a rabbit, a mouse to those of a turtle, a crab signify important psychophysiological and psychosociological processes of inversion and of the mounting indifference to the worlds of materiality and action: "Crustaceous—crab—ungainly turtle: that was how he thought of himself, that was how he saw himself—an old turtle trudging through dusty Indian soil" (11). But Baumgartner has not retreated to the life of apraxia, noninvolvement and indolence, for to accuse Baumgartner of sloth or acedia will be to misconstrue the meaning of the fable. The dramatic irony in the dominant symbol of the helpless and maimed cats and their keeper "the Billéwallah Pagal" reveals the psychological and philosophical complexities of Baumgartner's deeply ingrained suffering. His self-reflective protest against the normative values of modern culture becomes transposed into psychological pity for the maimed cats, the injured, the victimized and the orphaned of humanity. The poignant irony in this symbolism is that Baumgartner emerges as the keeper and the protector of the helpless cats of the world, that he himself goes begging for their food and that he has voluntarily identified himself with the littered condition of human existence. The poor, the homeless of Bombay or Berlin—and the circuitous irony is that Baumgartner himself is one of the world's homeless cats—can only helplessly mimic and resort to self-denial, pacifism and interiorization of their suffering and pain as moral alternatives amidst an otherwise morally delinquent world order. Baumgartner's growing sense of universal humanism evokes a feeling of sympathetic identity with the poverty and filth of migrant workers without attempting "to avoid contamination as the others did, but to hide his shame at being alive, fed, sheltered, privileged" (207). This moral awakening in Baumgartner enables him not only to recognize the ideological structure of classes and the magnitude of human suffering but also to comprehend perspicaciously the representational metaphors of the maimed cats and their keeper. The lowest dregs of society are the victimized and unsheltered cats. Thus by creating two interdependent metaphors, the cats and their mad keeper, Desai brings Baumgartner to the sphere of direct social involvement.

The idea of the "Pagal" or madman in *Baumgartner's Bombay* should remind one about Foucault's conception of Otherness in his *Madness and Civilization*.[53] We are told that, traditionally and historically, it is the leper—the madman, of course, is a continuation of the idea of the leper—whose psychosociological characteristics of impurity, impropriety and unacceptability have cumulatively defined Otherness, the alien and foreign elements in a civilization. Madness as a foreign and deleterious element in a civilization must be contrasted to reason, sanity, purity and acceptability. Thus in the binary opposition the madman (the Pagal) is considered a threat to society and hence judged, punished and excluded. In history, however, prophets and revolutionaries have often been characterized as Pagals because their imaginations were deemed as incendiary agents of revolutionary change and moral disintegration. Evidently, Baumgartner's position seems to be situated in neither of the two categories—he is somewhere in the middle. But one would argue that the structure of human values embedded in the conceptual model of the Pagal and his cats far surpasses any existing structure of Western materialistic philosophy. There is no ineluctability and irreconcilability in Baumgartner's position, except that he would give refuge to Kurt not in the name of the mistaken identity of German racism and nationalism, but only as a fellow human being, as a stray cat that needs food and shelter.

The narrative universalizes the problem of human conflict, of war and of the total structure of civilization in broad moral and psychological terms. Let us examine the following universalization, mainly originating from the political disturbances in the postwar Calcutta:

His war was not their war. And they had had their own war. War within war within war. Everyone engaged in a separate war, and each war opposed to another war. If they could be kept separate, chaos would be averted. Or so they seemed to think, ignoring the fact that chaos was already upon them. And lunacy. The lunacy of performing acts one did not wish to perform, living lives one did not wish to live, becoming what one was not. Always another will opposed to one's own, always another fate, not the one of one's choice or even making. A great web in which each one was trapped, a nightmare from which one could not emerge. (173)

This commentary cannot be dismissed merely as a simple authorial intrusion, a harangue or an apologia: the collocated analogies elaborate the psychosociological process of mass behavior called war. Baumgartner has experienced all these wars waged by collectivity—the war for the extermination of Jews, World War II and communal disturbances in India—and his extraordinary perception of violence and misery lead him to a Hegelian synthesis and universalization: "Baumgartner felt himself overtaken by yet another war of yet another people. Done with the global war, the colonial war, only to be plunged into a religious war. Endless war. Eternal War" (180). Baumgartner's mind, functioning beyond the level of simple cognitive awareness, helps him to see the "monumentalization" of human brutality: all wars—individual, national, colonial and imperial—are traps, webs, engineered by the same common principle. In his letter to Sigmund Freud, Albert Einstein refers to the latent tendency in man to hate and destroy, which can be "inflamed into a mass psychosis," and asks: "is it possible to so guide psychological development of man that it becomes resistant to the psychoses of hate and destruction?"[54] Of course, "the mass psychosis" is initially engineered and inflamed by a small cluster of individuals. Freud's lengthy response to Einstein mentions two major divisions of human emotions as the basis of a structure of civilization, Eros and the destructive instincts of hate and aggression, maintaining that "if readiness to go to war represents the discharge of destructive instincts, it is evident that we should oppose it with other instinct, Eros." But Freud has posed a more potent counterquestion for Einstein: "Why are we, you and I and so many others, so indignant about war?" And why has war as a form of collective human behavior "not yet been condemned by general human consent?"

One must ask if in terms of the narratological problems of the novel as an art form the onerous task of monumentalizing human brutality and aestheticizing history are mutually inclusive. Lukács points out that Scott has successfully achieved such a synthesis.[55] I would argue that Desai's *Baumgartner's Bombay,* though not quite in the line of Scott, also shows that, given the postcolonial and postmodern considerations, even the cruelest sections of human history can be rendered into a defensible art form and an aesthetic category that simultaneously explicate the progressive concerns of a civilization. Conrad's *Heart of Darkness* and Forster's *A Passage to India* are two bold and iconoclastic experiments of this century in the reconstruction of history and undoubtedly *Baumgartner's Bombay* belongs to this group. Ironically, *Baumgartner's Bombay* shows that a third-world text can be, canonically and aesthetically, a self-absorbent big belly of history that would simultaneously include both the first world and the third world, related to or contained by not only binary opposition of capital and labor but also the universal humanistic concerns of a civil society.[56] In a globalized and universalized structure of a new world order where spaces are now what Bhabha calls transnational and translational the fundamental problems of our civilization cannot be simply compartmentalized merely into the first world and second world or third world categories.[57] Forster's *A Passage to India* is one of the greatest literary achievements in one special sense: essentially a study in human relationships, the narrativized issues of textuality and contextuality are premised by an idealistic but contentious assumption that whatever else must be said about colonialism and imperialism a world community of independent minds could possibly evolve. In this sense alone, the formation of the text of *Baumgartner's Bombay* is a rewriting of Forster but with a singular difference: that theorizing India includes theorizing Europe, that Baumgartner's individual experiences have their validity in the universal context of the collectivity and that localized identities of race, gender and nationality are ultimately submerged in the world's body. The text's body and Baumgartner's consciousness absorb both Europe and India to show that the European war theater destroyed simultaneously one's faith in Western humanism and, quite ironically, the foundations of Western imperialism and colonialism. Historically and psychoanalytically, Baumgartner's rejection of Europe and his discovery of India define a process of locating truth and of identifying the Other that had been hitherto centered in the narratives of colonialism and imperialism. The tragedy of Baumgartner must be read as a symbolic act of aestheticizing the tyrannous obliquities and unresolvabilities of history; it is an embodiment of Desai's "post-Holocaust, post–World War II and post-colonial"[58] vision of history. The text of *Baumgartner's Bombay* seems to exhort humanity, in the words of Rabindranath Tagore, "to claim the right of manhood to be friends of men, and not the right of a particular proud race or nation which may boast of the fatal quality of being the rulers of men."[59]

Chapter 10 ⟐

Alienation, Identity and Structure in Arun Joshi's *The Apprentice*

The individual's alienation from his fellow man and from himself and his search for identity constitute the thematic center of Arun Joshi's *The Apprentice* and his other novels, *The Foreigner, The Strange Case of Billy Biswas* and *The Last Labyrinth*.[1] Alienation, sociological or psychological, is often the consequence of the loss of identity. Alienation and identity are closely intertwined: whether one seeks identity with a lover or a culture, the search has social, moral and spiritual dimensions, which are interrelated, especially in the sense that the focal point in each case is the discovery of the self. Ratan Rathor, the protagonist-narrator in *The Apprentice*, who narrates the story of his own life in a somewhat episodic and reflective manner, is initially an idealist like his father but is later obliged to sacrifice his idealism in the face of the harsh, frustrating realities of bourgeois existence. A sham, a crook, a debauch and a whore, Ratan Rathor ponders the cryptic loss of his idealism, aspiring to the awakening in himself of a perspective that will give meaning to his own existence and to this cruel, chaotic world, the classic example of which is the sensual image of the city that, burning in its own nakedness at night, subsumes all and everything. The Brigadier considers the world "a beautiful whore—to be assaulted and taken" (18).[2] Himmat Singh, the double of Ratan Rathor, provides another contextual meaning of the metaphor of whore by poignantly and ironically revealing the fact that his mother was a "maddening whore." In this flawed and perverted culture, everyone is whoring, knowingly or unknowingly: both the antagonist and the protagonist are maliciously engaged in whoring, and during this mechanical process they rob each other violently and inexorably of humanity and of the spirit that distinguishes man from beast. Ratan Rathor finally searches for the meaning of all this; he strives to find himself and to establish an equilibrium that balances man with himself and his fellow man in a communal fellowship.

It is in India of the 1940s where Ratan Rathor first confronts two worlds, the world of the father, one of idealism, patriotism and social and moral concern, and the crippled world of history and bourgeois filth, one of ravenous and money-hungry gods. Ironically, Ratan Rathor's mother is a staunch realist who, knowing fully the practical value of money, states categorically that without money life and all its idealism are totally meaningless. Rathor's mother had warned her husband not to give up his lucrative law practice for the sake of the falsetto idealism of the Mahatma. Following her husband's sacrificial death, she is more convinced about the value of money. Himmat Singh's mother who like most other helpless and destitute women was driven to prostitution by society had practically shared the same view. No doubt poverty is a fertile soil for breeding crime, but it is the rich and the bourgeoisie of the pre-independence and the post-independence periods who will do anything to gratify their indulgent lust for money. Joshi's astute analysis of the crumbling values of the bourgeoisie and of the complete absence of ethical concerns on the part of aristocracy reveals the nature of the moral and psychological conflict that people like Ratan Rathor face, especially in preserving their own idealism. In fact, one sees clearly that the structure of bourgeois values is as embarrassingly contrived and fake as is its prodigy Ratan Rathor: Himmat Singh calls him a "sham," "a bogus man." It is this structure that indubitably divests people of any sort of heroism, determination and the will to aspire for excellence.

The self-destructive confusion and moral ambivalence of Ratan Rathor, which finally make him succumb to the mounting temptation of accepting tainted money and to sacrifice his patriotism and honor, result from the spineless structure of bourgeois morality. By accepting the bribe from Himmat Singh, he has risked the lives of thousands of patriotic soldiers who will now be fighting the enemy with inferior weapons. Ironically, when it comes to rationalization—one of the last resorts of a criminal like our hero—Ratan Rathor is frantically obsessed more by his honor than by the severity and magnitude of his crime. But he is not alone, for the plot of selling inferior arms to the army has been cleverly and meticulously masterminded by none other than the Secretary and the Minister. What happened to the patriotic and nationalistic idealism for which his father had died? He is overwhelmed by the deceitfulness and wickedness of this illusory world, the world of appearance that envelops reality. The phenomenal universe with all its glittering nets and entrapments is like the world of the devouring mother archetype who ultimately eats her own children. This world is the body of history, the sum total of social energy and its representative modes and structures, the city and the cultural and social forces.

In any ideal conception of a culture and its representative social orders, whether sociopolitical or theological, man is supposed to be in harmony with nature; he seeks human fellowship to create a community of beings; and he endeavors to develop his individuality by seeking utmost perfection, so that he can comprehend the individuality of others. But in a modern cultural context that essentially derives its meaning and power from commerce, materialism and drudge luxury, man and the city happen to be the two warring adversaries that in the social and historical process dehumanize each other and are finally themselves dehumanized. In *Culture and Anarchy*,[3] Matthew Arnold defines anarchy more or less as a mental condition in which man accepts and perpetuates imperfection, mediocrity and grossness and in doing so loses his moral freedom. The greatest threat to cultural progress, as Arnold would have us believe, stems from the barbarians and the philistines, not from the populace. The uncouth, dehydrated mental structure of the philistines is evidently symptomatic of the decline and fall of culture. Philistines like Ratan Rathor, Himmat Singh, the Secretary and the Minister share full responsibility for the retrogradation of culture, and, hence, for such repugnant conditions as boredom, stagnation and vulgarity. Indeed, it is ironic that whereas Ratan Rathor can be redeemed, the retrievability of society remains morally ambiguous. In the theological conception of the city, whether Christian or Hindu, the vision of the City of God holds a promise of human perfection, but the view of historical decay of a culture is much more seriously self-deprecating and self-admonishing. While the mythic view of fallen humanity in history, of the decline and fall of cultures and their redemption as projected in some of the myths, is one of hope and optimism, the issue of cultural decline and the painful predicament of putrid human waste raise the larger issue of the origin of evil.

Whether we consider the Hobbesean or the Rousseauistic view, the problem of evil in man and society is a potent one, especially when we examine the nature of the ameliorative and redemptive forces and processes. London, Bombay, New York and Delhi are modern cities, but, like elegant and seductive whores, they rob such persons as Ratan Rathor of their individuality, conscience and imagination. In return, people like Ratan Rathor are equally engaged in the business of whoring—of forcefully disengaging the centrality and fulcrum of communal values and ideals, and of satiating their unquenchable desires for that which is an outright prevarication. Whoring implies both the gratification of lust as well as the commercial bargaining of means, but in either case pleasure and sex are commercial commodities to be carefully and schematically bartered. Psychologically, gratification of lust involves jealous possessiveness, abusive violence and corrosive perversion of emotion. In a sense, it is both masochistic and sadistic. The woman as a whore is the object-world, the "other," the "desexualized"[4] female body, for such a perception of woman carefully excludes the creative function of love as sexuality and eroticism. Likewise, the city as a whore is the object-world that worships only malevolent gods. No doubt whoring is morally offensive and spiritually degenerative, but it explicitly means that both man and society have been deprived of the central soul-force and the moral vision of good and perfection. While society traps the individual and seduces him, the individual takes advantage of society in much the same manner: society induces man to move in a certain direction and man in return forces himself upon society.

Ratan Rathor has seen two pictures of India, the colonial India that produced a nation of clerks, the pillars of Raj, and the post-independence India that in spite of fervent patriotism, ancient heritage and Gandhian moral zeal is still overwhelmed by the British colonial tradition. The unique class of clerks is ironically portrayed by Joshi as a class of emaciated men whose ambition and zeal do not extend beyond the constricting goals of clerkship, career-hunting, matrimonial game-planning, and other highly charged ritualistic games involving status and money. Hegel's view of history as a progressive synthesis of the dialectical forces is, indeed, optimistic, but it seems to preclude the stagnant and frozen condition of the bourgeoisie. Surprisingly enough, even the Marxist thesis of class struggle as a basis of revolutionary reform and progress does not extend much reassurance to the sociology and psychology of the bourgeoisie.[5] For one thing, the nature of the bourgeois discontent, if discontent be the seed of progress, is as embarrassingly repugnant and self-deprecating as is the nature of their aspiration or the absence of any aspiration at all. And, indeed, colonialism as a formidable and repressive force has been instrumental in restructuring the sociology and psychology of Ratan Rathor and his kind.

In a bourgeois structure the dehumanization of man, both as a target and as a social process, is not too difficult to imagine: the process inevitably engenders moral decrepitude, infelicitous vulgarity and unwholesome vitriolism. It is a diseased civilization in which Ratan Rathor and his mother "suffer from the same disease: discontent and discontent" (25). This discontent and despair stem from man's incapacity to fight against the precipitous forces of social determinism, the Hobbesean leviathan. Unless man responds to this monstrous social cannibalism heroically and resolutely to regain the moral freedom he had lost in the sociohistorical process of dehumanization, the disastrous consequence is the loss of faith, hope and humanity. The bourgeois social apparatus persistently emphasizes docility and obedience as values; and it is this pungent and castrated spirit of docility and obedience, whether enforced by the colonial masters or championed by the dogmatic tradition, "that makes the middle-class so blindly follow its masters" (38). Once man surrenders his own freedom to the obdurate collective will, subjecting himself to demoralization, dehumanization and defeatism, he automatically becomes a part of the tyrannizing social structure and its value system that approves marriage as a quick fix and a negotiable entity, engenders moral indifference to social evil, promotes career-consciousness at the cost of moral consciousness and expects an uncompromising obedience to its own constricted standards of social progress. Surely, both Marx and Freud talk about discontent as symptomatic of the sickness of modern civilization: in the Marxist thesis, discontent, like the Fall, is considered to be a fortunate phenomenon because it will bring about a revolution, a beneficial change that will replace the existing order. But in the Freudian context the nature of discontent is psychological, inner rather than outer. Ratan Rathor, it should be noted, is not a revolutionary; since the seed of discontent is much more of psychological and moral—indeed, existential— nature, it will not fructify into a social revolt. As a bourgeois, he seems to be a microcosm of the social order he represents.[6] But he lacks the will to rebel and transgress: inasmuch as he lacks the will to rebel against the bourgeois structure of values, which has crippled his moral idealism, he still remains a part of this stubborn structure and at times he seems to be speaking as a "[b]ourgeois speaks to bourgeois."[7]

The paradox is that in proposing a moral rectitude to the ironic predicament of Ratan Rathor, Joshi chooses to go to the very root of the problem of "bourgeois filth." By projecting into the interior consciousness of Ratan Rathor and by making the conflict finally center on moral sense, Joshi carefully avoids the possible loss of the hero to the leviathan of social determinism. One might argue that the course Joshi outlines for Ratan Rathor is more akin to the Hegelian idealism than to the Marxist view of man and society. Alienation, according to Hegel, results from the experience of the object-world as alien or "the other," for the external world is deemed a projection of consciousness. Thus, in Hegel's epistemology consciousness, by relating itself to the "objectified, alienated otherness,"[8] the object-world perceived as being out there, recognizes only itself. But since consciousness perceives only the appearance of the object, it must keep on perceiving layers of its own manifestation. Whereas in Hegel consciousness is the basis of realizing identity, in Marx the emphasis is placed on the recognition of autonomous existence of the object-world, on the objectification of the reality of the material world in such specific and concrete forms as property, things and value. Consciousness in man, according to Marx, should emerge from economics—property, value and things—and from collectivity and its supposed ideal structure. We have seen that Ratan Rathor in identifying himself with materialistic calculus of money becomes the author of a painful tragedy, experiencing privation, misery and suffering that he had not seen before.

It is clear from the narrative that in a society which is socially, economically and morally corrupt, no structure, including the Marxist structure, can guarantee individual freedom—man's deliverance from evil and his achievement of unity. "If alienation is the splintering of human nature into a number of misbegotten parts," wonders Ollman about Marx's conception of alienation, "we would expect communism to be presented as a kind of reunification."[9] The philosophical assumption is that in order to overcome various forms of estrangements man must return from the three "misbegotten parts"—property, industry and religion—back to the social order. Ratan Rathor has already stayed away from religion; his attempted identification with money has given him a rude awakening; and the social order to which he is supposed to return is merely a degenerated shell. In fact, Ratan Rathor and the social order have been at odds, although, finally, he becomes conscious of the "otherness": his consciousness begins to perceive the object-world as its own integral part. Ratan Rathor, it should be emphasized, is seeking moral freedom—the recovery of his consciousness and identity: whereas this search is incompatible with the Marxist thesis, it is only partially compatible with the Hegelian conception. Ratan Rathor the bourgeois, the victim of the system, can be redeemed, and yet the puzzling paradox is that the decadent bourgeois social order itself cannot be revolutionized all at once. Ratan Rathor recognizes this paradox of individual redemption without the redemption of collectivity and the possible limits of the projected social change.

Since the bourgeoisie is not faced with any significant and serious challenges of a Romantic hero and since it has no limits to transgress, it suffers from boredom, stagnation, alienation, anxiety and fear. For Ratan Rathor, the question of identity is imperceptible and hence irrelevant, for either the goals are identified much too readily or they are virtually nonexistent. The slow and sly process of history, the monstrosity of the city and the mechanistic and self-indulgent fatalism of the bourgeois have stripped Ratan Rathor of a vision and commitment. The rise to the clerkship and then to the superintendency is not the problem, nor does the acquisition of wealth, status and marriage mean anything but a trivial social routine. The resultant impact of all this is that life, based upon habit and conformity rather than on imagination, initiative and creativity, has become frightfully mechanical and ritualistic. Ratan Rathor's habitual handling of his position is as mechanistic and superficial as his marriage. Even the sexual act with his wife is nothing more than a mechanical and artless coition and is often confused with love. Ratan Rathor can accept a bribe because it is customary for people in his position to seek graft. And once he has become rich, he does not see much problem with debauchery, drinking and prostitution as possible cures for his loneliness and boredom. The upstarts and the bourgeois, it appears, can imitate blindly and habitually, strike compromises and enter into convenient wheeling-dealing propositions without any moral considerations. Evidently, these unwholesome tendencies of a bourgeois like Ratan Rathor reveal the psychopathological structure of his personality: in a sense, he is amoral and asocial, the lack of moral and social consciousness being the result of his emotional and mental disorientation.

It should be abundantly clear from the foregoing discussion that the modern bourgeois culture of the industrialized era subscribes to the morality of convenience and compromise. Even religion, including the tutelary knowledge of the *Gita* and other scriptures, is an empty and meaningless ritual. For Ratan Rathor bribery or graft is not morally wrong, but the unexpected accusation of bribery and fraud has threatened his honor, that prized possession of the status-conscious bourgeois, for which he is now determined to take revenge from Himmat Singh and then from the Secretary. That the nation was defeated because of the conspiracy of supplying defective weapons to the army, and that the Brigadier, his childhood friend, stands accused of voluntary desertion stir not his moral conscience but the muddled notion of the likely loss of a name. After all, he has taken a bribe only one time and should therefore be judged not as guilty as his other colleagues who have been routinely and habitually accepting bribes. It is as much a question of deconstructing the existing pattern of morality as it is of recognizing the absence of an ethical and spiritual basis of an evolving culture. The search for identity entails living not by presumptuous ignorance, impudent wickedness and willful deceitfulness but by the unstinted and implacable freedom from the bondage of illusion. That he may register legal confession simply to save the life of his friend, the Brigadier, as the police would want him to do, that he would vindicate his honor by killing Himmat Singh and the Secretary, and that he can hide the matter of bribery from his wife as a matter of convenience are some of the nontruths and half-truths. But the intriguing part of all that anxiety and frustration he experiences during the course of his schematic plan of living by deceiving, concealing and fabricating is that he does not recognize his crime.

Ratan Rathor is guilty of accepting a bribe that Dante would characterize as compound fraud, the sin against community. He persistently fails to regard his crime as sin, although he has now reached a point where he finds it impossible to withstand the pressure of police to confess. Like Dostoevsky's Raskolinkov in *Crime and Punishment*, Ratan Rathor has consistently denied his knowledge of the crime.[10] Ratan Rathor's apparent disintegration results from his failure to perceive social sin and is a part of the psychological process of his spiritual recovery. But there is a good deal of uncertainty in the epistemological process. Dostoevsky, as Philip Rahv maintains, uses "the principle of uncertainty or indeterminacy in the presentation of character," of "hyperbolic suspense," that "originates rather in Dostoevsky's acute awareness (self-awareness at bottom) of the problematical nature of the modern personality and its tortuous efforts to stem the disintegration threatening it."[11] Joshi's treatment of Ratan Rathor reflects that indeterminacy or "hyperbolic suspense" that dramatizes the complexity of modern man's psychic structure—the loss of his social and political faith, the degeneration of his moral consciousness and the fragmentation of his vision of identity. Ratan Rathor himself cannot perceive the process and structure of evil, nor can he comprehend the forces, both inner and outer, that have led to his disintegration. However, the suspenseful indeterminacy in either case is real, especially as it pertains to the dismantled personality of Ratan Rathor and the degenerated social order. The indeterminacy in Ratan Rathor's case serves as an ironic tool of revealing the fundamental nature of the incompatibility that persists between the dream of human progress and the stubborn social order that has not allowed for that progress. The system, it appears, will not prevent the process of disintegration, nor will it restore human dignity. We may no doubt condemn the social and cultural milieu that produces men like Ratan Rathor, Himmat Singh, the Secretary and the Minister, but the fact remains that such people cumulatively define the character of society. Ironically, Ratan Rathor cannot conceptualize the nature of social evil; his inability to define the forces that brought about his collapse is merely symptomatic of the insufficiency of our knowledge of human nature and, hence, of our helplessness and inability in general to define that which otherwise remains dark, inscrutable and indefinable.

By making Ratan Rathor confront the forces that have disintegrated his personality, Joshi employs the epistemology and metaphysics of social evil. Joshi's methodology includes, among other things, existential confrontation, individuation and reintegration. It is Himmat Singh who indomitably challenges Ratan Rathor to cast off his fear and cowardice and to face the situation courageously and boldly. Himmat Singh knows well that Ratan Rathor cannot pull the trigger on him and that he cannot dodge the authorities any longer. He overcomes anxiety and fear by going through several stages, finally recognizing the nature and degree of evil in which he had been an active participant all along. For awhile he had reflected upon the meaninglessness and absurdity of human existence, its disgusting hollowness and treacherous emptiness. But with the gradual recognition of his own self he has come to recognize the source of human baseness and depravity. He had been lonely because he had been entrapped by the illusory world of appearance and because he had hitherto denied himself the opportunity to know his own real self. Both Himmat Singh and Ratan Rathor had pawned their souls; they had made their shadowy choices self-righteously and without knowing the meaning of good and evil. Ratan Rathor had been a timid conformist in every respect, and lacked the will and courage to reject habit and tradition, the boring and ugly commerce of life, and to confront reality—the recognition that his life of 20 years has been a total loss, and that between good and evil he had himself opted for evil not knowing the meaning of the imprudent choice he made. Finally, now, there arise stern and agonizing reverberations of the inner voice, all reminiscent of a heavier guilt and enlightened remorse: he had pawned his soul in the dazzling game of "bourgeois filth" and fraudulent crookedness; he was a sham and his life had no purpose. But he now realizes that his soul is only pawned and not killed, and that life is not "a zero" (205). The word "honor" has a new and more comprehensive meaning: it means a recovery of an authentic and sincere consciousness—the casting off of self-centered seclusion and conceit and the reawakening of the spirit of self-redemptive social good.

It is strange that Joshi saves Ratan Rathor from committing suicide. The fact that Ratan Rathor does not have to opt for death as being the only freedom from dejection, anxiety and failure, a course clairvoyantly echoed by a modern school of existential philosophy, not only strengthens his fractured sense of identity but also gives an immediate sense of form to the digressional narrative. Ratan Rathor is guilty of incivism, but he does not suffer from permanent malignity and ill will; he has shown capricious gullibility to vice, even in its inchoate state, but he has also exhibited a remarkable sense of recovery; he can impute crime to Himmat Singh, but the ascribability of crime and the open expression of impudicity are essential to the cognitive process. Following the belabored and slow recognition of his guilt, Ratan Rathor's method of expiating the guilt, it should be noted, is more Gandhian than Vedantic:

Each morning, before I go to work, I come here. I sit on the steps of the temple and while they pray I wipe the shoes of the congregation. Then, when they are gone, I stand in the doorway. I never enter the temple. I am not concerned with what goes on in there. I stand at the doorstep and I fold my hands, my hands smelling of leather and I say things. Be good, I tell myself. Be good. Be decent. Be of use. Then, I beg forgiveness. Of a large host: my father, my mother, the Brigadier, the unknown dead of the war, of those whom I harmed, with deliberation and with cunning, of all those who have been the victims of my cleverness, those whom I could have helped and did not. After this I get into my car and go to office. And during the day whenever I find myself getting to be clever, lazy, vain, indifferent, I put up my hands to my face and there is the smell of a hundred feet that must at that moment be toiling somewhere and I am put in my place. (206–07)

It is only in the context of the philosophical disquisition of the *Gita,* more appropriately the Gandhianized *Gita,* that one would understand the asseveration: "Without vanity and without expectations and also without cleverness" (208). This voluntary injunction categorically purports that one should pursue the path of action without expecting any reward (*Nishkam Karma*), overcome indulgent desire and annihilate his ego voluntarily and unreservedly. Ratan Rathor is apprenticed to the challenging task of moral reconstruction of his own self: "If you can learn to wipe shoes well, who knows," as Rathor comments with unquestionable sincerity and insightful clarity, "you can perhaps learn other things. It is humiliating at times but apprentices need to be put in their place" (208). Ironically, this penitential process of seeking moral and spiritual identity goes on outside, not inside the temple, the inside of the temple having become "[f]rozen, petrified, like our civilization itself" (208). Admittedly, Ratan Rathor is facing an uphill task: actually, it is twofold, one of insuring his own recovery and progress, and the other of using his wisdom to redeem the "petrified" civilization. And yet there persists still another danger of the absence of a clear guarantee that during the course of future ameliorative endeavors and of a possible social interaction with the slumbering mass, the bourgeoisie, he may not slip down on the declivitous path and lose his identity. Does Ratan Rathor know that there are cycles and spirals of growth? Or, should he worry only about the present? Surely, Ratan Rathor knows that whereas social identity is vulnerable to moral hurricanes, only spiritual identity will endure.

The task of moral recovery and reconstruction presupposes a battle against human depravity, "The crookedness of the world; the crookedness of oneself" (205–06). Whereas the nature of evil is essentially social, the battle for eradication of evil must begin from within the individual self. In the case of Ratan Rathor, the psychology and epistemology of evil show that in the cognizance of evil and in his attempt to achieve perfection political programs and religious doctrines do not play any significant part:

How to get rid of it [crookedness]? Revolution or God? the Sheikh had said. But what do I know of either of them, my friend? Of Revolution; or of God? I know nothing. That is the long and the short of it. The Superintendent's God is no use. Of that I am sure. Whose God then? The God of Kurukshetra? The God of Gandhi? My father's God, in case he had any? And whose Revolution? The Russian? The Chinese? The American? My father's? Whose? Could they possibly be the same—Revolution and God? Revolution and *some* God? Coinciding at some point on the horizon. (206)

The interrogative sentence, "How to get rid of it?" like the continuous terrain of other interrogative sentences, posits serious moral and metaphysical issues, some of which are unresolvable and are undoubtedly beyond the limits of the narrative. For one thing, the moral anarchy of the Nietzschean mold and of certain other similar doctrines is not the answer. For the Marxist, evil is strictly a social phenomenon that will be overcome by a revolution, but for a Gandhian moralist, it is both inside and outside. While the battle against evil must be waged both inside and outside, it is the individual self that must become cognizant of evil, fortify his moral will and then wage a Promethean war against it on the outside. But the irony is that Ratan Rathor is not a Promethean hero: he is seeking identity with his own consciousness and not with the bourgeois collectivity, the culture that is basically disoriented and flawed. In a culture of this type, God and revolution, contrary to the idealistic position, are viewed as divergent, stereotyped and finite forces. But if ever the idea of God and the idea of revolution must coincide, it will happen only in the revelatory moment of inner grace and purity: after all, the moment of awakening to redemptive change is the moment of self-purification and, hence, of apprehending inner divinity. But Ratan Rathor is only an apprentice and he has a long way to travel in order to experience this type of fulfillment.

Does Ratan Rathor become penitent? Is his penitence sincere, voluntary and authentic? It is clear from the concluding section of the novel, which reads like a tightly structured moral discourse, that the path of connotive self-immolation and penance comes awfully close to the Christian outline of the recognition of guilt, remorse and penitence, for the Hindu ethical system, as has been observed in the case of Gandhi's moral philosophy, does not admit self-debasement as a form of penance and as a step in the process of moral reconstruction.[12] And yet the nature of Ratan Rathor's redemption, it must be noted, is blatantly unorthodox, especially in the sense that Joshi does not induct him into an austere yogic discipline of moral reconstruction and self-integration. Ratan Rathor's moral will is to be continuously and regularly fortified by an assiduous epistemological process that includes, among other things, a repetitive reminder of the rotten and filthy smell of the shoes of the visitors to the temple. The problem of a possible moral deviance has to be resolved by an iterative confrontation with the concrete form of human debasement—offensive odorous smell of the shoes, a bathetic image of self-debasement, that bears strong resemblance to that of bourgeois filth, and serves as a stern reminder of the sweat and blood of suffering humanity. Ratan Rathor has gradually recognized the problem of evil:[13] the nature of evil is no doubt social, but it has to be continuously recognized and purged by a disciplined process of confrontation with the individual self that has been debased in the social process.

There seems to be a much more subtle and comprehensive outline according to which Joshi realigns and reconstructs Ratan Rathor's moral will without subjecting him to any karmic illusion or a traditional ascetic discipline: Ratan Rathor is not now bargaining for salvation but is striving for a spiritual identity between the inner self and the social self. By constantly experiencing the odorous foulness—that is symbolic of collective human ugliness—Ratan Rathor continually annihilates his non-self, thus seeking a definitive relationship between his own moral conscience and social good. Inasmuch as his moral self participates in social good, his sense of identity becomes stronger, especially from the standpoint of his recognition of the difference between the criminality of bribery as merely a legal offense and the moral guilt as expressive of remorse and penitence. It must, however, be noted that in Joshi's theodicy Ratan Rathor's expiation of guilt does not reach the level of contrition, nor does it aspire to the supreme idealism of *ananda* and *moksha*. In rejecting the apocalypse and institutional religion, Ratan Rathor affirms the path of ethical humanism. Ratan Rathor does not seek ultimate liberation from the illusion of life; on the contrary, he seeks identity with life, his true self, and the very stuff of which life is made. And in this dual process of self-immersion in the foul smell and of participation in the public good, he insures a graduated progression of private good. In fact, for Ratan Rathor the public good and private good are inseparable. He has recognized the root of evil, which is desire or ego, the alloyed world of *tamas*:[14] he conquers this world of desire, ego, anxiety and fear by surrendering his own self—by deflating and "deconstructing" his ego self. He finally sees the dawn of enlightenment, the morning of rejuvenation and renewal. But ironically he is merely an "apprentice" to the more complex and esoteric art of finding truth, wisdom and equanimity.

It may be argued that *The Apprentice* is predominantly about money, power and politics, that it is basically about "a New Slavery with new masters: politicians, officials, the rich, old and new" (83) and that the narrative directly aims at exposing social and political corruption.[15] It could also be argued that the novel deals with the problem of character building, since Ratan Rathor the young idealist had authored an essay on the crisis of character. One inevitably derives these ambivalent impressions from the deep reflective broodings of the protagonist-narrator, but the fact remains that he moves into the heart of social reality without merging his self with bourgeois collectivity, that is, without losing his individual identity to perverted communal consciousness. His pervasive and lucid knowledge of the reality of his universe extends from the servile yoke of the bourgeois to the opprobrious acts of social sin and is finally summed up in the powerful image of the smell of the shoes of humanity. However, one must ask perplexingly if Ratan Rathor will ever overcome the penitential foulness of the smell and if Joshi would have considered softening the unusually harsh epistemology of moral recovery. The central theme of *The Apprentice* is undoubtedly the existential struggle of Ratan Rathor, the protagonist-narrator—his idealism and alienation, fall, expiation and recovery: the narrative pointedly centers on his search for identity, his true self. The structural problem, if there is a noticeable problem, is created by censorious limitation imposed on the theme: rightly or wrongly, Ratan Rathor is allowed only a limited victory. Admittedly, such a highly complex issue is directly related to a writer's moral vision and his view of human nature.

One may, however, legitimately and dispassionately assert that a criminal like Ratan Rathor should not be allowed total freedom and that in order to return to his place in community he must continue performing the interminable act of atonement, of cleansing and smelling the sweaty shoes of suffering humanity. Although Joshi must decide some of these matters in a larger cultural context, the question still remains open: will Ratan Rathor ever entitle himself to complete moral freedom? Is Joshi in his approach to the rehabilitation of Ratan Rathor an absolutist, a stern and uncompromising moralist? These problematic issues and even some other inconsistencies and uncertainties can cloud the narrative: that Ratan Rathor is still a bourgeois and not a revolutionary may be regarded as an irksome incongruity between the larger theme of spiritual identity and the configuration of social reality. Maybe, the single voice of the protagonist-narrator,[16] because of its characteristic limitation, cannot reveal the whole truth; maybe, too, the novel as a commentary on life and society does not provide exact mathematical analogues and inimitable causal truths, no matter how much harder a fabulator tries to fabulate a neatly designed fictional universe based upon the principle of truth and verisimilitude. But whatever we make of these thematic and structural difficulties, Joshi's vision effectively and successfully portrays the larger side of Ratan Rathor—his search for spiritual identity that includes his concern for humanity. Ratan Rathor is freed from the fear of a possible punitive judgment of society, but he remains bound to his own moral conscience in a voluntary attempt to mitigate the "otherness." Indeed, there are no guarantees of an apocalypse, nor is there a magical escape latch from existential commitment and reality. However, in the process of discovery of self there are magical moments when one sees congruence between social morality and individual consciousness.

The story of Ratan Rathor is the story of modern man's alienation—of his relentless struggle to conquer alienation and to achieve some form of identity with the object-world. The progress made by Ratan Rathor from whoring to experiencing the smelly shoes of humanity defines the art and methodology of expiation and recovery. His moral recovery remains incomplete, because he has just begun his apprenticeship to the arduous task of moral reconstruction. The contemporary philosophical thought, as Pappenheim argues, has tried to grapple with the problem of modern man's alienation, but nevertheless the issue has become only more sharply pronounced: can man, within the framework of modern civilization, conquer, by his own actions and will, alienation, and, hence, pain, anxiety and suffering?[17] If we consider Marx's belief that man's dream of self-realization is dependent upon the external forces in nature and society and especially upon the improvement of socio-economic institutions, we will unhesitatingly conclude that man is certainly not free to shape his destiny. In the case of Ratan Rathor, however, Joshi does not let him wait for his recovery until the social order has been reconstructed and revitalized. Furthermore, Joshi even bypasses society insofar as Ratan Rathor's criminality is concerned, assuming, of course, that perverted communal consciousness is not entitled to judge individual moral deviance. But the emphasis, as has been seen, is on the reawakening and strengthening of Ratan Rathor's inner consciousness, a methodology and an epistemology that, indeed, do not rely on the prodigious growth and idealization of a social order and that, therefore, do not subscribe to social determinism. Ratan Rathor's disciplined endeavor and his moral will have shown him the way of establishing spiritual identity with himself and with the object-world.

Chapter 11

The Metaphysics and Metastructure of Appearance and Reality in Arun Joshi's *The Last Labyrinth*

Arun Joshi, comparatively a younger Indian novelist, has been following in the footsteps of philosophical novelists like Tolstoy and Dostoevsky.[1] The moral problems of Rattan Rathor, the protagonist of *The Apprentice*, are expanded and intensified in the figure of Som Bhaskar, the "antihero" of *The Last Labyrinth*. Both characters confront the problems of alienation and identity with one significant difference: whereas Rattan Rathor finds an answer to his moral guilt and returns to the community, Som Bhaskar fails to find answers to his moral and cultural alienation and cannot return to society. The tragedy of Som Bhaskar is the tragedy of modern man who, being at odds with himself and his cultural environments, is confronted by moral and psychological fragmentation and by a persistent struggle between the two worlds, the two types of hunger—"Hunger of the body. Hunger of the Spirit" (11).[2] The dramatic conflict between the two intricate worlds of appearance and reality as portrayed in *The Last Labyrinth* constitutes the basis of fictional discourse and the structural principle of the narrative.

In many ways, Som Bhaskar is a Freudian figure whose discontent with his civilization and with himself, reiterated in the frequently repeated expression, "I want. I want. I want" (78), defines the structural principle of the narrative. Som Bhaskar has received a prestigious education at Harvard, has inherited the family business and fortune after his father's death, and has become a comfortable millionaire at the age of 25. Apparently, Bhaskar is fully at home with the Western intellectual tradition, and one of the central issues in the process of his self-discovery is the role and place of Indian religious thought. Will Bhaskar's scientism help him to understand Krishna? The narrative of *The Last Labyrinth* seems to be a continuous dialectical confrontation between the main currents of Western intellectual thought and the Indian religious thought, with one significant difference: Joshi's method of participating in the Western intellectual discourse is one of epistemological transvaluation. Considered in this context, *The Last Labyrinth* is essentially a document in the history of ideas. One may argue that it is probably inevitable that writers like Mulk Raj Anand, Raja Rao and Arun Joshi, to name only a few, would participate in the Western intellectual discourse. One could easily read in *The Last Labyrinth* the loose threads of Samuel Butler's argument between religion and science in *The Way of All Flesh;* and on the subject of sex, love and women D. H. Lawrence's *Sons and Lovers* bears a fairly plausible resemblance.

In his discriminating self-analysis, Bhaskar outlines the issues boldly and clearly:

> I knew that money was dirt, a whore. So were houses, cars, carpets. I knew of Krishna, of the lines he had spoken; of Buddha at Sarnath, under the full moon of July, setting in motion the wheel of Righteousness; of Pascal, on whom I did a paper at Harvard: 'Let us weigh the gain and loss in wagering that God is, let us estimate these two chances. If you gain, you gain all, if you lose, you lose nothing.' All this I knew and much else. And yet, at the age of thirty-five, I could do no better than produce the same rusty cry: I want. I want (11–12).

Bhaskar had inherited the business and wealth at 25, but now he is 35. It is interesting to note that during these ten years his perception of life has not changed and he seems, one would assume, to be getting closer to the idea of Krishna. He had known that the Pascalian thesis about the existence of God is distinctly different from Descartes's dualistic philosophy of matter and spirit. Leela Sabnis, a Ph.D. from Michigan and a professor of philosophy, with whom Bhaskar has occasional sex, is a follower of Descartes. Sabnis explains somewhat assertively that in Descartes's philosophy the world of matter and the world of spirit are two separate worlds that cannot be united. Bhaskar is, of course, very quick to refer to the philosophy of Spinoza according to whom "both matter and spirit embraced in God, and flowed from Him" (81). When Bhaskar undertakes the gruesome journey to the top of mountains to recover the shares of Aftab Rai's company, he meets Gargi, a mystic, who reminds Bhaskar that "there is no harm in believing that God exists" (213). And Bhaskar comments unreservedly and unintimidatingly: "So I was back with Pascal! . . . It is easier to believe that He does not exist. It is more convenient that way." (213)

Historically, Pascal's polemical reply to Descartes's controversial philosophy rests on his theory of the wager or wagers, which is essentially epistemological. Indeed, the characterization of Leela Sabnis and her rejection of Bhaskar are allegorical of Pascal's rejection of Descartes's ideas. It is true that for an adequate understanding of Pascal one must know Descartes or possibly Montaigne or even St. Augustine, the intellectual milieu of Pascal, but the fact remains that Joshi takes the complex epistemological and theological debate to the seventeenth and eighteenth centuries, and further to the nineteenth and twentieth centuries. Significantly, the debate centers on the reading of Som Bhaskar, a modern intellectual who had been deeply immersed in all these ideas—he even wrote a paper on Pascal—but who cannot accept Pascal's wager. Yet the paradox is that Bhaskar keeps on thinking about Krishna: "No, there was nothing simple about this thing. There was nothing simple about Krishna. Had it been so, He would not have survived ten thousand years. He would have died along with the gods of the Pharaohs, the Sumerians, the Incas. Krishna was about as simple as the labyrinths of Aftab's Haveli" (173).

Bhaskar's father had also been searching for truth and the first cause. In a dialogue with Bhaskar, he says: "There was neither death nor immortality, then . . . Who knows the truth? Who can tell whence and how arose the universe. The gods are later than its beginning: Who knows, therefore, whence comes this creation?" (155) Evidently, the argument about the first cause and about the Idea or Reality is ancient in origin, although modern scientific thought has not helped to bridge the gap between science and religion. But Bhaskar's father had reminded his son that in the metaphysics of the first cause and the Spirit scientific reasoning is of very little or no help. The best poetic reconciliation in the narrative comes from Anuradha: "Maybe Krishna begins where Darwin left off" (132). But does Anuradha comprehend the intellectual implications of such a condensed restatement of the long debate in the history of ideas—a sort of linear and direct unity and continuity between science and religion? Or is Joshi ironically suggesting the limits of science? In an answer to Aftab's question, Bhaskar states: "The point is that this Spirit is there. And if it is there, if Man has inherited it, then what is he to do with it?" (132) But he does not share Aftab's view that "it is a matter of visions" (132). "Visions," remarks Bhaskar somewhat contemptuously, "are dime a dozen" (132).

It is abundantly clear from the narrative that Bhaskar has constantly subjected himself to rigorous and discursive self-analysis and at times this tyrannizing process has proved to be primitive, demoralizing and self-destructive. On his way to the temple in the mountains, he calls himself a leper, the one who "needed a cure" (126). His insatiable hunger for Anuradha, Aftab's mistress, his compulsive fornications, his puzzling relationship with his wife Geeta, and his powerful desire to acquire control of Aftab's business only partially define his muddle. In fact, Leela Sabnis has frankly called him a fornicator and neurotic. But I believe the serious conflict in the book is between the Cartesian world of reason and the world of intuition. Aftab Rai along with Anuradha, Gargi and the dancing girls of Lal Haveli represents the mysterious world of intuition, of pain and pleasure and of balance and harmony. It is only in the context of the spiritual morality of Lal Haveli, including its labyrinths, that one can understand Anuradha's relationship with Aftab and Bhaskar, the pain of the history of Lal Haveli and the impending takeover of Aftab's business by Bhaskar.

It is virtually impossible for Bhaskar to understand the undaunted morality and complexity of Anuradha's statements—that she is not unfaithful to Aftab and that "you can't marry everyone you love" (43)—and her sacrificial act of giving up her jewels and shares in Aftab's company. Anuradha's conception of love belongs to the category of idealistic and spiritual love that implies the notions of good, sympathy and sharing. Anuradha boldly emphasizes the obsolescence of the institution of marriage by disclosing somewhat laughingly that she has "never been married" (43), and later by commenting reflectively: "I can imagine I am married to Aftab. I can imagine I am married to you. My mother used to imagine she was married to Krishna" (128).

In contrast, Leela Sabnis's relationship with Bhaskar is very short-lived. She believes that the sexual act is concerned only with the body, the world of matter. Her ideologies of free love and feminism, it should be noted, are distinctly different from Anuradha's ideas of love and sexuality. Anuradha's incorruptible notion of love corresponds to the idea of love as bhakti (selfless devotion), a kind of spiritual love that is commonly implied in the relationship between Krishna and his cohorts in the mythical legend. The tragedy and the paradox are that Som Bhaskar and Leela Sabnis belong to the same materialistic world of empiricism, rationalism and intellectualism. Bhaskar is convinced that in Leela Sabnis's rational world "Descartes and *tantras* [do] not mix" (54). Although Leela Sabnis urges Bhaskar to understand and accept the Cartesian thesis, Bhaskar seems to believe firmly that "what [he] needed, perhaps, was something, somebody, somewhere in which the two worlds combined" (82).

In *The Will To Power*, Nietzsche divides the history of ideas into three centuries: (1) "Aristocratism," the era of Descartesian reason and will; (2) "Feminism," the age of superiority and supremacy of feeling, as advanced by Rousseau; and (3) "Animalism," the era of Schopenhauerian will and therefore "the sovereignty of animality."[3] "The nineteenth century," adds Nietzsche, "is more animalic and subterranean, uglier, more realistic and vulgar, and precisely for that reason 'better,' 'more honest' . . . but sad and full of dark cravings, but fatalistic."[4] Considering that the twentieth century is only a logical extension of the nineteenth century, we find that a work like *The Last Labyrinth* and the figure of Som Bhaskar belong to Nietzsche's third category. At least, Som Bhaskar is honest and truthful about matters pertaining to his libidinousness and other desires and the ensuing moral and psychological problems. His life is heavily punctuated by embarrassing and debasing vulgarity and an irrecoverable sense of vanity and powerplay. The more Bhaskar craves the gratification of his desires to gain control over Aftab's company and complete possession of Anuradha, the more excruciating and uglier the situation becomes. But Som Bhaskar can find neither the truth nor the remedy for his suffering, since he has combined sex with power, money and authority.

Bhaskar is no doubt familiar with Pascal's philosophical formulation of the relationship between moral conscience and the ability to comprehend truth, but his ravenous pursuit of the world of desire has destroyed his reasoning power. Evidently, the matter of ascertaining moral conscience has been expediently obviated, for the convoluted structure of reality in which Bhaskar's praxeological values are defined, has no reference to such terms as conscience or moral conscience. Money, wife and children, successful business and prestigious education have given Som Bhaskar neither freedom nor happiness. The more he runs after Anuradha, the more he finds out the invincibility of the situation. After all, the central metaphor of Lal Haveli suggests indecipherable and invincible illusion in which Bhaskar is caught as a helpless prisoner of Aftab's business and Anuradha's sexuality. Earlier, Bhaskar was a prisoner of the Cartesian voids, the vacant spaces in nature and hence in one's own mind. And paradoxically, his business of manufacturing plastic pails is a big monster, a leviathan that will devour the creative energies of an intellectual like Som Bhaskar.

It may be argued that in a moralistic discourse the most gruesome situation in the structure of civilization represented by the narrative is Bhaskar's marriage to Geeta. Bhaskar, considering his own embarrassing deviations, frankly recognizes that Geeta too has every right to "the adulteries of the body," though she has "only taken to cleansing of the soul" (63). In accepting the position of the insignificant other and her husband's Don Juanish affairs with other women, Geeta has patronized her husband's lustful indulgences, recognizing at the same time her pathetic helplessness and self-deprecation. She has known of her husband's affair with Anuradha; in fact, during her husband's illness Geeta and Anuradha had jointly prayed for his recovery. While Geeta suffers and perseveres through her husband's womanizing and boozing, Anuradha gets the upper hand in dealing with Aftab and Bhaskar. Although Gargi has called Anuradha Bhaskar's shakti, Bhaskar rightly calls her his "dark and terrible love" (157), more in the sense of the Freudian id. Ironically, the tantric metaphor of shakti for Anuradha basically remains incomplete, actually dysfunctional. It is of course true that Anuradha electrifies, vivifies and controls Bhaskar's life, thus enabling Bhaskar to know his subconscious self.[5] But as Eros she does not lead Bhaskar to the recognition of Krishna in himself.

Bhaskar's unconquerable desire for Anuradha and Anuradha's own sexuality are paradigmatic much more in the Freudian sense and the Jungian sense of the anima than in the Indian sense of the shakti.[6] The mythical-poetical world of Lal Haveli, with its mysterious voids and labyrinths, remains illusory to the scientific-rational mind of Bhaskar, but it is undoubtedly Anuradha who, with her evocative physicality and sexuality, is the principal creator of illusion. One would surmise that Bhaskar's complete and perfect union with Anuradha could have given him spiritual wholeness, the state in which sexual anxiety and spiritual consciousness are fully integrated. But in this complex psychoanalytical-theological argument Anuradha remains merely Bhaskar's projection. As Bhaskar acknowledges somewhat helplessly: "There was more to her than met the eye. A world spinning all by itself. I was infatuated with this mysterious world" (189). Bhaskar, as is clear from the thrust of the narrative, cannot reconcile the worlds of ego and id. It must not be forgotten that Bhaskar's inexorable use of power to possess Aftab's business and Anuradha simply adds to her inextricability. There is an obvious analogy between the two phases: the first phase when Bhaskar simply tries to take over Aftab's business, and the second phase when Anuradha as personification of Bhaskar's desire becomes the creator of illusion, the veil of Maya in the Schopenhauerian sense.[7] Imprisoned in this world of Maya, Bhaskar has totally lost the focus and perspicacity of his own vision and will. While Bhaskar's own ego lets him believe that he can conquer the world around him, his unethical and unjust conduct of repressive dominance and authoritarian tyranny clearly show the nature of degeneration in him.

In his introduction to Pascal's *Pensées*, T. S. Eliot makes the following observation: "But I can think of no Christian writer, not Newman even, more to be commended than Pascal to those who doubt, but who have the mind to conceive, and the sensibility to feel, the disorder, the futility, the meaninglessness, the mystery of life and suffering, and who can only find peace through a satisfaction of the whole being."[8] But Nietzsche in his shrewd observation has compared Pascal and Schopenhauer: "'*Our inability to know the truth* is the consequence of our corruption, our moral decay'; thus Pascal. And thus, at bottom, Schopenhauer. 'The deeper the corruption of reason, the more necessary the doctrine of salvation'—or, in Schopenhauer's terms, negation."[9] I must also refer to Thomas Mann's famous essay in which he compares Schopenhauer with Freud. Freud's world of id, as Mann explains, is very much identical with Schopenhauer's world as Will.[10] Som Bhaskar's world, whether Freudian or Schopenhauerian or Pascalian, is a study of mental, moral, and emotional disorder, resulting from man's inability to know the world of id or the world as Will. The knowledge of Krishna or truth presupposes complete harmony of all discordant and hidden forces and the complete annihilation of the ego. Bhaskar cannot know Krishna because spiritual knowledge is an intuitive recognition of the worlds of flesh and intellect, matter and spirit. Bhaskar's thinking is still divisive, rather fragmented, because he continues to seek logicality in the power of his uncontrollable desire and in the existence of the Spirit. The ironic difference in his mental and moral development is evident in his inability to read poetic mythology and symbolism in which Krishna and Shiva are symbolic centers of truth and consciousness.

In his scientific and rational thinking Bhaskar can only read of the third eye of Shiva as the third eye of the lizard Hatteria and Krishna only as a gas flame. It is only when the world of flesh, spirit and intellect are unified that sexuality, eroticism and pleasure approximate the condition of truth. Pleasure, considered in relation to itself or to any kind of power or power-wielding characteristics, is merely a form of indulgent sensuality. Does Bhaskar understand the metaphysics of *ananda* in Indian thought? The worst type of vulgarity from which Bhaskar suffers is his senseless pride of wealth and intellectual superiority, which obstructs his mind and heart from envisioning reality. His unbridled sensuality and invidious pride lead him only to despair and meaninglessness in life, and hence to the impulsive decision to commit suicide. Although it had become clear to him that "Leela Sabnis was a muddled creature. As muddled as me" (77) and that "like Aftab [he], too, had wanted to start life all over again" (169), he is unable to forge ahead.

With the disintegration of Bhaskar's dream world, the narrative crumbles. Quite surprisingly, the narrative does not include any plans for the recovery and redemption of Som Bhaskar. One cannot help observing that in the conceptual framework of a poetic tragedy people like Som Bhaskar, Geeta and Leela Sabnis are ineffective players. Nevertheless, Anuradha's sudden and unceremonial disappearance from the narrative, Geeta's dehumanized existence, and Leela Sabnis's emaciated rationalism are a commentary on the vitiated social order of which Som Bhaskar is a tragic product. Bhaskar's lust for Anuradha has not changed into love, nor has his repugnant and vituperative attitude toward Aftab mellowed. Bhaskar's anxiety, fear and pain, stemming from his own mental and emotional fragmentation, are clearly echoed in these lines: "Anuradha, if there is a God and if you have met Him and if He is willing to listen, then, Anuradha, my soul, tell Him, tell this God, to have mercy upon me. Tell Him I am weary.

Of so many fears; so much doubting. Of this dark earth and these empty heavens" (223).

Evidently, here one finds an element of the Kierkegaardian epistemology of experiencing truth and of expostulating that there is perhaps a greater power, even though the intermediary of this power is supposed to be Anuradha. Unable to comprehend the structure of reality, especially the matters of unity and continuity and also of certitude, penetrability and permanence, Bhaskar's clogged mind struggles with the problem of the limits of knowledge. Bhaskar has now finally come to realize that the gap between the self and reality cannot be closed. Bhaskar's self has been lost to the overabundance of fear and pain. Strangely, however, Bhaskar continues to wonder about the validity and meaning of these "strange mad thoughts": "Are they the harbingers, the pilot-escort, of melancholia? Of insanity? Faith?" (223) Of course, Bhaskar has not forgotten that his father had died of melancholia. Foucault points out that melancholia, variously considered from the sixteenth century to Descartes to modern times, is a form of disorder or madness.[11] Nevertheless, melancholia and insanity belong to the realm of unreason or non-reason—as perhaps does faith. But it remains to be argued if Bhaskar can recover from delirious madness and self-debilitating anxiety and fear. It also remains to be argued if Bhaskar fully shares Pascal's "moral pessimism" that, as Nietzsche wonders, may have its possible affinities: "But where does the moral pessimism of Pascal belong? the metaphysical pessimism of the Vedanta philosophy? the social pessimism of the anarchists (or of Shelley)? the pessimism of sympathy (like that of Leo Tolstoy, Alfred de Vigny)?"[12] Does Bhaskar comprehend the metaphysics of karma, of action and non-action, as expounded in Krishna's discourse in the *Gita?* Is it acedia, non-action, the indifference to individual and communal good, that finally leads to melancholia, or is it melancholia, the psychological degeneration, especially occasioned by a withdrawal from *vita activa,* that deconstructs moral will and engenders irretrievable conditions of estrangement and acedia?[13]

Notes

CHAPTER 1

1. Refer to some of the assumptions in Fredric Jameson, "Third-World Literature in the Era of Multinational Capitalism," *Social Text* 15 (1986): 65–88. Also see Aijaz Ahmed, "Jameson's Rhetoric of Otherness and 'National Allegory,'" (1987), *Marxist Literary Theory,* ed. Terry Eagleton and Drew Milne (Oxford: Blackwell, 1996) 375–98. "These two propositions [Jameson's and Ahmed's]," maintains Sara Suleri, "remain necessary misreadings of both each other's claims and of the situatedness of nationalism in the colonial encounter . . ." (*The Rhetoric of English India* [Chicago: U of Chicago P, 1992] 14).
2. K. R. Srinivasa Iyengar, *Indian Writing in English,* 5th ed. (New Delhi: Sterling, 1990).
3. See Marilyn Butler's commentary on the consolidation of the British Empire in her "Plotting the Revolution: The Political Narratives of Romantic Poetry and Criticism," *Romantic Revolutions,* ed. Kenneth R. Johnston et al. (Bloomington: Indiana UP, 1990) 134–35.
4. Iyengar, *Indian Writing in English* 24–25.
5. *Indian Writing in English* 30.
6. See his essay "Goethe as the Sage," *On Poetry and Poets* (New York: Octagon, 1975) 240–64.
7. See Laurence Binyon, "Introductory Memoir," *Songs of Love and Death* by Manmohan Ghose, ed. Laurence Binyon, 3rd ed. (Calcutta: U of Calcutta, 1968) 1–15.
8. See Bloom's essays "Introduction" and "Clinamen or Poetic Misprision," in *The Anxiety of Influence: A Theory of Poetry* (New York: Oxford UP, 1973) 5–16, 19–45.
9. Cited by Iyengar in *Indian Writing in English* 653.
10. G. H. Langley, *Sri Aurobindo: Indian Poet, Philosopher and Mystic* (London: David Marlowe, 1949) 19.
11. Cited in Langley 17.
12. Langley ix.
13. See Meenakshi Mukherjee's discussion in chapter 2 of *The Twice Born Fiction: Themes and Techniques of the Indian Novel in English,* 2nd ed. (New Delhi: Arnold-Heinemann, 1974).

14. See Margaret Atwood's psychosociological treatment of nationalism, alienation and identity in the struggles of Elaine and Josef in *Cat's Eye* (New York: Bantam, 1989). Note Josef's observation: "I come from a country that does not exist . . . and you come from a country that does not yet exist" (324).

15. In V. S. Naipaul's *A House for Mr Biswas*, introd. Ian Buruma (London: Penguin, 1992), the historical containment of the Hanuman House and the oppositional issue of Mr Biswas's homelessness are significant aspects of coloniality.

16. Khushwant Singh's *Train to Pakistan* (London: Chatto, 1956) appeared in the United States as *Mano Majra*. See my discussions of India's division in chapters 7 and 9.

17. See Fredric Jameson's discussion in his *The Seeds of Time* (New York: Columbia UP, 1994) 150–51. But also see Anand's letter of August 11, 1971 to Saros Cowasjee in *Author to Critic: the Letters of Mulk Raj Anand*, ed. Saros Cowasjee (Calcutta: Writers Workshop, 1973): "I wished to write about human beings who were not known or recognized as human at all, or admitted into society—such as the outcastes. . . . I not only tried to reveal things which the middle class did not accept but the hypocrisy of the bourgeoisie—by going below the surface to the various hells made by man for man . . ." (115).

18. E. M. Forster, preface to *Untouchable* by Mulk Raj Anand (London: Penguin, 1940) v, vi-vii.

19. K. Nagarajan cited in Dorothy M. Spencer, *Indian Fiction in English* (Philadelphia: U of Pennsylvania P, 1960) 36–37.

20. For Anand's treatment of the Gandhi-Ambedkar controversy see Gauri Viswanathan, *Outside the Fold: Conversion, Modernity, and Belief* (Princeton: Princeton UP, 1998) 220. "In adopting Gandhi's perspective," remarks Viswanathan, "Anand's narrative alienates and marginalizes the assertion of dalit will, and totally ignores the debate initiated by Ambedkar . . ." (220). But Viswanathan seems to have missed Anand's subtle irony, for none of the answers offered, including the Gandhian resolution, is the ideal answer. Also see Teresa Hubel's "Gandhi, Ambedkar, and *Untouchable*," *Whose India? The Independence Struggle in British and Indian Fiction and History* (Durham: Duke UP, 1996) 147–178.

21. "Under Ben Bulben," *W. B. Yeats: Selected Poetry*, ed. A. Norman Jeffares (London: Macmillan, 1967).

22. See Iyengar, *Indian Writing in English* 438.

23. *The Twice Born Fiction* 189.

24. *Indian Writing in English* 748.

25. See P. Lal's reference to T. S. Eliot's comment on *Hatterr* cited in Meenakshi Mukherjee, *The Twice Born Fiction* 127 n5.

26. H. M. Williams, *Indo-Anglican Literature 1800–1970: A Survey* (New Delhi: Orient Longman, 1976) 69.

27. Introduction, *Mirrorwork: 50 years of Indian Writing 1947–1997*, eds. Salman Rushdie and Elizabeth West (New York: Holt, 1997) xx.

28. Murray Krieger, "From Theory to Thematics: the Ideological Underside of Recent Theory," *Deconstruction: A Critique*, ed. Rajnath (London: Macmillan, 1989) 30.

29. See Northrop Fye, *The Critical Path: An Essay on the Social Context of Literary Criticism* (Bloomington: Indiana UP, 1971).

30. See Frye, *The Critical Path* 27.

31. See D. P. Chattopadhyaya, *History, Society and Polity: Integral Sociology of Sri Aurobindo* (New Delhi: Macmillan, 1976).

32. See Fredric Jameson, *The Political Unconscious: Narrative as a Socially Symbolic Act* (Ithaca: Cornell UP, 1981) 68–74.

33. See Jacques Barzun, *Darwin, Marx, Wagner: Critique of a Heritage*, rev. 2nd ed. (New York: Doubleday, 1958).

34. The intellectual argument in *The Critical Path* focuses on two myths, the myth of concern and the myth of freedom, in relation to critical theory. The work deals with the history of ideas in the social context from Kant to Marx and Morris.

35. Cited by Brook Thomas in the epigraph to his essay "Preserving and Keeping Order by Killing Time in *Heart of Darkness*," *Heart of Darkness: A Case Study in Contemporary Criticism*, ed. Ross C. Murfin (New York: St. Martin's, 1989) 237.

36. See Georg Lukács, *The Historical Novel*, trans. Hannah and Stanley Mitchell, preface by Irving Howe (Boston: Beacon, 1963) 171ff.

37. *The Political Unconscious* 35. For Jameson's interpretation of history in *The Political Unconscious* see Samuel Weber, "Capitalising History: Notes on *The Political Unconscious*," *The Politics of Theory*, ed. Francis Barker et al. (Colchester: U of Essex, 1983) 248–64.

38. Charles Taylor, *Hegel* (Cambridge: Cambridge UP, 1975) 470.

39. Cited in Taylor, *Hegel* 152. The unidentified quotations pertaining to Hegel are from Taylor.

40. See Helen Tiffin, "Post-Colonialism, Post-Modernism and the Rehabilitation of Post-Colonial History," *Journal of Commonwealth Literature* 23 (1988): 169–81. Also see Homi K. Bhabha, *The Location of Culture* (London: Routledge, 1994).

41. J. Jorge Klor de Alva, "The Postcolonization of the (Latin) American Experience: A Reconsideration of 'Colonialism,' 'Postcolonialism,' and 'Mestizaje,'" *After Colonialism: Imperial Histories and Postcolonial Displacements*, ed. Gyan Prakash (Princeton: Princeton UP, 1995) 245.

42. See Homi K. Bhabha, "Difference, Discrimination and the Discourse of Colonialism," *The Politics of Theory*, ed. Francis Barker et al. 194.

43. Marilyn Butler's term used by her in "Repossessing the Past: the Case for an Open Literary History," *Rethinking Historicism: Critical Readings in Romantic History*, ed. Marjorie Levinson et al. (Oxford: Blackwell, 1989) 66.

44. See Helen Tiffin's discussion of postcolonialism, postmodernism and poststructuralism in "Post-Colonialism, Post-Modernism and the Rehabilitation of Post-Colonial History"; and Stephen Selmon and Helen Tiffin, introduction, *After Europe: Critical Theory and Post-Colonial Writing*, eds.

Stephen Selmon and Helen Tiffin (Sydney: Dangaroo, 1989) ix-xxiii. For a philosophical perspective on postmodernism see Fredric Jameson's foreword to Jean-Francois Lyotard's *The Postmodern Condition: A Report on Knowledge,* trans. Geoff Bennington and Brian Massumi (Minneapolis: U of Minnesota P, 1984) vii-xxi.

45. Jerome McGann, "The Third World of Criticism," *Rethinking Historicism: Critical Readings in Romantic History,* ed. Marjorie Levinson et al. 85. The unidentified quotations in this paragraph are from McGann. Of course, McGann refers to Frantz Fanon's famous study *The Wretched of the Earth,* trans. Constance Farrington, preface by Jean-Paul Sartre (New York: Grove, 1963).

46. Walter Benjamin cited in McGann 86.

47. McGann 100. For a discussion of Aurobindo's and Balachandra Rajan's assessment of Milton see discussions in chapters 4 and 7.

48. See Ramkrishna Mukherjee, "Introductory," *The Rise and Fall of the East India Company: A Sociological Appraisal* (London: Monthly, 1974) xiii.

49. John Clive, series editor's preface, James Mill's *The History of British India,* introd. William Thomas (Chicago: U of Chicago P, 1975) viii.

50. William Thomas's introduction to Mill's *The History of British India* xxi. All unidentified quotations in the discussion that follows are from Thomas.

51. Eric Stokes, *The English Utilitarians and India* (Oxford: Clarendon, 1963) 54.

52. See Stokes's dominant assumption in *The English Utilitarians and India* and also the discussion in chapter 3.

53. Stokes 320–21.

54. Stokes 321.

55. Sir Alfred Lyall cited in Stokes 321–22.

56. See Edward Said's discussion of universalism in the context of imperialism in his *Culture and Imperialism* (New York: Knopf, 1993) 276ff.

57. Alfred Cobban, *Edmund Burke and the Revolt Against the Eighteenth Century* (London: Allen, 1962) 106.

58. Cobban 249.

59. See, for example, S. N. Mukherjee, *Sir William Jones: A Study in Eighteenth-Century British Attitudes to India,* 2nd ed. (Bombay: Orient Longman, 1987); and P. H. Salus, preface to *Sir William Jones: A Reader,* ed. Satya S. Pachori (Delhi: Oxford, 1993) 3–11.

60. See Edward Said's *Orientalism* (New York: Pantheon, 1978) 328.

61. Edward W. Said, *The World, the Text, and the Critic* (Cambridge: Harvard UP, 1983) 28.

62. *The World, the Text, and Critic* 29.

63. Ronald Inden, *Imagining India* (Oxford: Blackwell, 1990) 104.

64. Northrop Frye, *Fearful Symmetry* (Boston: Beacon, 1967) 173.

65. See Stuart Curran, *Shelley's Annus Mirabilis: The Maturing of an Epic Vision* (San Marino: Huntington, 1975) 213, 225–27. Can culture or religion as a structure of knowledge claim to be noncoercive, nonhegemonic and non-

manipulative? Historically, Akbar had used syncretism to strike some sort of unity between Hinduism and Islam and had initiated miscegeny, adaptation, assimilation and diffusion as techniques. See, for example, Gauri Viswanathan's "Beyond Orientalism: Syncretism and the Politics of Knowledge," *Stanford Humanities Review* 5.1 (1995): 19–34.

66. Cobban 217.
67. See Marilyn Butler's "Repossessing the Past: the Case for an Open Literary History," *Rethinking Historicism* 80.
68. William Blake, "The Marriage of Heaven and Hell," pl. 27, *The Complete Poetry and Prose of William Blake,* rev. ed. David V. Erdman (New York: Doubleday, 1988).
69. Introduction, *After Colonialism* 13.
70. See John Barrell, *The Infection of Thomas De Quincey: A Psychopathology of Imperialism* (New Haven: Yale UP, 1991) 6–7; and Nigel Leask, *British Romantic Writers and the East: Anxieties of Empire* (Cambridge: Cambridge UP, 1992) 5–6.
71. Ronald Inden 45.
72. Inden 47.
73. Patrick Brantlinger, *Rule of Darkness: British Literature and Imperialism, 1830–1914* (Ithaca: Cornell UP, 1990) 106–07.
74. John Stuart Mill, *On Liberty:* Annotated Text, Sources and Background, Criticism, ed. David Spitz (New York: Norton, 1975) 11.
75. Cited in Robert J. C. Young, *Colonial Desire: Hybridity in Theory, Culture and Race* (London: Routledge, 1995) 55.
76. Matthew Arnold, *Culture and Anarchy,* ed. J. Dover Wilson (Cambridge: Cambridge UP, 1966) 70.
77. Cited in Shlomo Avineri, *The Social and Political Thought of Karl Marx* (Cambridge: Cambridge UP, 1969) 170.
78. See Avineri's discussion of Marx's views on India 168–71; and Ramkrishna Mukherjee, *The Rise and Fall of East India Company: A Sociological Appraisal* 423ff. The unidentified quotations in this paragraph are from Avineri.
79. For divergent critical interpretations of E. M. Forster see Lisa Lowe, *Critical Terrains: French and British Orientalisms* (Ithaca: Cornell UP, 1991). As for Kipling, V. S. Naipaul seems to be a new endorser of Kipling's representation of India. See Rana Kabbani's discussion in his *Europe's Myths of Orient* (Bloomington: Indiana UP, 1986) 129–33.
80. *Culture and Imperialism* 60.
81. *The Historical Novel* 344.
82. See Henri Peyre's introduction, *The Failures of Criticism,* 2nd ed. (Ithaca: Cornell UP, 1967) 1–25.
83. Richard Ellmann, *The Identity of Yeats* (New York: Oxford UP, 1964) viii.
84. Tagore and Nehru cited in Ramkrishna Mukherjee 427–29.
85. I am primarily referring to Coleridge's theory of poetic creation as enunciated in *Biographia Literaria,* 2 vols., ed. J. Shawcross (Oxford: Oxford UP, 1965), chapters 13, 14 and 15; and the two essays "On the Principles of

Genial Criticism Concerning the Fine Arts" (2.219–46) and "On Poetry or Art" (2.253–63). The Romantic writers firmly believed in the power of the imagination to create, to mediate, to transmute and to reconstruct. See my discussion in chapters 2 and 4.

86. See Lukács's discussion in chapter 1 of *The Historical Novel.*

87. Coleridge cited in Alan Liu, *Wordsworth: The Sense of History* (Stanford: Stanford UP, 1989) 27. In *Manfred, Poetical Works* (London: Oxford UP, 1967), Byron portrays Napoleon as "The Captive Usurper" (2.3.16).

88. *Indian Writing in English* 410.

89. Cited in *Indian Writing in English* 404.

90. Introduction, *After Colonialism* 11–12.

91. Cited in Gyan Prakash, introduction 11.

92. Young 161.

93. See Meena Alexander, "Shelley's India: Territory and Text, Some Problems of Decolonization," *Shelley: Poet and Legislator of the World,* eds. Betty T. Bennett and Stuart Curran (Baltimore: John Hopkins UP, 1996) 169–78.

94. I am essentially referring to Fanon's monumental work *The Wretched of the Earth.* See n45 above. Also see Jean-Paul Sartre's important preface to *The Wretched of the Earth.*

95. See Gayatri Chakravorty Spivak, *The Post-Colonial Critic: Interviews, Strategies, Dialogues,* ed. Sarah Harasym (New York: Routledge, 1990) 158.

96. Gauri Viswanathan, "Coping with (Civil) Death: The Christian Convert's Rights of Passage in Colonial India," *After Colonialism* 185.

97. W. J. T. Mitchell cited in Biodun Jeyifo, "On Eurocentric Critical Theory: Some Paradigms from the Texts and Sub-Texts of Post-Colonial Writing," *After Europe: Critical Theory and Post-Colonial Writing,* eds. Stephen Selmon and Helen Tiffin 107–08. Note M. Keith Booker's observation on W. J. T. Mitchell's position: "For Mitchell, postcolonial literature and contemporary Western criticism are in a sense natural allies, given that both tend to situate themselves in opposition to the official ideology of the Western tradition" (*A Practical Introduction to Literary Theory and Criticism* [New York: Longman, 1996] 150).

98. See E. P. Thompson's discussion of the metaphorical usage "charter'd" in Blake's poem "London" in *Witness Against the Beast: William Blake and the Moral Law* (New York: New, 1993) 176–77, especially n5. On the subject of the control of creativity in the peripheries by imperial centers see Meenakshi Mukherjee, "The Center Cannot Hold: Two views of the Periphery," *After Europe* 41–57. Note Khushwant Singh's important question: should Indian writers be expected "to route their work through centers of light, like London, Paris or New York before they could be expected as good or great literature?"—cited in R. Sitaramiah, "The State of Literary Criticism," *Writing in India: The Seventh P. E. N. All India Writers' Conference, Lucknow 1964 (Proceedings),* ed. Nissim Ezekiel (Bombay: P. E. N.,1965) 200.

99. All textual references are to the Birth Centenary Library Edition of the Collected Works, to be referred as *BCL.*

100. Rabindranath Tagore, *Nationalism* (New York: Macmillan, 1917) 32.
101. Mulk Raj Anand, *Is There A Contemporary Indian Civilisation?* (London: Asia, 1963) 178. On the other hand, it can be argued that one should look at the predicament of a postcolonial critic. Note, for example, Gayatri Spivak's observation: "I cannot understand what indigenous theory there might be that can ignore the reality of nineteenth-century history. As for syntheses: syntheses have more problems than answers to offer" (*The Post-Colonial Critic* 69).
102. See J. M. Blaut's conceptualization of diffusionism or Eurocentric diffusionism in *The Colonizer's Model of the World: Geographical Diffusionism and Eurocentric History* (New York: Guilford, 1993).
103. Cited in Ruth Aproberts, "Nineteenth-Century Culture Wars" (a review article on the Yale edition of Matthew Arnold's *Culture and Anarchy*), *American Scholar* 64 (1995): 146.

CHAPTER 2

1. All textual references, unless otherwise indicated, are to the *Sri Aurobindo Birth Centenary Library Edition of the Collected Works,* to be referred as *BCL.* Shelley has also classified the world's great poets into three classes. In *Adonais,* Milton is "the third among the sons of light" (36). In *A Defence of Poetry,* Shelley says that "Milton [is] the third epic poet," Homer being the first and "Dante the second epic poet" (7.130). All references from Shelley are to *The Complete Works of Percy Bysshe Shelley,* 10 vols., eds. Roger Ingpen and Walter E. Peck (New York: Gordian, 1965).
2. For further biographical details see K. R. Srinivasa Iyengar, *Sri Aurobindo: A Biography and A History,* 2 vols., 3rd rev. ed. (Pondicherry: Sri Aurobindo International Centre, 1972); Prema Nandakumar, *Sri Aurobindo: A Brief Biography* (New Delhi: Government of India, 1972); and A. B. Purani, *The Life of Sri Aurobindo,* 4th ed. (Pondicherry : Sri Aurobindo Ashram, 1978). Iyengar notes two interesting facts: Aurobindo's "Christianized" name was Aravinda Ackroyd Ghose; and the favorite work of the young Aurobindo was Shelley's *The Revolt of Islam.*
3. See, for example, Sudhir Kakar's analysis of the relationship between culture and personality in his *The Inner World: A Psycho-analytic Study of Childhood and Society in India,* 2nd ed. (Delhi: Oxford UP, 1981), especially chapters 2 and 5. In chapter 5, Kakar has attempted a psychoanalytical study of Vivekanand. Also see A. S. Dalal, "Sri Aurobindo and Modern Psychology," *Journal of South Asian Literature* 24.1 (1989): 154–67. Dalal convincingly argues that Aurobindo's "concept of the vital is more inclusive than even Jung's concept of the libido" (165n), that Aurobindo's view of psychology "as the science of consciousness and its states and operations in Nature" anticipated the modern movements of humanistic psychology and transpersonal psychology and that Aurobindo's view of psychology as a discipline "by which man purifies and perfects himself" (164) is similar to the conception of psychology "as a self-knowledge discipline."

4. See, for example, D. P. Chattopadhyaya's remarks in his introduction to *History, Society and Polity: Integral Sociology of Sri Aurobindo* (New Delhi: Macmillan, 1976).

5. See C. T. Indra's essay "The Use of the Andromeda Myth in 'Perseus The Deliverer'" *Journal of South Asian Literature* 24.1 (1989): 50.

6. "Sri Aurobindo's Letters on 'Savitri,'" *Savitri: A Legend and a Symbol,* 3rd ed. (Pondicherry: Sri Aurobindo Ashram, 1970) 737.

7. It could very well be that despite the postcolonial developments the judgmental image of colonial India as advanced by Macaulay and the "India House Utilitarians" still persists in certain quarters. See Edward W. Said's interesting discussion of the problem in his "Introduction: Secular Criticism," *The World, the Text, and the Critic* (Cambridge: Harvard UP, 1983). "New cultures, new societies, and emerging visions of social, political, and aesthetic order," remarks Said, "now lay claim to the humanist's attention, with an insistence that cannot long be denied" (21).

8. Terry Eagleton, *Literary Theory: An Introduction* (Minneapolis: U of Minnesota P, 1983) 66. I have taken these three questions from Eagleton's commentary on Hans-Georg Gadamer's *Truth and Method* (1960). Gadamer, maintains Eagleton, is Heidegger's "most celebrated successor" (66). Eagleton distinguishes between Heidegger's philosophy of "hermeneutical phenomenology" and Husserl's "transcendental phenomenology": the fundamental difference between the two forms is that Heidegger's philosophy "bases itself upon questions of historical interpretation rather than on transcendental consciousness" (66).

9. *An Introduction to Metaphysics,* trans. Ralph Manheim (New York: Anchor, 1961) 86.

10. See Northrop Frye, "The Romantic Myth," *A Study of English Romanticism* (New York: Random, 1968) 3–49.

11. Rabindranath Tagore cited in K. R. Srinivasa Iyengar, *Sri Aurobindo* 1.29.

12. Cited in Prema Nandakumar, *A Study of 'Savitri'* (Pondicherry: Sri Aurobindo Ashram, 1962) 4–5. For an interesting exposition of a synthesis of East and West in Aurobindo see Charles E. Moore, "Sri Aurobindo on East and West," *The Integral Philosophy of Sri Aurobindo: A Commemorative Symposium,* eds. Haridas Chaudhuri and Frederic Spiegelberg (London: Allen, 1960) 81–110.

13. Cited in *The Moving Finger: An Anthology of Essays in Literary and Aesthetic Criticism by Indian Writers,* ed. V. N. Bhushan (Bombay: Padma, 1945) 1.

14. See, for example, K. D. Sethna's review of some of the criticism of Sri Aurobindo in his *Sri Aurobindo—The Poet* (Pondicherry: Sri Aurobindo International Centre, 1970) 403ff. Speaking of his standing as a poet and especially of his relationship to the "modern consciousness," Sisirkumar Ghose admits that Aurobindo "remains a controversial, even an enigmatic figure" ("Sri Aurobindo—Poet as Seer," *Sri Aurobindo: An Interpretation,* ed. V. C. Joshi [Delhi: Vikas, 1973] 43).

15. Cited in Nandakumar, *A Study of 'Savitri'* 436.

16. Cited in Nandakumar, *A Study of 'Savitri'* 540.
17. See chapter 7, "*Savitri:* A Cosmic Epic," in Nandakumar, *A Study of 'Savitri'*.
18. See, for example, Northrop Frye's criticism of T. S. Eliot in "The Archetypes of Literature," *Fables of Identity: Studies in Poetic Mythology* (New York:
Harcourt, 1963) 8–9.
19. See Aurobindo's discussion of Milton in chapter 12 of *The Future Poetry,* and
his "Letters on 'Savitri,'" appended to *Savitri: A Legend and a Symbol.* Also see
my discussion of Aurobindo's assessment of Milton in chapter 5. In "Milton
and Sri Aurobindo," *Journal of South Asian Literature* 24.1 (1989): 67–82, K. R.
Srinivasa Iyengar, while tracing parallels between Milton's life and Aurobindo's life, especially the circumstances governing the creation of *Paradise
Lost* and *Savitri,* rightly calls attention to Aurobindo's keen and quick recognition of Milton's achievement in *Paradise Lost.* And yet "Milton's comparative failure to project in convincingly resplendent terms Adam, Eve or the
Heavenly Father, and in later works Christ or Samson," maintains Iyengar,
"was simply due to 'a failure of vision'" (70). In considering *Savitri* along with
the world's great epical poems, such as the *Commedia* and *Paradise Lost,* we
will be quick to note that the direct relationship, if there is one, especially in
terms of style and epic structure, is between *Savitri* and *Paradise Lost.* Is *Savitri*
Miltonic? Aurobindo's answer to the charge of "Miltonism" is a categorical
"no." Keats, it may be noted, had also denied the charge of Miltonism.
20. See Northrop Frye, "Polemical Introduction," *Anatomy of Criticism: Four
Essays* (Princeton: Princeton UP, 1957). "Criticism," maintains Frye, "is a
structure of knowledge . . ." (*The Critical Path: An Essay on the Social Context of Literary Criticism* [Bloomington, Indiana UP, 1971] 27).
21. See *A Defence of Poetry* 7.124.
22. See Harold Bloom, *The Anxiety of Influence: A Theory of Poetry* (New York:
Oxford UP, 1973).
23. See, for example, S. K. Maitra's comparison between Sri Aurobindo and
Goethe in his *The Meeting of the East and the West in Sri Aurobindo's Philosophy* (Pondichery: Sri Aurobindo Ashram, 1956) 336–98. There is also
Nandakumar's important study *Dante and Sri Aurobindo: A Comparative
Study of The Divine Comedy and Savitri* (Madras: Affiliated, 1981), comparing the *Divine Comedy* with *Savitri.*
24. See Aurobindo Ghose's excellent essay "On Quantitative Metre," *BCL*
5.341–87. Sethna cites Banning Richardson's comments on Aurobindo's
essay, which appeared in *The Aryan Path* of March 1944: "[This essay] deserves wide currency and consideration by all those interested in the future of English poetry and of poetry in general. . . . In it he [Aurobindo]
seems to have struck at the root of the problem which modern poets have
been attempting to solve by recourse to free verse forms. Both argument
and example are convincing, and one wonders whether poets like Eliot,
Auden and Spender have reached similar conclusions. At least they should
be made aware of this considerable contribution to English prosody by an
Indian poet" (*Sri Aurobindo—The Poet* 116 n1).

25. K. D. Sethna, *Sri Aurobindo—The Poet* 131. It is significant to note that Herbert Read considers *Ilion* "a remarkable achievement by any standard," further noting "the skillful elaboration [of the English language] into poetic diction of such high quality" (Letter of June 5, 1958, cited by Sethna in *Sri Aurobindo—The Poet* 132).

26. Note the following observation made by Aurobindo in one of his letters appended to *Savitri*: "But if I had to write for the general reader I could not have written *Savitri* at all. It is in fact for myself that I have written it and for those who can lend themselves to the subject-matter, images, technique of mystic poetry" (*BCL* 29.735).

27. This seems to be a fairly standard approach to the study of *Savitri*. See, for example, Nandakumar, *A Study of 'Savitri'*. But the new critics, including I. A. Richards, advocate the independent character of a poem, divested of all other addenda, appendices and aids, including the biography of a poet. In his essay on Dante, T. S. Eliot also raises some very pertinent questions about the relationship between Dante's theology and Dante's poetry as well as the place of *Summa Theologica* in the study of Dante. See Eliot, "Dante," *Selected Essays,* new ed. (New York: Harcourt, 1960) 199–237.

28. See my essay "Myth and Symbol in Aurobindo's *Savitri*: A Revaluation," *Journal of South Asian Literature* 12.3 and 4 (1977): 67–72.

29. In *Dawn to Greater Dawn: Six Lectures on Sri Aurobindo's Savitri* (Simla: Indian Institute of Advanced Studies, n.d.) 62ff., Iyengar notes the difference between the original Mahabharata legend and Aurobindo's treatment of it. Nandakumar (*A Study of 'Savitri'* 288–99) and P. C. Kotoky (*Indo-English Poetry : A Study of Sri Aurobindo and Four Others* [Gauhati: Gauhati UP, 1969] n40, 188–89) also refer to some of the differences. It should be noted that Toru Dutt and Manmohan Ghose had shown interest in this legend of conjugal love. In "'The air is holy': Holst's *Savitri,*" *South Asian Review* 8.5 (1984): 86–89, Peter Garvie notes that Gustav Holst had written a chamber opera "Savitri." But whether or not Aurobindo was familiar with the opera cannot be ascertained.

30. It is significant to note that in the metaphysics of death Aurobindo seems to echo some of the issues posed by scientific materialism, and especially by Darwinism—issues that had preoccupied the Victorians. For example, Tennyson in his epic elegy *In Memoriam* treats questions pertaining to the soul's immortality, identity of the individual soul and the cleavage between science and religion.

31. It should be clearly understood that in Aurobindo's thought it is *not* annihilation or negation but transformation that is the way of discovering one's self. Aurobindo, as G. H. Langley maintains, does not believe in the negation of one's individuality: "What must be negated are the egocentric motives that, in his present condition, so largely dominate man's activity and purpose. Union with the Divine does not abolish individual existence; it transforms the individual being and nature by revealing to individuals their true significance. Enjoyment by man of his union with the Divine is, in

fact, the only means to fulfillment of his individual being" (*Sri Aurobindo: Indian Poet, Philosopher and Mystic* [London: David Marlowe, 1949] 56). In *Worthy is the World: The Hindu Philosophy of Sri Aurobindo* (Rutherford: Farleigh Dickinson UP, 1971), Beatrice Bruteau notes "Aurobindo's thesis of the three poises of Brahman," and observes: "He [Aurobindo] has no difficulty in admitting the union of the human spirit with the Absolute and at the same time preserving the individuality of man" (243).

32. In *Evolution in Religion: A Study in Sri Aurobindo and Pierre Teilhard de Chardin* (Oxford: Clarendon, 1971), Zaehner remarks that Aurobindo during his stay in England "had come to accept Darwinism and Bergson's idea of *creative* evolution" (10). But Sethna in *The Spirituality of the Future: A Search apropos of R. C. Zaehner's Study of Sri Aurobindo and Teilhard de Chardin* (Rutherford: Farleigh Dickinson UP, 1981) contradicts Zaehner's contention that Aurobindo was influenced by Bergson's theory of creative evolution (29).

33. *Evolution in Religion* 35.

34. Cited in Purani, *The Life of Sri Aurobindo* 160.

35. For a discussion of Aurobindo's theory of evolution see R. S. Srivastava, "The Integralist Theory of Evolution," *The Integral Philosophy of Sri Aurobindo,* eds. Chaudhuri and Spiegelberg 133–42.

36. See Zaehner, *Evolution in Religion;* Sethna, *The Spirituality of the Future;* and Frank J. Korom, "The Evolutionary Thought of Aurobindo Ghose and Teilhard de Chardin," *Journal of South Asian Literature* 24.1 (1989): 124–40.

37. See S. K. Maitra, "Sri Aurobindo and Spengler: Comparison between the Integral and the Pluralistic Philosophy of History," *The Integral Philosophy of Sri Aurobindo,* eds. Chaudhuri and Spiegelberg 60–80.

38. See Maitra, "Sri Aurobindo and Spengler" 69.

39. See my essay "The Woman Figure in Blake and the Idea of Shakti in Indian Thought" *Comparative Literature Studies* 27.3 (1990) 193–210; and introduction to my *The Vision of "Love's Rare Universe": A Study of Shelley's Epipsychidion* (Lanham: UP of America, 1995) 1–12.

40. For the conception of Saccidanand as Reality or Absolute Reality see Maitra, *The Meeting of the East and the West in Sri Aurobindo's Philosophy* 9, 217. Ultimate Reality as Saccidanand is existence, knowledge and bliss. See Steve Odin's explanation of Saccidanand in terms of the Vedantic concept of reality and the Hegelian Absolute in "Sri Aurobindo and Hegel on the involution-evolution of Absolute Spirit" *Philosophy East and West* 31.2 (1981): 179–91. But Aurobindo's "conception of the Absolute," maintains Odin, "is thus closer in nature to the Absolute described by F. H. Bradley in terms of the 'Felt Totality' as an undivided 'suprarational' whole of sentient feeling or an indivisible continuum of experiential immediacy existing anterior to or beyond the subject-object division of cognitional awareness" (180). Also see A. C. Das's interpretation of Saccidanand as Reality in his essay "Sri Aurovinda's Theory of Superman," *Sri Aurovinda* (Calcutta: Asiatic Society, 1976) 10–25.

222   *The Indian Imagination*

41. See George Steiner, *Language and Silence: Essays on Language, Literature, and the Inhuman* (New York: Atheneum, 1967) 36ff.; and Harold Coward, "Language in Sri Aurobindo," *Journal of South Asian Literature* 24.1 (1989): 141–53.

42. For a discussion of Aurobindo's theory of poetry as mantra see S. K. Prasad, *Sri Aurobindo* (Patna: Bharati, 1974), chapter 5.

43. Note Shelley's lament in *Epipsychidion:*

> Woe is me!
> The wingéd words on which my soul would pierce
> Into the height of Love's rare Universe,
> Are chains of lead around its flight of fire—
> (587–90)

44. See *The Future of Poetry, BCL* 9.125.

45. The conceptual term "*ananda*" is extensively used by Aurobindo in his poetics and metaphysics. In one of his letters (*BCL* 29.802ff.) Aurobindo explains the conception of the "Overhead" poetry and of the "Overhead aesthesis": The "universal Ananda," "the parent of aesthesis," "is the artist and creator of the universe witnessing, experiencing and taking joy in its creation" (810).

46. The modern poet, according to Aurobindo, "must preserve as jealously and satisfy by steeping all that he finds in his wider field in that profoundest vision which delivers out of each thing its spiritual Ananda, the secret of truth and beauty in it for which it was created; it is in the sense of that spiritual joy of vision, and not in any lower sensuous, intellectual or imaginative seeing, that Keats' phrase becomes true for the poet, beauty that is truth, truth that is beauty, and this all that we need to know as the law of our aesthetic knowledge" (*BCL* 9.247). The "Overhead aesthesis" in Aurobindo is somewhat similar to "spiritual sensation" in Blake. Note Kathleen Raine's interesting observation: "The poem *Infant Joy,* in appearance so simple, is in truth the fine flower of this philosophy. 'Joy is my name' does not so much describe as define a child. Joy is not an attribute of life: life is joy, *ananda;* and all lives delight in the play of their own existence in the divine Being" (*Blake and Tradition* [Princeton: Princeton UP, 1968] 2.130).

47. Sri Aurobindo, as Sethna contends in *The Spirituality of the Future,* "explicitly declared that his Yoga and his Ashram had nothing to do with any religion as such" (73).

48. See, for example, Eliot's essay "The Unity of European Culture," *Christianity and Culture: The Idea of a Christian Society and Notes towards the Definition of Culture* (New York: Harcourt, 1949), where Eliot maintains that the "dominant force in creating a common culture . . . is religion" (200). Hence, the conception of Christian culture as a basis for the progress and unity of the Western world. But Eliot clearly enunciates his social biology in the following distinction: "If Christianity goes, the whole of our culture goes"; and

also, "If Asia were converted to Christianity tomorrow, it would not thereby become a part of Europe" ("The Unity of European Culture" 200). Why should an ideal culture appropriate for itself "the structurally closed character of political societies and of languages?" Note Lacombe's important observation: "Wisdom, science, moral values, values of art *tend* to overcome by themselves territorial boundaries. The higher the pitch of a civilization, the greater is its force of appeal, the more radiant its universalism" ("The Problem of Human Unity," *Sri Aurobindo: A Centenary Tribute*, ed. K. R. Srinivasa Iyengar [Pondicherry: Sri Aurobindo Ashram, 1974] 230).

49. "T. S. Eliot," *Abinger Harvest* (New York: Harcourt, 1964) 94.

50. Iyengar's reference is to the famous lines in *The Waste Land:* "Ganga was sunken . . ."; but it is with reference to the last passage ("Then spoke the thunder"—the passage where Eliot employs the fable of the Thunder from the *Brihadaranyaka Upanishad*) that leads Iyengar to say that "the issue is left in doubt" (*Dawn to Greater Dawn* 59).

51. I am using the expression in the same sense as is used by Northrop Frye in *The Critical Path*. But can we look beyond the simple sociology of a myth? Is it possible to combine the two myths, the myth of concern and the myth of freedom, into a larger and more comprehensive myth that encompasses the total dream of man? Does literature create mythologies or patterns of civilization, that allow for the spiritualization of the human race? In *Savitri* and elsewhere, Aurobindo the poet and thinker addresses these and other issues with unique clarity and boldness. See, for example, Sisirkumar Ghose's discussion in his *Sri Aurobindo: Poet and Social Thinker* (Dharwar: Karnatak,1973).

52. Langley ix.

CHAPTER 3

1. See Karan Singh, *Prophet of Indian Nationalism: A Study of the Political Thought of Sri Aurobindo Ghosh, 1893–1910* (London: Allen, 1963); Vishwanath Prasad Varma, *The Political Philosophy of Sri Aurobindo* (New York: Asia, 1960); and Sisirkumar Mitra, *Sri Aurobindo* (New Delhi: Indian Book, 1972). R. C. Majumdar notes: "Today Arabinda is known more as a Rishi or a spiritual leader than anything else. But we can look upon him as a great political seer and leader who played the most important role in the last phase of India's struggle for independence. . . . He was indeed the prophet of Nationalism. For the two chief characteristics of nationalism which brought about a radical change in our politics were initiated by Arabinda. These were a clarion call to look upon complete independence of India as our goal and to substitute for the policy of mendicancy followed by the then Congress, a policy of self-help and passive resistance to achieve the goal" (qtd. by Mitra, *Sri Aurobindo* 115–16).

2. See, for example, the views expressed in the *Bande Mataram* of Feb. 6, 1908: "Nationalism is itself no creation of individuals and can have no respect for

persons. It is a force which God has created, and from Him it has received only one command, to advance and advance and ever advance until He bids it stop, because its appointed mission is done. It advances, inexorably, blindly, unknowing how it advances, in obedience to a power which it cannot gainsay, and every thing which stands in its way, man or institution, will be swept away, or ground into powder beneath its weight. Ancient sanctity, supreme authority, bygone popularity, nothing will serve as a plea" (*Bande Mataram: Early Political Writings,* vol. 1, *Sri Aurobindo Birth Centenary Library Edition of Collected Works* [Pondicherry: Sri Aurobindo Trust, 1970–72] 669). A more expanded and comprehensive analysis of this conception appears in *The Human Cycle.* All textual references, unless otherwise indicated, are to the Birth Centenary Library edition of collected works, to be referred to as *BCL.*

3. See S. K. Maitra, "Sri Aurobindo and Spengler: Comparison between the Integral and Pluralistic Philosophy of History," *The Integral Philosophy of Sri Aurobindo: A Commemorative Symposium,* eds. Haridas Chaudhuri and Frederic Spiegelberg (London: Allen, 1960) 60–80. Maitra argues that Aurobindo's philosophy of evolution is not cyclical in the same sense as is Spengler's, although Aurobindo himself calls the pattern cyclical. For an exposition of the "cyclical" pattern in Aurobindo see Kishore Gandhi, *Social Philosophy of Sri Aurobindo and the New Age,* 2nd ed. (Pondicherry: Sri Aurobindo Society, 1991).

4. R. C. Zaehner, *Evolution in Religion: A Study in Sri Aurobindo and Pierre Teilhard de Chardin* (Oxford: Clarendon, 1971) 4.

5. I believe Zaehner's point is that Marxism was one of several possibilities—Vedanta, Christianity and others—that during the process of transvaluation and synthesis should have converged into a common structure of reality. For a detailed comparison between Aurobindo and Marx see D. P. Chattopadhyaya, *History, Society and Polity: Integral Sociology of Sri Aurobindo* (New Delhi: Macmillan, 1976). For a criticism of Zaehner see K. D. Sethna, *The Spirituality of the Future: A Search apropos of R. C. Zaehner's Study in Sri Aurobindo and Teilhard de Chardin* (Rutherford: Farleigh Dickinson UP, 1981).

6. In *Nationalism: A Religion* (New York: Macmillan, 1960), Carlton J. H. Hayes notes that "modern nationalism, as we know it today, had its original seat in England" (39), that nationalism which was supposed to be a spiritual force degenerated into an intolerant and belligerent force (chapter 7), that nationalism became "the seed and product of the New Imperialism" (chapter 8) and that nationalism was a cause of World War I (chapter 9).

7. Robert H. Murray, *Studies in the English Social and Political Thinkers of the Nineteenth Century,* 2 vols. (Cambridge: Heffer, 1972) 2.210.

8. Colonization, according to Coleridge, is "not only a manifest experiment, but an imperative duty in Great Britain. God seems to hold out His finger to us over the sea. But it must be a national colonisation" (Cited by Murray 1.177). In Carlyle's writings, notes Murray, there is a strong note of a

happy imperialist (1.350–51); and Disraeli, according to Murray, "was always an imperialist, anxious to consolidate the empire by evoking the sympathies of the colonies for the Mother Country" (1.231).

9. The issue of the origin and growth of colonialism is, indeed, controversial. Marx, for example, considers colonialism originating from economic imperialism or capitalism. Moin Shakir observes that Marx had "firmly established a correlation between colonialism and capitalism ("Karl Marx on Colonialism," *Colonial Consciousness in Commonwealth Literature,* eds. G. S. Amur and S. K. Desai [Bombay: Somaiya, 1984] 260). British imperialism in India, according to Marx, proved "regenerative" (Chattopadhyaya 96).

10. Murray 2.211.

11. See Alfred Cobban, *Edmund Burke and the Revolt Against the Eighteenth Century* (London: Allen, 1962) 48. Burke had spearheaded the impeachment proceedings against Warren Hastings; and "[had] called on the country [England] to fit itself for world-wide dominion by abandoning old parochial limitations, or rather by expanding them to the utmost limits of Empire" (Cobban 48). Concerning the allegations against Hastings, "George III wrote of 'shocking enormities in India that disgrace human nature'" (P. J. Marshall, introduction, *The Impeachment of Warren Hastings* [London: Oxford UP, 1965] xviii).

12. Note Aurobindo's poignant criticism of Lord Morley, "The Radical philosopher, the biographer of Voltaire and Rousseau": " . . . for the life of John Morley is a mass of contradictions, the profession of liberalism running hand in hand with the practice of a bastard Imperialism which did the work of Satan while it mouthed liberal Scripture to justify its sins" (*BCL* 1.863).

13. See Eric Stokes, *The English Utilitarians and India* (Oxford: Clarendon, 1963) 286–322.

14. Stokes 298.

15. See Rabindranath Tagore, *Nationalism* (New York: Macmillan, 1917) 32. Tagore maintains that the famous statement, "East is east and the West is west and never the twain shall meet," is clearly an expression of "arrogant cynicism" (32).

16. Joseph Conrad, *Heart of Darkness:* Complete Authoritative Text with Biographical and Historical Contexts, Critical History, and Essays, 2nd ed., ed. Ross C. Murfin (New York: St. Martin's, 1996) 66. I agree with Meenakshi Mukherjee's main thesis that Africa in Conrad's *Heart of Darkness* and India in Forster's *A Passage to India* "are in each case metaphors for a larger human experience," but I do not agree with her observation when she says that these works are "basically not about racial and political issues at all" ("Caliban's Growth: Impact of Colonialism," *Colonial Consciousness in Commonwealth Literature* 219). If India and Africa are comprehensive metaphors, then political reality must be an integral part of the total structure of reality that these metaphors represent.

17. Note Nehru's observation: "It is significant to note that great political mass movements in India have had a spiritual background behind them. In Sri Aurobindo's case, this was obvious . . . Mahatma Gandhi's appeal to the people of India . . . was essentially spiritual" (foreword, Karan Singh's *Prophet of Indian Nationalism* 7). In *Metaphysical Foundations of Mahatma Gandhi's Thought* (New Delhi: Orient Longmans, 1970), Surendra Verma maintains that Gandhi "makes religion his soul objective. . . . What he really wants to achieve is self-realization and his ventures in political field are directed towards this very goal" (9).

18. For these two divergent positions, the extremists and the moderates see John R. McLane, *Indian Nationalism and the Early Congress* (Princeton: Princeton UP, 1977) 152–78; and Jim Masselos, *Indian Nationalism: An History* (New Delhi: Sterling, 1985) 93–118. Aurobindo did accept the idea of passive resistance, but the type of passive resistance he advocated meant a categorical moral war against slavery and exploitation. In this connection, see "The Doctrine of Passive Resistance" and "The Morality of Boycott," *BCL* 1.85–128. Also see "Revolutions and Leadership," *BCL* 1.668–70; and the play "The Slaying of Congress," *BCL* 1.671–96. Even after his retirement from active political struggle, his position on the subject remained unchanged. For example, in his letter of December 1, 1922 to Barindera Kumar Ghose, he reiterates: "As you know, I do not believe that the Mahatma's principle can be the true foundation or his programme the true means of bringing out the genuine freedom and greatness of India, her Swarajya and Samrajya. On the other hand others would think that I was sticking to the school of Tilakite nationalism. That also is not the fact, as I hold that school to be out of date" (*BCL* 26.438).

19. "In November 1886, before the second Congress met," remarks Anil Seal, "Syed Ahmed Khan publicly declared India unready for representative or popular government, and condemned Congress as 'seditious'" (*The Emergence of Indian Nationalism: Competition and Collaboration in the Later Nineteenth Century* [Cambridge: Cambridge UP, 1968] 320). Indeed, it was the interest of Muslims—the fear of Muslims being reduced to the status of a perpetual minority—that led Sir Syed Ahmed Khan to support the colonial regime.

20. Aurobindo's withdrawal from the active political scene has been a subject of some speculation and concern. But Aurobindo, as this essay explicitly shows, did not divorce himself from the social and political problems of India. Although the writings in the *Arya* from 1915–18, which later appeared as *The Psychology of Social Development* and *The Ideal of Human Unity* (*BCL* 15), sufficiently show the nature and scope of Aurobindo's commitment, we may especially refer to the following excerpt from his letter of the Pondicherry period: "Pondicherry is my place of retreat, my cave of tapasya, not of the ascetic kind, but of a brand of my own invention. I must finish that, I must be internally armed and equipped for my work before I leave it. . . . I do not at all look down on politics or political action or con-

sider I have got above them. I have always laid a dominant stress and I now lay an entire stress on the spiritual life . . . all human activity is for me a thing to be included in a complete spiritual life, and the importance of politics at the present time is very great. But my line and intention of political activity would differ considerably from anything now current in the field. I entered into political action and continued it from 1903 to 1910 with one aim and one alone, to get into the mind of the people a settled will for freedom and the necessity of a struggle to achieve it in place of the futile ambling Congress methods till then in vogue. . . . I hold that India having a spirit of her own and a governing temperament proper to her own civilisation, should in politics as in everything else strike out her own original path and not stumble in the wake of Europe" (Letter to Joseph Batista in response to his invitation to accept the editorship of an English daily newspaper, *BCL* 26.430–31). There is enormous evidence, as D. Mackenzie Brown notes, concerning Aurobindo's active interest in India's political development: synthesis of East and West into an international brotherhood; his open expression of support for the Allies during World War II; his fear of German aggression of Asia; his enthusiastic support of the Cripps's Mission Proposal; and the formation of linguistic provinces under the new constitution (*The White Umbrella* [Berkeley: U of California P, 1958] 123).

21. In *Social Philosophy of Sri Aurobindo and the New Age,* Kishore Gandhi maintains that after the first few chapters of *The Human Cycle* Aurobindo did not follow Karl Lamprecht's rigid categorization that was based on "materialistic-economic conception of history and society" (86) and that he subsequently used his own broad divisions, namely, infrarational, rational and suprarational. The infrarational stage includes Lapmrecht's three stages, symbolic, typal and conventional; the rational stage is common to both; and the "suprarational stage is a wider extension of the subjective age of the earlier sequence" (87).

22. Spencer, observes Ernest Barker, learned from Coleridge that life is "a transcendental principle, in virtue of which nature as a whole, and society as a part of nature, evolve from within outwards towards a final 'individuation'": " . . . but it was Coleridge, and Schelling through Coleridge, who gave precise form to the hypothesis [of evolution]. In all nature, he came to argue, and therefore in human society, there is transcendental and divine force of life. Hence it follows that nature and society are living organisms: it follows that in virtue of their immanent life they develop; and this development may be regarded as a process of individuation or differentiation, which is combined with co-ordination of the differentiated elements" (*Political Thought in England, 1848 to 1914,* 2nd ed. [London: Oxford UP, 1963] 74).

23. Aurobindo, as V. Madhusudan Reddy maintains, "steers clear of two extreme views of evil. The first extreme view, sponsored by India, looked upon evil as unreal and as product of ignorance. . . . The other extreme

view . . . is one which has generally found favour in the west and which treats evil as a permanent feature of the world" (*Sri Aurobindo's Philosophy of Evolution* [Hyderabad: Institute of Human Study, 1966] 324–25). For a lucid discussion of the problem of evil in Aurobindo see S. K. Maitra, *The Meeting of the East and the West in Sri Aurobindo's Philosophy* (Pondicherry: Sri Aurobindo Ashram, 1968) 111–50. For Aurobindo's own view of evil see *The Life Divine, BCL* 18, chapter 14. It should be noted that while denying absolutism of evil, Aurobindo readily admits absolutism of good.

24. In *The Religious Roots of Indian Nationalism* (Calcutta: Mukhopadhyay, 1974), David L. Johnson, for example, raises the issue of the failure of synthesis between political goals and spiritual goals. "And given the complete isolation from politics, as well as the duration of that isolation," remarks Johnson, "I would maintain that Aurobindo was convinced of a basic incompatibility between spiritual goals and political goals" (119). See June O'Connor's comment on Johnson's criticism in *The Quest for Political and Spiritual Liberation: A Study in the Thought of Sri Aurobindo Ghose* (Rutherford: Farleigh Dickinson UP, 1977) 123ff.: "But in the later (spiritual) period, to integrate the two was no longer necessary, for Aurobindo no longer viewed political involvement as a value to be nourished. His vision of the supramental provoked to devalue the political forum as an 'impure form' unworthy of one's energy. To say that Aurobindo dramatically exemplifies an 'ideal blending of social-political activism and spiritual discipline' at most refers to chronological sequence, not to matured philosophical conviction nor intended contribution" (137). I am inclined to believe that both Johnson and O'Connor have contradicted themselves, and have not shown adequate and clear understanding of Aurobindo's spiritual vision of human progress and unity. Furthermore, it is difficult to see the relevance of social and political activism to the nature and scope of a poet's or a philosopher's vision, for a poet or a philosopher does not have to prove the validly of his vision by his activism.

25. "[Is] it possible," wonders June O'Connor, "that Aurobindo's impact might delay or even impede the progress of social reform in India?" (138)

CHAPTER 4

1. Cited in D. MacKenzie Brown, *Indian Political Thought from Manu to Gandhi* (Berkeley: U of California P, 1958) 124.
2. See, for example, C. D. Narasimhaiah's essay "Aurobindo: Inaugurator of Modern Indian Criticism," *Journal of South Asian Literature* 24.1 (1989): 87–103 where he criticizes K. R. Srinivasa Iyengar for not paying adequate attention to Aurobindo's work as a critic. See S. K. Prasad, *Sri Aurobindo (with special reference to his poetry)* (Patna: Bharati Bhawan, 1974); and K. D. Sethna, *Sri Aurobindo on Shakespeare* (Pondicherry: Sri Aurobindo Ashram, 1965).
3. See Mulk Raj Anand's "Sri Aurobindo the Critic of Art," *Journal of South Asian Literature* 24.1 (1989): 104–13. For the relationship between Au-

robindo's literary and critical conceptions as expounded in *The Future Poetry* and classical Indian aesthetic see V. Raghavan, "Sri Aurobindo's Aesthetics," *Sri Aurobindo: A Centenary Tribute,* ed. K. R. Srinivasa Iyengar (Pondicherry: Sri Aurobindo Ashram, 1974).

4. See my brief commentary on Dilip Kumar Chatterjee's article "Cousins and Sri Aurobindo: A Study in Literary Influence," *Journal of South Asian Literature* 24.1 (1989): 114–23 in "Observations," *Journal of South Asian Literature* 24.1 (1989): 1–9. A study like James H. Cousins's *The Work Promethean* (Port Washington: Kennikat, 1970) may suggest that there are certain similarities in the thinking of the two minds, but it is incorrect to suggest that Aurobindo was influenced by Cousins.

5. See Aurobindo's introductory essay in *The Future Poetry,* vol. 9 of *Sri Aurobindo Birth Centenary Library Edition of Collected Works,* 30 vols. (Pondicherry: Sri Aurobindo Ashram, 1970–72). All references to *The Future Poetry (FP)* and other works of Aurobindo are to *Sri Aurobindo Birth Centenary Library Edition of Collected Works (BCL).* It should be noted that the section "Letters on Poetry, Art and Literature" of vol. 9 contains extended references to Yeats, D. H. Lawrence, Bernard Shaw and Bertrand Russell.

6. Cited in Basil Willey, *Samuel Taylor Coleridge* (New York: Norton, 1973) 15.

7. "Observations" 3. Also see my essay "Sri Aurobindo As A Poet: A Reassessment," chapter 2. Undoubtedly, Aurobindo was deeply immersed in Indian literatures, ancient and modern. See, for example, Aurobindo's three important essays: "Bankim Chandra Chatterjee," *BCL* 3.73–102; "Valmiki and Vyasa," *BCL* 3.136–209; and "Kalidasa," *BCL* 3.212–301. Given his enviable scholarly background in European and Indian literatures, both classical and modern, and in English literature, Aurobindo is incontestably best suited for a comparativist examination and a possible synthesis of paradigmatic structures of thought and language.

8. Of course, one must consider the impact of several other disciplines. Admittedly, there is a long line of philosophers from Plato to the contemporary scene—Plato, Aristotle, Rousseau, Kant, Hegel, Nietzsche, Heidegger and Husserl. One needs to look into Derrida's philosophy of deconstruction. See Vincent B. Leitch's historical survey in his *Deconstructive Criticism: An Advanced Introduction* (New York: Columbia UP, 1983). Also see John M. Ellis's discussion in chapters 1 and 2 of *Against Deconstruction* (Princeton: Princeton UP, 1989).

9. I am particularly referring to the critical theory of Northrop Frye as formulated in *Anatomy of Criticism* (Princeton: Princeton UP, 1957). I must also refer to some of the essays in *Fables of Identity: Studies in Poetic Mythology* (New York: Harcourt, 1963), notably the first four essays in section 1.

10. Frye, "The Archetypes of Literature," *Fables of Identity* 8. Also see the two very generic essays in this argument: Matthew Arnold's "The Function of Criticism at the Present Time," *Selections from the Prose Works of Matthew Arnold,* ed. William Savage Johnson (New York: Houghton, 1913); and T. S.

Eliot's "The Function of Criticism," *Selected Essays,* new ed. (New York: Harcourt, 1964) 12–22.

11. K. D. Sethna rightly notes the main points of Aurobindo's candid criticism of Cousins (*Sri Aurobindo on Shakespeare* 5–6). See Aurobindo's criticism of Cousins as a critic, *BCL* 26.276–77. It is abundantly clear that Aurobindo does not regard any form of persiflage and adverse criticism as genuine literary criticism. Section 6 "The Poet and Critic," *BCL* 26.220–347, contains some important observations, showing Aurobindo's critical acumen and intellectual capacity for enlightened practical criticism. See, for example, his observation on Hopkins and Kipling: " . . . he [Hopkins] is a poet, which Kipling never was nor could be. He has vision, power, originality; but his technique errs by excess; he piles on you his effects, repeats, exaggerates and in the end it is perhaps great in effort, but not great in success. Much material is there, many new suggestions, but not a work realised, not a harmoniously perfect whole" (*BCL* 26.344). In fact, Aurobindo has drawn a clear distinction between a good critic and a bad critic. In this regard, compare Aurobindo's conception with Eliot's in the first two chapters of *The Scared Wood: Essays on Poetry and Criticism* (London: Methuen, 1967) 1–46.

12. See S. T. Coleridge, *Biographia Literaria,* 2 vols., ed. J. Shawcross (London: Oxford UP, 1965), chapter 14. "The Poet, described in i*deal* perfection," remarks Coleridge, "brings the whole soul of man into activity . . ." (2.12). Note Coleridge's engagement with three basic questions: What is Poetry? What is a Poem? What is a Poet? See the discussion in chapter 15 on "the specific symptoms of poetic power" (2.13).

13. Ananda K. Coomaraswamy, *The Dance of Shiva,* rev. ed. (New York: Noonday, 1969) 51. See Coomaraswamy's extended discussion of *rasa* 35–53. Coomaraswamy maintains that absolute beauty like other absolutes exists only in terms of *rasa;* thus the highest and the most exalted *rasa* is the vision of absolute beauty. Also see Prasad's discussion of *rasa* and Katharsis 229.

14. The reader-response theory is formalistic in nature; it allows inclusion of such theories as New Criticism, new historicism, feminism and Marxism. See, for example, *Reader-Response Criticism: From Formalism to Post-Structuralism,* ed. Jane Tompkins (Baltimore: Johns Hopkins UP, 1980).

15. See *A Defence of Poetry, The Complete Works of Percy Bysshe Shelley,* vol. 7, eds. Roger Ingpen and Walter E. Peck (New York: Gordian, 1965) 138–39.

16. See D. P. Chattopadhyaya's introduction to *Sri Aurobindo and Karl Marx: Integral Sociology and Dialectical Sociology* (New Delhi: Motilal, 1988). Some of Chattopadhyaya's basic assumptions have been voiced earlier by R. C. Zaehner in chapter 2 of *Evolution in Religion: A Study in Sri Aurobindo and Pierre Teilhard de Chardin* (Oxford: Clarendon, 1971).

17. See Robert A. McDermott's discussion in "The Absolute as a Heuristic Device: Josiah Royce and Sri Aurobindo," *International Philosophical Quarterly* 18 (1978): 171–99.

18. See Grace E. Cairns's essay "Aurobindo's Conception of the Nature and Meaning of History," *International Philosophical Quarterly* 12 (1972): 206.
19. Karl Jaspers, *Nietzsche and Christianity* (Henry Regnery, 1967) 102–03. Note Jaspers's rhetorical question: "What is the source of the other way of thinking, the exciting, soul-stirring way, which confers either a crushing feeling of impotence or a sense of extraordinary power over the course of events—depending upon the circumstances?" (51)
20. See Stephen Greenblatt's essay "The Politics of Culture," *Falling into Theory: Conflicting Views on Reading Literature,* ed. David H. Richter (Boston: St. Martin's, 1994) 289–90. Concerning Aurobindo's political radicalism and nationalism, see my essay "The Social and Political Vision of Sri Aurobindo," chapter 3. Greenblatt's reading probably extends itself to Frank Kermode's sociohistorical explication of Eliot's view of the classic, with special reference to the role of Virgil, in chapter 1 of *The Classic: Literary Images of Permanence and Change* (Cambridge: Harvard UP, 1983) 15–45. Kermode maintains that Eliot's treatment of the classic is based on the doctrine of "*imperium sine fine.*" The classic is *imperium,* and Eliot, according to Kermode, sees this pattern in Kipling's vision, "almost that of an idea of empire laid up in heaven" (*The Classic* 38). Ironically, various trendsetters in the contemporary discourse on culture, especially in so far as theorizing on colonialism, imperialism and postcolonialism is concerned, seem to have rested their case on marginalized sociohistoricity and cultural anthropology as instruments of restructuring and redefining the text.
21. See S. K. Maitra's profound discussion in "Sri Aurobindo and Spengler: Comparison between the Integral and the Pluralistic Philosophy of History," *The Integral Philosophy of Sri Aurobindo: A Commemorative Symposium,* eds. Haridas Chaudhuri and Frederic Spiegelberg (London: George Allen, 1960) 60–80.
22. Note Aurobindo's interesting observation: "His [Blake's] occasional obscurity,—he is more often in his best poems lucid and crystal clear,—is due to his writing of things that are not familiar to the physical mind and writing them with fidelity instead of accommodating them to the latter . . ." (*BCL* 9.529). Aurobindo himself acknowledges that "it took the world something like a hundred years to discover Blake . . ." (*BCL* 29.799). But in order to be fair to Aurobindo it must be recognized that he is raising a question about Blake's vision, myth and language, a question that the figure of Los in Blake debates extensively. Can language communicate adequately and fully the immensity and totality of a poet's vision, "its originality and purity," to use a phrase from Shelley? Note Shelley's important observation in the *Defence:* " . . . the most glorious poetry that has ever been communicated to the world is probably a feeble shadow of the original conception of the Poet" (135). Dante at the end of the *Divine Comedy* and Shelley at the end of *Epipsychidion* voice their respective frustrations about the inadequacy of the poetic language.

23. *Conversations with Eckermann (1823–1832),* trans. John Oxenford (San Francisco: North Point, 1984) 104.

24. See Eliot's essay "Byron," *On Poetry and Poets* (New York: Octagon, 1957) 223–39. In "Byron and the Anonymous Lyric," *Romanticism: A Critical Reader,* ed. Duncan Wu (Oxford: Blackwell, 1995), Jerome J. McGann refers to T. S. Eliot's denigration of Byron (243). In "*Don Juan* and Byron's Imperceptiveness to the English Word," *Romanticism: A Critical Reader,* ed. Duncan Wu, Peter J. Manning also refers to Eliot's accusation of Byron's "imperceptiveness . . . to the English word" (217).

25. Edward Caird cited in Carl Woodring's "Wordsworth and the Victorians," *The Age of William Wordsworth: Critical Essays on the Romantic Tradition,* eds. Kenneth R. Johnston and Gene W. Ruoff (New Brunswick: Rutgers UP 1987) 266.

26. See M. H. Abrams's discussion of Wordsworth in *The Mirror and the Lamp: Romantic Theory and the Critical Tradition* (New York: Norton, 1958) 103ff.

27. See Frank Kermode's discussion of an artist's isolation and despair in chapter 1 of *Romantic Image* (New York: Vintage, 1964).

28. See Basil Willey's *Samuel Taylor Coleridge* 93.

29. Cited by Basil Willey in *Samuel Taylor Coleridge* 253.

30. Herbert Read, *The True Voice of Feeling: Studies in English Romantic Poetry* (London: Faber, 1968) 181.

31. I must hasten to add that this is a broad and provisional classification. See, for example, Cousins's *The Work Promethean* and Stephen Spender's introduction to *A Choice of Shelley's Verse* (London: Faber, 1971). For a discussion of some of the critical valuations of Shelley see Newell F. Ford's introduction to *The Poetical Works of Shelley* (Boston: Houghton, 1975) xvii-xxxii.

32. Robert Browning, *Pauline,* line 1020, *Poetical Works 1823–1864,* ed. Ian Jack (London: Oxford UP, 1970). For a discussion of Browning's allusion to Shelley see Donald Smalley's introduction to *Poems of Robert Browning* (Boston: Houghton, 1956) x-xi.

33. Sisirkumar Ghose, *The Poetry of Sri Aurobindo: A Short Survey* (Calcutta: Chatuskone, 1969) 49.

34. See Indra Sen's essay "Sri Aurobindo's Theory of the Mind," *Philosophy East and West* 1 (1952): 45–52; Stephen H. Phillips's *Aurobindo's Philosophy of Brahman* (Leiden: Brill, 1986); R. C. Zaehner's *Evolution in Religion;* Rama Shanker Srivastava's *Sri Aurobindo and The Theories of Evolution* (Varanasi: Chowkhamba, 1958); K. D. Sethna's *The Spirituality of the Future: A Search apropos of R. C. Zaehner's Study of Sri Aurobindo and Teilhard de Chardin* (Rutherford: Farleigh Dickinson UP, 1981); and H. P. Sullivan's, "Sri Aurobindo on the Supermind and the Creative Process," *Sri Aurobindo: A Garland of Tributes,* ed. Arbinda Basu (Pondicherry: Sri Aurobindo Research Academy, 1973). It must be understood that Aurobindo's theory of the mind ultimately defines his evolutionary philosophy. In this concerted discussion it is important to understand Aurobindo's conceptual terms "Brahman," "Saccidanand" and "Supermind" in the total context of his theory of

mind and philosophies of Brahman and evolutionary progress. A. C. Bhat-tacharya, in *Sri Aurobindo and Bergson: A Synthetic Study* (Gyanpur: Jaga-bandhu, 1972), maintains that Aurobindo does not make a clear and precise distinction between the philosophical terms "Saccidanand" and "Super-mind" (260). For comparison between Aurobindo's conception of the Ab-solute and that of Hegel, or of F. H. Bradley see Steve Odin's essay "Sri Aurobindo and Hegel on the involution-evolution of Absolute Spirit," *Phi-losophy East and West* 31.2 (1981): 179–91.

35. See Sethna's *Sri Aurobindo on Shakespeare* 8–9. I have followed Sethna's clas-sifications and numbers. The first part of Aurobindo's letter of March 31, 1932 (*BCL* 9.521) does not include the names of Vyasa and Sophocles, but the second part of the aforementioned letter contains a suggestion for the addition of these two names to the original classifications. Note Au-robindo's criteria for the occupants of the first row of the "world's supreme singers": "supreme imaginative originality, supreme poetic gift, widest scope and supreme creative genius" (*BCL* 9.521). In an answer to a ques-tion about the exclusion of Shelley, Keats and Wordsworth from one of the three categories, Aurobindo remarks candidly: "If Keats had finished *Hype-rion* (without spoiling it), if Shelley had lived, or if Wordsworth had not pe-tered out like a motor car with insufficient petrol, it might be different, but we have to take things as they are" (*BCL* 9.521–22).

36. *Adonais,* line 36, *The Complete Works of Percy Bysshe Shelley,* vol. 2. In the *Defence* Shelley states: "Homer was the first and Dante the second epic poet . . . Milton was the third epic poet" (130).

37. See canto IV, lines 88–102, *The Inferno,* trans. John Ciardi (New York: Men-tor, 1954).

38. Note Northrop Frye's comment in "The Archetypes of Literature": "The literary chit-chat which makes the reputations of poets boom and crash in an imaginary stock exchange is pseudo-criticism. That wealthy investor Mr. Eliot, after dumping Milton on the market, is now buying him again; Donne has probably reached his peak and will begin to taper off . . ." (*Fa-bles of Identity* 8–9).

39. *The Classic* 22.

40. "The Function of Criticism at the Present Time" 30.

41. The phrase "the Indian virtue of detachment" is Arnold's. "Criticism," re-marks Arnold, "must maintain its independence of the practical spirit and its aims" (48). Note Arnold's definition of criticism: "*a disinterested endeavor to learn and propagate the best that is known and thought in the world*" (52; Arnold's emphasis). If there is a distinction between the literature of knowledge and the literature of value, can there be, one must ask, a simi-lar distinction between the criticism directed toward the creation of knowledge and the criticism directed toward the examination and preser-vation of values?

42. See K. R. Srinivasa Iyengar, "Milton and Sri Aurobindo," *Journal of South Asian Literature* 24.1 (1989): 67–82.

43. See Abrams's succinct analysis of the Romantic writers' views of Milton in *The Mirror and the Lamp* 250ff. In the twentieth century, however, the movement for "Milton's dislodgment," as F. R. Leavis explains in "Milton's Verse," *Revaluation: Tradition & Development in English Poetry* (New York: Norton, 1963), was spearheaded by T. S. Eliot (42). Note Northrop Frye's important observation, in "Criticism, Visible and Invisible," *The Stubborn Structure: Essays on Criticism and Society* (Ithaca: Cornell UP, 1970): "Ezra Pound, T. S. Eliot, Middleton Murry, F. R. Leavis, are only a few of the eminent critics who have abused Milton. Milton's greatness as a poet is unaffected by this: as far as the central fact of his importance in literature is concerned, these eminent critics might as well have said nothing at all" (78).

44. *A Defence of Poetry* 129.

45. *Blake's Fourfold Vision* (Wallingford: Pendle Hill, 1956) 14.

46. See his *The Burden of the Past and the English Poet* (New York: Norton, 1972).

47. *The Anxiety of Influence: A Theory of Poetry* (New York: Oxford UP, 1973) 11. Also see Bloom's discussion in chapter 1.

48. *A Defence of Poetry* 124, 129, 140. In "The Function of Criticism," Eliot reiterates his previous position about the relationship between the past and the present—"that the past should be altered by the present as much as the present is directed by the past" (12). Eliot further speaks about this pattern of relationship in Coleridgean terms: "'organic wholes,' as systems in relation to which, and only in relation to which, individual works of literary art and the works of individual artists, have their significance" (12–13).

49. See M. H. Abrams's discussion in *Natural Supernaturalism: Tradition and Revolution in Romantic Literature* (New York: Norton, 1971) 221–25.

50. In the Derridean metaphysics of deconstruction the primary concern in writing is not the communication of truth, especially since logocentric writing cannot communicate truth. See Leitch 35ff.; and Ellis 34ff.

51. See Vinayak Krishana Gokak's discussion in *Sri Aurobindo: Seer and Poet* (New Delhi: Abhinav, 1973) 107ff. The verbal structures "mantra" and "sutra" seem to have gained wide currency. See, for example, Northrop Frye's observation about Blake's *Jerusalem*: "The beauty of *Jerusalem* is the beauty of intense concentration, the beauty of the Sutra, of the aphorisms which are the form of so much of the greatest vision, of a figured bass indicating the harmonic progression of ideas too tremendous to be expressed by a single melody" (*Fearful Symmetry : A Study of William Blake* [Boston: Beacon, 1967] 359).

52. See Coleridge's discussion of the Platonic principles of beauty (as "multeity in unity") and joy (as achieved "through the medium of beauty")—and Coleridge cites the relevant lines from the "Dejection" Ode—in "On the Principles of Genial Criticism Concerning the Fine Arts," *Biographia Literaria* 2.219–42.

53. For Aurobindo's own exposition of the Overhead and Overmind states and of the meaning of various types of *ananda* see letters 5 and 6 on *Savitri* (*BCL* 29. 785–816).

54. F. H. Bradley, in *Appearance and Reality: A Metaphysical Essay,* 2nd ed., introd. Richard Wollheim (London: Oxford UP, 1969), notes the problem of "human-divine self-consciousness" in these lines of Shelley's poem (396 n1).
55. Oscar Wilde cited by Laurence Binyon in his "Introductory Memoir," *Songs of Love and Death* by Manmohan Ghose, 3rd ed. (Calcutta: U of Calcutta, 1968) 15.
56. This is Northrop Frye's term; see his "Criticism, Visible and Invisible," *The Stubborn Structure* 79.
57. See Terry Eagleton's conclusion in *Literary Theory: An Introduction* (Minneapolis: U of Minnesota P, 1983) 194ff.
58. *A Defence of Poetry* 140.
59. *Sri Aurobindo and Karl Marx* 285.
60. *Sri Aurobindo and Karl Marx* 313–14.
61. *The Stubborn Structure* 172.
62. Evidently, I am echoing the persistent debate in history on the function of criticism. See, for example, Shelley's *Defence,* Arnold's "The Function of Criticism at the Present Time" and Eliot's "The Function of Criticism."

CHAPTER 5

1. Ronald Dewsbury, rev. of *Coolie, Life and Letters To-Day* 15.4 (Autumn 1936): 208–10.
2. Peter Burra, rev. of *Coolie, The Spectator* 26 June 1936: 1186.
3. See Mulk Raj Anand, *Untouchable* (London: Wishart, 1935); and *Coolie* (London: Wishart, 1936). *Untouchable* had been written in 1930, but was not published until 1935. However, following the dramatic success of *Untouchable, Coolie* was readily accepted by Laurence & Wishart and appeared in 1936. See Saros Cowasjee's *Coolie: An Assessment* (Delhi: Oxford UP, 1976) 5–6. Cowasjee mentions about the "ecstatic" reviews of *Coolie* in England (18). Significantly, Laurence & Wishart published Anand's third novel *Two Leaves and a Bud* in 1937.
4. Stephen Spender, rev. of *Two Leaves and a Bud, Life and Letters To-day* 16.8 (1937): 155. Note George Orwell's response to a critic's review of Anand's *The Sword and the Sickle:* "It is quite true that in a political sense Mr. Anand is anti-British. . . . And if Mr. Anand makes it plain that he is anti-imperialist and thinks that India ought to be independent, is he not saying something which almost any English intellectual would echo as a matter of course?" (TLS 23 May 1942)
5. See Marlene Fisher, "Mulk Raj Anand and Autobiography," *South Asian Review* 15.12 (1991): 12–17. For a more comprehensive treatment of the relationship between psychobiography and fiction in Mulk Raj Anand see Fisher's *The Wisdom of the Heart: A Study of the Works of Mulk Raj Anand* (New Delhi: Sterling, 1985).
6. *Apology for Heroism,* 3rd. ed. (New Delhi: Arnold-Heinemann, 1975) 79.
7. See Friedrich Nietzsche, "From 'On Truth and Lie in an Extra-Moral Sense'," *The Portable Nietzsche,* ed. Walter Kaufmann (New York: Viking,

1968) 42–47. "We still do not know," remarks Nietzsche, "where the urge for truth comes from; for as yet we have heard only of the obligation imposed by society that it should exist: to be truthful means using the customary metaphors—in moral terms: the obligation to lie according to a fixed convention, to lie herd-like in a style obligatory for all . . ." (47).

8. "If our great revolution is to succeed," remarks Stapledon, "it must consist not merely of an economic change, though this is indeed necessary, but also of a widespread deepening of our consciousness of ourselves and one another. And unless that deepening consciousness controls the economic revolution, all will have been in vain" (cited in John Huntington, "Olaf Stapledon and the Novel about the Future," *Contemporary Literature* 22.3 [Summer 1981]: 356).

9. *Apology* 203.

10. I am indebted to Harold Bloom for the central thesis of his essay "The Internalization of Quest-Romance," *Romanticism and Consciousness,* ed. Harold Bloom (New York: Norton, 1970) 3–24. "If I know my relation to myself and to the external world," says Goethe, "I call that truth. And thus every man can have his own truth, and yet truth is still one" (cited by Ernst Cassirer in "Goethe and the Kantian Philosophy," *Rousseau, Kant and Goethe: Two Essays,* trans. James Gutmann et al. [Princeton: Princeton UP, 1970] 97).

11. *William Wordsworth,* ed. Stephen Gill (New York: Oxford UP, 1984) 606.

12. See Shelley's famous statement about the moral nature of the imagination in *A Defence of Poetry, Shelley's Prose and Poetry,* eds. Donald H. Reiman and Sharon B. Powers (New York: Norton, 1977) 487–88.

13. See Suresh Raval's valuable discussion of some of the critical theories in his *Metacriticism,* especially chapter 3, "Intention and Contemporary Literary Theory" (Athens: U of Georgia P, 1981).

14. Herbert Read, *The True Voice of Feeling: Studies in English Romantic Poetry* (London: Faber, 1968) 272.

15. See Alan Liu's argument in the introductory chapters, "The History in 'Imagination'," and "History, Literature, Form," of *Wordsworth: The Sense of History* (Stanford: Stanford UP, 1989).

16. In "Myth, Fiction, and Displacement," *Fables of Identity: Studies in Poetic Mythology* (New York: Harcourt, 1963), Northrop Frye explains the process and meaning of displacement. In a special sense, subversion, displacement and reconstruction are interchangeable terms.

17. In *So Many Freedoms: A Study of the Major Fiction of Mulk Raj Anand* (Delhi: Oxford UP, 1977), Saros Cowasjee has ably traced various influences on Anand. However, George Orwell's "Inside the Whale," a succinct and witty survey of the English literary scene during the twenties and thirties, in his *Inside the Whale and Other Essays* (Harmondsworth: Penguin, 1966), may be helpful to our understanding of the making of Anand the novelist. See, for example, Orwell's controversial statement: "The novel is practically a Protestant form of art; it is a product of the free mind, of the autonomous

individual" (39). Also see Marlene Fisher, *The Wisdom of the Heart: A Study of the Works of Mulk Raj Anand* 3–45.

18. See *Inside the Whale and Other Essays* 31.
19. For the American scene, I am indebted to Frederick J. Hoffman's *The Twenties: American Writing in the Postwar Decade,* rev. ed. (New York: Free, 1962); and Edmund Wilson's two essays, "Dos Passos and the Social Revolution" and "The Historical Interpretation of Literature," *The Portable Edmund Wilson,* ed. Lewis M. Dabney (Harmondsworth: Penguin, 1983).
20. Introduction to Elizabeth Gaskell's *Mary Barton: A Tale of Manchester Life* (Harmondsworth: Penguin, 1975) 15.
21. See my essay "The Social and Political Vision of Sri Aurobindo," chapter 3, where I have discussed in some details the ideologies of colonialism and imperialism in relation to India's freedom from Great Britain.
22. The essay appears as an "Afterword" in Gobinda Prasad Sarma's *Nationalism in Indo-Anglican Fiction* (New Delhi: Sterling, 1978) 347–48.
23. *The Marriage of Heaven and Hell,* pl. 27, *The Complete Poetry and Prose of William Blake,* rev. ed., ed. David V. Erdman (New York: Doubleday, 1988).
24. See n8 in my essay referred to in n21 above: "Colonisation, according to Coleridge, is 'not only a manifest experiment, but an imperative duty in Great Britain. God seems to hold out His finger to us over the sea. But it must be a national colonisation' (cited by Murray, I.177). In Carlyle's writings, notes Murray, there is a strong note of a happy imperialist (I.350–51); and Disraeli, according to Murray, 'was always an imperialist, anxious to consolidate the empire by evoking the sympathies of the colonies for the Mother Country' (I.231)."
25. In "The New Historicism and *Heart of Darkness," Joseph Conrad: Heart of Darkness: A Case Study in Contemporary Criticism,* ed. Ross C. Murfin (New York: St. Martin's, 1989), Murfin refers to Jerome McGann's "sociohistorical" approach and quotes Conrad's statement from the epigraph to Brook Thomas's essay: "Fiction is history, human history, or it is nothing" (237). Murfin, however, sounds a note of caution that one must, without being dogmatic, be open to other approaches.
26. James Joyce, "Daniel Defoe," *Daniel Defoe: Robinson Crusoe: An Authoritative Text, Backgrounds and Sources [and] Criticism,* ed. Michael Shinagel (New York: Norton, 1975) 356.
27. See Edward W. Said's *The World, the Text, and the Critic* (Cambridge: Harvard UP, 1983) 48. "Joyce's work," remarks Said, "is recognition of those political and racial separations, exclusions, prohibitions instituted ethnocentrically by the ascendant European culture throughout the nineteenth century. The situation of discourse, Stephen Dedalus knows, hardly puts equals face to face" (48–49).
28. See Samuel Taylor Coleridge, *Shakespearean Criticism,* 2 vols., ed. Thomas Middleton Raysor (New York: Dutton, 1961) 1.120.
29. Sandra Clark, *William Shakespeare: The Tempest* (London: Penguin, 1986) 76. Clark of course refers to W. H. Auden's use of Shakespeare's play in his *The*

Sea and the Mirror. "For Auden," says Clark, "Caliban represents the physicality of life which Prospero, abetted by Ariel, has unwisely neglected and suppressed" (75).

30. *Conversations in Bloomsbury* (New Delhi: Arnold-Heinemann, 1981) 74. All textual references are to this edition of the text.

31. See Gayatri Chakravorty Spivak's discussion of the subaltern in chapters 12 and 14 of *In Other Worlds* (New York: Methuen, 1987).

32. P. N. Furbank, *E. M. Forster: A Life,* 2 vols. (New York: Harcourt, 1981) 1.220.

33. See Gayatri Chakravorty Spivak's discussion of colonialism and imperialism in "Imperialism and Sexual Difference," *Contemporary Literary Criticism: Literary and Cultural Studies,* 2nd ed., eds. Robert Con Davis and Ronald Schleifer (New York: Longman, 1989) 517–29. Also see Janet Powers, "Mulk Raj Anand: The Text in Response to Colonialism," *South Asian Review* 15.12 (1991): 57–65.

34. See C. Northcote Parkinson, *East and West* (New York: New American, 1965) 236ff.

35. See Jawaharlal Nehru, *The Discovery of India* (New Delhi: Asia, 1969) 287, 297.

36. In *The Eighteenth Century: The Intellectual and Cultural Context of English Literature, 1700–1789* (New York: Longman, 1986), James Sambrook refers to Cowper's "The Task" and Goldsmith's "The Travellers." "Berkshire," notes Sambrook, "seems to have been a regular hunting-ground for nabobs in search of country estates, local influence and parliamentary seats; it had five Anglo-Indian sheriffs between 1772–1789, and was called 'the English Hindoostan'" (76).

37. Brook Thomas, "Preserving and Keeping Order by Killing Time in *Heart of Darkness*," *Joseph Conrad: Heart of Darkness, A Case Study,* ed. Ross C. Murfin 244, 245.

38. George Orwell, "Rudyard Kipling," *Five Approaches of Literary Criticism: An Arrangement of Contemporary Critical Essays,* ed. Wilbur S. Scott (New York: Collier, 1979) 163. Orwell maintains that Kipling "was the prophet of British Imperialism in its expansionist phase" and that he was "also the unofficial historian of the British Army, the old mercenary army which began to change its shape in 1914" (163). Note T. S. Eliot's observation on "the development of his [Kipling's] view of empire" in his essay "Rudyard Kipling," *On Poetry and Poets* (New York: Octagon, 1975): "He had always been far from uncritical of the defects and wrongs of the British Empire. . . . He is more concerned with the problem of the soundness of the *core* of empire . . . But at the same time his vision takes a larger view, and he sees the Roman Empire and the place of England in it. The vision is almost that of an idea of empire laid up in heaven" (286). Significantly, Eliot denies the charge that Kipling is racist, maintaining that the later Kipling, "in his middle years, is 'the development of the imperial imagination into historical imagination'" (289). In contrast, see Edward W. Said's interesting

reading of Kipling in *Culture and Imperialism* (New York: Knopf, 1993) 133–62. Kipling's relationship with India and Kipling's standing as a literary figure, it must be admitted, are extremely controversial issues. In his preface to *Conversations,* Anand remarks that "the talks evoke some of those lovable, liberal Englishmen and women, who compensated us for Rudyard Kipling's contempt for the 'lesser breeds', with inspirations for free thinking" (6). Spivak quotes the following lines from Nirad Chaudhuri: "I read Kipling's *Jungle Book* first at the age of ten in an East Bengal village, but never read anything else by him for fear of being hurt by his racial arrogance" ("Imperialism and Sexual Difference" 259).

39. See Dorothy Figuiera, "Mulk Raj Anand's *Across the Black Waters:* Europe as an Object of 'Orientalist Discourse,'" *South Asian Review* 15.12 (1991): 51–56.

40. See Hoffman's excellent analysis in chapter 2, "The War and the Postwar Temper," *The Twenties.*

41. Bonamy Dobrée, rev. of *Across the Black Waters, The Spectator* 22 Nov. 1940: 560.

42. Figuiera 54.

43. See Ian Watt, "Robinson Crusoe as a Myth," *Daniel Defoe: Robinson Crusoe,* ed. Michael Shinagel 311ff.

44. "Daniel Defoe," *Daniel Defoe: Robinson Crusoe* 355.

45. *Roots and Flowers: Two Lectures* (Dharwar: Karnatak UP, 1972) 15.

46. See Mary Shelley's "Note on Shelley's *Prometheus Unbound,*" *Shelley: Poetical Works,* ed. Thomas Hutchinson (London: Oxford UP, 1967) 271.

47. M. K. Naik, *Mulk Raj Anand* (New York: Humanities, 1973) 183, 185.

48. *So Many Freedoms* 153.

49. K. D. Verma, "An Interview with Mulk Raj Anand," *South Asian Review* 15.12 (1991): 38. See William Blake's poems "The Divine Image" and "The Human Abstract," *The Complete Poetry and Prose of William Blake,* ed. David V. Erdman: "The Divine Image" combines the ideals of mercy, pity, peace and love, but "The Human Abstract" contains the very antithesis of the aforementioned moral values. Anand of course claims that he is indebted to Guru Nanak, Kabir, Tagore, Gandhi and the *Gita.* See the following excerpt from Anand's letter: "I began by destroying all traditions, ideas, clichés, claptrap of organised religions, to suggest a 'religion without religion,' 'a religion of love itself.' I am with J. Krishnamurti much of the way. Leave the past clichés and start afresh. Give up the greed, the envy, the slavery, with the consumer society. Cultivate the capacity and the depth of love, which is in all of us. It doesn't need anything more than the spark to make it into a 'fire.' And then one begins to dance in the circle of fire— dancer becomes the dance, 'burning and melting,' like Nataraj. This was Nietzsche's longing for ecstasy. The Shiva bronze is not a mere work of art: it is the symbol of rhythm of the Cosmos itself . . ." (*Old Myth and New Myth: Letters from Mulk Raj Anand to K. V. S. Murti* [Calcutta: Writers Workshop, 1991] 60).

50. See Margaret Berry's *Mulk Raj Anand: The Man and the Novelist* (Amsterdam: Oriental, 1971) 18ff. Also see S. C. Harrex's interesting reading of Anand in his "Western Ideology and Eastern Forms of Fiction: The Case of Mulk Raj Anand," *Asian and Western Writers in Dialogue: New Cultural Identities,* ed. Guy Amirthanayagam (London: Macmillan, 1982) 142–58.

51. *Is There a Contemporary Indian Civilization?* (London: Asia, 1963) 158.

52. Leon Edel, "The Question of Exile," *Asian and Western Writers in Dialogue: New Cultural Identities,* ed. Guy Amirthanayagam 52.

53. Note Joyce's definition of a spiritual exile in his play *Exiles:* "that food of the spirit by which a nation of human beings is sustained in life" (cited by Leon Edel 53). See Meenakshi Mukherjee's observation on Anand's alienation in "Beyond The Village—An Aspect of Mulk Raj Anand," *Critical Essays On Indian Writing in English,* ed. M. K. Naik et al. (Delhi: Macmillan, 1977) 244–45. Of course, the psychosociological problem of alienation must be understood in the larger context of the debate on identity.

54. Mulk Raj Anand, "Tradition and Modernity in Literature," *Journal of South Asian Literature* 10.1 (1974): 49, 50.

55. *So Many Freedoms* 132. Note Marlene Fisher's observation: "*The Private Life of an Indian Prince* remains one of Anand's most well crafted novels and testifies to his ability, at its best, to transform felt experience into art" (*The Wisdom of the Heart* 117).

56. See P. K. Rajan's interview with Mulk Raj Anand in *Studies in Mulk Raj Anand* (New Delhi: Abhinav, 1986) 110. Even *The Bubble* invites Butlerian reading. See, for example, Krishan Chander's letter of January 30, 1927, to his father in *The Bubble* (New Delhi: Arnold-Heinemann, 1984) 583–96. The following lines would have been written by Butler's Ernest Pontifex: "You ask me to cultivate love for our family. How can one cultivate love? It is either there or not there. And my love for you and mother is there. I owe my existence to you both. But the flow of feeling was obstructed by the abuse, the constant denigration and the harsh words you have always uttered since I grew up" (583). For a more recent study of Butler's position see Phyllis Greenacre, *The Quest for the Father: A Study of the Darwin-Butler Controversy, As a Contribution to the Understanding of the Creative Individual* (New York: International, 1963).

57. Dieter Riemenschneider, "*The Bubble:* A Literary Achievement," *The Novels of Mulk Raj Anand,* ed. R. K. Dhawan (New Delhi: Prestige, 1992) 214.

58. *The Wisdom of the Heart* 122.

59. See Philip Rieff, "Two Honest Men," *D. H. Lawrence: Sons and Lovers, Text, Background, and Criticism,* ed. Julian Moynahan (New York: Penguin, 1977) 518–26.

60. "Tradition and Modernity in Literature" 47. Undoubtedly, Anand's statement should find ample support in the ideas of Freud and Jung. See, for ex-

ample, Carl Gustav Jung, "Psychology and Literature," *The Creative Process: A Symposium,* ed. Brewster Ghiselin (Toronto: Mentor, 1967) 208–23.

61. Mulk Raj Anand, dedication to *Morning Face* (New Delhi: Arnold-Heinemann, 1980) vii.

62. See Jessie Chamber's comment on D. H. Lawrence in *D. H. Lawrence: Sons and Lovers,* ed. Julian Moynahan 480.

63. See E. M. Forster's letter to Mulk Raj Anand about *Untouchable, South Asian Review* 15.12 (1991): 93.

64. E. M. Forster, preface to *Untouchable* by Mulk Raj Anand (London: Penguin, 1940) vii.

65. Inder Nath Kher, "The Emerging Woman in Mulk Raj Anand's *Gauri,*" *South Asian Review* 15.12 (1991): 43.

66. For a discussion of *ars erotica* and *scientia sexualis* see Michel Foucault, *The History of Sexuality: vol. 1: An Introduction,* trans. Robert Hurley (New York: Pantheon, 1978) 53ff.

67. Basically, I am referring to Barthes's conception of pleasure and Kristeva's notion of *jouissance.*

68. Mulk Raj Anand, *Gauri* (New Delhi: Arnold-Heinemann, 1981) 263.

69. Inder Nath Kher 43.

70. Note Dieter Riemenschneider's observation in "Mulk Raj Anand," *Essays on Contemporary Post-Colonial Fiction,* eds. Hedwig Bock and Albert Wertheim (Munchen: Verlag, 1986): "With Gauri, Anand clearly propagates an image of a woman totally different from that of traditional Hindu society by emphasizing her right to personal freedom and individual choice against the structures imposed on women by religion in a patriarchal society" (184).

71. See *The Wisdom of the Heart* 171–73. Also see Jag Mohan, "Mulk Raj Anand's *Marg:* A History and Perspective," *South Asian Review* 15.12 (1991): 83–90.

72. *The Wisdom of the Heart* 168, 171.

73. See, for example, Morris's prophetic voice in the following lines from *The Pilgrims of Hope:* "Hope is awake in the faces angerless now no more. / Till the new peace dawn on the world, the fruit of the people's war. . . ." See E. P. Thompson, *William Morris: Romantic to Revolutionary* (New York: Pantheon, 1977) 671.

74. Northrop Frye, *The Critical Path: An Essay on the Social Context of Literary Criticism* (Bloomington: Indiana UP, 1971) 102.

75. This is Blake's phrase. Note Anand's observation in a letter to Saros Cowasjee: "I wrote this novel [*The Big Heart*] at the end of the Second World War in London, when the machines of western civilization had nearly destroyed the world. I was convinced that if India also went the same way, after freedom, without controlling the machine, but allowed it to become the instrument of exploitation, then we would also produce the same horrors" (*Author to Critic: The Letters of Mulk Raj Anand,* ed. Saros Cowasjee [Calcutta: Writers Workshop, 1973] 121).

76. Note Edmund Wilson's comment on his discussion with E. M. Forster
" . . . I [Wilson] shared his enthusiasm for his [Forster's] three favorite
books: *The Divine Comedy,* Gibbon, and *War and Peace.* . . . But, I thought
that *Das Kapital* almost belonged in the same category" (*Edmund Wilson:
The Fifties,* ed. Leon Edel [New York: Farrar, 1987] 117). Does the larger
issue in this debate rest on the difference between aesthetic attitudes and
moral valuations? See Northrop Frye's interesting discussion in chapter 4
of *The Critical Path* 79–103.
77. Mulk Raj Anand, *Kama Kala: Some Notes on the Philosophical Basis of Hindu
Erotic Sculpture* (Geneva: Nagel, 1963) 8.
78. See Mulk Raj Anand, *The Hindu View of Art,* with an introductory essay
on "Art and Reality" by Eric Gill, 2nd ed. (Bombay: Asia, 1957). The work
was first published in 1933 by George Allen and Unwin, London. Ananda
Coomaraswamy's essay under reference appears as appendix 1, 91–110.
79. *Seven Little-Known Birds of the Inner Eye* (Vermont: Tuttle, 1978) 98–99.
80. See Carl Gustav Jung's essay "Approaching the unconscious," *Man and His
Symbols* by Carl G. Jung et al. (New York: Doubleday, 1983) 18–103.
81. *Seven Little-Known Birds of the Inner Eye* 19.
82. *Seven Little-Known Birds of the Inner Eye* 56.
83. See Ebrahim Alkazi's foreword to *Contemporary Indian Sculpture: The Madras
Metaphor,* ed. Josef James (Madras: Oxford UP, 1993) 5–6.
84. Coomaraswamy has raised a very important question: "What are the paintings even of Michelangelo compared with the paintings on the walls of the
cave temples of Ajanta?" "These works," answers Coomaraswamy, "are not
the work of a man, 'they are the work of ages, of nations'" ("The Philosophy of Ancient Asiatic Art," *The Hindu View of Art* 110).
85. See Mulk Raj Anand's comments on Dhanapal in his essay "S. Dhanapal,"
Contemporary Indian Sculpture: The Madras Metaphor 54.

CHAPTER 6

1. About Anand's circle of friends and acquaintances see Marlene Fisher's *The
Wisdom of the Heart: A Study of the Works of Mulk Raj Anand* (New Delhi:
Sterling, 1985) 34ff. One may, however, question the logic behind Anand's
choice of these names, unless, of course, Anand's statement in the preface
is taken at its face value. See Anand's preface to *Conversations in Bloomsbury*
(New Delhi: Arnold-Heinemann, 1981). All textual references, unless otherwise indicated, are to this edition of *Conversations.*
2. Northrop Frye, *Fearful Symmetry: A Study of William Blake* (Boston: Beacon,
1967) 87.
3. "*Conversations,*" remarks Marlene Fisher, "presents us with the autobiogra-
pher's shaping of the significance that the events—the conversations—re-
counted have both to his past and his present selves" ("Mulk Raj Anand
and Autobiography," *South Asian Review* 15.12 [1991]: (15).
4. Martin Heidegger, *An Introduction to Metaphysics,* trans. Ralph Manheim
(New York: Doubleday, 1961) 87ff. Also see Suresh Raval's discussion of

Gadamer's attempt in "developing Heidegger's ontology of understanding into a dialectical hermeneutics" (*Metacriticism* [Athens: U of Georgia P, 1981] 100). I am particularly indebted to Daniel T. O'Hara's discussion of the acceptance by Derrida via Heidegger and Nietzsche of the conception of aesthetic representation in his essay "The Approximations of Romance: Paul Ricoeur and Ironic Style of Postmodern Criticism," *Philosophical Approaches to Literature: New Essays on Nineteenth-and-Twentieth-Century Texts,* ed. William E. Cain (Lewisburg: Bucknell UP 1984).

5. T. S. Eliot, "Dante," *Selected Essays,* new ed. (New York: Harcourt, 1964) 217. Incidentally, C. S. Lewis, in his essay "Shelley, Dryden, and Mr. Eliot," *English Romantic Poets: Modern Essays in Criticism,* ed. M. H. Abrams (New York: Oxford UP, 1965) 262, concurs with Eliot's classification.

6. Curiously, Huxley's perception of India is much clearer and more accurate and his attitude toward Anand is more sympathetic.

7. *The Textual Condition* (Princeton: Princeton UP, 1991) 15.

8. See chapters "Bloomsbury Philosophy" (20–45) and "Bloomsbury Aesthetic" (46–95) in J. K. Johnstone's *The Bloomsbury Group: A Study of E. M. Forster, Lytton Strachey, Virginia Woolf, and their Circle* (London: Secker, 1954). Also see Virginia Woolf's impassioned defense of Bloomsbury, especially in terms of their commitment to humanitarian ideals, in her letters 3633 and 3634 to Benedict Nicholson, *The Letters of Virginia Woolf,* vol. vi: 1936–1941, eds. Nigel Nicolson and Joanne Trautmann (New York: Harcourt, 1982).

9. *Bloomsbury* (New York: Basic, 1968) 12.

10. Anand has not treated all the internal feuds in the Bloomsbury Circle. The role and position of Roger Fry and the alleged maltreatment of Wyndham Lewis are two specific cases in point. Note Quentin Bell's observation in *Bloomsbury:* "It is hardly astonishing that, for the rest of his life, Lewis believed that he was being persecuted by Bloomsbury and, above all, by Roger Fry; it is after all more comfortable to suppose that one is being persecuted than to believe that one is disregarded, and this anguished sense of injustice finds its echo in the violent fantasies of Lewis's friend and recorder, Sir John Rothenstein" (56). It is significant to note that F. R. Leavis and his friends who had been excluded from Bloomsbury were "the sworn enemies of aestheticism and intellectuality in general and of Bloomsbury in particular" (Frederick C. Crews, *E. M. Forster: The Perils of Humanism* [Princeton: Princeton UP, 1962] 170). Dr. Leavis's hero was Lawrence and not Forster, and Lawrence's problems with Bloomsbury had now come out in the open.

11. *Bloomsbury* 85.

12. P. N. Furbank, *E. M. Forster: A Life,* 2 vols. (New York: Harcourt, 1981) 2.163.

13. E. M. Forster, *Abinger Harvest* (New York: Harcourt, 1964) 94–95.

14. *Abinger Harvest* 95.

15. Undoubtedly, I am referring to Wordsworth's theory of poetry as enunciated in the preface (1802) to *Lyrical Ballads:* "I have said that Poetry is the

spontaneous overflow of powerful feelings: it takes its origin from emotion recollected in tranquillity: the emotion is contemplated till by a species of reaction the tranquillity disappears, and an emotion, kindred to that which was before the subject of contemplation, is gradually produced, and does itself actually exist in the mind" (*William Wordsworth*, ed. Stephen Gill [Oxford: Oxford UP, 1984] 611). I have also drawn from David Perkin's discussion of the difference between history and literary history in *Is Literary History Possible?* (Baltimore: Johns Hopkins UP, 1992) 175ff.

16. For an understanding of such conceptual terms as *sat, cit, ananda* and maya in Shankara's metaphysics see Raphael's *Self and Non-Self: The Drig-drisyaviveka Attributed to Samkara,* trans. and commentary by Raphael (London: Kegan Paul, 1990); and for the concept of Maya in Indian thought see Donald R. Tuck's perceptive study *The Concept of Maya in Samkara and Radhakrishanan* (Columbia: South Asia, 1986). According to Raphael, " . . . *sat, cit* and *ananda* belong to the sphere of the absolute *Brahman* and therefore can not be considered as qualifications, attributes, conditions or causes except from the empirical point of view . . . *Ananda* represents an innate, natural modality of pure Bliss and absolute Fullness of *Brahman*" (11).

17. See F. O. Matthiessen, *The Achievement of T. S. Eliot: An Essay on the Nature of Poetry,* 3rd ed. (New York: Oxford UP, 1965) 145.

18. Matthiessen 144.

19. For a more detailed discussion of this important point see D.E.S. Maxwell's *The Poetry of T. S. Eliot* (London: Routledge, 1970); William Skaff's *The Philosophy of T. S. Eliot: From Skepticism to a Surrealist Poetic 1909–1927* (Philadelphia: U of Pennsylvania P, 1986); and William M. Chace's *The Political Identities of Ezra Pound & T. S. Eliot* (Stanford: Stanford UP, 1973). Especially refer to chapter 8 of Chace's work. Chace refers to René Wellek's opinion of Eliot's choice of classicism: "Eliot's classicism is a matter of cultural politics rather than literary criticism" (131).

20. See my essay "The Woman Figure in Blake and the Idea of Shakti in Indian Thought," *Comparative Literature Studies* 27.3 (1990): 193–210.

21. Skaff also notes the Freudian view of such an experience: "But unlike Eliot, and Jung, Freud contends that myths are symbolic expressions and rituals are symptomatic behavior of mental disorder caused by an inability to adjust to sexual desire. Religious experience is, therefore, reduced to a psychological disease" (73). See Chace's comment on the subject: "Baudelaire's imagination was impaired, as was Eliot's, in attempting to recreate the Dantesque worlds of spiritual anguish and spirited ecstasy" (149). But note the following observation by Matthiessen: " . . . the way in which she [the Lady in 'Ash Wednesday'] is described in distinct definite images and yet left at the same time indefinite and suggestive, she can stand at once as Beatrice or a saint or the Virgin herself, as well as being an idealized beautiful woman" (116).

22. Skaff, *The Philosophy of T. S. Eliot* 19.

23. Introduction, *Appearance and Reality: A Metaphysical Essay* by F. H. Bradley, 2nd ed. (London: Oxford UP. 1969) viii–ix.

24. *Myth, Rhetoric, and the Voice of Authority: A Critique of Frazer, Eliot & Campbell* (New Haven: Yale UP, 1992) 68.

25. *The Philosophy of T. S. Eliot* 72.

26. Jerome Christenson, "Philosophy / Literature: The Associationist Precedent for Coleridge's Late Poems," *Philosophical Approaches to Literature*, ed. William E. Cain 27.

27. See Ernst Cassirer's essay "Goethe and the Kantian Philosophy" in *Rousseau, Kant and Goethe: Two Essays*, trans. James Gutman et al., introd. Peter Gay (Princeton: Princeton UP, 1970).

28. Christopher Ricks, *T. S. Eliot and Prejudice* (Berkeley: U of California P, 1988) 106.

29. See especially P. S. Sri, *T. S. Eliot, Vedanta and Buddhism* (Vancouver: U of British Columbia P, 1985); and Cleo McNelly Kearns, *T. S. Eliot and Indic Traditions* (Cambridge: Cambridge UP, 1987). It is needless to mention that the Indian literary scene has shown significant interest in Eliot. See, for example, the discerning rhetorical question posed by Makarand R. Paranjape in his essay "T. S. Eliot Through Indian Eyes: Mulk Raj Anand's *Conversations in Bloomsbury*," *The Literary Criterion* 24.3 &4 (1989): "Why have we taken to—or should I say, been taken in—by T. S. Eliot in such a big way?" (50) It remains to be argued whether this extraordinary attention given to Eliot is because of his poetic modernism or his interest in Indian thought. The critical debate, as Anand seems to suggest in *Conversations*, must focus on the structure and fundamental originality of Eliot's poetic vision.

30. *T. S. Eliot and Indic Traditions* 190.

31. B. Rajan, "The Unity of the Quartets," *T. S. Eliot: A Study of His Writings by Several Hands*, ed. B. Rajan (New York: Russell, 1966) 87.

32. "*The Waste Land*: An Analysis," *T. S. Eliot: A Study of His Writings by Several Hands*, ed. B. Rajan 28.

33. Edward W. Said, *The World, the Text, and the Critic* (Cambridge: Harvard UP, 1983) 176–77.

34. *Abinger Harvest* 64.

35. *Abinger Harvest* 63.

36. See my two essays "The Social and Political Vision of Sri Aurobindo," chapter 3; and "Understanding Mulk Raj Anand: An Introduction," *South Asian Review* 15.12 (1991): 1–11.

37. Vincent P. Pecora, *Self & Form in Modern Narrative* (Baltimore: Johns Hopkins UP, 1989) 141.

38. Cited in Ross C. Murfin, "Introduction: The Critical Background," *Joseph Conrad: Heart of Darkness*, A Case Study in Contemporary Criticism, ed. Ross C. Murfin (New York: St. Martin's, 1989) 110.

39. T. S. Eliot, *Christianity and Culture: The Idea of a Christian Society and Notes towards the Definition of Culture* (New York: Harcourt, 1949) 20.

40. *Christianity and Culture* 100.

41. See Maxwell's *The Poetry of T. S. Eliot,* chapter 6, "The Humanist Criticism."

42. *Christianity and Culture* 167, 139.

43. *Christianity and Culture* 167.

44. *Christianity and Culture* 166.

45. Furbank, E. M. *Forster: A Life* 2.123.

46. See, for example, Henry James's introduction to the *Selected Works of Rudyard Kipling,* vol. 3 (New York: Collier, n.d.). James seems to think that Kipling's "freshness" and charm as a writer primarily come from his skillful portrayal of the primitive and lowly life in India. There is hardly any argument about Kipling's standing as a right writer and as a known defender of the empire. Christopher Ricks maintains that Eliot was indebted to Kipling; however, Kipling's anti-Semitism—and for that matter Eliot's own—had become extremely controversial and indefensible. Ricks also notes the public exchange between Trilling and Eliot (*T. S. Eliot and Prejudice* 25–27). As opposed to Eliot's rightist view of Kipling, there are the views of the left writers—Orwell, Anand and others. See my essay "Mulk Raj Anand: A Reappraisal," chapter 5. In his preface to *Conversations,* Anand refers to "Kipling's contempt for the 'lesser breeds'" (6).

47. *T. S. Eliot* (New York: Capricorn, 1972) 12.

48. Octave Mannoni, *Prospero and Caliban: The Psychology of Colonization,* trans. Pamela Powesland and new foreword by Maurice Bloch (Ann Arbor: U of Michigan P, 1990) 106. Also see Alden T. Vaughan, "Caliban in the 'Third World': Shakespeare's Savage as Sociopolitical Symbol," *The Massachusetts Review* 29.2 (1988): 289–313.

49. *Prospero and Caliban* 108.

50. *T. S. Eliot* 8.

51. Chace, *The Political Identities of Ezra Pound & T. S. Eliot* 110.

52. Mulk Raj Anand, *Apology for Heroism* 185.

53. See my "An Interview with Mulk Raj Anand," *South Asian Review* 15.12 (1991): 36.

54. "The Dry Salvages," *Four Quartets* (New York: Harcourt, 1943).

CHAPTER 7

1. For a convenient summary of some of the critical opinions see Uma Parameswaran's *A Study of Representative Indo-English Novelists* (New Delhi: Vikas, 1976); and A. N. Dwivedi, "*The Dark Dancer:* A Critique," *Studies in Indian Fiction in English,* ed. G. S. Balarama Gupta (Gulbarga: JIWE, 1987) 68–76.

2. This still remains the standard view, although the roots of the issue are actually traceable to the Anglicist-Orientalist controversy.

3. *The Yale Review* 48 (1958): 123. Note Spear's important observation: "Balachandra Rajan's *The Dark Dancer* is the first Indian novel I have read that employs the full resources of the Impressionist school whose great masters in English are Conrad and James" (122).

4. See, for example, Georg Lukács's interesting discussion of the historical novel and his unusually warm praise of Walter Scott in *The Historical Novel*, trans. Hannah and Stanley Mitchell (Boston: Beacon, 1963).
5. See S. C. Harrex, "Dancing in the Dark: Balachandra Rajan and T. S. Eliot," *World Literature Written in English* 14.2 (1975): 310–21; and George Wood-cock, "Paradise Lost and Regained in the Novels of Bal[a]chandra Rajan," *Canadian Literature* 132 (Spring 1992): 136–44. Also see Woodcock's earlier essay "Balachandra Rajan: The Critic as Novelist," *World Literature Written in English* 23.2 (1984): 442–51. Note Harrex's interesting but contestable observation: "Moreover, the novel [*The Dark Dancer*] serves as a rewarding reminder that, however valuable and interesting comparative studies can be, whenever the question of 'influence' is raised the critic must distinguish (as did Eliot) between imitation without assimilation, and assimilation without imitation, as well as determining a writer's masticating prowess when chewing his master's cud. Eliot sought in Indian mysticism confir-mation of his own visions; some may think it more than generous of In-dian writers to find in T. S. Eliot support for their indigenous metaphysical tradition" (320).
6. For Yeats's search for identity and the general discussion of identity see George Bornstein, "Romancing the (Native) Stone: Yeats, Stevens, and the Anglocentric Canon," *The Romantics and Us: Essays in Literature and Cul-ture*, ed. Gene W. Ruoff (New Brunswick: Rutgers UP, 1990) 108–29. Yeats has raised a fundamental question: "Have not all races had their first unity from a mythology that marries them to rock and hill?" (Bornstein 113) Balachandra Rajan, in his "Remarks on Identity and Nationality," *Literature East and West* 9 (1965): 91–94, has quoted the following lines from Yeats's "Under Ben Bulben": "Many times man lives and dies / Between his two eternities, / That of race and that of soul / And ancient Ireland knew it all" (93). While Whitman and Stevens tried to establish their unique American identities by "de-Anglicizing" English (Bornstein's argument), Eliot on the other hand, it can be readily construed, made a "regressional" journey back to England. Can Krishnan "de-Anglicize" his consciousness? Can issues of nationalism and patriotism—the rock-and-hill identifications—be rele-gated to the innermost voice of one's conscience?
7. "The Indian Virtue," *The Journal of Commonwealth Literature* 1 (1965): 80, 85.
8. "Remarks on Identity and Nationality" 93.
9. Several important studies to which I am indebted are F. H. Bradley, *Ap-pearance and Reality*, 2nd ed. (London: Oxford UP, 1969); Baruch A. Brody, *Identity and Essence* (Princeton: Princeton UP, 1980); Martin Heidegger, *Identity and Difference*, trans. Joan Stambaugh (New York: Harper, 1969); Je-remy Hawthorn, *Identity and Relationship: A Contribution to Marxist Theory of Literary Criticism* (London: Lawrence, 1973); Robert Langbaum, *The Mysteries of Identity* (New York: Oxford UP, 1977); and Manfred Putz, *The Story of Identify: American Fiction of the Sixties* (Stuttgart: Verlagbuchhan-dung, 1979).

10. Especially see chapter 26, "The Absolute and its Appearances." "Appearance without reality," remarks Bradley, "would be impossible, for what then could appear? And reality without appearance would be nothing, for there certainly is nothing outside appearances" (432).

11. *The Mysteries of Identity* 7.

12. See D. H. Lawrence, "Morality and the Novel," *Selected Literary Criticism,* ed. Anthony Beal (New York: Viking 1966). "The business of art," says Lawrence, "is to reveal the relation between man and his circumambient universe, at the living moment" (108). Also see Rajan's views on the subject in "Remarks on Identity and Nationality."

13. Balachandra Rajan, *The Dark Dancer* (Westport: Greenwood, 1970) 1–2. All textual references are to this edition of the work.

14. See Gauri Viswanathan's enlightened discussion of the system of education in British India in her *The Masks of Conquest: Literary Study and British Rule in India* (New York: Columbia UP, 1989). For a discussion of Macaulay's famous Minute on Education (1835) see Eric Stokes, *The English Utilitarians and India* (Oxford: Clarendon, 1963) 45–47. James Mill's Utilitarianism, Macaulay's "radical liberalism" and Trevelyan's "fusion of the Evangelical and Radical outlook" supposedly furthered the cause of creating "an English-educated middle class 'who may be interpreters between us and the millions whom we govern—a class of persons Indian in colour and blood, but English in tastes, in opinions, in morals, and in intellect' [Macaulay]" (Stokes 46). Note William Walsh's interesting observation in *Commonwealth Literature* (London: Oxford UP, 1973): "Rammohan Roy (1774–1833) was as much responsible for this policy [for the advancement of European learning] on the Indian side as Macaulay was on the British" (1). But it remains debatable if Indian liberals, including Rammohan Roy, shared Macaulay's—and the empire's—general objectives.

15. Meenakshi Mukherjee, in *The Twice Born Fiction,* 2nd ed. (New Delhi: Arnold-Heinemann, 1974), notes Naipaul's disillusionment with writers who have ignored the commoner and the reality of life (123). But this is a debatable point. I agree with the general feeling, however, that with the democratization of the country Indo-Anglian writers would discover the Crusoes, the Moll Flanders, the Joe Gargerys, the Pips, the Mary Bartons and the Adam Bedes. It must be noted that, historically, the domain of the Indo-Anglian writer, with the singular exception of Mulk Raj Anand, has been the privileged class.

16. Mukherjee notes that the analogy with Karna "is not extended far enough to become significant" (*The Twice Born Fiction* 132).

17. This is Frank Kermode's term. See Manfred Putz 25.

18. See Lionel Trilling's discussion in his "Art and Neurosis," *Art and Psychoanalysis,* ed. William Phillips (New York: World, 1963) 502–20.

19. Cited in Brewster Ghislen, *The Creative Process: A Symposium* (Toronto: Mentor, 1967) 13.

20. Lionel Trilling, "Manners, Morals, and the Novel," *Approaches to the Novel,* rev. ed., ed. Robert Scholes (San Francisco: Chandler, 1961) 127.

21. See Mrs. Bennett's portrayal in chapter 1 of Jane Austen's *Pride and Prejudice,* Norton critical ed., ed. Donald J. Gray (New York: Norton, 1966). Note especially the opening sentence of *Pride and Prejudice:* "It is a truth universally acknowledged, that a single man in possession of a good fortune, must be in want of a wife" (1).

22. See Lewis Gannett's rev. "Novel of New India's Conflicts," *The New York Tribune* 27 July 1958.

23. See Anand Lall's rev. of the novel in "Dilemma of an In-Betweener," *Saturday Review* 41 (1958): 14.

24. See Northrop Frye, "Fictional Modes and Forms," *Approaches to the Novel,* ed. Robert Scholes 23–42.

25. See, for example, Maulana Abul Kalam Azad, *India Wins Freedom* (New York: Longmans, 1960), especially the introduction; and S. R. Mehrotra, "The Congress and the Partition of India," *The Partition of India: Policies and Perspectives 1935–47,* eds. C. H. Philips and Mary Doreen Wainwright (London: Allen, 1970). On the general background of India's struggle for independence see Jawaharlal Nehru, *The Discovery of India,* ed. Robert L. Crane (New York: Doubleday, 1960); and Rupert Emerson, *From Empire to Nation* (Cambridge: Harvard UP, 1962). Also see K. K. Sharma and B. K. Johri, *The Partition in Indian-English Novels* (Ghazibad:Vimal, 1984); and my discussion in chapter 9.

26. See Rajat K. Ray, "Three Interpretations of Indian Nationalism," *Essays in Modern Indian History,* ed. B. R. Nanda (Delhi: Oxford UP, 1980) 36. It could also be argued that the creation and strengthening of communalism in the pre-independence British India had economic basis—not necessarily a justification. See, for example, P. C. Joshi, "The Economic Background of Communalism in India—A Model of Analysis," *Essays in Modern Indian History,* ed. B. R. Nanda 167–81.

27. The cases of Coleridge, Aurobindo and Gandhi, to name only a few, show that in the history of social and political thought, especially in the evolution of the Enlightenment and post-Enlightenment ideologies, religion, as distinguished from communalism, has played a dominant role. See my "The Social and Political Vision of Sri Aurobindo," chapter 3. If the foundation of Gandhian thought, as has been commonly argued, is rooted in a moral force, what is the genesis of such a moral force? For an interesting discussion of Gandhi's thought see Partha Chatterjee, *Nationalist Thought and the Colonial World: A Derivative Discourse?* (London: Zed, 1986) 85–130.

28. "Afterword," Gobinda Prasad Sarma's *Nationalism in Indo-Anglian Fiction* (New Delhi: Sterling, 1978) 355.

29. Percy Bysshe Shelley, *Prometheus Unbound, Shelly: Poetical Works,* ed. Thomas Hutchinson (London: Oxford UP, 1967) 1.305.

30. See Ananda K. Coomaraswamy, *The Dance of Shiva,* rev. ed. (New York: Noonday, 1969) 66–78. Coomaraswamy's interpretation of the dance of

Shiva combines these two views. For other interpretations of this commonly used Indian myth see C. G. Jung, *Symbols of Transformation*, 1, trans. R. F. C. Hull (New York: Harper, 1956); Heinrich Zimmer, *Philosophies of India*, ed. Joseph Campbell (Princeton: Princeton UP, 1969); and Stella Kramrisch, *The Presence of Śiva* (Princeton: Princeton UP, 1981). Hermann Hesse, it should be noted, uses the image in *Magister Ludi (The Glass Bead Game)*, trans. Richard and Clara Winston (New York: Bantam, 1986) 291–92. Note the following: "It is wonderful—how these Indians, with an insight and capacity for suffering scarcely equalled by any other people, looked with horror and shame upon the cruel game of world history, the eternally revolving wheel of avidity and suffering; they saw and understood the fragility of created being, the avidity and diabolism of man, and at the same time his deep yearning for purity and harmony; and they devised these glorious parables for the beauty and tragedy of the creation: mighty Siva who dances the completed world into ruins, and smiling Vishnu who lies slumbering and playfully makes a new world arise out of his golden dreams of gods" (*Magister Ludi* 291–92).

31. For Byron's response to the Apollo Belvedere and Shelley's response to da Vinci's Medusa see John Hollander, "The Gazer's Spirit: Romantic and Later Poetry on Painting and Sculpture," *The Romantics and Us: Essays on Literature and Culture*, ed. Gene W. Ruoff 130–67. For Keats's treatment of the Grecian Urn see Geraldine Friedman, "The Erotics of Interpretation in Keats's 'Ode on a Grecian Urn': Pursuing the Feminine," *Studies in Romantism* 32 (Summer 1993): 225–43.

32. See John Hollander 130ff.

33. See Herbert Read, "The Notion of Organic Form: Coleridge," *The True Voice of Feeling: Studies in English Romantic Poetry* (London: Faber, 1968) 15–37. Also M. H. Abrams's discussion in his *Natural Supernaturalism: Tradition and Revolution in Romantic Literature* (New York: Norton, 1971) 190–91.

34. See Mircea Eliade, *Myth and Reality*, trans. Willard R. Trask (New York: Harper, 1968) 89.

35. *The Dance of Shiva* 77. Coomaraswamy's emphasis.

36. *The Presence of Śiva* 283.

37. *The Presence of Śiva* 282.

38. E. M. Forster, *Abinger Harvest* (New York: Harvest, 1964) 137.

CHAPTER 8

1. See P. Lal's introduction to Nissim Ezekiel's *The Unfinished Man: Poems Written in 1959* (Calcutta: Writers Workshop, 1960); and Rajeev Taranath and Meena Belliappa, *The Poetry of Nissim Ezekiel* (Calcutta: Writers Workshop, 1966). All textual references, unless otherwise indicated, are to the poems included in this edition of *The Unfinished Man*.

2. For a somewhat different interpretation of the metaphor of journey see Michael Garman, "Nissim Ezekiel—Pilgrimage and Myth," *Critical Essays on Indian Writing in English*, ed. M. K. Naik et al. (Dharwar: Karnatak UP,

1968) 106–21; and Inder Nath Kher, "'That message from another shore':
The Esthetic Vision of Nissim Ezekiel," *Mahfil* 8 (1972): 17–28.

3. See Northrop Frye's two essays "Historical Criticism: Theory of Modes"
and "Archetypal Criticism: Theory of Myths" in *Anatomy of Criticism: Four
Essay* (New York: Athenaeum, 1967). For the conception of the displace-
ment of myth see Northrop Frye, "Romantic Myth," in *A Study of English
Romanticism* (New York: Random House, 1968); and Susanne K. Langer,
Philosophy in a New Key: A Study in the Symbolism of Reason, Rite, and Art
(New York: American Library, 1951) 224ff.

4. See David McCutchion, *Indian Writing in English* (Calcutta: Writers Workshop, 1969) 100.

5. See Frye, *Anatomy* 141ff.

6. See F. H. Bradley, *Appearance and Reality: A Metaphysical Essay*, 2nd ed., intro.
Richard Wollheim (London: Oxford UP, 1969) 403ff.

7. See William Blake's "London," *Blake: Complete Writings*, ed. Geoffrey
Keynes (Oxford: Oxford UP, 1979) 276.

8. See Frye's interpretation of Arnold's three classes in *Anatomy* 347.

9. See W. H. Auden's two interesting and generic essays "The Virgin & the
Dynamo" and "The Poet & the City" in *The Dyer's Hand* (New York: Vintage, 1968) 61–71, 72–89.

10. K. R. Sirinivasa Iyengar, in his *Indian Writing in English* (Bombay: Asia,
1962), remarks that there is "a miniature *Anabasis*" (397).

11. We may recall the last lines of Shelley's "Ode to the West Wind," *Shelley's
Poetry and Prose,* ed. Donald H. Reiman and Sharon B. Powers (New York:
Norton, 1977): "O Wind, / If Winter comes, can Spring be far behind?
(69–70) Cf. Stephen Spender's Prose Poem:

> Bring me peace bring me power bring me assurance. Let me reach the
> bright day, the high chair, the plain desk, where my hand at last con-
> trols the words, where anxiety no longer undermines me. If I don't
> reach these I'm thrown to the wolves, I'm a restless animal wandering
> from place to place, from experience to experience.
>
> Give me the humility and the judgment to live alone with the deep
> and rich satisfaction of my own creating: not to be thrown into doubt
> by a word of spite or disapproval.
>
> In the last analysis don't mind whether your work is good or bad
> so long as it has the completeness, the enormity of the whole world
> which you love.
>
> —*The Making of a Poem* (New York: Norton, 1962) 60.

12. See, for example, Yeats's "A Prayer for My Daughter," *W. B. Yeats: Selected
Poetry,* ed. A. Norman Jeffares (London: Macmillan, 1967) 100–03.

13. See P. Lal's observation in his introduction to *The Unfinished Man:* " . . . that
honesty married to simplicity adds up to poetry that is prayer."

14. See the concluding section of Coleridge's poem *The Rime of the Ancient
Mariner, Samuel Taylor Coleridge,* ed. H. J. Jackson (Oxford: Oxford UP,
1985).

15. The woman seems to be associated with sin, but the suggestion is rather very mild, especially when we consider it in the context of marriage. Sin in this context means fallen perception. Moreover, "the mark of Cain" appears on both of them. However, in his later poetry, Ezekiel takes a more positive view of woman. Cf. "A Woman Admired," *Quest* 66 (1970): 67–69.

16. See Richard Ellmann, *The Identity of Yeats* (New York: Oxford UP, 1964) 71–74.

17. See *The Exact Name: Poems 1960–1964* (Calcutta: Writers Workshop, 1965).

18. See my *The Vision of "Love's Rare Universe": A Study of Shelley's Epipsychidion* (Lanham: UP of America, 1995).

CHAPTER 9

1. Anita Desai's *Baumgartner's Bombay* (London: Penguin, 1989) 10. All textual references are to this edition of the text.

2. See Homi K. Bhabha, *The Location of Culture* (London: Routledge, 1994), especially the discussion in chapters 1 and 2; Curtis M. Hinsley, "Strolling through the Colonies," *Walter Benjamin and the Demands of History*, ed. Michael P. Steinberg (Ithaca: Cornell UP, 1996) 119–40; and Ackbar Abbas, "Hyphenation: The Spatial Dimensions of Hong Kong Culture," *Walter Benjamin and the Demands of History*, ed. Michael P. Steinberg 214–31.

3. I am referring to some of the fundamental assumptions in chapter 1 of Georg Lukács's *The Historical Novel*, trans. Hannah and Stanley Mitchell, preface by Irving Howe (Boston: Beacon, 1963).

4. See Matthew Arnold, *Culture and Anarchy: An Essay in Political and Social Criticism*, ed. Ian Gregor (New York: Bobbs, 1971) 81–106.

5. See Frederic Jameson, *The Political Unconscious: Narrative as a Socially Symbolic Act* (Ithaca: Cornell UP, 1981), chapter 1.

6. For commentary on Kipling and Forster see Edward W. Said, *Culture and Imperialism* (New York: Knopf, 1993) 132–62, 200–06; and for Desai and Forster see Judie Newman, "History and Letters: Anita Desai's *Baumgartner's Bombay*," *World Literature Written in English* 30.1 (1990): 37–46. Note Newman's observation: "In *Baumgartner's Bombay* Desai takes the Imperial convention for representing the colonised (immaturity) and refines it as a property of Europe" (39). For variant responses to Forster's *A Passage to India* see Lisa Lowe, *Critical Terrains: French and British Orientalists* (Ithaca: Cornell UP, 1991). See n35 below.

7. For Thackeray's representation of India see Patrick Brantlinger, *Rule of Darkness: British Literature and Imperialism, 1830–1914* (Ithaca: Cornell UP, 1990) 73–107.

8. See Corrine Demas Bliss, "Against the Current: A Conversation with Anita Desai," *Massachusetts Review* 29 (Fall 88): 521–37; John Clement Ball and Chelva Kanaganayakam, "An Interview with Anita Desai," *The Toronto South Asian Review* 10.2 (Winter 1922): 30–41; and Feroza Jussawalla and

Reed Way Dasenbrock, *Interviews with Writers of the Post-Colonial World* (Jackson: UP of Mississippi, 1992) 156–79. Of course, one of the most important questions in these paratexts and subtexts—interviews, notebooks, diaries, margin notes and first drafts—is how much of the private world an artist has disclosed truthfully and candidly.

9. See Lukács 289.
10. See Lukács 30.
11. Michael Valdez Moses, *The Novel and the Globalization of Culture* (New York: Oxford UP, 1995) 192. But freedom for Popper, adds Moses, is means of achieving truth (192).
12. Lukács 29. In this debate about historiography and the role of history, it is important to consider other positions, such as those advanced by Schopenhauer, Burckhardt, Taine, Nietzsche, Croce and Flaubert. For a convenient summary of various positions see Lukács 172ff. Schopenhauer, it must be noted, was critical of Hegel's view of history and human progress. Note Lukács's observation: "It was Schopenhauer who discovered for Germany that Indian philosophy was the appropriate antidote to Hegel's 'superficial' view of human progress. And since then this theory has been re-echoed in every possible variation in the philosophy and literature of the German intelligentsia and the intelligentsia of other countries" (290).
13. Lukács 343.
14. Hinsley 119.
15. Moses 11.
16. Irving Wohlfarth, "Smashing the Kaleidoscope: Walter Benjamin's Critique of Cultural History," *Walter Benjamin and the Demands of History*, ed. Michael P. Steinberg 200.
17. Cited in Michael Löwry, "'Against the Grain': The Dialectical Conception of Culture in Walter Benjamin's Theses of 1940," *Walter Benjamin and the Demands of History*, ed. Michael P. Steinberg 209.
18. Löwry 210.
19. Cited by Christopher Ricks in *T. S. Eliot and Prejudice* (Los Angeles: U of California P, 1988) 197.
20. For the figure of Urizen see William Blake's *The Four Zoas* and *Jerusalem* in *The Complete Poetry and Prose of William Blake*, ed. David V. Erdman, rev. ed. (Berkeley: U of California P, 1982); and for the figure of Jupiter see Percy Bysshe Shelley's *Prometheus Unbound, Shelley: Poetical Works*, ed. Thomas Hutchinson (London: Oxford UP, 1967).
21. In this respect, the fundamental premise of the Romantic-Hegelian vision of reconstruction can hardly be ignored. See Jameson's forceful argument about the Marxist view of reconstruction in chapters 1 and 6 of *The Political Unconscious*. Especially see Jameson's commentary on Northrop Frye's critical theories: Jameson thinks that Frye's theories of the four phases of literature and of archetypes essentially focus on the redemptive view of the community, thus reconciling the world of history and the world of desire (68–74).

22. See Jameson, *The Political Unconscious* 35.

23. *The Political Unconscious* 19.

24. Sigmund Freud, *Civilization and its Discontents,* trans. Joan Riviere, ed. James Strachey, rev. ed. (London: Hogarth and the Institute of Psycho-Analysis, 1975).

25. Daniel Jonah Goldhagen, *Hitler's Willing Executioners: Ordinary Germans and the Holocaust* (New York: Knopf, 1996), especially chapters 1–5. It should be noted that the central thesis of Goldhagen's book is not based on the theories of collective guilt and the inevitability of history.

26. For some of these details I am indebted to "Anti-Semitism," *Encyclopedia Britannica* 2 (1963) 81ff. "The charges made against the Jews by anti-Semitic writers and agitators," we are told, "revolved around three main points: (1) the claim that Jews were a disintegrating force in the political, moral and cultural life of the countries in which they resided; (2) charges of Jewish economic domination and monopoly; and (3) a claim of Jewish world conspiracy. (Paradoxically, the Nazis later sought to liquidate Jews because of Judaism's spiritual values and its vision of the universal relatedness of all human beings)" (85).

27. See Octave Mannoni, *Prospero and Caliban: The Psychology of Colonization,* trans. Pamela Powesland (Ann Arbor: U of Michigan P, 1990). In the general discourse on colonialism, the standard theoretical assumptions underlying the Hegelian model of the lord-bondsman relationship and the Marxist model of the master-slave relationship should be compared to the Lacanian psychoanalytical conception of the Other. "In 1952, it was Fanon," remarks Bhabha in *The Location of Culture,* "who suggests that an oppositional, differential reading of Lacan's Other might be more relevant to the colonial condition than the Marxist reading of the master-slave dialectic" (32).

28. I am suggesting that such clusters of power in a civilization as Nazism, Fascism, racism and imperialism are governed by similar fundamental philosophical and psychosociological motivational forces. In a larger context, Jean-Paul Sartre, in his preface to Frantz Fanon's *The Wretched of the Earth,* trans. Constance Farrington (New York: Grove, 1968), refers to the phenomenon of "racist humanism" and the process by which "the European has only been able to become a man through creating slaves and monsters" (26). Significantly, Sartre elucidates Fanon's psychoanalytical terms, the colonized's neurosis and the colonizer's (Europe's) narcissism.

29. See Robert E. Park, "Human Migration and the Marginal Men" (1928), *Theories of Ethnicity: A Classical Reader,* ed. Warner Sollors (New York: New York UP, 1996) 156–67.

30. It is commonly argued that internationalization or cosmopolotization is essential to enlarging one's consciousness and to establishing a world community. In Baumgartner's case, however, the difference is between true consciousness and false consciousness. The peremptory renunciation of German nationality turns out to be a matter of epistemological and moral

recognition of false consciousness. In this sense and also in the Hegelian sense, Baumgartner has discovered the meaning of true freedom. The notion of true freedom is fundamentally rooted in the universalization of one's consciousness, a process in which the deterritorialized and decolonized mind, freed from fear, subjugation and hegemony, ultimately comprehends the meaning of truth.

31. See Renate Zahar, *Frantz Fanon: Colonialism and Alienation*, trans. Willfried F. Feuser (New York: Monthly, 1974) 65.

32. See my "The Nature and Perception of Reality in Hermann Hesse's *Siddhartha*," *South Asian Review* 11 & 12.8–9 (1988): 26–40.

33. See Philip Gleason, "Identifying Identity: A Semantic History" (1983), *Theories of Ethnicity: A Classical Reader*, ed. Warner Sollors 461.

34. Anita Desai has repeatedly emphasized the psychobiographical fact of her German past and its integration with her Indian experiences. Note her statement: "I feel about India as an Indian, but I suppose I think about it as an outsider [like my mother]" (interview with Bliss 527). Elsewhere she says: "I see India through my mother's eyes, as an outsider, but my feelings for India are my father's, of someone born here. . . . If I feel at home in any society, it is such a society where nobody really belongs, everyone is in the same way uprooted" (Andrew Robinson, "Anita Desai," *Beyond the Glass Ceiling*, ed. Sian Griffiths [Manchester: Manchester UP, 1966] 80). She has persistently maintained that *Baumgartner's Bombay* has provided her an opportunity to unload her German past. The dichotomous split between feeling and thought, not necessarily oppositional or dialectical, must remind one of the ideas of Locke and Hume on identity of the self (see n33 above) and of Freud on art and neurosis. In the Freudian sense, of course, the rendering of biography into art is essentially therapeutic. Clearly, there are three pictures of India in Desai, the India of her father, the India of her mother and the India of her own experiences. The whole issue of her German past, especially her relationship with her mother who, as we are told, had partly accepted India and partly questioned it somewhat skeptically from the viewpoint of a European, a viewpoint that remains deeply embedded in her, is important to the examination of her work and art. One must remember the problems of splintered consciousness and identity in such figures as James Joyce and T. S. Eliot and in the expatriate experience in general. Can individual consciousness be submerged in universal consciousness? Can the issue of identity with a historically defined space and hence of nationalism and patriotism have any relevance to a new emerging consciousness? If cultural identify is not a possibility, should one try to achieve psychological identity through a process of individuation? Can one form of identity be realized without the other? See Bhabha's *The Location of Culture* 38–39. William Phillips, in introduction to *Art and Psychoanalysis* (New York: Meridian, 1963), notes that "such themes as loneliness, self-doubt, hypersensitivity, loss of identity, estrangement from the community—all have their counterparts among the common neuroses . . ."

(xix). Refer to the two very important essays on the subject included in this volume: Thomas Mann, "Freud and Future" 369–89; and Lionel Trilling, "Art and Neurosis" 503–20. For different perspectives on the subject of alienation and identity, especially in the case of "half and halfers" see my discussion of Balachandra Rajan's *The Dark Dancer,* chapter 7. Also see my "Alienation, Identity and Structure in Arun Joshi's *The Apprentice,*" chapter 10.

35. See n6 above. It can be safely assumed that in the European discourse on India the standard conventional groupings are almost along ideological lines. For varied representations of India see Eric Stokes, *The English Utilitarians and India* (Oxford: Clarendon, 1963); Raymond Schwab, *The Oriental Renaissance: Europe's Rediscovery of India and the East, 1680–1880,* trans. Gene Patterson-Black and Victor Reinking (New York: Columbia UP, 1984); Kate Teltscher, *India Inscribed: European and British Writing on India 1600–1800* (Delhi: Oxford UP, 1995); John Barrell, *The Infection of Thomas De Quincey* (New Haven: Yale UP, 1991); John Drew, *India and the Romantic Imagination* (Delhi: Oxford UP, 1987); Ronald Inden, *Imagining India* (Oxford: Blackwell, 1990); Donald F. Leach, *India in the Eyes of Europe* (Chicago: U of Chicago P, 1968); Nigel Leask, *British Romantic Writers and the East: Anxieties of Empire* (Cambridge: Cambridge UP, 1992); Sara Suleri's *The Rhetoric of English India* (Chicago: U of Chicago P, 1992); and Jean Sedlar, *India in the Mind of Germany: Schelling, Schopenhauer and their Times* (Washington, D.C.: UP of America, 1982). For my discussion of T. S. Eliot's and E. M. Forster's treatment of India see "Ideological Confrontation and Synthesis in Mulk Raj Anand's *Conversations in Bloomsbury,*" chapter 6. Note Said's extremely important observation in *Culture and Imperialism:* "Indians are a various lot, they need to be known and understood, British power has to reckon with Indians in India: such are Kipling's coordinates, politically speaking. Forster is evasive and more patronizing; there is truth to Parry's comment that '*A Passage to India* is the triumphant expression of the British imagination exploring India,' but it is also true that Forster's India is so affectionately personal and so remorselessly metaphysical that his view of Indians as a nation contending for sovereignty with Britain is not politically very serious, or even respectful" (204).

36. In an interview with Jussawalla Desai mentions Tagore's "Tolstoyan personality" (Jussawalla and Dasenbrock 171). Tagore's reputation as a writer—poet, novelist, playwright and essayist—had been well established in India, Europe and North America. The most significant work that was introduced by Yeats and that earned him the Nobel prize is of course *Gitanjali.* See Anita Desai, "Re-Reading Tagore," *Journal of Commonwealth Literature* 29.1 (1994): 5–14. Tagore is said to have been known to such luminaries as Yeats, Einstein, Rolland and Wells. See *A Tagore Reader,* ed. Amiya Chakravarty (Boston: Beacon, 1967).

37. Khushwant Singh's *Train to Pakistan* (London: Chatto, 1956) appeared in the U.S. in 1956 as *Mano Majra.* Bapsi Sidhwa's *Cracking India* (Minneapolis: Milkweed, 1991) had originally appeared as *Ice-Candy-Man* (1988).

38. See Graham Huggan, "Philomela's Retold Story: Silence, Music, and the Post-Colonial Text," *Journal of Commonwealth Literature* 25.1 (1990): 12–23; Prafulla C. Karr, "Khushwant Singh: *Train to Pakistan*," *Major Indian Novels: An Evaluation*, ed. N. S. Pradhan (Atlantic Highlands: Humanities, 1986) 88–103; and my discussion of this subject in "Balachandra Rajan's *The Dark Dancer:* A Critical Reading," chapter 7. Also see K. K. Sharma and B. K. Johri, *The Partition in Indian-English Novels* (Ghaziabad: Vimal, 1984).

39. It is no doubt true that Rushdie in *Midnight's Children* has transformed history into a mythical fantasy, probably after the *Mahabharata* model, but Forster in *A Passage to India*, according to Said, has used India "to represent material that according to the canons of the novel form cannot in fact be represented—vastness, incomprehensible creeds, secret motions, histories, and social forms" (*Culture and Imperialism* 200). For Rushdie's view of history see David Lipscomb, "Caught in a Strange Middle Ground: Contesting History in Salman Rushdie's *Midnight's Children*," *Diaspora* 1.2 (1991): 3–29.

40. Dorothy Figuiera, "Mulk Raj Anand's *Across the Black Waters:* Europe as an Object of 'Orientalist Discourse,'" *South Asian Review* 15.12 (1991): 51–56. Also see Percival Spear's description of the country's "mood," in *The Oxford History of India 1740–1947* (Oxford : Clarendon, 1965) 376. Note Spear's modestly phrased question: "How could India assist the cause of liberty abroad without first obtaining her freedom at home?" (376)

41. See E. M. Forster's treatment of the epistemology of reality in "Part I: Cambridge," *The Longest Journey* (New York: Vinatage, 1962). Ansell raises the issue of the reality of the cow's existence: "The cow is there. . . . The cow is *not* there" (1). In fact, Forster, through Ansell, covers the history of the European intellectual thought from Plato to modern times. ,

42. Desai's persistent interest in Indian metaphysics is evident from her recent novel *Journey to Ithaca*. Andrew Robinson believes that "in writing the novel, Desai was influenced by her knowledge of Krishnamurti, of the famous Mother at the Aurobindo ashram in Pondicherry and by two postwar books about India often regarded as classics of spiritual autobiography" ("Anita Desai" 79). Also see Pico Iyer's "The Spiritual Import-Export Market: *Journey to Ithaca* by Anita Desai" (1995), in his *Tropical Classical: Essays from Several Directions* (New York: Knopf, 1997) 164–77.

43. For the idea of ekphrastic poetry see John Hollander, "The Gazer's Spirit: Romantic and Later Poetry on Painting and Sculpture," *The Romantics and Us: Essays on Literature and Culture*, ed. Gene W. Ruoff (New Brunswick: Rutgers UP, 1990) 130–67.

44. See Mircea Eliade, *Myth and Reality*, trans. Willard R. Trask (New York: Harper, 1968) 187–93, about the myths of the elite.

45. Joseph Conrad, *Heart of Darkness: Complete Authoritative Text with Biographical and Historical Contexts, Critical History, and Essays*, 2nd ed., ed. Ross C. Murfin (New York: St. Martin's, 1996) 86.

46. Quoted in P. N. Furbank, *E. M. Forster: A Life*, 2 vols. (New York: Harcourt, 1981) 2.125.

47. *E. M. Forster: A Life* 2.125 n2. The discussions of the cave symbolism in *A Passage of India*—of Miss Quested's experience in the cave—undoubtedly suggest that Forster was more knowledgeable about Indian thought than is generally conceded. See, for example, Wilfred Stone, *The Cave and the Mountain: A Study of E. M. Forster* (Stanford: Stanford UP, 1969) 298ff. Note Said's statement: "Hindus, according to the novel [*A Passage to India*], believe that all is muddle, all connected, God is one, is not, was not, was" (*Culture and Imperialism* 202). Incidentally, in an interview with Ball and Kanaganayakam Desai remarks: "Life is muddle, even history is a muddle . . ." (34). Undoubtedly, the allusion is to the philosophy of Illusionism or Maya in Indian metaphysics. And yet there is, as Said notes, another type of India's incomprehensibility in *A Passage to India:* "'nothing in India is identifiable' . . ." (*Culture and Imperialism* 201). Bhabha has referred to the following lines from *A Passage to India:* "How can the mind take hold of such a country? Generations of invaders have tried, but they remain in exile. . . . She has never defined. She is not a promise, only an appeal" ("Articulating the Archaic: Notes on Colonial Nonsense," *Literary Theory Today,* ed. Peter Collier and Helga Geyer-Ryan [Ithaca: Cornell UP, 1990] 203). For the symbology of Shiva I am indebted to Heinrich Zimmer, *Philosophies of India,* ed. Joseph Campbell (Princeton: Princeton UP, 1969); Ananda K. Coomaraswamy, *The Dance of Shiva,* rev. ed. (New York: Noonday, 1969); and Stella Kramrisch, *The Presence of Śiva* (Princeton: Princeton UP, 1981). Also see my discussion of the icon in "Balachandra Rajan's *The Dark Dancer:* A Critical Reading," chapter 7.

48. It remains to be argued if Baumgartner's cold-blooded murder by Kurt reflects Desai's own ambivalence, if such an abrupt ending follows the archetypal pattern of the martyred Jew in myth and history and if it is consistent with the moral of the fable. Desai has said that while she "was playing with two alternative endings," she finally decided to play the destiny card by having him die at the hands of a Nazi. The obvious model for her final choice, as she explains, was that of Greek tragedy. His death, maintains Desai, "gave me a certain satisfaction, that he had met the kind of death which fate had devised for him anyway" (Jussawalla and Dasenbrock 176). Also see Desai's discussion of the ending in Ball and Kanaganayakam 34–35. Will it be reasonable to suggest that such a presumptive ending was directed by Desai's conception of time as a fourth dimension? In a discussion with Ramesh K. Srivastava ("Anita Desai at Work: An Interview") about the use of the fourth dimension of time in her novel *Clear Light of Day,* Desai refers to Eliot's notion of time in *Four Quartets.* "What I have tried to prove," remarks Desai, "is that although Time appears to damage, destroy and extinguish, one finds instead that nothing is lost, nothing comes to an end, but the spiral of life leads as much upwards as downwards and is in perpetual circular motion, both the past and future existing always in time present" (*Perspectives on Anita Desai,* ed. Ramesh K. Srivastava [Ghaziabad: Vimal, 1984] 225). It must be noted that Shelley's poetization of the idea of the West Wind as

destroyer and preserver in "Ode to the West Wind" and later Eliot's treatment of time as destroyer and preserver in "The Dry Salvages" are directly related to the symbology of Shiva in Indian metaphysics.

49. See, for example, Malashri Lal, "The Shift from Female Centered to Male Centered Narrative in the Novels of the 1980s: A Study of Anita Desai and Nayantra Sahgal," *The New Indian Novel in English: A Study of 1980s*, ed. Viney Kirpal (New Delhi: Allied, 1990) 279–86; and Harveen Sachdeva Mann, "'Going in the Opposite Direction': Feminine Recusancy in Anita Desai's 'Voices in the City,'" *Ariel* 23.4 (1992): 75–95.

50. See the discussion in part 5 of Michel Foucault's *The History of Sexuality: vol. 1: An Introduction,* trans. Robert Hurley (New York: Pantheon, 1978).

51. M. Keith Booker, *A Practical Introduction to Literary Theory and Criticism* (New York: Longman, 1996) 91. Booker provides a convenient summary of the major ideas of feminist literary critics, but I find Julia Kristeva's discussion of agape, eros, transubstantiation and consubstantiation extremely relevant to my discussion. See her "Identification and the Real," *Literary Theory Today,* ed. Peter Collier and Helga Geyer-Ryan 167–76.

52. See Sigmund Freud, "Dostoevsky and Parricide," *Art and Psychoanalysis,* ed. William Phillips 13.

53. See Michel Foucault, *Madness and Civilization: A History of Insanity in the Age of Reason,* trans. Richard Howard (New York: Pantheon, 1965), especially chapter 1.

54. Albert Einstein's letter to Sigmund Freud in *The Correspondence between Albert Einstein and Sigmund Freud,* trans. Fritz and Anna Moellenhoff (The Chicago Institute for Psychoanalysis, n. d.). Sigmund Freud's remarks summarized and cited here are from his reply to Albert Einstein included in the aforementioned *Correspondence.* The unidentified quotations in this paragraph are from *Correspondence.*

55. See Lukács 399. Lukács refers to Scott's *Heart of Midlothian* as a characteristic example of such a synthesis and balance. But note Lukács's basic assumption in chapter 1 of *The Historical Novel:* "Scott's greatness lies in his capacity to give living human embodiment to historical-social types" (35).

56. The idea of the metaphor of belly comes from Aijaz Ahmed's "Jameson's Rhetoric of Otherness and the 'National Allegory'" (1987), *Marxist Literary Theory: A Reader,* ed. Terry Eagleton and Drew Milne (Oxford: Blackwell, 1996) 375–89.

57. *The Location of Culture* 172. See also Anita Desai's response to theorizing India in terms of the commonly misappropriated politico-economic categories, first world, second world and third world, in "The Other Voice: A Dialogue between Anita Desai, Caryl Phillips and Ilan Stavans," *Transition* 64 (1994): 77–89.

58. This phrase is a reconstruction of Diana Brydon's title of her essay "A Post-Holocaust, Post-Colonial Vision," *International Literature in English: Essays on the Major Writers,* ed. Robert L. Ross (New York: Garland, 1991) 583–92.

59. Rabindranath Tagore, *The Religion of Man* (Boston: Beacon, 1966) 163.

CHAPTER 10

1. We may also include in this group *The Survivor* (1975), a collection of short stories.
2. Arun Joshi, *The Apprentice* (New York: Asia, 1974). All textual references, unless otherwise indicated, are to this edition of *The Apprentice*.
3. See Arnold's *Culture and Anarchy*, ed. J. Dover Wilson (Cambridge: Cambridge UP, 1966); Lionel Trilling's *Matthew Arnold* (Cleveland: Meridian, 1968); and Patrick J. McCarthy's *Matthew Arnold and the Three Classes* (New York: Columbia UP, 1964). Note Trilling's conception of culture: "Culture is not merely a method but an attitude of spirit contrived to receive truth. It is a moral orientation, involving will, imagination, faith; all of these avowedly active elements body forth a universe that contains a truth which the intuition can grasp and the analytical reason can scrutinize. Culture is reason involving the whole personality; it is the whole personality in search of the truth" (241).
4. I am indebted to Roland Barthes's essays "Striptease" and "The World as Object," *A Barthes Reader*, ed. and introd. Susan Sontag (New York: Noonday, 1988). "Woman," remarks Barthes in his essay "Striptease," "is desexualized at the very moment when she is stripped naked" (85). As metaphors there is very little difference between a striptease and a whore, for they both represent the "desexualized" female.
5. See Marx's criticism of the bourgeoisie in Shlomo Avineri's *The Social and Political Thought of Karl Marx* (Cambridge: Cambridge UP, 1969). Of course, the only alternative to bourgeois society is the communist society. "For Marx's theory of history," remarks Jacques Barzun, "is above all a theory of things, distinction between the 'real' base and superstructure of appearance. . . . But Marx enlarges this insight into a general proposition: the way in which men earn their livelihood is fundamental to everything else" (*Darwin, Marx, Wagner: Critique of a Heritage* [New York: Doubleday, 1958] 133). And Barzun cites Marx: "The method of production in material life determines the general character of the social, political, and spiritual processes of life. . . . It is not the consciousness of men that determines their being, but, on the contrary, their social being determines their consciousness. In the first view, one proceeds from the consciousness as the living individual; in the second, which conforms to real life, one proceeds from the really living individuals themselves and regards consciousness only as *their* consciousness" (133).
6. "If civilizations are macrocosms of human nature," remarks David Daiches, "individual characters are microcosms of civilizations . . ." ("Fiction and Civilization," *The Modern Critical Spectrum*, eds. Gerald Jay and Nancy Marmer Goldberg [Englewood: Prentice-Hall, 1962] 114).
7. In "George Bernard Shaw: A Study of the Bourgeois Superman," *Five Approaches of Literary Criticism*, ed. Wilbur S. Scott (New York: Collier, 1979), Christopher Caudwell uses this expression for Shaw (149).

8. Avineri 97.
9. Bertell Ollman, *Alienation: Marx's Conception of Man in Capitalist Society* (Cambridge: Cambridge UP, 1973) 135.
10. There are general echoes of Dostoevsky, especially of the psychological process through which Dostoevsky takes Raskolnikov to help him recognize his crime and recover his consciousness. But it must be noted that with the exception of the psychology and sociology of the criminal—transgression, confession and penance—the two situations are otherwise greatly dissimilar: Raskolnikov kills for a principle, whereas Ratan Rathor's crime of bribery is a case of blatant social and moral deviance. See the epilogue, *Crime and Punishment* by Feodor Dostoevsky, Norton critical ed., 2nd ed., ed. George Gibian (New York, 1975) 459.
11. "Dostoevsky in *Crime and Punishment*," *Crime and Punishment* by Feodor Dostoevsky, ed. George Gibian 542.
12. Referring to Gandhi's view of man's inferiority or superiority based on the Hindu hierarchical structure of castes, Aurobindo remarks: "The view taken by the Mahatma in these matters is Christian rather than Hindu— for the Christian, self-abasement, humility, the acceptance of a low status to serve humanity or the Divine are things which are highly spiritual and the noblest privilege of the soul" (*Letters on Yoga,* vol. 22, Sri Aurobindo Birth Centenary Library Edition [Pondicherry: Sri Aurobindo Ashram, 1970] 486).
13. The Indian thought admits two positions on evil, the monistic and the dualistic. The *Bhagavadgita* traces the origin of evil to the *gunas:* evil belongs to the lower order of nature, *Prakriti,* and does not have any absolute and independent existence. See Radhakrishanan's "Introductory Essay" appended to the *Bhagavadgita,* Sanskrit Text, trans. and Notes by S. Radhakrishanan, (London: Allen, 1949) 11–78. The Christian view of evil is essentially dualistic. In the history of the European intellectual thought, the Hobbesean view presupposes that man by nature is basically depraved. But evil, according to Rousseau, is a product of society and does not have any independent existence of its own.
14. In the *Bhagavadgita,* the three *gunas, sattva, rajas* and *tamas,* as Radhakrishanan explains, "are the three tendencies of prakrti or the three strands making up the twisted rope of nature" (317). *Tamas,* the lowest of the three *gunas,* signifies "darkness and inertia" (317).
15. See, for example, Gobinda Prasad Sarma's peremptory assertion (in his *Nationalism in Indo-Anglian Fiction* [New Delhi: Sterling, 1978] 276ff.) that *The Apprentice* is basically about the social and political corruption in the post-independence India. Indeed, the issue with all its ramifications is controversial. Is the novelist mainly concerned with social and political reform or is he committed to the communication of universal truth? What makes a work of art more enduring? Is art capable of absorbing historicity? Does art have to destroy historicity in order to create illusion? Will it be utterly inappropriate to suggest that Conrad's *Heart of Darkness* and Forster's *A*

Passage to India are treatises on imperialism and colonialism? Admittedly, in each of these works, there are deeper, subtler and more profound issues—universal truths of human nature—although they remain rooted in history. In his preface to *The Nigger of the "Narcissus," Three Great Tales* (New York: Vintage, n. d.), Conrad defines art "as a single-minded attempt to render the highest kind of justice to the visible universe, by bringing to light the truth, manifold and one, underlying its every aspect. It is an attempt to find in its forms . . . what of each is fundamental, what is enduring and essential—their one illuminating and convincing quality—the very truth of their existence" (vii).

16. There is no authorial intrusion, editorial analysis or direct commentary, nor are there any multiple voices of a dramatic narrative, that we normally get from an omniscient narrator. The entire narrative of *The Apprentice* comes from Ratan Rathor, the protagonist-narrator.

17. My question is an extended paraphrase of Fritz Pappenheim's question: "Can alienation be overcome?" (*The Alienation of Modern Man: An Interpretation Based on Marx and Tonnies* [New York: Modern, 1968] 115) Marx, notes Pappenheim, had believed that the "forces of commodity production . . . had brought about modern man's alienation" (116) and had "rejected the attempt 'to overcome alienation within the framework of alienation,' to conquer alienation within a society geared to commodity relations" (134).

CHAPTER 11

1. In my discussion of Joshi's earlier work *The Apprentice,* I have pointed out the similarities between the narratives of *Crime and Punishment* and *The Apprentice,* especially the difficulty of fictional representation of life's larger issues and the interior quests pertaining to moral, psychological and philosophical matters. See my essay "Alienation, Identity and Structure in Arun Joshi's *The Apprentice,*" chapter 10.

2. Arun Joshi, *The Last Labyrinth* (New Delhi: Orient, 1981). All textual references noted in parenthesis are to this edition of the work.

3. Friedrich Nietzsche, *The Will To Power,* trans. W. Kaufmann and R. J. Hollingdale (New York: Vintage, 1968).

4. *The Will To Power* 59.

5. See Arun Joshi's own remarks cited by R. K. Dhawan in *The Fictional World of Arun Joshi* (New Delhi: Classical, n.d.) 46.

6. For the idea of Shakti in Indian thought see my essay "The Woman Figure in Blake and the Idea of Shakti in Indian Thought," *Comparative Literature Studies* 27:3 (1990): 193–210.

7. See Thomas Mann, "Schopenhauer," in his *Essays of Three Decades,* trans. H. T. Lowe-Porter (New York: Knopf, 1968) 388ff.

8. T. S. Eliot, introduction, *Pascal's Pensées* (New York: Dutton, 1958) xix. Also see some enlightening essays and Harold Bloom's introduction in *Blaise Pascal,* ed. Harold Bloom (New York: Chelsea, 1989).

9. *The Will To Power* 52.

10. Thomas Mann, "Freud and the Future," *Essays of Three Decades* 415ff.

11. See Michel Foucault, *Madness and Civilization: A History of Insanity in the Age of Reason,* trans. Richard Howard (New York: Random, 1965), especially 117ff.

12. *The Will To Power* 528.

13. Indeed, I am referring to Walter Benjamin's theorization of melancholia. See Francoise Meltzer, "Acedia and Melancholia," *Walter Benjamin and the Demands of History,* ed. Michael P. Steinberg (Ithaca: Cornell UP, 1966) 141–63.

Index

Printed in the USA
CPSIA information can be obtained
at www.ICGtesting.com
LVHW091834021223
765388LV00004B/43